neck, pulled her against him and kissed her, hard.

She gave him exactly what he wanted, melting into him with a little gasp of admiration.

"There's more where that came from," he said, rising from his chair. "You stay right where you are."

He strutted off like a peacock, all broad shoulders and jutting chin. He thought he'd won the prize with his natural charm and good looks. Men like him always assumed that any girl, even the most sophisticated flapper, would fall for them if they so much as crooked their fingers…

CHASING MIDNIGHT

BY
SUSAN KRINARD

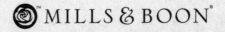

First published in Great Britain 2009
Harlequin Mills & Boon Limited,
Eton House, 18-24 Paradise Road, Richmond, Surrey TW9 1SR

© Susan Krinard 2007

ISBN: 978 0 263 87625 3

89-1109

Harlequin Mills & Boon policy is to use papers that are natural, renewable and recyclable products and made from wood grown in sustainable forests. The logging and manufacturing processes conform to the legal environmental regulations of the country of origin.

Printed and bound in Spain
by Litografia Rosés S.A., Barcelona

Dear Reader,

What is it about the nineteen twenties?

For me, the fascination began with my first viewing of the movie *Chicago*, starring Catherine Zeta-Jones. Before then, I'd never given the decade much thought. I knew about Prohibition, of course, and flappers, but it all came alive when Ms Zeta-Jones performed "All That Jazz." I was hooked.

The Roaring Twenties was a remarkable period. It was the time when the old rules of Victorian America gave way to the new rules of the twentieth century. It was the age when women first began to vote, when the "working girl" came into her own, when music and art were undergoing startling transformations. The West was still recovering from the trauma of the Great War, finding its way into a strange new world. In New York and Chicago and the other great cities, mobsters made fortunes from bootlegging. There was a flourishing underworld of clubs and speakeasies where the daring and fashionable could quench their thirst for alcohol and excitement.

What better place to set a story about werewolves and vampires in conflict but Prohibition-era New York, where the mobs of three very different races compete for dominance? The first image that immediately sprang into my head was one of a vampire flapper with a Louise Brooks bob, dressed in a short skirt and high-heel pumps…a young woman who couldn't be bothered with the restrictions of either human society or her own vampire clan. And who should her romantic interest be but a rather old-fashioned and chivalrous werewolf who has his own issues with the *loups-garous* of New

York…and who finds himself falling for a girl who seems to be doing everything possible to drive him crazy?

With those characters and situations firmly in my mind, *Chasing Midnight* was born. I've seldom had so much fun writing a book. I hope you'll give the Roaring Twenties a try; I'll be revisiting them in my next paranormal romance novel for Mills & Boon® Super Nocturne™, which will be arriving on book shop shelves in December 2009.

Susan Krinard

CHASING MIDNIGHT

PROLOGUE

New York City, 1924

SHE WOKE TO THE SOUNDS of the street: the honking of horns as taxicabs, sedans and roadsters jockeyed for position; the rattle and rumble of trucks bearing cargo both legitimate and illicit; the shouts of the newsboy on the corner, trumpeting the scandalous details of the latest police raid on Joe Bocelli's Club Desirée.

She lay quietly for a moment, eyes closed, trying to decide what was different. It wasn't only that the sounds were so distinct, falling on her ears like drumbeats, or that she could feel the shift of every current of air as it brushed against her skin. It wasn't only that, for the first time in so many years, her body didn't hurt.

With a groan of pleasure she extended her arms over her head, feeling muscles stretch and bones pop. Her toes tingled. She wiggled them, delighting in the touch of the satin sheets against her skin.

And then she froze as the realization struck her so hard and fast that it stole her breath.

She had moved. Not with stiff, painful jerks, her limbs refusing to obey her simplest commands. Not with withered muscles wasting away, prisoners in a cage of flesh. She had moved easily, smoothly, strength flowing through her like cascades of fresh cool water.

Slowly she opened her eyes. The room should have been dark; no lamps were on, and the shades and curtains were drawn over the windows. But she saw everything with crystal clarity, as if the entire world were bathed in light. Every detail of the Persian carpet stood out in elegant relief. The pattern of the wallpaper seemed to dance a geometric ballet. And the man in the chair…

Alice sat up, her heart bounding beneath her ribs. The man in the chair gazed at her with a faint smile, his pale eyes reflecting a dim red glow.

"Alice," he said, "do you remember?"

She rubbed her eyes, caught by a wave of dizziness that made the bed roll and heave beneath her. An hour, a week, a year ago, she had been lying in this same bed, her limbs like dead weights among the sheets, her mouth filled with words she could barely speak. *He* had been there, looking down at her with an expression both kindly and grim, and she had been afraid.

"There is always a risk," he'd said back then. "Especially to one in your condition. But the rewards…" He'd gestured at her twisted body. "The rewards are beyond calculation. You will walk again, Alice. You will be free."

And alive. If she should awaken from the long sleep he had told her about, she would no longer be facing imminent death at the age of twenty-four. She wouldn't spend another year in bed, her legs no longer able to support her body, her hands too weak to hold a book, listening to the sounds of life passing by her window. There would be a new existence awaiting her, one she could scarcely imagine. She would be better than before, even better than if she'd grown up without the disease that had stolen her friends, her family, her hope.

"You will have a new family," he'd told her. "The old loyalties will fall away, the old rules by which you lived. You will never be able to go back."

She'd shivered. "I have…nothing to lose," she'd said, pushing the sounds past the thickness in her throat.

He'd nodded, as if he had expected no less from her. "Make no mistake," he'd said, "you will die. You will no longer breathe. Your heart will cease to beat. If a doctor were to enter this room, he would pronounce you deceased."

Tears had leaked from the corners of Alice's eyes. "I understand."

"I doubt that you do," he'd said sadly, "but there is no other way for your body to undergo the change. Either you will wake in this bed, or…"

Or she would not wake at all. But she would have died knowing that she had taken the ultimate gamble and spat in the eyes of all the pitying, privileged "friends" who had deserted her to the slow descent into hell.

Mother won't even know I'm gone, she'd thought. And if she ever comes looking for me…

Alice had smiled, her mouth too stiff for laughter. "I'm ready."

He'd taken the chair beside the bed and looked into her eyes. "There will be no pain. You will become very sleepy. Don't fight it, my dear. Let it take you." He'd bent close, his not-unpleasant breath drifting over her cheek. "Close your eyes and dream of paradise.…"

Alice snapped back to the present, her hands shaking on the bedsheets. She clenched her fists and listened to the steady, strong beat of her heart…her heart, still doing what hearts were supposed to do. Her lungs still took in air. Except for the easy movements of her limbs and throat and face, she seemed to be the same as before.

"To most humans you will seem normal," Cato said. "Despite certain fairy tales to the contrary, you are not 'undead.'" He rose from the chair, came to her bedside and took her hand in his, checking her pulse like a kindly physician. "You may eat and drink in moderation, so long as you do not neglect your most essential needs. You may walk in daylight so long as you wear tinted glasses and cover your skin. Even brief exposure will result in serious burns. That is why most of us prefer to conduct our public business after sunset."

Alice stared at the window. Only the tiniest sliver of light entered past the heavy curtains. "How—" she cleared her throat, startled by the smooth, musical sound of her own voice "—how long was I…"

"Dead?" He patted her hand. "Two weeks. I was not entirely certain that you would wake. But now…" He stood back. "Rise and walk, AliceCharles."

Her mouth as dry as cotton, Alice began to move. She slid her legs along the mattress and cautiously let them drop over the side of the bed. The ground seemed very far away. She flexed her feet on the carpet.

"Your body has the strength," Cato said. "Far more strength than you need to walk across this room." His words took on a strange hum, like some powerful generator crackling with energy. "Prove that you are worthy of this gift. Walk!"

Compelled by a force far stronger than fear, Alice pressed her weight down, felt her muscles tighten and grow firm at her command. She stood, swayed, straightened. She took one step, and then another. Her legs carried her to the opposite wall and back again without a single stumble.

I can walk, Alice sang silently. *I can walk, I can walk, I can walk....*

"Yes," Cato said, a distant look in his eyes. "I need no further proof." He took her shoulders and steered her toward the huge mirror that dominated the wall above the dressing table. "Look," he urged. "See what you have become."

She looked, though she had not viewed her own reflection in many years. The face that stared back at her was almost unrecognizable, as if some skilled and prudent sculptor had taken her features and rearranged them into something that was partly AliceCharles and partly something...other. Something beautiful. The lines of her features were clean and regular, her skin smooth, her brow unlined over vivid aqua eyes. Her hair, black and shining, hung down her back like ebony silk. And her body, clearly outlined by the sheer drape of her night robe, was both strong and intensely—unmistakably—female.

"Lovely," Cato said, lifting her hair in his hands and letting it sift through his fingers. "So much more than I had hoped."

He gestured Alice back to the bed and sat down beside her. "There is still a great deal for you to learn, my dear, and I will be your teacher until you have passed beyond your infancy...shall we say." He lifted her chin with his fingertips. "Do you remember what we discussed?"

Alice nodded. There was more than one price to pay for this miracle, and she had resolved to settle the debt without complaint. She began to remove her nightgown.

Cato laughed. "My dear, you misunderstood. It is quite true that we are now bound by blood…as you will learn should either of us find ourselves long separated or in a life-threatening predicament, unlikely as that may seem. But I am far too old to find the prospect of rolling about between the sheets in the least appealing."

Alice released her breath. "Then how can I repay you for what you've done?"

He held her gaze, and she felt the power of his great age work its way into her mind. "You shall make a new life," he said. "You will have all the money you could possibly require, all the freedom you have lacked since the coming of your illness. I ask only that you protect your secret, as our kind must, and come to me when I call you."

Alice angrily scrubbed at her cheeks. "Why? Why have you helped me?"

"Your father and I were friends, brothers in science in spite of our obvious differences. He never learned of my true nature, but he would have appreciated my intervention in more ways than one. And I…I consider your Conversion one of the great achievements of my latter years." He kissed her forehead and rose. "Rest now. It will be a few days before your instruction can begin. You may spend the time composing a name for yourself. Until then, everything you need will be supplied by my servants."

He left, closing the door behind him. Alice lay still, half-afraid that if she moved she might wake to find it had all been a dream. But the moments passed, and nothing changed. After a while she got up again and wandered about the room, stopping before the mirror once more.

Perhaps this was what she might have been like if the disease hadn't claimed her at so young an age. Perhaps she might have attended parties and outings with other young people on Long Island, gone riding and sailing, even married.

Or perhaps they would have snubbed her anyway, knowing that all she and her mother had left was the decaying mansion and two servants to manage the entire estate. She couldn't have afforded the expensive frocks or given the right kinds of soirées.

No, she would always have been an outcast among the fashionable set to which her mother had once belonged. Alice smiled at herself, imagining Lucy Shearer and Wilson Hinds, Johnnie Macklin and Oralie Gray, all the neighbors and former friends who had found even pity too taxing an emotion. Outcast they had declared her, and outcast she would remain. To hell with them all. She would learn to live in a way they couldn't begin to imagine.

Tossing her hair over her shoulders, she turned toward the window. Cato had reminded her of one of the basic rules of her new existence: one must not walk in daylight without layers of protective clothing. A rule that must be obeyed. A law that meant survival.

Just another set of chains to choke and bind.

She walked slowly toward the window, her gaze fixed on the sliver of light at the edges of the shade. She passed her hand through the narrow band of illumination. There was no pain. With a swift jerk she drew back the dark, heavy curtains. The shade was triple thick, utterly safe. Alice raised it with a sharp tug on the cord.

Heat and light flooded into the room, bathing Alice's face and hands, penetrating her thin gown as if it were tissue. She braced herself for the burning, the punishment she had risked by daring to defy the rules.

Strangely, nothing happened. Her skin remained smooth and unmarred, with no blisters or blackening, no agony as the world of humanity took its toll. Only the soft and gentle caress of warmth stroking her cheek like a long-absent lover.

She pressed her palms to the window and looked down into the street. Few of those people passing on the sidewalks were aware that they shared their city with beings that looked very like them but were not human. None of them knew what had transpired in this room today. They had never heard the name Alice Emil Charles.

That would change. She would choose a new name, and New York would come to know it, rules or no rules. She would have fun. And she would laugh… laugh so long and loud that even the snooty debs and fancy chaps would hear her in their pricey mansions.

Alice turned her face up to the sun. Let them try and pity her now. Let them keep their rarified world of knowing the right people and wearing the right clothes. She wanted no part of it.

She would never go back again.

CHAPTER ONE

New York City, 1926

GRIFFIN DURANT STEPPED out of the elevator, strode across the polished lobby floor and slipped through the revolving doors, fortifying himself for the assault of smell and sound that crouched on Broad Street like an attentive predator awaiting its next victim. He pushed his hat lower on his head, wrinkling his nose against the acrid blend of gasoline, fermenting refuse and human sweat. His ears buzzed with the grinding of engines and the wildly varying pitch of human voices…but, as always, it was only a matter of moments before he was able to bring his senses under control and face the world with reasonable calm.

"Mr. Durant?"

A hand tugged at his coat, and he looked down at the smudged, familiar face of the corner newsboy.

"Paper, Mr. Durant?"

Griffin reached inside his pocket and pulled out a coin. "Here you are, Bobby," he said, tucking the paper under his arm.

Bobby stared at the coin and gave a joyful whoop. "Gee, thanks, Mr. Durant!"

Griffin sighed. It took so little to make a difference in this boy's life, yet he was only one of millions who called this city their home…teeming multitudes cast up on the shores of the biggest city in America. A metropolis that was rapidly becoming a place of corruption, violence and sudden death.

You could have chosen another city, he thought.

A city without such a thriving bootleg trade, for instance—though one couldn't escape the traffic in illicit drink anywhere in the United States. New York's business was simply bigger and more notorious than in any other municipality except Chicago.

You could have stayed in England. But then Gemma might never have come to know her native country. And he would never have escaped the reminders of the Great War that haunted him every time he read the latest news from Europe.

Griffin shook off the crawling sensation that raised the hairs on the back of his neck, took a firm grip on his briefcase and flagged down a taxi to take him to East Forty-second Street near Grand Central Station. The cabbie let him off a few blocks from the dressmaker's shop. As he walked, Griffin dispassionately examined the women with whom he shared the sidewalk: soberly dressed dowagers with small dogs clutched in their arms; working girls in conservative suits; tycoons' daughters in afternoon frocks from Worth or Chanel…and the flappers in their brazenly short dresses, daring anything male to gawk at their rolled stockings and rouged lips.

Frowning in disapproval, Griffin averted his gaze. Thank God Gemma had only left her English boarding school a few months ago and hadn't yet been exposed to what passed for fashion among the fast set. The gown he'd ordered for her birthday was elegant, expensive and eminently tasteful. He had meant to commission a frock from Molyneux, but there simply hadn't been time to have anything made overseas. With any luck, Gemma wouldn't notice the difference.

A short walk brought him to the couturière's. He summoned up a smile for the salesgirl who hurried to meet him.

"Mr. Durant," she said, "you've come for the gown?"

"I have, Miss Jones. Is Madame Aimery available?"

"Of course, Mr. Durant. If you will excuse me…" She vanished through the back door, leaving Griffin alone with the shop's other customer.

The young woman was slim and pretty, her warm brown skin a pleasant contrast to the pale green of her frock. Griffin tipped his hat to her, and she smiled in return.

"A very pleasant day, Mr. Durant," she said.

Griffin started. "I beg your pardon…have we met before?"

She laughed, a soft, rich chuckle. "I heard Miss Jones speak your name…and who hasn't heard of Mr. Griffin Durant?"

"Am I as notorious as all that, Miss…"

"Moreau. Louise Moreau." She offered her hand, and he took it. Her grip was firm. "Your notoriety is of the salutary variety, Mr. Durant. I—"

She broke off as Madame Aimery emerged from the back room with Miss Jones and another assistant, both assistants laden with ribbon-tied boxes.

"I beg your pardon for the wait, Monsieur Durant," Madame Aimery said in her light French accent.

"No trouble at all," Griffin said. He glanced at Miss Moreau. "Please attend to this young lady first. I'm in no hurry."

Madame Aimery gestured to her assistant, who approached Miss Moreau with three wide boxes. "Good afternoon, Miss Moreau," she said briskly. "Would you care to examine the dresses?"

Miss Moreau smiled slightly, matching Madame Aimery's almost imperceptible coolness. "That will not be necessary. I'm certain that Miss Chase will find the dresses very much to her liking."

"Mademoiselle Chase must not hesitate to call if we may be of further service."

"I shall so inform her." Miss Moreau took the boxes and tucked them under her arms. "Thank you for your time, Madame Aimery."

The couturière nodded and signaled Miss Jones to fetch the remaining box. "Monsieur Durant—"

"A moment, if you would. Miss Moreau…"

The young woman paused at the door. "Mr. Durant?"

"May I call a taxi for you?"

She smiled, her eyes crinkling at the corners. "Thanks so much, Mr. Durant, but I'm to meet my employer at a café down the street. The boxes aren't heavy."

He moved to open the door for her. "If you're quite certain…"

"I'm stronger than I look." She winked at him and swept through the door.

Madame Aimery gave a discreet cough. "Monsieur Durant, if you are ready…"

Griffin accepted Gemma's gown, paid in full and escaped into the cool breeze of twilight. Tall buildings cast long shadows that darkened the streets well before the sun went down, but for Griffin it was still as bright as noon. He considered hailing a taxi to take him to Penn Station, but he found that he, like Miss Moreau, preferred to walk.

With the coming of dusk, the dark-loving creatures crawled out of the woodwork: bootleggers and racketeers strutting out on the town with their painted floozies; truck drivers whose innocuous-looking vehicles contained a wealth of contraband cargo; laughing young men and their short-skirted dates seeking the latest hot spot to indulge in their passion for illegal booze; crooked policemen patrolling their beats, ready to lend their protection to the "businesses" that so generously augmented their meager salaries.

Griffin remained relaxed but alert, sifting the air for the scents of those denizens of night he preferred to avoid. He almost missed the faint cry from the alley as he passed. The smell of fear stopped him in his tracks; he tossed Gemma's box among a heap of empty crates at the alley's mouth and plunged into the dim canyon, unbuttoning his coat as he ran.

Two men in dirty clothing were circling a slight figure crouched between a pair of overflowing garbage cans, knives clenched in their fists. One of them looked up as Griffin approached. He grabbed his companion by the sleeve. "Joe," he hissed, "we got company."

Griffin slowed to a walk, keeping on eye on the muggers as he edged toward the garbage cans. "Are you all right?" he called.

"Yes," came the muffled female voice.

Joe's friend glared at Griffin, passing his knife from hand to hand. "What we got here, Joe? Some cake-eater who's lost his way to the Cotton Club?"

"Sure looks that way, Fritz," Joe said. He rubbed his thumb along the ugly scar that ran from the corner of his eye to his chin. "Listen, chump, and take some friendly advice. Get outta here and mind your own business."

"That's right," Joe said with a grin, "or me 'n' Fritz'll carve you up real nice."

"It seems we're at an impasse," Griffin said. "But I'll give you one chance to avoid possible serious injury. Leave now."

Joe and Fritz exchanged incredulous glances. Fritz dropped his shoulders and hung his head as if in defeat. Joe lowered his knife. They held their submissive poses for all of five seconds before Fritz attacked.

Griffin closed his eyes. It would have been so easy then to become the wolf, and take these hoodlums down with teeth and claws and sheer lupine strength. So easy to lapse into the killer's mind that had so often consumed him during the War, when he had taken revenge on those who'd slain his men in battle.

But he wouldn't give in. Not this time. Not while he had the safety of the civilized world around him.

Griffin caught Fritz's arm on its downward swing, applied a little pressure and neatly snapped the hoodlum's wrist. Fritz's shriek filled the alley like a siren. Griffin kicked his knife away and gently sidestepped Joe's charge. He slipped up behind Joe before the mugger could catch his balance, seized his waistband and collar and tossed him into a thick heap of refuse piled in the corner.

"I'll kill her!"

Griffin looked up. Fritz was standing with one arm hanging limp at his side and the other wrapped around the young woman's throat, the edge of a switchblade pressed against her delicate skin.

The victim was none other than Miss Louise Moreau.

She met Griffin's gaze, her eyes brave and calm in spite of her precarious situation. Griffin nodded slightly and returned his attention to Fritz.

"Let her go," he said softly, "and I may let you live."

Fritz tried to laugh and only managed a squeak. "Make one move," he growled, "and I'll slit her throat."

"You'll do nothing of the kind," Griffin said. "You see, you're much too slow to stop me, Fritz. I'll reach you before you can so much as twitch your little finger."

"You're crazy." Fritz licked his lips. "I've got—"

He never finished his sentence. Griffin crossed the space between them in one leap, wrenched the switchblade from Fritz's hand and flung him against the brick wall. Fritz slumped to the ground. Griffin grabbed Miss Moreau just as she began to fall and guided her to one of the empty crates.

"Sit down, Miss Moreau," he said. "I'll make sure these men are incapable of any further mischief."

Miss Moreau took a deep breath. "Thank you so much, Mr. Durant."

He squeezed her arm and walked back into the shadows, his legs shaking with reaction from the fight and the memories it had evoked. Joe still lay unconscious in the refuse heap; Griffin found a bit of rope and tied his hands behind his back. A moaning Fritz lay where he'd fallen, nursing his wrist. He wouldn't be molesting anyone soon.

Just as he finished tying Fritz's ankles together, Griffin sensed a sudden, unexpected motion behind him. He jumped to his feet and found himself staring into the concealed face of a woman, her head and body swathed in dark veils and a black velvet coat that fell to her ankles. Her tantalizing scent seeped into Griffin's skin and raced through his blood like a dangerous drug.

"Lou," the woman said, crouching to take Miss Moreau's hands, "are you all right?"

Miss Moreau passed a shaking hand over her hair. "I'm fine, Allie. Thanks to this gentleman."

The woman—Allie—scrutinized Miss Moreau's face and touched the narrow line of blood at the base of her neck. "They hurt you."

"It's nothing. I'd just like to go home."

"Of course. Just give me a minute." Allie rose, glanced toward the hobbled men and then fixed her attention on Griffin. "I owe you one, mister," she said in a voice half silk and half steel, "but I can handle it from here."

Griffin shook himself—hard. "I beg your pardon, Miss—"

"You don't have to beg anything. Just leave the rest to me."

His equilibrium somewhat restored, Griffin turned back to Miss Moreau. "Is this the employer of whom you spoke?"

"Yes." She began to rise. "Mr. Durant, may I present Miss Allegra Chase. Allegra—"

"Sit down, Lou, before you fall down," Miss Allegra Chase said sharply. She faced Griffin again. "What's your name?"

He tipped his hat, not without a touch of irony. "Griffin Durant."

"Oh, yes...the morally upright multimillionaire." Her mockery belied her terse thanks. "Well, Mr. Durant, if you'd like to keep playing the gentleman, you could do me a favor and escort Lou out to the street until I've finished here."

Griffin's bemusement turned to foreboding. "Finished with what, Miss Chase?"

"Merely what you started. Making sure these hoodlums don't try this kind of thing again."

Griffin stood very still, studying Miss Chase with astonishment. Such a casual reference to confronting a pair of street toughs would ordinarily have seemed absurd coming from a female swathed in a trailing black coat and tottering on high-heeled pumps. She was petite, her head hardly reaching his shoulder, yet the swiftness of her appearance and the way she'd taken him by surprise spoke volumes; he'd been caught off guard that way only a few times in his life, and never by an ordinary woman.

Nevertheless...

"I would prefer not to leave you alone, Miss Chase," he said firmly.

The blue-green eyes behind her veil glinted red. "Are your kind always so protective of people they've never met?"

Your kind. So she knew, as she must realize that he recognized her inhuman nature.

"I don't regard a situation like this as a matter of species," he said. "I wouldn't leave any woman with men such as these...not even one of *your* kind."

Miss Chase feigned surprise. "My kind, huh? What do you suppose he means by that, Lou?" She took Griffin's elbow, sending an almost electric current through his arm, and drew him aside.

"Come on, Mr. Durant," she said, purring his name. "Do you really think I can't put a scare into a couple of humans?"

Griffin shivered as he felt the stirrings of physical sensations he usually kept under strict control. He remembered when his father had told him how leeches attracted their prey: something in their smell had an overwhelmingly erotic effect on humans, enticing them as certain carnivorous plants lured hapless insects into their gullets. Griffin had never had occasion to witness the phenomenon himself, but now it was all too evident that what worked on humans could also affect *loups-garous*.

His mind, however, was still clear enough to recognize that Miss Chase's seductiveness was a pretense. She couldn't help herself, any more than she could help preying on hapless humans. As little as Griffin knew about the female of the vampire species, he presumed they were driven by the same instincts as their male counterparts.

Oh, this one could definitely put a scare into Joe and his companion. But she might not stop at that. Miss Chase undoubtedly possessed ten times the strength of the strongest human, quite possibly greater than Griffin's own. And she was surely more than capable of the casual violence that lurked beneath the handsome appearance and elegant demeanor with which so many of her breed deceived the world.

Unless, of course, she was discouraged from proceeding any further.

Griffin carefully freed his arm. "Better leave justice to the authorities, Miss Chase."

Her easy manner vanished. "Sure," she snapped. "That will work. Because if these guys work for a boss, they'll get off in no time."

"I have a contact in the police department. He can see to it that they don't escape so easily."

"A cop who isn't corrupt? That I've gotta see."

He held her gaze through the netting of the veil. "You're too young for cynicism, Miss Chase. Your soul won't profit by it."

"How do you know how young I am? And what makes you think I have a soul?"

"A hunch, Miss Chase."

"And how did you come to be so wise?"

"When you've lived a few more years—"

"Until I become a doddering old graybeard, like you?"

"I trust you'll never grow a beard, Miss Chase. It would not be an improvement." He tested the steadiness of his hand and extended it to her. "Come along...."

She slapped his hand aside. Her coat flew open to reveal long legs in flesh-colored silk stockings, exposed from ankle to knee by her short dress. He was momentarily distracted by the brazenness of her garments and the flash of bare skin at her upper thigh.

"Enjoying the view?" she taunted. "Want a better look?"

With one slender hand she lifted the veil from her face, and he finally saw the mysteries he had only guessed at before.

She was beautiful. Fair skin, so pale that it rivaled the moon at its whitest. Full lips enhanced with dark lip-rouge, contrasting vividly with the rest of her face. Aqua eyes, large and expressive, rimmed with kohl. Dark brows beneath the bangs of sleek black hair cut in a Louise Brooks bob just at the level of her stubborn, dimpled chin.

Griffin's breath stopped. He knew the leeches tended to be handsome creatures, their appearances enhanced by transformation and the power of their natural magnetism. But in his rare dealings with them, he'd never met one quite so magnificent.

"Seen enough?" Allegra Chase demanded.

"More than enough." He turned and offered his hand to Miss Moreau, helping her to her feet. "You and your mistress are leaving now."

Allegra detached Miss Moreau from Griffin's light hold and put her arm possessively around the other woman's shoulders. "This isn't over, Durant."

"It is for you, Miss Chase."

"You…you son of a—"

"You may regale me with every curse in your vocabulary, but it won't do you any good. Even if you believe yourself capable of harming these men, which I seriously doubt, I won't permit you to follow your less admirable proclivities."

"Permit?" She laughed again. "You think I want *your* permission, much less admiration?"

"No. Nor do I require yours." He caught her eyes. "Trust me. I'll see that these men are sent to jail."

"Ha." She brooded for a moment, and then her posture loosened like that of a cat pretending disinterest in a careless bird. "Isn't it a shame, Lou, that the world won't know of our savior's admirable chivalry?"

Miss Moreau glanced from Allegra to Griffin, frowning. "I doubt that Mr. Durant requires the world's approbation."

"True," Allie purred. "He's known as a recluse, isn't he? Not the sort to seek publicity." She leaned close to Griffin. "The gossip columns love to speculate as to who you really are under that straitlaced reputation. Wouldn't they just love to know *what* you are?"

Griffin clung to his patience. "They'd be highly unlikely to believe such a story, Miss Chase."

"Bet it would cut down on the list of scheming gold diggers hot on your trail."

"I haven't met these gold diggers. They must be chasing another man."

"No fiancée? No lover?"

"That's really none of your concern."

Her expression softened. "You're truly alone, aren't you?"

"Miss Chase, this is hardly—"

"Is that why you spend your time rescuing damsels in distress?"

Griffin looked pointedly toward the street. "I suggest that you see a doctor at once, Miss Moreau," he said. "If you and Miss Chase will—"

"Your hands are shaking," Allegra interrupted. "Are you sure you're not hurt?"

Cold sweat trickled under Griffin's collar. "I'm perfectly well."

"Could have fooled me. Still, it doesn't seem—"

The sound of an engine drowned out her words. Griffin glanced up to see a battered delivery truck backing into the alley. Instinctively he placed himself between the ladies and the vehicle.

"What is it?" Miss Moreau asked.

"Bootleggers," he said. "No doubt here to make a delivery."

Allegra Chase moved up to stand beside him, her body tense and alert. "What perfect timing," she murmured.

No sooner had she finished speaking than a pair of hatchet men jumped from the back of the truck, took up positions facing the street and stood watch while several other men began to unload crates into the alley. A door near the mouth of the alley opened to receive the shipment.

The last of the crates had just been passed into the building when another man, dressed from head to toe in black wool and leather, emerged from the truck and spoke to someone inside the door. After a moment the door shut, and the man turned to look at Griffin. His upper face was completely covered by his black fedora and sunglasses.

Griffin advanced a dozen paces, his hands loose at

his sides, and stopped a few yards from the man in black. He felt the leech's eyes on him, eyes as keen in the dark as his own.

The leech's lips curled. He signaled to a pair of henchmen armed with tommy guns.

"You shouldn't be here, dog," he said.

"It wasn't intentional, I assure you." Griffin spread his hands. "We have no interest in your business."

"You are pack—"

"My name is Griffin Durant. I don't belong to the pack."

The leech made a sound of disbelief and glanced toward Miss Chase. He hissed through his teeth.

"Allegra."

The lady in question strolled past Griffin and assumed an insolent pose, pushing her coat away from her dress to expose her shapely legs, one hip thrust out, her hand perched at the curve of her waist.

"Bendik. How *nice* to see you."

Griffin stepped in front of her again. "A friend of yours, Miss Chase?"

"A friend? That's a laugh." She returned her attention to her fellow vampire. "Quit your glaring, Bendik. No one here's going to cause any trouble, so why don't you just wander on home?"

The leech looked Miss Chase up and down with scarcely less hostility than he'd shown Griffin. "What are you doing with a dog?"

"He's woman's best friend. Or hadn't you heard?"

"Raoul…"

"Worried he might not approve? Too bad he can't decide who I spend my time with."

"You'll go too far, Allegra. I look forward to the day Raoul puts you in your place."

She yawned, stretching her body sensuously. "I'll see you at the funeral, Bendik. Send him my best wishes."

Bendik lingered a moment longer, looking as if he would have dearly loved to spray the alley with bullets, then retreated with an audible snarl. His henchmen jumped back into the truck, and the vehicle pulled out of the alley.

Griffin faced Allegra, his palms slick with perspiration. "That was very foolish, Miss Chase," he said.

"Why? Did you think I was in danger?"

Anger choked him. "That…man was clearly not well disposed toward you."

"He's one of Raoul's lieutenants, and Raoul isn't happy with me these days."

Griffin had heard the name Raoul more than once. The leech ruled the city's vampire clan, but the authorities naturally assumed him to be human.

"Raoul is your patron," he said.

"No!" Allie's vehemence made it evident that she was telling the truth. "My patron…he's nothing like Raoul."

Griffin almost asked her to explain but stopped himself. He had no desire to become involved in vampire politics.

"A pity your patron isn't here to caution you against your habit of imprudence," he said.

"Ha. You don't know anything about my habits. I—" She paused, regarding him through narrowed eyes. "Hey. You're as white as a sheet." She lay a hand against Griffin's cheek. "Your heart's beating like a jackhammer."

Her touch wasn't cold, as he'd expected a vampire's would be. He moved away. "I didn't savor the prospect of further violence, Miss Chase."

"Don't tell me you were scared. Bendik and his men would as soon have shot you as looked at you, but you were ready to take them on single-handedly."

He stepped away. "Only if every other method failed."

She shook her hair beneath the veil. Silky skeins settled about her face like black feathers. "So modest, isn't he?" she said to Miss Moreau. "A paragon of virtue."

Refusing to dignify Allegra's provocation with a reply, Griffin gathered up his and Miss Moreau's packages and asked the ladies to wait while he hunted down a policeman. Much to his surprise, Allegra and Miss Moreau were still in the alley when he returned with an officer of the law.

After the patrolman had briefly questioned Miss Moreau and taken the hoodlums into custody, Griffin flagged down a taxi and handed the ladies into the backseat. Allegra gave the cabbie an address that made Griffin raise his brows. It was one of the finest apartment buildings on Fifth Avenue, directly across from Central Park.

Miss Chase leaned out of the cab, her eyes unreadable behind the veil. "Thank you, Mr. Durant," she said coolly, "for Lou's sake."

"You're welcome, Miss Chase." She began to close the door, but he locked his fingers around the handle, holding it open.

She lifted the veil and gazed up at him, dark brows high. "Well?"

"May I telephone you? At your convenience, of course."

She grasped the card he offered between two slender, red-nailed fingers. "Why?"

"To inquire after Miss Moreau's recovery."

"Ah. Of course." She smiled slyly. "Do you like me, Mr. Durant?"

Her blunt question left him mute. There was no sensible answer, no response that was more than witless babble. They'd only just met. They were of different breeds, races that had been enemies far more often than not. All the prejudices of his species should make Griffin regard her with suspicion and loathing.

But Allegra Chase had a subtle charisma that was something more than the glamour others of her kind possessed…something complex and passionate beneath the brash, seemingly careless exterior. She was fiercely protective of her employee, a quality that must be rare among creatures who viewed humans as servile inferiors. She was brave…and dangerously reckless.

The fact that she belonged—quite literally—to another man had oddly little impact on Griffin's heart. He hadn't felt such an instinctive attraction to any woman in nine long years. It was utterly mad. And undeniable.

"It isn't real, you know," Allegra said softly. "It's just what we do." Abruptly her features changed, taunting him with an air of casual indifference. "It's a good thing for you that I have obligations that can't be broken. You don't want to know me, Griffin Durant." She let his card fall into the gutter. "You must have a nice, quiet life. Don't let anyone complicate it for you."

He backed away from the cab, his throat tight under the knot of his tie. "I should certainly not wish to interfere with yours."

"You already have. I hope you're far away next time I want to have a little fun."

She closed the cab door, and he caught only a brief glimpse of her face before the automobile drove away.

Deeply shaken by the fight and what had come after, Griffin walked aimlessly until well past sunset. Only then did he remember that Gemma would be wondering where he was. He stared at the slightly dented box in his hands and thought of the sweet, pristine dress inside it.

Gemma would never know a woman like Allegra Chase. And that was just the way Griffin wanted it. Miss Chase had done him a tremendous favor by reminding him just how untouchable she truly was.

CHAPTER TWO

THE CEREMONY wasn't anything a human would have recognized as a funeral. There were no clergymen, no pallbearers, no weeping relations. There would be no eulogies, no flowers thrown on the grave. The members of the clan stood in silent rows, sinister in their stillness, and draped in dark clothing that made them indistinguishable from the night sky and the black silhouettes of oak and chestnut trees.

Allie wore red. Cato would have appreciated her choice. She stood apart from the others, as befitted the one who'd been closest to the old scientist; she would scatter the ashes and speak the final words. And when it was over, not a single *strigoi* in the city could tell her what to do or how to do it.

She let her gaze wander away from her fellow mourners and drift to the buildings with their hundreds of windows glittering like stars. If any of the people in those buildings should wander into Central Park tonight, they would be in for a bit of a shock. Not that they would be killed; there were less drastic ways of dealing with inquisitive or thoughtless humans. Of course, Boucher didn't have to conduct his cremation ceremonies in Central Park; he did it because it was his way of claiming his part of the city. At night, the park belonged to the clan.

A cool breeze ruffled the fringed hem of Allie's dress. Her skin prickled, and she looked up to meet Raoul's stare. He held the vessel out to her. She took it, careful not to touch his skin, and hugged it to her chest.

So this is all that's left of a lifetime, Cato. How many hundreds of years, reduced to ashes.

How did you die, my friend? Raoul says it was the weakness left by the influenza that killed so many of us after the War. I don't believe it. You would never tell me what you were working on, that secret research for Raoul. But you gave me a great gift, and I still wonder if that had anything to do with your passing....

She remembered the moment when she'd felt his death...the terrible, devastating shock that had washed through her like molten lava, a monster that ripped her heart from her chest with jagged steel claws. The blood-bond had been severed, yet the ghost of it had lingered, leaving her helpless while her world shattered and slowly reassembled itself again.

Cato is dead.

Grief made a hard knot in her chest, but she didn't weep. She'd learned not long after her rebirth that vampires didn't—couldn't—cry, another one of those "anatomical changes" Cato had warned her about. But that was all right. The last thing she wanted was for Raoul to see her weak.

She nodded to the Master, reached into the vessel and gathered a handful of ashes. They felt dry and cool in her palm. She withdrew her hand, spread her fingers and scattered the ashes on the breeze, letting them fall where they might. No one made a sound. The others were here because Raoul demanded it, not because they cared that Cato was gone. They didn't like being reminded that even *strigoi* could die.

Allie emptied the vessel quickly and let it fall. She faced the clan members with a raw-edged smile.

"Cato was my patron," she said. "But he was also my friend. I know that doesn't mean much to most of you. The funny thing about Cato was that he hadn't forgotten that there are a few good parts about being human."

Someone hissed, a sound of derision and contempt. Raoul's head snapped around, seeking the source of the comment. The ensuing silence was deafening.

Allie laughed. "I always did enjoy a good argument." She grabbed her wrap from the tree branch where she'd hung it and threw it over her shoulders. "Rest in peace, Cato Petrovic."

She'd walked halfway to Fifth Avenue when a man stepped out from among the trees along the path and gestured to her frantically. She paused as she recognized his face, pursed her lips and went to join him.

"Elisha Hatch," she said. "I didn't think you'd be here."

The human looked right and left, his nervousness palpable. "I watched," he said. "Cato was my friend, too."

Friend? Perhaps, Allie reflected. But Elisha had primarily been Cato's laboratory assistant, the one human her mentor had trusted to help him in his mysterious work. He reminded Allie too much of a mouse…or more likely a rat, with his beady eyes and furtive movements. Not every human could live comfortably among vampires.

"What is it?" she asked, eager to be gone.

He rubbed his arms repeatedly, though the night was warm. The tattoos on the back of his right hand jumped and quivered. "Did Cato…did he give you anything before he died?"

The question caught her unawares. "What do you mean?"

"There was something…something he was supposed to leave to me if anything happened to him. It's missing. I thought you might have it."

Allie narrowed her eyes. "If something happened to him?"

Elisha risked a glance at her face. "The old weakness, you know."

Just as Raoul had claimed, but Allie was far from satisfied. "Was he in some kind of danger?"

"No, no. Nothing like that."

"And what was he supposed to give you?"

Once again Elisha looked carefully about them. "Papers," he said. "Notes from his research. He didn't want them to be misplaced if he…if he couldn't work on them anymore. He knew I was the only one who could understand them."

Allie weighed his answer. It seemed reasonable enough. "Why do you think he would have given them to me?"

Elisha shifted from foot to foot. "Maybe he thought they'd be safe with you."

"Safe from what?"

But Elisha had scarcely begun a hesitant reply when he saw something that shut him up fast. He melted back into the trees, leaving Allie to wait alone for Raoul.

The Master glanced toward the trees as Allie returned to the path. "Talking to someone?" he asked.

"I thought I saw an intruder hanging around."

"And did you?"

"I must have imagined it."

Raoul regarded her with a half smile. "Your imagination is as troublesome as your impertinence, Allegra."

"Impertinence? Is that what they call it?" She began to walk, and Raoul fell into step beside her, his shoes soundless on the path.

"Impertinence," he said. "Rashness. Foolhardy defiance."

Allie yawned behind her hand. "Glad I made an impression."

"Oh, you most certainly did." He moved almost imperceptibly, and suddenly he was in front of her, walking backward with casual ease. "I had hoped you would stay for a little chat."

"I don't think there's anything to talk about, Raoul. Not anything we haven't discussed before."

Raoul's handsome, ageless face altered before Allie's eyes, becoming more animal than human. "I'm not satisfied with the outcome of our discussion."

"I guess even the great Master will have to get used to the occasional disappointment."

With a flash of white teeth, Raoul came to a stop. Allie caught herself in midstride. They stood face-to-face, inches apart, gazes locked.

"I think not," Raoul said. "I've ruled the clan for thirty years. I have no intention of allowing a rogue protégée to foster anarchy and disrupt the organization I've built here."

"I'm not a protégée any longer, Raoul."

He leaned closer, bathing her face with his breath. "You will submit. There is no other way for you."

"I know the law as well as you. No one, not even the Master, can compel me to accept a new patron once I'm free."

"Free to spend your nights among humans."

"With anyone who doesn't think that the last good hooch was distilled during the Roman Empire."

"Does that include dogs?"

She remembered Bendik and his threats. "So what if it does?"

For a moment his eyes glinted red, and his body seemed to lift off the ground. Then he relaxed, the muscles under his perfectly fitted suit smoothing out with supple grace.

"You're afraid, Allie," he said. "There is no need for fear. If you give yourself to me, I will care for you. You'll want for nothing. You will belong."

Allie gazed into his eyes, feeling his power like hot, fresh blood flowing over her tongue. It would be so easy to agree. One bite, and she would be bound to Raoul as she had been to Cato…his offspring, his student, his property. She would be part of the *strigoi* hierarchy in which every member knew his or her place, virtually incapable of challenging the Master's control. No need to make decisions or worry about spending the long centuries alone. No need for anything but obedience….

She shook her head, casting off Raoul's subtle influence. "Nice try," she said. "But I'm not likely to want for anything with the money Cato left me. And by clan law you can't touch it, as long as I pay the settlement."

"You think that's enough?" He grabbed her arm and tightened his grip until she felt her pulse pound beneath her skin. "You'll never leave this city or rise from your lowly rank. You won't ever be permitted to create your own protégés, Allegra…not if you live a thousand years."

Allie pulled his hand away. "You think that's the

ultimate ambition of everyone like us? To make more? It may be the only way to gain status in the clan, but I don't care. Get it? *I don't care.*"

She pushed past him and continued toward Fifth Avenue, bracing herself for another assault. But Raoul didn't follow. That didn't mean he'd given up, not by a long shot. She would have to keep fending him off until he got the message, even if it took the rest of the century to do it. Of course, there was always the possibility that he would resort to illegal force, but that was a chance she was willing to take.

And how far are you willing to go, Allie? She slowed her angry stride, her thoughts returning to the strange encounter earlier that evening. Funny that she was still thinking of Griffin Durant. She should have been able to put him out of her mind easily enough; she'd spoken no less than the truth when she'd told him that he wouldn't want to know her. She'd done the right thing by implying that she was still blood-bound. One look at Griffin Durant and anyone would realize he was the old-fashioned type, still clinging to his Victorian morals, chivalrous to the core.

The problem was that she'd taken more than one look, and he had somehow become imprinted on her mind. There was no doubt he was handsome, and not in the pretty-boy way of so many among the pampered rich set. His slightly wavy dark brown hair tumbled over his forehead as if he hadn't the patience to slick it down into the usual style. He had a small scar on his chin. His wolf-yellow eyes had been haunted with some past suffering.

He was the right age to have served in the War, and that would explain a great deal. Allie couldn't imagine that many werewolves had volunteered to fight. Certainly no vampire would have done so. But Griffin Durant wasn't a member of the pack, and that in itself was highly unusual. The pack could be every bit as jealous as the clan. The fact that he'd kept his independence hinted at a powerful will and considerable courage.

Allie frowned as she stepped into the street and crossed to her building. Griffin Durant was a bit of a paradox. But then, so was she. Someone who didn't know better might have thought they were much alike, but they were worlds apart.

You wanted to protect me from myself, Mr. Durant, she thought. *You said I was too young, as if I couldn't know my own mind. But you're the one who's naive. No one can save anyone else. All of us, breeder and dog and leech...we all go through this life alone.*

With an impatient toss of her head, Allie dismissed Durant from her thoughts. She smiled at the night doorman and took the stairs all the way up to the eighth floor, relishing the exercise after the unpleasantness with Raoul. Almost the moment she touched the door-knob to her flat, the door swung open.

"Lou!" Allie said, shocked by the look on the other woman's face. "What's wrong?"

Lou retreated, letting Allie into the flat. "Something has happened, Allie...someone has—"

"Sit down, for God's sake." Allie grabbed Lou's arm and led her to the nearest chair. "I should never have left you alone. Let me get you a drink, and then you can tell me what—"

"I'm all right." Lou took a deep breath and clasped Allie's hand. "Someone has been in the apartment. I lay down as you suggested, and I must have fallen asleep."

She made a mute gesture at the room, and Allie

looked. At first glance there didn't seem to be anything wrong, but then she noticed the chair sitting off kilter, the pictures hanging crooked on the walls, the knick-knacks scattered across the floor. A glass vase lay shattered beside the sofa.

"I didn't move anything, in case you wanted to call the police," Lou said. "I didn't know where to find you, or I'd—"

"I know. You did the right thing, Lou." Allie pounded her fist on her thigh. "For you to suffer two attacks in one day…"

"They weren't after me. It's obvious that the intruder was looking for something, something he wanted very badly." Lou rose and took a few agitated steps toward the hall. "I think I woke up when the vase broke. I must have interrupted the thief, because he had barely started in your bedroom."

Allie clenched her teeth. "How did he get out?"

"Your bedroom window was open. He must have climbed up somehow."

"What did he take?"

"Only a few pieces of jewelry, as far as I can tell." Lou turned in a slow circle, her arms folded tightly across her chest as if she were fighting the urge to clean, scour and polish until every trace of the trespasser was consigned to the dustbin. "I'm so sorry. If only I'd woke up sooner…"

"Don't be ridiculous." Allie put her arm around Lou's shoulders and steered her into the kitchen. "I'm glad you didn't, or the bastard might have hurt you."

She pushed Lou into a seat at the small dining table and searched the cupboards for the tea Lou preferred to anything stronger. Once she'd prepared a steaming cup and left Lou to enjoy it in peace and quiet, she made a thorough examination of the flat from door to bathroom.

Lou had been right; it didn't seem that much had been taken. Allie's jewelry box had been upended and the contents scattered over her dressing table. The closet door stood open, boxes strewn and spilling mothballed clothing and last year's hats across the carpet.

Allie opened her window and looked out. There was just enough of a ledge for a very skilled acrobat to make his way to the fire escape.

A *very* skilled acrobat.

Allie sat on the edge of the mattress, working her fingers into the quilted satin bedspread. After her conversation with Elisha, she couldn't help but suspect that the "papers" he was looking for might be of interest to Raoul, as well. Elisha had said Cato had willed these mysterious papers to him purely because he was the only one who could understand them. But in the park he'd been scared to death that someone would see him. What exactly had those notes contained?

And who had been in Allie's apartment?

Was it you, Raoul? Do you want something else from me besides my submission?

If Raoul was behind this invasion, he'd obviously had reason to make it appear as if a common thief were responsible. Whatever it was he hoped to discover, she intended to find it first.

If you're spoiling for a fight, Raoul Boucher, she thought, *you'll get it.*

Because Griffin Durant was wrong. If it came down to choosing a soul or survival, she would pick survival every time.

"I CAN'T GO BACK."

The Master heard Elisha Hatch's puerile excuses with a calm that the human had every reason to mistrust. Hatch cringed, his defiance a matter of one fear pitted against another. The Master could spare him no sympathy.

"I must have them," he said coldly, holding Hatch still with the power of his gaze.

The human swallowed. "I tried. I asked her. She wasn't lying…she really doesn't know."

"Why should I trust your judgment?"

"I've known her ever since she was Converted. She's never been like the rest."

"Skilled at prevarication, you mean?"

The human blanched. "I don't intend any offense."

"Naturally not." The Master leaned back in his chair. "Even if she knows nothing of the papers, they may still be in her possession. You must finish searching her apartment."

"I think I was seen. They're looking for me already. If I go back now, they'll find me and question me, and then I won't be of any further use to you."

A certain slyness had entered the human's voice, a pathetic attempt at negotiation he had no hope of carrying off. "Let me wait a couple of weeks," he said, "so they think I'm really gone. *He'll* have enough to worry about soon enough, and then I can slip in with no one the wiser."

The Master traced his finger over his lower lip. "Perhaps you're right," he said. "But if he gets the papers first, I will hold you entirely responsible."

Hatch literally shook in his shoes. "I…understand."

Of course he did. All the Master's human employees were well aware of the penalty for failure. They were tools to be used and discarded, their petty dreams of wealth and power destined to end along with their short and miserable lives.

"Leave me," the Master told Hatch. "Stay out of my sight until you're prepared to complete your task, or I may lose my patience."

Hatch bowed. "I understand, My Liege." He scrambled from the room. After a moment the Master rose and went to visit the laboratory, reminding himself that what he sought was almost within his grasp.

Patience, he thought. *You have waited thirty years. You can wait another few weeks.*

A few weeks, a taste of ambrosia, and the new age of glory would truly begin.

"I JUST DON'T UNDERSTAND what's happened to her, Grif," Malcolm Owen said, dropping his head into his hands with a sigh. "It's been three months since I've spoken to her. Three months! I don't care what De Luca says…she wouldn't just give me the brush-off like that."

Griffin steepled his fingers under his chin, regarding his friend with sympathy. "You're absolutely sure her father didn't send her away?" he asked, signaling for Starke to refresh Mal's drink. "Just because he didn't object before, that doesn't mean he approved of your plans. It's one thing for you to take his daughter out to nightclubs and speakeasies, and quite another to marry her."

Mal laughed bitterly. "You talk as if De Luca was a real father to her instead of a mobster more interested in his profits than any genuine human emotion. He could have stepped in long ago if he'd wanted to put the kibosh on our engagement." He leaned forward, meeting Griffin's gaze. "Margot wanted it as much as

I did, Grif. She was sick of being a bootlegger's daughter. She was ready to throw it all away…the furs, the jewelry, the automobiles, everything."

And live happily ever after in your humble apartment off Washington Square, scraping by on a playwright's income, Griffin thought. *If she was that much in love with you, my friend, why did she disappear?*

He frowned. Mal was a passionate lover, just as he was passionate about his plays and music and art and life itself. He threw himself into every scheme with a wide-eyed enthusiasm and guilelessness that belied his experiences overseas. There had been times during the War when only his high spirits and optimism had kept Griffin sane. Mal had been sixteen then…hardly more than a boy, but as courageous as they came.

He was nothing at all like Griffin, but there wasn't much Griffin wouldn't do for the man who'd saved his life.

Mal snatched up his glass and downed half his brandy in one swallow. "I don't think I can go on without her, Grif," he said. "She's everything to me." He ran his hands through his fair hair. "Should I go back to De Luca and grill him again? He doesn't scare me. I'd do it in a second if I though it would make any difference."

"I doubt it would help," Griffin said. "The best you can hope for is that he'll throw you out on your ear, and the worst…" He shook his head. "No, Mal. Recklessness won't get you anywhere."

"Then what will?" The young man's eyes snapped with indignation. "I'm certain something has happened to her, and I won't sit idly by if she's in trouble."

Griffin got up and walked to the window, pulling the heavy drapes away from the mullioned glass. Late-morning light beat a path over the aged Persian carpet but did little to brighten the study, encumbered as it was with dark paneling and heavy oak furnishings.

"I doubt she'd be in the kind of trouble you're envisioning," Griffin said. "De Luca has too much power." He debated whether or not to speak his mind and decided to err on the side of mercy. "From all you've said, I still think it most probable that her father sent her away. And since he isn't likely to tell you anything more…" He turned away from the window. "Let me look into it. I have a few…connections in the city. Someone may know more than De Luca is telling."

Mal's eyes filled with hope. "Would you, Grif? That's awfully good of you."

"Don't thank me yet. It may take me a few days to track down my sources."

"These sources…are they—" Mal cleared his throat "—are they like you?"

"The less you know about that the better."

"But you *will* tell me as soon as you hear anything?"

"Of course."

Mal grabbed Griffin's hand. "You're the best pal a guy could have, Grif."

Griffin stepped back and gently freed his hand. "Will you stay at Oakdene tonight, or should I have Fitzsimmons drive you to the station?"

"Thanks for the invite, Grif, but I have that play to finish…and I think I might actually do it now that I know you're on the case."

"I'm glad to hear it." Griffin gestured to Starke. "Uncle Edward, will you please ask Fitzsimmons to—"

"Mal!"

Gemma's voice cut across Griffin's like sunlight through shadow. She bounded into the room, flashed

Starke a smile of apology and came to a halt before Mal.

"Why didn't you tell me Mal was coming, Grif?" she demanded. "He must think I'm terribly rude for not greeting him."

"Nothing of the kind, Gem," Mal said with a fond grin.

"It was just business…nothing that you would have found of interest," Griffin said. "Are you already done with your lessons?"

Gemma took a sudden interest in the toes of her sensible shoes. "Miss Spires had a headache," she said.

"I see. I wonder what brought that on?"

Gemma glanced up at him from under her thick brown lashes. "I'm making excellent progress."

"I hope so. I'd hate to think that I made a mistake in extracting you from that boarding school."

Gemma shuddered. "Mal, tell my brother how much I love America, and that I never want to go back to those horrid—" She broke off and put on a prim expression. "I'll be forever grateful for the education I received in the convents and boarding schools, but I am nearly seventeen. Isn't it time that I should see something of the world?"

"If that's your aim," Mal said helpfully, "New York is the place to do it."

"Thank you, Mal," Griffin said dryly. "Gemma, don't you think you should take some tea up to Miss Spires? It might make her feel better."

Gemma pulled a face. "Tea." She looked toward the sideboard. "Brandy would do her more good, or maybe whiskey…"

"You know very well that Miss Spires doesn't drink."

"Only because she's an old—" Gemma bit her lip.

"Don't you think I should be allowed to try it, big brother? My birthday is in less than a week."

"Out of the question."

"Why?"

Mal stared at the ceiling. Griffin sighed. "You're too young, Gemma, and alcohol is illegal."

"It's only illegal to sell it, not drink it. And anyway, you keep it here."

"Only for guests. You know I don't drink."

"You shouldn't keep the stuff around just for my sake, Grif," Mal said.

"Thank you, Mal. Your concern is appreciated but entirely unnecessary." Griffin turned back to Gemma. "I'm not going to argue the merits of the Volstead Act with you, Gemma. You aren't to drink in this house."

Gemma glared for a moment, turning undoubtedly rebellious thoughts about in her head. It was amazing how quickly she'd gone from obedient schoolgirl to willful young woman. Griffin could still remember the day of the fire, when he'd held a wailing two-year-old in his arms and watched, helpless, as their parents and elder brother were consumed by the flames. She had been so tiny then, so desperately in need of his protection....

"You can't keep me locked up forever," Gemma said in a deceptively calm voice. "In a few more years I'll be able to make my own decisions, and then…"

"Gemma, Gemma—" Griffin cupped her chin in his hand "—why are you in such a hurry to face the world? It's not as pretty as you imagine."

She met his gaze. "I know how hard it was for you…in the War, I mean…all the things you had to do—"

He dropped his hand as if she had burned it. "You

know nothing about it, and I never want you to learn. You'll have a good life. Nothing will ever hurt you, Gemma. That I promise."

"A good life." She flounced away from him, banging her heels on the carpet. "You mean, a life among the stuffy, boring, proper members of New York society. You want me to marry an ordinary man and become a good, obedient wife who gives respectable teas and occasionally plays tennis with the other young matrons." She swung back to face him. "What if *I* don't want that kind of life? What if I want jazz and dancing and fast motor cars? What if I want to be free?"

"Gemma…"

"Don't you see? We aren't *like* other people, Grif! We can't just pretend we are. What would happen if I married some nice, upstanding young man and he found out what I really am? Or will I have to hide it for the rest of my life?"

Griffin looked away, knowing she had hit on the one point he could not refute. He thought of another woman who would probably represent Gemma's ideal of the liberated, modern woman: a certain long-legged vamp with a black bob and aqua eyes and a throaty voice made for whispering seductive promises; a brash and brazen young woman who considered herself the equal of any male, human or otherwise—who'd made Griffin remember that he was still very much a man.…

"Why can't you just let me meet the others in New York?" Gemma demanded, cutting into his thoughts. "Why can't we be with our own kind?"

"The pack would hardly permit you the freedom you crave," he said.

"How do you know what they'd permit? You say

you don't trust them. I know it has something to do with what happened in San Francisco, but that was a different place. They aren't the same!"

"They're bootleggers," Griffin said grimly. "They break the law every day."

"But that isn't—"

"Please go to your room, Gemma."

She opened her mouth, closed it again and retreated with the air of one who had suffered only a temporary defeat. Griffin gave Mal a weary smile.

"I'm sorry about that little contretemps," he said. "You shouldn't be subjected to our family squabbles."

"It's nothing, really," Mal said. "You should have seen me and my sisters."

"I don't enjoy such disagreements," Griffin said. "She's so much younger than I. She never knew our parents."

"You had to raise her yourself."

"Starke took care of us after the fire, until I was old enough to assume responsibility for the administration of our inheritance."

"That's why you call him Uncle Edward?"

"He was like a second father to us." Griffin glanced away. "A few years later came the War. After that, Gemma spent more time with governesses or away at school than with me." He walked with Mal toward the door. "It's my own fault if she doesn't see things as I do."

"It's not your fault, Grif. Change is in the air. It's not the way it was before the War. There are so many girls just like Gemma…girls who won't go back to the way our mothers lived."

Griffin stopped at the foot of the staircase. "Gemma won't be that kind of girl, not as long as I have anything to say about it." He gripped the newel post, tightening his fingers until they ached. "My life has no purpose if I can't protect my sister."

"No purpose? Your money does plenty of good in the world."

"What I do is a drop in the bucket." The newel post creaked under his hand. "Gemma has no resources to face the harsh realities of a mad and violent world. I intend to see that she reaches womanhood with her innocence unspoiled."

Mal glanced at the floor and then back at Griffin, his expression guarded. "I hope it turns out the way you want it to, Grif, but don't blame yourself if it doesn't. Gemma isn't an ordinary girl, and not even you can control everything." He scuffed his shoe on the parquet floor. "I know it isn't any of my business…"

"No. It isn't." He heard the harsh tone of his own voice and managed a smile. "Don't worry about us, Mal. You have enough problems of your own, and I intend to help you as best I can."

"You know I'm grateful."

"There are no debts between us, Mal…not now and not ever."

They continued on to the door, where Fitzsimmons could be seen waiting in the drive with the limousine. Griffin sent Mal off to Manhattan and returned to his study, his thoughts bleak and troubled.

Despite what he'd told Mal, he wasn't at all confident that he could control Gemma. She had abilities far beyond those of a human girl her age. She was also far too inexperienced to fully grasp the consequences of employing them recklessly.

Griffin picked up the brandy snifter and swirled the liquor around and around, flaring his nostrils at the strong, sweet scent. Gemma would have been delighted to drink what Mal had left, but alcohol was the least of the dangers she faced. Maintaining Gemma's respectability would be easy in comparison to holding her wolf nature in check. For Gemma, just like her brother, could become an animal in the blink of an eye.

And once the animal was free, there could be no certainty of restraining it.

The smell of the liquor went sour in Griffin's nostrils. He'd been speaking no less than the truth when he'd told Mal that his life's only remaining purpose was to protect Gemma. God knew, nothing else seemed very important. Any competent businessman could take his place administering the Durant estate, charities and commercial holdings. He had little interest in politics and even less in high society, beyond what was required to secure Gemma's future.

And as for women…

He closed his eyes, drawn once again to the alley and his unconventional meeting with Allegra Chase. *"You're truly alone, aren't you?"* she'd said. *"Is that why you spend your time rescuing damsels in distress?"*

Her question had been intended as a gibe, but somehow she'd sensed that he'd cut himself off from the opposite sex, unwilling to embark on empty liaisons with the kinds of women who gave themselves freely for a handful of expensive trinkets or a few months of sexual gratification.

Allegra Chase was exactly that sort of woman, or would have been if she were human. She had her "obligations," her powerful ties to the vampire who had Converted her, as well as to the rest of the clan—literal ties of blood even more binding than those that governed the world of the pack. Yet Griffin was still thinking about her, still remembering the fire in her eyes and the curves of her shapely legs. He'd dreamed of her last night, and awakened this morning hard and aching with need.

It was ridiculous. Allegra had been honest enough to warn him that the attraction he'd felt wasn't real when he was too muddled to think for himself. She obviously had no more interest in him than she might have had in an African ape.

He should have been grateful. At the time, he'd thought she'd done him a favor. Allegra Chase was only a fantasy, and such visions eventually faded.

But this one hadn't. If the attraction hadn't been real, it surely would have died a quiet death by now.

Griffin scowled with self-disgust, nearly cracking the snifter in his hand. The only cure for these irrational thoughts and feelings would be time…time and the inevitable distance ensured by two very different lives.

Time and distance made no difference to Mal, he reflected. Once his friend had given his heart, nothing would shake him from his course. And that was why Mal deserved his happiness, he and the dreamers like him. No one—except for a few ambitious debutantes and their mothers—would notice or care if Griffin Durant cut himself off from the society that had kept him civilized.

Shaking off his grim mood, Griffin picked up the telephone receiver and gave the operator a number he hadn't called in far too long.

"Kavanagh," the man on the other end answered.

"Ross?"

"Griffin? Griffin Durant?"

"Hello, Ross. I know it's been quite a while—"

"Hell, man. Far too long. How is life among the

polo players and stuck-up debutantes of the North Shore?"

"The same as always. Nothing much changes here."

"So I've heard. How is Gemma?"

"Her seventeenth birthday is just around the corner."

"That old? You must be watching her like a hawk."

"I do what I can."

"And the pack? They aren't giving you any more trouble?"

"No more than usual. I can handle them."

Ross Kavanagh laughed, an edge to his voice. "Yeah. I'll bet."

"And you?"

"I'm dead to them. They leave me alone, and I don't tell the other cops or my friends in the Prohibition Bureau about their little operation."

"Good." Griffin sat in the chair next to the telephone stand, forcing his muscles to relax. "Listen, Ross…I have a favor to ask."

"What is it, brother?"

Succinctly Griffin recounted the situation with Margot De Luca. "Mal's already been to see her father, and asked around every club he and Margot frequented, all with no success. If you could keep your ear to the ground, I'd appreciate it."

"Sure. Mal's a good kid."

"Honest, honorable and the bravest man I've ever known."

"That's saying a lot, coming from you." Griffin heard the sound of a pencil scratching on paper. "I'll give you a call if I turn up anything."

"Thanks, Ross."

"Don't be such a stranger, Grif."

As he hung up and walked to the window, Griffin

wondered if he would ever be anything but a stranger. He had chosen his course, and he had no one to blame but himself.

With a snap of his wrist, Griffin closed the drapes and let the darkness enfold him.

CHAPTER THREE

LULU'S WAS JUMPING tonight, and the hottest table in the joint belonged to Allie Chase.

She relaxed in her chair, an unlit cigarette dangling from her lips, and watched Pepper Adair dance the Charleston on the tabletop, red hair bouncing to the jazz band's hectic rhythm. Bruce and Nathan were clapping in time, shouting encouragement as the tempo increased, while Nikolai stared into his drink with a feigned air of gloom and pretended he wasn't having a good time. Sibella scribbled furiously in her sketchbook, deftly working to capture Jimmy McCrae in action as he balanced an empty glass on his nose.

"It is all so meaningless," Nikolai said in his heavy Russian accent. "Must we always fiddle while Rome burns?"

Allie laughed. "Is there a fire somewhere I haven't heard about, Kolya?"

He gazed at her from dark, soulful eyes. "There is the one in my heart, which only you can extinguish."

"Oh, knock off the mushy talk, comrade," Jimmy said, tossing his glass from hand to hand. "You know Allie ain't interested."

Allie smiled sweetly. "What would I do if I didn't have you to tell me all about myself, Jimmy?"

"Good question." He grinned and loosened his

collar. "What I don't get is why you haven't fallen for me."

"Because she has better taste than that," Bruce said. "Such good taste, in fact, that I doubt any guy will meet with her approval in the foreseeable future."

"Don't listen to him, Allie," Nathan said, his gentle face achingly sincere. "Sometimes he just likes to hear the sound of his own voice."

Bruce snorted. "Allie would be the first to agree with me."

The music had stopped. Pepper jumped down from the table and plopped into a chair, her face flushed and her eyes bright. "What are y'all talkin' about?" she demanded. "Come on, tell!"

Allie signaled to the waiter to bring another round of drinks. "It's nothing very interesting, really," she said lightly. "Just a discussion of my love life."

Pepper leaned forward, the neckline of her frock falling open to reveal a sliver of her fashionably flat bust line. "How excitin'! Who is he, darlin'?"

"Nobody, Pep," Jimmy said. "Just the usual string of one-night stands."

"That's right," Allie said. "I believe in keeping things uncomplicated." She accepted a whiskey from the waiter and took a long drink. "I'm not the kind to settle down like Bruce and Nathan."

"Who says I've settled down?" Bruce said.

"Don't you be mean to Nathan, darlin', or you'll regret it. Won't he, Allie?"

Allie gave Bruce a long look, and he acquired a sudden interest in his drink. Kolya heaved a great sigh. Sibella chewed on her pencil, oblivious. The jazz band struck up another number.

Pepper seized Jimmy's hand and hauled him onto

the dance floor. After a moment, Bruce and Nathan wandered off together, while Kolya began to feel the effects of his drinking and sprawled across the table. Allie smiled fondly and ruffled his dark hair.

"Look after him for me, Sibella," she said. "I've got some business to attend to."

Sibella mumbled agreement, and Allie strolled away from the table. She felt the eyes on her… covetous eyes, hungry eyes, eyes that saw a length of leg in a rolled silk stocking, the sway of hips beneath a low-waisted black satin dress, and thought nothing of the woman to whom they belonged.

That suited her just fine. The men who watched her, who assumed she was a hot little number who would jump into bed with the first big six to pass her a line…they were her rightful prey. The boldest fish were the easiest of all to hook.

She allowed her gaze to wander from table to table, seeking the most likely mark. A young man in Oxford bags, his face as yet fresh and unblemished by years of dissipation, tried to catch her eye. She ignored him and passed on, pretending boredom as she examined the darkest tables in the back of the room. An otherwise appealing mobster grinned in her direction, but when he lit his cigarette she crossed him from her list.

At last she found the perfect donor: a good-looking man in his early thirties, his cynical expression hinting at experience, his body firm and fit. She sauntered toward him, dipping her finger in his gin and slowly licking it clean.

"Buy me a drink?" she asked, sliding into a chair beside him.

He looked her up and down. "What'll you have, baby?"

She picked up his half-empty glass, drained it and gave him a heavy-lidded stare. "Whiskey and soda," she drawled. "And make it fast."

He ran his fingertip from her bare shoulder to her wrist. "Why're you in such a hurry?"

"I don't believe in wasting time when I find what I want."

"I can see that."

"Then let's have that drink."

He signaled to a waiter, his attention focused on Allie. When the waiter failed to appear at the table, he glanced reluctantly toward the bar.

"Promise me you won't go anywhere, baby," he said, an edge to his voice.

She stretched luxuriantly, letting him glimpse several inches of bare thigh. "Now, why would I do that?" she purred.

He wrapped his fingers behind her neck, pulled her against him and kissed her, hard. She gave him exactly what he wanted, melting into him with a little gasp of admiration.

"There's more where that came from," he said, rising from his chair. "You stay right where you are."

He strutted off like a peacock, all broad shoulders and jutting chin. He thought he'd won the prize with his natural charm and good looks. Men like him always assumed that any girl, even the most sophisticated flapper, would fall for them if they so much as crooked their fingers.

Let him keep his illusions. He would awaken from their encounter believing he'd had the best sex of his life, which meant that she could come back for more and he would be happy to oblige.

Allie rolled her toes inside her pumps and let her

thoughts wander to yesterday's fruitless search. She and Lou had practically turned the apartment upside down looking for the papers Elisha—and obviously someone else, as well—believed Cato might have given her. They hadn't found anything but dust and a pair of earrings Allie had thought she'd lost last winter.

In a way, their failure had relieved Allie. She hadn't solved the mystery of why those notes were so valuable, but at least she could honestly say she didn't know where they were if someone questioned her again. And that might buy her time to keep looking into the circumstances of Cato's death.

The watch on Allie's wrist ticked out the minutes, and lover boy still hadn't returned. She glanced toward the table where she'd left Kolya and Sibella. Kolya had fallen asleep over his vodka; Sibella was still sketching the various speakeasy patrons, her tongue between her teeth. Beyond them, at the entrance to the club, the doorman had just admitted a single girl in a cheap, overlarge yellow dress and a long string of very expensive-looking pearls.

Allie tapped her fingers on the tabletop. During her two years of hunting in Manhattan's various clubs, speakeasies and dives, she had learned how to read people with almost perfect accuracy. For someone in her position, such a skill was essential. She'd used it to pick friends, like Bruce and Nathan and Pepper, who weren't apt to question her peculiarities, and she relied on it to help her select her donors.

Now she looked at the girl in the yellow dress, all wide eyes and red lipstick, and knew exactly what was about to happen.

Get out, Allie thought. *Get out while you still can.*

The girl took a few steps farther into the room,

staring about her with an expression that practically begged the worst of the roués and lady-killers to go for the throat. Fresh meat…that was all she would be to them. Easy to get drunk, since she'd probably never tasted anything stronger than near-beer, if that. Easy to win over with compliments and pretty words of admiration. All a man had to do was appeal to her desire to be daring and rebellious, and soon she would be eating out of his hand.

And then…

Hissing between her teeth, Allie folded her arms and turned away. It wasn't any of her business if inexperienced girls who thought they wanted a fast life came slumming where they didn't belong. The pearls suggested that this one had come from a privileged background. She'd probably never known a single day of suffering in her entire life.

Pampered and spoiled, Allie thought. *She's nothing like I was.*

But Allie's rationalizations didn't improve her unexpectedly dark mood. She swiveled to watch as the girl walked up to the bar with an air of forced bravado and ordered a drink. The bartender asked her a question; she tossed her head and laughed. With a shrug, he moved to fill her order.

A moment later the first of the tomcats arrived…a handsome Valentino with slicked-back hair and a smile too full of teeth. He sidled up to the girl and engaged her in conversation, not quite touching her, playing the good old pal for all he was worth. The girl picked up her glass, gingerly sipped and nearly choked on the liquor, her fair skin turning scarlet with chagrin. Valentino laughed companionably and gave her a brotherly hug. She gazed at him with gratitude and the beginnings of real interest.

Lousy taste, Allie thought. *At least find someone closer to your age. Like that boy in the Oxford bags....*

But the girl wouldn't be interested in some collegiate type. She wanted the bad men, the dangerous ones her parents wouldn't approve…just like the ones who were beginning to circle the bar like sharks smelling blood.

Maybe she'll get out of it all right. Maybe she's smarter than she looks....

"Miss me, baby?"

Allie's own chivalrous suitor set a fresh pair of drinks on the table and settled into his seat beside her. "Where were we?" he drawled. "Oh, yeah…you were saying that you don't like to waste time."

"That's right. I'm a regular bearcat when my interest is aroused."

"No kidding." He licked his lips, as his hand snaked under the table and came to rest on her knee. "I admire a doll who gets right to the point."

Suddenly Allie was sick of his clumsy lovemaking. She stopped his hand in its progress and pulled him out of his seat. "Let's go."

He gaped at her. "Now?"

She smiled mockingly. "Having second thoughts?"

"Don't you even want to know my name?"

"Why? You don't know mine."

"Sure I do. You're Allie Chase. Everyone knows you."

"Isn't that nice." She ran her fingernails up the length of his sleeve. "Are you coming or not?"

He surrendered to her tug and followed her to the back door. "Where are we—"

"The alley."

"You want to do it there?"

"Why not?"

He grinned, excitement replacing surprise. "All right, baby. Fast and hard it is."

Allie had barely stepped out into the alley when he lunged at her and pushed her against the brick wall, one eager hand pushing the skirt of her dress up to her hips, while the other fumbled with his trousers. She felt the hard bulge of his cock pressing against her belly. With a little sigh she pressed her face against his neck and kissed him, unbuttoning his shirt and loosening his collar. By the time he had worked her step-ins down around her thighs, she had pulled his coat and shirt away from his shoulders.

The hunger swept over her, demanding immediate relief. She kissed him at the juncture of his throat and shoulder, finding the veins closest to the skin. He forced her thighs apart. She bit him—gently, so gently that he would feel no more than the slightest pinch. She licked the small wound in his neck, tasting blood and releasing the chemicals her own body produced, waiting while they went to work…drew back and watched in astonishment as the slack face before her began to change, taking on strikingly different lines, brown eyes changing to gold, alight with fierce desire.

Allie swayed, startled by the sheer power of her own imagination. Her body grew hot and wet; she could almost feel Griffin Durant's hands on her flesh, stroking, exploring, touching her breasts and her thighs. His mouth was on hers, savage and possessive; he pressed against her, demanding entrance, and she could think of nothing but taking him inside, making him a part of her for all time.…

Her nameless prey gave a soft groan and let go of her shoulders. Griffin Durant vanished. Seized by desire that had become a raging thirst, Allie shook off her confusion and focused on the reality of the man in her grip. While he stood smiling in an erotic stupor, she took what she needed. The blood was both tart and sweet on her tongue. She felt new strength seep into her bones and muscles and organs, the first rush of euphoria that always came with a good feeding but was all too often so quick to evaporate.

When she was finished, she steered him to the wall and let him slump there while his wound began to heal. "That's all, friend," she said, patting his stubbled cheek. "You just sleep it off right here."

His knees buckled, and he slid to the dirty pavement. Allie stepped over his sprawled legs and tapped on Lulu's back door. A waiter opened it, glanced past her at the body and hastily stepped aside.

Everything was much as Allie had left it. Pepper was up on the table again; the jazz band was playing "Sugar Foot Stomp." Allie found herself searching the crowd for a yellow dress with a string of pearls. She didn't have far to look.

It was a lot worse than she'd thought. Valentino had been ousted from his favored position by a notorious womanizer who was known to prefer rape to any sort of consensual sex. Jake Greco was one of Carmine De Luca's hatchet men, a bully of the worst kind—immensely handsome, ruthless and consummately capable of deceiving any woman naive enough not to know his reputation.

Miss Yellow-Dress had been completely taken in. Several empty glasses stood before her on the table she shared with Greco, and she had another in her hand. She giggled as she drank, nearly dropping the glass when she attempted to put it down. Greco laughed and dabbed at her mouth with his handkerchief. She draped her arms over his shoulders and whispered in his ear.

Whatever she'd said gave Greco the encouragement he needed. He groped at her small breasts. She squirmed, still half smiling as she made some mild protest. Greco didn't listen. He pulled her hard against him and kissed her roughly. She braced her hands on his shoulders, trying to pull away. He made some comment that penetrated the girl's inebriated haze. Suddenly her smile was gone, her pretty face aghast with the dim realization of what she had done.

Allie ran her tongue over her teeth. She knew what came next: Greco would strong-arm the girl out of the club, and he would get away with it, because the few people who might give a damn wouldn't risk provoking his anger.

From the look of her, the girl wasn't going to go quietly. Greco clamped his hand around her arm and started for the door; she leaned away with all her insubstantial weight, the heels of her pumps scraping along the floor. The jazz band played on with furious abandon, and every pair of eyes in the place was focused on something as far away from Greco and his victim as possible.

Every pair except Allie's.

She strolled to her table, pulled her compact and lipstick from her tiny beaded pocketbook and carefully reapplied the vivid color. Jake Greco and the girl were halfway to the door. Allie fluffed her hair, gave her body a little shake and walked directly into Greco's path.

"Why in such a hurry, handsome?"

He stopped, briefly startled by her abrupt appearance. "Allie Chase," he said, digging his fingers into the girl's tender skin. "What do you want?"

Allie examined her nails. "Oh, nothing. I was just wondering why you always go after half-grown schoolgirls who can't fight back."

A look of pure fury crossed his face, and then his mouth twisted in a smirk. "Why would any girl want to fight me?" He yanked Miss Yellow-Dress around to face him. "They all love me. Ain't that true, doll?"

The girl averted her eyes, every muscle in her thin frame straining against him. "Let me go," she whispered.

Greco laughed. "They always say that. It don't mean nothing." He fixed Allie with a hard stare. "Get outta my way, bitch."

"Give me one good reason why I should."

He raised his fist. "I'll give you five."

She lifted her hand to her forehead and feigned a swoon. "Oh, deah. Whatevah shall Ah do?"

Greco swore and barreled forward, shoving Allie aside. She spun around and seized the back of his collar, jerking him to a halt.

"Come on, Jake," she said. "You can do better than that, even if you do like to rape little girls."

In one motion he released Miss Yellow-Dress and swung on Allie, his fist slicing the air like a meat cleaver. Allie moved lightly out of the way, grabbed Jake's arm and twisted. With a cry of pain, Jake fell to his knees. Allie held his arm behind his back and kicked him in his posterior.

"Want to try again?" she asked.

He snorted like a bull, his face beet red. "I'll kill you, bitch."

"No, you won't." Bruce came to stand beside Allie, Nathan at his back. "Allie's got too many friends, and you've got too many enemies."

"That is right," Kolya said, his heavy-lidded eyes flat with hostility. "You had best find another place to do your hunting, *svoloch*."

"And remember you ain't the only one who carries protection," Jimmy said, patting his coat suggestively. "Them that live by the sword die by the sword, so they say."

Allie's heart warmed at her friends' support. She didn't need their help, but it meant something that they were willing to give it.

"You heard them, Jakey," she said, blowing her breath into his ear. "You can get up and walk out of here…alone. If you pull your gun, you'll never make it to the door." She glanced up. "Pepper?"

"I'm here, darlin'."

"Look after the girl, will you?"

"I'll do that little thing. Come on, sugar."

Allie heard the tap of two pairs of pumps moving away. When she was certain the girl was out of harm's reach, she released Jake. He scrambled to his feet and thrust his hand inside his coat. Allie struck him across the face so hard that he crashed into the nearest table.

"One last chance," she said. "Get out."

Jake pawed at the broken table and hauled himself up, swaying like a drunken bear. Allie could see the thoughts plodding through his head as he weighed his chances. In the end he must have decided that Allie Chase was too strange a creature to fight. He staggered out the door.

Allie brushed at her dress and muttered a curse when she noticed the run in her left stocking.

"Send Jake the bill," Bruce suggested. His eyes twinkled with appreciation. "That was quite a show, honey. Hard to believe a little thing like you can fight so well."

"You did it for the girl," Nathan said, glancing toward the table where Pepper sat with Miss Yellow-Dress.

Allie smoothed her hair. "Jake needed taking down a peg, that's all." She kicked off her pump and removed the ruined stocking. "Get me a drink, Kolya, would you?"

Kolya sauntered off, and Allie went to join Pepper and Miss Yellow-Dress. It was obvious that the girl had been crying, and Pepper was doing her best to comfort her. The girl's long hair had fallen out of its pins, and her rouge was smeared. A fresh drink sat on the table before her.

"It's all over now, sugar," Pepper was saying. "That bad man won't hurt you again. Allie made sure of that." She looked up with a smile. "And here she is now."

Allie slid into a chair opposite the girl, pushing aside the empty glasses. "You mind giving us a little privacy, Pep?"

"Sure thing, darlin'." Pepper went off to join a friend at a nearby table, leaving Allie alone with the girl.

"Are you all right?" Allie asked.

Miss Yellow-Dress met her gaze, and for the first time Alley saw that her eyes were a rich combination of brown, gold and green, large and expressive and filled with confusion.

"I…" She swallowed. "Thank you so much for what you did." Her voice held the slight trace of an accent, made somewhat indistinct by the lingering effects of alcohol.

But Allie barely heard her. She was struck by a realization that had utterly escaped her until this moment, an awareness that made her skin prickle in a way it hadn't done since a certain meeting in an alley off East Forty-second Street.

"What's your name?" she asked.

The girl hesitated. "Ruby."

"Ruby what?"

"Du…Dubois. Ruby Dubois."

Kolya arrived with Allie's drink, and she took a fortifying mouthful before she spoke again. "This is your first time at a speak, isn't it?"

"Y-yes."

"How old are you, Ruby?"

"Six…almost seventeen."

"Do you understand the risks you took tonight?"

The girl stared at Allie's glass. "Yes."

"Does your family know where you are?"

"No."

"Then hadn't you better call them and let them know?"

"No! I mean…" Ruby hunched her shoulders. "I don't want him to find out. Anyway, I'll be home before he knows I was gone."

"He?"

"My brother. He'd kill me if he knew I'd come here."

I'll just bet he would, Allie thought. "Why didn't you fight harder when Jake tried to take you out? You could have overpowered him, just as I did."

"I beg your—"

"I know what you are, Ruby."

The girl's eyes widened. "You do?"

"Sure. Amazing how easy it is to tell once you've got the knack."

"Then you…you're one of us?"

"Try again."

"Oh." Ruby flushed with mingled fear and excitement. "You're a—"

Allie pressed her finger to Ruby's lips. "You're the only person here who knows."

"Not even your friends?"

"That's right."

"But the way you fought… Didn't anyone notice?"

"It's amazing what people will accept if you act casual enough about it."

Ruby considered that for a moment, chewing on her lower lip. "If you're…one of *them,* why did you help me?"

"You mean, those old, outdated prejudices?" Allie buffed her nails on her thigh. "They bore me."

"Oh." Another thought captured her attention. "Do you know any other *loups-garous?*"

Once more Allie thought of golden eyes and a strong, grave face. "Not many."

"I've never met anyone from the pack," Ruby said eagerly. "My brother won't let me."

"Your brother?"

"Gerald. Gerald Dubois."

"Don't know him. Anyway, I thought all werewolves belonged to the pack."

"Not us." She sighed. "My brother doesn't trust many people. He likes living alone."

It was painfully obvious that Ruby was desperate to confide in someone, desperate enough that she would reveal all sorts of personal information to the first person who seemed to be on her side. Allie found herself prepared to encourage the girl for reasons she couldn't quite acknowledge.

"What's he like, your brother—besides being so eager to protect you?"

"He's always serious. He almost never laughs. I know a lot of it's because of the War. He was my age when he went over. I hardly remember what he was like before." She ran her finger through a puddle of whiskey on the table. "He wants me to marry a rich man and become a member of New York society."

"*Human* society?"

"He thinks I'll be safer that way."

"Because he doesn't trust other werewolves."

"Yes."

"But you want to be one of them."

"I want to be free."

Allie felt an unwelcome stab of pity. She knew what it was like to feel trapped, confined to a narrow life with the oblivious world going past you day after day. She'd been confined by her own body. Ruby was being asked—by her own kin, no less—to deny her very nature.

They had more in common than Allie cared to admit.

"Don't worry, kid," she said gently, "when you're a little older, you'll find a way to become what you were meant to be."

Ruby sat straighter in her chair, as if bracing for an argument. "Will *you* teach me?"

"Teach you what?"

"To be like you." She scooted forward, the pulse beating fast at the base of her throat. "To be beautiful and sophisticated and free."

At another time Allie might have been amused, but the situation was beginning to get far too complicated. "I don't take apprentices," she said. "And your brother…"

"But he doesn't have to find out! I was careful. Miss

Spires is on my side. We're not far from the train station, so it's easy for me to get here."

"And easy for you to get into trouble."

Ruby lifted her chin. "It's better to take risks and try new things than spend your whole life afraid of anything different."

Like your brother is afraid, Allie thought. She leaned back in her chair. "You're right," she said, "you can't spend your life running away."

"Then you'll let me stay, just for tonight? I promise I won't be any bother."

"Oh, let her, Allie," Pepper said, returning to the table. "No one is goin' to bother her now."

"Sure," Jimmy said, sprawling into an empty chair. "Poor kid probably never has any fun." He grinned at Ruby. "Where d'you live, infant?"

"On Long Island," Ruby said, gazing at Jimmy's platinum hair.

"There you go," Jimmy said. "Give her a break, Allie."

Sibella pulled up another chair and took the pencil out of her mouth. "I'd like to sketch her," she said.

"And I," Kolya announced, "shall compose a poem on the death of innocence. She must remain as my inspiration."

Allie frowned. It wasn't as if Ruby—if that was really her name, which she doubted—would suffer any real harm from remaining with the group for a few more hours, now that she'd gotten through the worst of the night. And if "Gerald Dubois" really did have her future planned out for her—which Allie didn't doubt in the least—*she* wouldn't deny the girl the chance to experience a little precious freedom beforehand.

"All right," she said. "You can stay. As long as you don't give me any grief when it's time to go home."

Ruby grinned. "I won't, I promise!" She practically danced with excitement, all memories of her ugly encounter with Greco happily forgotten. Everyone crowded close to welcome her into Allie's circle.

The night was loud, bright and raucous. Pepper set about teaching Ruby the Charleston, while Kolya drank vodka and scribbled scraps of poetry on his notepad. Allie showed her how to apply lipstick with a few quick strokes of the finger and coached her in how to kick a troublesome skirt chaser in the groin. The girl learned quickly, her innocent charm and unfeigned pleasure a surprisingly welcome change in such a jaded atmosphere.

Allie had been naive in many ways when Cato had Converted her. Ruby aroused feelings she'd almost forgotten…just like Griffin Durant. And maybe that wasn't such a terrible thing after all.

By 3:00 a.m. Allie was beginning to regret that she would have to send Ruby home. She pushed through the gang of admirers who had become a permanent fixture around the girl and found Pepper standing over Ruby with a pair of shears in her hands. Half of Ruby's luxuriant brown tresses lay on the ground at her feet; the other half still hung over her shoulders.

"There, now," Pepper said. "We're halfway there…"

"Pepper!" Allie snatched the shears out of Pepper's hands. "What do you think you're doing?"

Pepper's small pink mouth dropped open. "Why, I… Ruby wanted a nice little bob, and I've had some experience with—"

"With angry brothers?" Allie stood in front of Ruby, hands on her hips. "This was your idea?"

Ruby was utterly unrepentant. "I hate my hair. I want it to be short, like everyone else's. What's wrong with that?"

"I thought the idea was to hide tonight's adventures from your brother? That won't exactly be possible now, will it?"

"I'll tell him I just went to a barbershop."

"In the middle of the night? I'm sure *that* will appease him." Allie weighed the shears in her hand. "You don't mind if I finish it, Pepper?"

Pepper stepped back, and Allie took her place behind Ruby. She was just putting the finishing touches on Ruby's new bob when a sudden commotion began at Lulu's front door. The doorman and a couple of bouncers were attempting to prevent a man from entering, but it was quickly obvious that they were having little success. The man cast them off like a dog shaking water from its coat and charged into the room, looking sharply this way and that.

Ruby let out a soft gasp and started up from her chair. Allie didn't have to study the newcomer to know who he was or why he was here. Her heart began to race with unaccustomed anticipation.

She steered Ruby back to the table, took her own seat and waited while her friends settled around her. An instant later the newcomer's eyes found Allie— yellow eyes filled with startling intensity and seething emotion—and then focused on Ruby. He strode toward them, long legs eating up the distance, and came to a halt beside Allie's chair.

"Miss Chase," he said, "what in God's name are you doing with my sister?"

CHAPTER FOUR

ALLEGRA CHASE STOOD UP SLOWLY, undeniably majestic in spite of her scandalously short dress and painted face. She met Griffin's gaze without flinching, and he felt alarm and astonishment give way to very different feelings over which he had not the slightest command.

He had never expected to see her again, and certainly not like this. Oh, he'd known at their first meeting that she was wild—a true child of the bold new generation, no matter when she'd been Converted. But he'd assumed that she had briefly escaped the authority of her patron and would soon return to the protection of her own kind.

He'd clearly been wrong. Whoever her patron might be, he must have no objection to his protégée making a spectacle of herself in a very human public place. And Allegra Chase *was* a spectacle, flaunting her nearly naked legs, commanding the attention of every male in the room. Griffin understood at once that she ruled this seamy hotbed of Bohemians, dissipates and addicts.

It would have been disconcerting enough to meet her again under such circumstances, but to find her with Gemma was nearly inconceivable. What were the odds of such an occurrence?

What were the odds that Allegra Chase could

plunge him into confusion with a single glance of those remarkable eyes?

"Your sister is perfectly safe," she said, her voice cool and reasonable, as if nothing were at all out of the ordinary. "Why don't you join us, Mr. Durant?"

He steeled himself against the powerful allure of her nearness. "Did you bring Gemma to this place, Miss Chase?"

She lifted one dark, sculpted brow. "I never met her before tonight. She walked in on her own. My pals and I just happened to be here at the time."

"Yet you don't seem surprised to see me," he said, keeping a tight rein on his anger.

"Ruby—Gemma—mentioned that she had a brother, and I put two and two together. There *is* a family resemblance, if you hadn't noticed."

"You know each other?" Gemma said in a small voice.

Griffin's glare silenced her immediately. "Our acquaintance has been brief, Miss Chase, but I had assumed you to be an intelligent woman. If my arrival has failed to surprise you, you must have guessed that I would hardly approve of my sister coming to a dive in the middle of the night. Or are you so accustomed to the habitués of such sordid environments that you mistook Gemma for one of them?"

A muscular young man rose from the table. "Hey, you—"

"It's all right, Bruce." Miss Chase toyed with the oddly old-fashioned locket that was her only jewelry, swinging the chain between her fingers. "It's no wonder she has to sneak around, Mr. Durant, if this is the way you treat her. And anyway, since she'd already gotten here by herself, I didn't figure she would become much more corrupt if she stayed for a few hours."

One of Allie's "pals" smothered a laugh. Griffin gazed at the faces about the table, men and women who considered illegal clubs their natural homes. Gemma, in her flimsy dress and bright-red lipstick, did indeed, look just like one of them.

A woman like Allegra Chase would draw Gemma to her as a blossom lures a bee. She was beautiful, witty, willful…and obviously contemptuous of the civilized standards that gave life its structure. It would be an easy matter for her to lead an innocent girl like Gemma to her ruin, even if she weren't a vampire.

Griffin circled the table, ignoring Miss Chase, and stood over Gemma with folded arms. "Miss Spires admitted everything," he said. "What do you have to say for yourself?"

Gemma sank down into her chair. "I…I didn't mean—"

"Do you know how many places like this Mal and I have searched tonight? I was beginning to think you…" He took a steadying breath, remembering that he mustn't let any of them, his sister least of all, see him lose his composure. He picked up one of the numerous empty glasses on the table. "How much have you been drinking, Gemma?"

"We haven't given her a thing," Allegra said.

Gemma cast Allegra such a look of gratitude that Griffin was sure she was lying. He carefully replaced the glass and stared at Gemma until she lowered her gaze. "Where did you get that dress?"

"I…I ordered it two weeks ago. Griffin—"

"And your hair. How did that come about, might I ask?"

"I cut it for her," Allegra said. "I think it's very becoming."

Griffin swung toward her, his tongue tripping on harsh words he couldn't bring himself to speak. "You had no right," he said. "She is my sister. My responsibility."

Miss Chase continued to gaze at Griffin through half-lidded, kohl-rimmed eyes. "What bothers you most, Mr. Durant, Gemma's clothes and hair, or the fact that she slipped out of your control for a few brief hours?"

"I beg your—" He broke off, refusing to take her bait. He cupped Gemma's chin in his hand. "Do you have any conception of the trouble you've caused?"

"I...I didn't think it would be dangerous...."

"You could have been hurt, Gemma. Don't you understand that?"

All at once the noisy room seemed very quiet. Gemma set her jaw. "Allie wouldn't let anyone hurt me."

Griffin hesitated. Perhaps Gemma didn't know what Allie was. Not all *loups-garous* could recognize *strigoi* by sight or smell. "Did you go out tonight expecting you'd find someone to take care of you? Is that it?"

"She didn't come running to me," Allegra said. "But if she were to find herself in a position where she couldn't fight back, whose fault is that?"

"I don't believe I take your meaning, Miss Chase."

She shrugged, as if to dismiss her own comment, but the redheaded woman across the table snorted loudly and pulled a face. "You ought to know, sugar, that if it hadn't been for Allie, you'd have had a real reason to worry."

Griffin's mouth went dry. "Gemma," he said, "did someone...bother you tonight?"

"Allie took care of it," said the man called Bruce, his mouth twisted in contempt.

"That's why she took your sister under her wing," said the slender man seated next to Bruce. "None of us meant any harm, Mr. Durant."

Griffin well remembered how Miss Chase had been prepared to take on the muggers for the sake of her maid, but he found it hard to believe that any of these people knew of Allie's true nature. "Who was this person?" he asked.

"It doesn't matter," Allegra said. "He's gone, and he won't be back."

"I see." He held her gaze. "It seems I owe you an apology, as well as my thanks, Miss Chase."

She smiled with familiar mockery. "I accept your apology."

"I hope you'll allow me to repay the debt."

"Let's just say we're even now, Mr. Durant."

He looked away so she wouldn't see how much he'd felt the sting of her rebuff. "In that case," he said stiffly, "Gemma and I will be leaving."

He helped Gemma out of her seat and draped his overcoat around her. She shivered in the crook of his arm. As he started for the door, he heard raised voices outside the building, and suddenly the men standing guard at the entrance turned and dashed for the bar. The bartender and waiters scrambled toward the darkened rear of the speakeasy. Men and women at the tables shouted questions and craned their necks to determine the source of the disturbance.

Allegra appeared beside Griffin. "It's a raid," she said. "The cops won't arrest any of us, but you probably don't want Gemma involved."

"A raid?" Gemma said. "I want to see—"

"Out of the question," Griffin said. "Do you have any suggestions, Miss Chase?"

"Come with me."

She started at a fast pace toward the back of the room, leaving her friends chattering at the table. There was a scarred wooden door behind the bar, barely visible behind stacks of seemingly innocent fruit crates. Allegra opened the door and moved aside, ushering Griffin and Gemma into an unlit alley. The sour stink of urine struck Griffin with the force of a storm. A drunken man lay sprawled across the filthy ground; Griffin lifted Gemma in his arms and carried her to the end of the alley, setting her down on the sidewalk.

"You don't have anything to worry about now," Allegra said. She pushed a stray lock of hair out of Gemma's face. "Your brother is right. You've had enough adventure for one night."

Gemma tried to assume a sophisticated air, but it dissolved in a helpless yawn. Allegra's eyes sparkled with a devastating combination of mischief and sympathy. Griffin looked at her and did his best not to let his body control his mind.

"Once again I owe you a debt of gratitude," he said. "Even if you refuse to accept my obligation."

She laughed. "You wouldn't like it if I held you to that obligation. Anyway, Gemma made the evening considerably more amusing."

"Is that truly all that matters to you, Miss Chase? Amusement?"

"What else is there?"

Her insouciant response troubled him past all reason. He'd seen plenty of evidence that she was a most unusual vampire, but he'd also begun to realize that she was not as lacking in character as he had at first chosen to believe.

"May I ask you a personal question?" he said.

"Shoot."

He began to walk in the direction of the street, where Fitzsimmons waited a few blocks away with the limousine, supporting a sleepy Gemma with his arm about her waist. "There weren't any other vampires at Lulu's when I came in."

"So?"

"So where is your patron, Miss Chase? It was my understanding that vampire patrons are notoriously jealous of their protégés and hardly encourage them to wander loose around the city."

She fell into step beside him. "That may be true of most protégés, but not me."

"How is it that you have a choice?"

She hesitated, obviously weighing her answer. "My patron's dead."

Griffin missed a step. "But you told me—"

"I know. It got rid of you, didn't it?" Her voice lost a little of its lightness. "Even when Cato was alive, he let me live as I chose. And that's exactly what I'm doing."

"How long since you were…altered?"

"Two years. And you don't have to dance around the word. It doesn't offend me."

And why should it, Griffin thought, when she so obviously hadn't suffered from the transformation? "So now you choose to associate with humans rather than your own kind."

"Just like you." She cast him a sideways look. "You're curious, aren't you…about how we live and what we do? Even though you hate us."

"I hardly hate you, Miss Chase."

"But it disgusts you, the blood drinking and all. That's one of the reasons you were so upset that I was with Gemma."

Griffin glanced down at Gemma's tousled head, regretting the direction the conversation had taken. "Surely you couldn't Convert her."

"Couldn't even if I wanted to. We're of different species, after all, and I'm not mature enough to create my own protégés. That usually takes a few years."

"But you could have...taken her—"

"Blood? That would have been a novel experience. But I'd already fed, and we don't have to drink more than a couple of times a week."

"I see." He tugged at his collar, reluctant to hear any more such confidences. "Whatever your personal habits, I don't think Lulu's is an appropriate venue for my sister."

"You really think bobbed hair and a short dress will ruin her?"

"Rebellion for rebellion's sake is not an admirable quality."

They walked half a block in silence. "She guessed what I was, you know," Allegra said. "She wasn't afraid."

"I'm hardly surprised, Miss Chase. Gemma has no experience of your worlds, either of them. You were compelled to rescue her from someone who meant her harm. That's proof enough that she doesn't belong here."

"Only because she doesn't know how to *be* what she really is."

Gemma muttered a garbled protest and subsided back into her half sleep. Griffin lowered his voice. "She isn't an animal, and I don't intend to let her behave like one."

"An animal? Is that what you think you are?"

Griffin remembered how tempted he had been in the alley...tempted to Change and rid the world of two humans the city would never miss. "I prefer civilization, Miss Chase."

"Civilization as in the rich snobs on Long Island."

"If you like."

"Then you do plan to keep Gemma locked away."

"Is that what she told you?"

"Isn't it true?"

"I dislike being rude, Miss Chase, but—"

"You'd prefer I kept my nose to myself." She shook her head. "Where did you get such a hard view of the world, Mr. Durant? Was it the War?"

Griffin forced himself to keep walking. "What drives you to waste your life on fleeting pleasures and unthinking nonconformity?" he asked.

She said nothing. The sound of her footsteps stopped, and for a moment he thought he had driven her away with his inexplicable rudeness. But then he heard the tap of her heels coming up behind him, and her sweet, earthy fragrance swirled about his head.

"I know what it's like to live in a small room with no hope of escape," she said. "I swore I'd never go back to that room." She caught the sleeve of his coat. "What's your cage, my friend?"

Her question left Griffin mute. He estimated the distance left to the limousine. Once he had Gemma safely transferred to Fitzsimmons's care, he would wait for Mal at their rendezvous site on Sixth Avenue. Miss Chase would surely become bored with baiting him and go back to her friends. They would go their separate ways once and for all.

He would find nothing to miss in her unfeminine frankness, her brazen choice of clothing, the firm curve of her calf, the obsidian silk of her hair, the sparkle of aqua eyes....

His thoughts stuttered to a halt. He lifted his head, detecting the faint scent that threaded its way among the city's common odors of gasoline, steel and refuse. The hairs on the back of his neck stood erect.

"What is it?" Allegra asked. "What's wrong?"

He took her wrist in a rigid grip. "Stay close to me," he said. "Don't interfere."

"But—" Her eyes searched the darkness as she sensed the others' approach. Gemma's face emerged from Griffin's overcoat.

"Griffin?" she murmured.

"It's all right, Gemma," he said. "Keep still."

"Good advice," a voice said.

A tall figure rounded the corner of a narrow tenement building, his shadow preceding him. At his side loped two enormous canines, eyes reflecting yellow from a distant streetlight. They ran ahead and came to a stop a few dozen feet from Griffin, pacing back and forth with lolling tongues.

Griffin pushed Allegra behind him and shook out his shoulders, flexing his muscles and breathing deeply. "Ivar," he said. "To what do I owe the pleasure?"

Ivar strolled forward. "I came to talk business, Durant," he said, "but not with *that* around."

Allegra brushed against Griffin, air hissing between her teeth. Griffin forcibly restrained her with one arm, holding Gemma close with the other.

"I'm afraid I don't understand you, Ivar," he said. "Perhaps it would be more convenient if we meet at another time and place."

Ivar laughed. The wolves stopped their pacing and faced Griffin, lips pulled back from ivory fangs. "Since when did you start consorting with leeches, Durant? You think *that's* better than us?"

"You want me to show you, dog?" Allie purred. A cloud of hostile scent rose from her body. It struck Griffin full force, and even Ivar blinked.

"Easy," Griffin whispered. He met Ivar's gaze. "It's none of your business what company I keep," he said.

"Oh, yeah?" Ivar snapped his fingers, and the wolves sat on their haunches, ready to lunge at the slightest provocation. "It *is* our business if what you do endangers the rest of us."

Griffin gently turned Gemma and passed her, coat and all, into Allegra's arms. "Keep her safe," he said. "No matter what you have to do."

"You're going to fight?"

"I may not have a choice."

Allegra nodded, though her eyes blazed with fury. She backed away, half carrying Gemma with her. The wolves leaped up and circled behind the women, giving Griffin a wide berth.

"You should know how little Garret approves of your attitude," Ivar said.

Griffin stalked toward Ivar, black anger churning in his belly. "Sloan isn't here."

"He takes my advice, and you'd better take mine. You're like a man walking down the middle of Broadway on a Saturday night, thinking he'll never get hit. It's a very dangerous way to live, brother."

"If you want to discuss my life, that's fine with me. But let Gemma go. This doesn't concern her."

"Oh, but it does." Ivar glanced toward the wolves, who continued to pace around Allegra and Gemma. "It has everything to do with her."

"If it's a fight you want, Ivar, I'll be happy to give it to you."

"And bring the whole pack down on your head? I

think you'd rather listen to what I have to say." Ivar withdrew a silver case from his pocket and selected a cigarette. "You've been out looking for Gemma all night, haven't you? She slipped her leash and got all the way to Fifty-second Street before you even knew she was gone." He put the cigarette in his mouth and produced a lighter. "Some of us picked up her scent and followed her to Lulu's. We saw how your sister walked right into the place as if she had nothing to hide." He sucked on the cigarette. "Very bad form, Durant."

Griffin clenched his fists, sickened by the thought that the pack had found Gemma before he did. "Gemma didn't do any harm."

"But she could have." Ivar blew a curl of smoke toward Griffin, smacking his lips. "All she had to do was reveal her strength or speed or one of our other useful talents, and someone might begin to ask questions. The kinds of questions we don't like."

Despite Ivar's bluster, the threat he represented was very real. Griffin fought to subdue his rage. "It won't happen again," he said.

"On your word of honor?" Ivar chuckled. "Maybe that's not good enough anymore. If you can't control your own kin, maybe it's time someone else did it for you."

Gemma fought Allegra's hold. "I can speak for myself," she said, facing Ivar with naive courage. "It's my fault, not Griffin's."

Ivar looked her up and down with an open leer. "You want to save your brother a lot of trouble? Come with us right now. We'll take good care of you."

Griffin snarled. "Get back, Gemma."

"But, Grif—"

"Back." He bared his teeth at Ivar. "You think you can take her, you slinking jackal?"

"I'll take her, all right. And she'll beg for more."

For an instant Griffin stood poised between man and beast, the man begging him to remember all his fears for Gemma, his solemn vows to civilization and peace. But the beast was aroused and would not be denied. He removed his tie, kicked off his shoes, shed his shirt and trousers and tossed them aside.

"Go ahead," he taunted. "I'm waiting, belly-scraper."

Ivar's eyes narrowed in fury. He lifted a hand. "Tibor. Caleb."

The wolves answered to their names, closing in on Allegra and Gemma. Griffin Changed, spun around and raced toward them. The larger of the two pack members faced him with tail high and ears flat, ready to spring. Griffin charged. He caught Caleb's thick mane in his jaws and twisted hard, forcing his opponent to the pavement. With sheer strength he held Caleb down, enduring the furious scrape of nails that sliced through his fur. Fangs snapped within inches of his face. He didn't flinch, staring into Caleb's yellow eyes until the *loup-garou's* struggles slowed and finally ceased. Caleb whined and licked Griffin's chin, going limp in Griffin's grip.

He released Caleb and turned to face the smaller beast, preparing himself for another fight. Tibor turned his head from side to side, tucked his tail between his legs and stretched his mouth in a grimace of submission. Griffin quickly Changed again and hurried to join Allegra and Gemma.

"Are you all right?" he asked.

"Why shouldn't we be?" Allegra said. "You did all

the fighting." She looked him over, keen interest in her eyes, and Griffin was suddenly very much aware of his nudity. Far worse, however, was his shame at what he had been forced to do. He left Allegra with Gemma and returned to Ivar, who had thrown his cigarette into the street and looked seconds away from Changing himself.

"Very impressive," he said. "You've made your point, Durant, but don't think you did yourself any favors. Your deal with the pack can be canceled anytime. The minute your lone wolf act becomes a threat to us, it's over."

"And the minute that happens," Griffin said, "the moment anything happens to Gemma or me, the generous remittance the pack receives from my estate will dry up forever."

The toe of Ivar's highly polished shoe struck the discarded cigarette, sending it rolling across the street. "I came here to warn you, Durant. Next time you won't get off quite so easy." He turned on his heel, striding away until his silhouette was swallowed up in darkness. The wolves loped after him, their bodies low to the ground.

Griffin closed his eyes and felt the tension drain out of his muscles. He'd bluffed his way through this time, but things could easily have gone the other way. He could have killed in defense of the ones he loved.

The ones he loved. He shivered at the slip, gathered his wits and looked for his clothes.

Allegra already had them in her arms, an ambiguous smile curving her lips. "*Very* impressive," she said, her gaze lingering a little too long on the area below his waist. "I've never seen one of your kind Change before."

The wolf was still very close to the surface. Griffin snatched his trousers away before his body could betray him.

"You really don't like fighting, do you?" she asked quietly.

His fingers fumbled at the buttons. "No."

"You didn't do anything wrong."

He ignored her and pulled on his shirt. She placed both hands on his chest before he could fasten the shirt.

"No wounds," she said.

His breath came faster. "The Change heals them."

"We heal fast, too. Something you and I actually have in common."

He pushed her hands aside and buttoned his shirt. "Gemma…"

His sister slunk toward him, her head low. "I'm so sorry, Grif," she said. "It's all my fault."

"I'm glad you recognize that actions have consequences." He took her face between his hands. "Now you see why we can't trust the pack. Why we can't give in to our other side."

"But you had to do it. Allie's right. There was nothing wrong with—"

"There is nothing romantic in becoming a beast, Gemma." He lowered his voice. "You must promise me never to come to Manhattan again."

"Oh, lay off," Allegra said. "You can give her the lecture after she's had a good day's sleep."

Griffin let Gemma go and faced Allegra. "Miss Chase, your interference is—" He stopped, clearing his throat. "It seems I owe you another debt of gratitude."

"I don't remember doing anything to be grateful for. The least you could have done was let me handle that idiot Ivar."

"And risk sparking an all-out war between vampires and werewolves? The truce is fragile enough as it is."

"That's just an excuse. You really wanted to make sure we helpless females were kept out of harm's way."

"If that was my intent," he said grimly, "I failed."

"If you'd only teach me how to fight," Gemma broke in, "I could help you next time. You wouldn't have to protect me."

"There won't be a next time." Griffin took her firmly by the shoulder, eager to forget what had happened. "Miss Chase, my driver is waiting a few blocks away. The least I can do is take you home…unless you would prefer to return to the club."

Allie shrugged. "My friends will have cleared out by now."

"Then we should hurry. It's nearly dawn."

Allie glanced at the sky. She had lost track of the time…an easy thing to do when she had no schedules to keep or responsibilities to tie her down. Griffin had provided certain other distractions, as well. He naturally believed that she was as vulnerable to daylight as any other *strigoi,* and she didn't see any reason to let him in on the secret. Not yet.

"I'll take the lift," she said.

Griffin nodded, firmly gripped Gemma's hand and set off again. They had gone another couple of blocks when they were accosted once more, this time by a thin young man with earnest features and wavy blond hair.

"Grif!" he said. "Thank God you found her. I'd finished searching the—" He broke off, his gaze settling on Allie. "Allegra?" he said. "Allegra Chase?"

Allie stepped forward. "Mal," she said. "It's been a long time."

Griffin looked from her to Mal and back again. "You know each other?"

"Mal used to frequent some of the same clubs as my friends and I," Allie said. "Sometimes he and—" She caught herself, remembering that there were some topics it was wiser not to mention. "We saw quite a bit of each other."

"The good old days," Mal said with a cheerless smile. "How've you been, Allie?"

"Grand, thanks." She didn't ask Mal how he was; one look at him told her all she needed to know. "I didn't realize you knew Mr. Durant."

"It never occurred to me to mention it. Your world and Griffin's…they always seemed miles apart."

That, Allie thought, was an understatement. "Funny how these things happen," she said. "Mr. Durant and I met by chance a few days ago, and then Gemma showed up at Lulu's tonight."

Mal raised a brow. "What was Gemma doing at Lulu's?"

"Biting off more than she could chew," Griffin said. "Miss Chase intervened when one of the patrons accosted her."

"I'm not surprised. Allie likes to pretend she's a world-weary cynic, but she's not nearly as hard-boiled as she makes out."

"You're going to ruin my reputation," Allie said, then looked pointedly toward the eastern horizon. "We'd better keep going, don't you think?" she asked Griffin.

"Of course. You're welcome to return with us to Oakdene, Mal. Stay for a few days if you like. Gemma's birthday party is on Saturday—"

"You mean, you're still going to have the party?"

Gemma asked. "Even though…even after what happened tonight?"

"If you give your word not to come to Manhattan alone," Griffin said, "I'll consider tonight's folly to be an isolated lapse of judgment."

Gemma nodded, but her expression didn't suggest any particular pleasure at Griffin's leniency. Allie could imagine what such a party might be like if Griffin had the planning of it.

And no wonder. Griffin's so afraid of the wolf part of himself that he goes too far in the other direction.

Allie had never heard that werewolves were intrinsically more violent than humans—or vampires, for that matter—but in Griffin's case, it was as if he would prefer to deny his inhuman nature entirely, as he seemed bent on denying Gemma's. *Being old-fashioned and forcing his sister to associate only with humans lets him convince himself that his "civilized" side is in control. Conservative, safe, hemmed about by rules and traditions.*

Still, he'd proven again tonight that he was willing to get rough when the situation demanded it…and Allie couldn't help but feel that the wolf was much closer to the surface than he would ever admit. Now that she'd seen Griffin in action, she'd begun to grasp what it must feel like to turn into an animal. If it had happened to her, *she* wouldn't be afraid. So much power, beauty and strength…

None of which he was willing to accept as the gift it was.

What would it take to teach you to glory in what you are, the senses and the speed and the freedom?

Allie laughed. That sort of project seemed far too much work for anyone but the most devoted martyr.

And anyway, why should she care? She'd tried to get rid of Durant at their first meeting by warning him that his attraction to her wasn't real. That should have been that.

But it wasn't. The joke was on her. She'd thought she would be able to forget about him. She hadn't been, although it seemed he'd taken her advice very much to heart. He certainly hadn't done much to encourage their further acquaintance. He was able to resist her, and that was a new and not entirely pleasant experience.

So, Allie Chase. What are you going to do about it? It's been a long time since you've had a real challenge.

They began to walk again. The smells of morning crept into the city air: baking bread; stale seawater from the docks; exhaust from milk and produce trucks making their first deliveries of the day. Men and women staggered, laughing, from hidden doorways as they ended their night's revels and prepared to retire to their comfortable beds on the Gold Coast. Longshoremen yawned as they left their tenements for a day's work at the docks. Ragged boys lingered on street corners hoping to gain employment, legal or otherwise, for a few hours or a day. Gunsels on mysterious errands patrolled the sidewalk, their coat collars turned up about their ears, and bootleggers' vehicles idled in alleyways.

This was Allie's world—more than the cold, beautiful mansions owned by Raoul and his most favored vassals, far more than the gilded, exclusive milieu of the Hamptons. It was, as Mal had said, miles away from anything Griffin Durant judged desirable for himself or his sister.

"Here we are," Griffin said, interrupting Allie's reflections. He indicated a handsome limousine, whose uniformed driver stood beside the passenger door awaiting his employer's instructions.

"Ladies," Griffin said, gesturing Gemma and Allie into the backseat. Gemma climbed in first. Allie slid onto the seat beside her, not bothering to adjust the hem of her dress when it inched well above her knee. She knew Griffin noticed; he stared for a dozen heartbeats, then hastily looked away. Mal joined her and Gemma in the rear, while Griffin took a seat beside his driver in the front.

Whatever Griffin might think of certain parts of Manhattan, he employed a driver with an obvious talent for finding the most direct routes through the city. They stopped first at a street off Washington Square, where Mal took his leave and promised to attend Gemma's party. In a remarkably short time—just as the first streaks of sunlight were beginning to sift among the buildings— the limousine pulled up in front of Allie's apartment.

Griffin jumped out and asked Gemma for the return of his overcoat. He removed his hat and offered it and the coat to Allie as he helped her from the car.

"The fit is hardly ideal," he said, "but they should provide adequate protection for a few moments."

She placed the overlarge hat on her head and wrapped the coat around herself, enveloped in Griffin's masculine, earthy scent.

"Can she come to my party?" Gemma said, leaning out of the car. "Please, Grif. I promise I'll behave."

Griffin looked as if he'd been cold-cocked by an invisible fist. He stared past Allie's shoulder, muscles flexing under the skin of his jaw.

"Doubtless a woman of experience like Miss Chase would find a Long Island party extremely uninteresting," he said.

"Oh, I don't think so," Allie said. "After all, you'd be there. What more fascinating entertainment could a girl ask for?"

He cast her a dark glance. "In that case," he said flatly, "we would be pleased if you would join us."

Allie performed a mocking curtsy. "I would be delighted to accept your generous invitation, kind sir."

Griffin bowed like a heel-clicking aristocrat out of a moving picture. "May I escort you to your door, Miss Chase?" He offered his arm, and Allie accepted it. The night doorman, about ready to surrender his duties to his daytime counterpart, hardly blinked at her masculine attire.

Griffin accompanied her into the lobby and stopped beside the elevator. "I…hope the night's events have not proven too troubling for you, Miss Chase," he said.

"Troubling? Because of Ivar? Or because I saw you turn into a wolf?"

"I regret that you were compelled to witness such unpleasantness."

"I've seen plenty of that on the vampire side of things."

"I'm sorry to hear it."

"You are, aren't you?" She removed the hat and twirled it around on the tip of her finger. "Do you really think I'll go wild and attack all your boring human friends?"

"I beg your pardon?"

"At the party. Is it because of Gemma that you don't want me there, or because I'm a leech?"

If he was taken aback by her bluntness, he managed to hide it. "You obviously have excellent control over your…needs, Miss Chase."

"At least you must admire that quality in me." She chuckled at his expression. "We don't exactly go around assaulting humans in public places. If we were that indiscreet, we'd hardly survive in a human world…any more than your kind would if you changed shape in the middle of Macy's Thanksgiving Day Parade."

He flushed and glanced at his shoes. "I apologize. My personal experience of vampire behavior is somewhat limited."

"And what knowledge you do have is tainted by prejudice."

"You've expressed some pride in being unlike other vampires, Miss Chase."

"You just said you didn't know much about vampires. Anyway, I didn't say I approve of everything my fellow *strigoi* do. I don't take responsibility for them, only myself."

A glimmer of some emotion she couldn't identify flickered in Griffin's eyes. "In that case, perhaps we should call a truce."

"I'm all for that, bub."

His shoulders relaxed as if he'd just released an intolerable burden. "The party will be held out of doors, in the afternoon…but you may certainly remain inside the house without attracting undo attention. If you dress for travel in daylight, I'll send Fitzsimmons to collect you on Saturday at 1:00 p.m."

"That's most convenient, thank you." She touched her finger to his chin. "Very gallant of you to worry so much about my safety."

"You didn't seem to welcome it before."

"Maybe I changed my mind."

"Why do I find it difficult to believe you?"

"You mean, you still don't trust me, after all we've been through together?"

He looked away. "Miss Chase—"

"Don't you think we should be on a first-name basis by now…Griffin?" She reached up and set his hat on his head, remaining on tiptoe so that her face was very close to his. "Say my name," she whispered. "Say it."

"Miss—"

"Why are you so afraid of a little word?"

His gaze met hers, embarrassed and angry. "Allegra."

"My friends call me Allie."

He stepped back abruptly, looking for all the world like a man who had nearly tumbled over a precipice. "I must take my sister home," he said. "Saturday, Miss Chase."

"I'll be there." She tossed him the coat and laughed as the elevator doors opened.

He hesitated, pulled his hat lower on his head and strode briskly toward the door. Allie stepped into the elevator as the attendant gaped at her sleepily.

"He should know by now that he's no match for Allie Chase," she said to the boy.

He grinned at the bills she pressed into his hand. "Yes, ma'am!"

CHAPTER FIVE

"I HOPE YOU LIKE IT," Griffin said, presenting the be-ribboned box to Gemma.

She examined the box with excitement she did her best to conceal, convinced—as were so many girls her age—that any outward sign of enthusiasm would betray a lingering attachment to childish things. She untied the ribbons with deliberate slowness, then slipped them off the box and laid them in a neat pile on the sofa. Her eyes sparkled as she lifted the lid.

"Oh," she whispered, stroking the soft yellow georgette with her fingertips. Abruptly she removed the dress from the box and stood, letting the silk tumble down over her body.

There was a moment of silence as Gemma examined the gift. The moment stretched far too long, and even before she looked up Griffin knew she was disappointed.

"It's lovely, Grif," she said, smiling with only a hint of strain. "The silk is…lovely. And the color…" She smoothed the long skirt over her legs. "Shall I wear it to the party?"

He returned her smile, knowing how embarrassed she would be if she suspected that he'd seen through her pretense. "That's your decision," he said.

She folded the dress, replaced it in the box and

leaned over to kiss him on the cheek. "Of course I'll wear it," she said. "In fact, I think I'll go upstairs and try it on right now."

"By all means," Griffin said. "You have plenty of time before the first guests arrive."

With a brief, self-conscious move, she touched her short hair. "Griffin, do you think—" She shook her head, gathered up the box and headed for the staircase.

Griffin rose from his chair. "Gemma…"

She paused at the foot of the stairs. "Yes, Grif?"

"I hope you understand why I don't want you to go into Manhattan alone."

Her gaze dropped to the floor. "Sure. I understand."

"Members of the pack believe in their absolute right to behave like animals when it suits them. I will not have that become your fate."

"It's not as if they go around killing people."

"But the temptation is always there."

Gemma pushed the toe of her foot against the carpet runner and sighed. "If you say so, Grif."

"I do." He waved his hand. "That's all. Go and change."

She ascended the stairs with elaborate dignity, leaving Griffin to stare after her with sadness and frustration. Only recently had Gemma taken up the idea that she had to radically change in order to claim her adulthood. She lacked a mother who could give her the counsel he wasn't equipped to provide…who could explain that the sort of dress she might have liked to wear on her birthday would not be in the least appropriate.

He walked to the window, looking out at the preparations Starke and Brenda, the maid, were making for the party. The lawn was a vivid green, the formal garden was in bloom and the weather could not have been more perfect. Soon the limousines would begin to arrive, spilling out the socially desirable young men and women who would be Gemma's peers when she married. Their parents had also been invited, though Griffin didn't expect many of the fathers to put in an appearance. They weren't the ones who generally made the crucial decisions about marital alliances.

Starke entered the room and inclined his head. "Everything is on schedule, Mr. Durant," he said. "Shall I ask Fitzsimmons to collect Miss Chase?"

Griffin rubbed the back of his neck. "I suppose you'd better. I'd rather that she showed up early than make a grand entrance in the middle of the party."

Starke, who had been told something of Gemma's escapade and Miss Chase's part in it, assumed a sympathetic air. "I quite understand, sir. I deeply regret that I was not aware of Miss Durant's plans that evening, and that I failed to hear—"

"I told you not to blame yourself, Uncle Edward. Any culpability belongs to Miss Spires, who was willing to accept a bribe from a child." *And to me, for failing to be an effective guardian.* "I expect Miss Chase to spend most of her time indoors, so perhaps we can encourage the other guests to take advantage of the fine weather."

Starke nodded and left to find Fitzsimmons. Griffin dropped by the kitchen to look in on Demetria, who was up to her elbows in tea sandwiches and hors d'oeuvres, and then went upstairs to change his clothes. He didn't ordinarily spend a great deal of time on his appearance, at least not beyond what was required to look neat and respectable. But now he couldn't seem to concentrate on the simplest activities.

His collar refused to stay in place, his tie wouldn't knot and his hair flew every which way no matter how carefully he brushed it.

It was all because of Allegra Chase. He couldn't forget the way she'd stood so close to him that night…the throaty sound of her voice as she'd challenged him to speak her name…the fact that she was about to show up in the one place he would have thought safe from her and her wild ways.

Seeing her again had simply confirmed what he'd been afraid to admit even to himself: he still felt the same overwhelming desire as he had that evening in the alley. Even his anger with her hadn't quenched his hunger. But *she* seemed to have changed her mind about him between their first and second meetings. Instead of fobbing him off with cynicism and prevarication, she was making an active attempt to seduce him.

And that made it all the more vital that he resist her blandishments. She had seen the worst of him; he had no desire to see the worst of her. In any case, everything she did was obviously a game to her, so he would simply refuse to play.

Committed to his fresh resolve, Griffin finished dressing and went back downstairs to read the *Times* and wait for Fitzsimmons and Miss Chase. Presently Gemma came down to join him, wearing the disappointing tea dress that fell so decorously to her ankles.

The limousine had still not returned when Mrs. Betancourt and her daughter, Clarice, arrived from Kings Point. Clarice was two years older than Gemma and had already made her debut; Mrs. Betancourt viewed Griffin with a predatory eye as he and Gemma ushered them into the garden and offered refreshments. There were any number of mothers who still considered Griffin fair game; he wasn't married, he was rich, and—as far as anyone knew—he had no peculiar proclivities.

As always, Griffin was unfailingly polite, but also careful not to give the girl and her mama the least bit of hope. The musicians finally made their appearance, and Starke supervised their disposition on the walkway between the lawn and garden. One by one the other guests drove up, elegantly alighted from their vehicles and left their gifts with Brenda to be displayed on one of the tables outside. Mal walked in at half past three. Almost everyone had arrived by four, and there was still no sign of Fitzsimmons and Allegra Chase.

Griffin instructed Starke to inform him immediately upon Miss Chase's arrival and did his brotherly duty, circulating among the guests. He asked Mrs. Dearing about her prize-winning rose garden, complimented Miss Groves on her afternoon frock, shared a mild joke with the elderly Mr. Nordstrom and had a brief discussion of polo ponies with young David Scribner. Gemma smiled and laughed and accepted birthday wishes with the poised bearing of a well-bred young lady. The women stared at her hair, but no one offered a comment on its altered appearance. The string quartet played Lehar waltzes in the background, while Starke and Brenda replenished the punch bowl and kept the trays of sandwiches and hors d'oeuvres continuously supplied with fresh delicacies.

Two hours after the party began, Starke approached Griffin with a too-blank expression on his impassive face. "Fitzsimmons has just pulled into the drive," he said. "Shall I detain Miss Chase in the hall?"

"I'll be right there, Starke." Griffin smoothed his expression to match Starke's for sheer blandness, offered some excuse to the matron with whom he was speaking and hurried back into the house. He'd passed through the summer parlor and was halfway to the vestibule when he heard her voice.

"Don't apologize, Fitzy. I don't mind being late, and I'm sure Mr. Durant feels the sa—" She stopped as she saw Griffin, and a grin spread across her face. "Speak of the devil."

Griffin came to a halt, his mouth gone dry. "Miss Chase."

She wagged her finger. "Allie, remember?"

"Allegra." He examined her from the crown of her dark head to the high heels of her scarlet patent leather pumps. His first response was dismay at her choice of garments: an elaborately beaded, sleeveless red party frock that actually fell *above* the knees, rolled flesh-colored stockings, and a blazing orange bandeau embellished with an enormous aigrette. But he was horrified by his own reaction to the sight of her—the violent rhythm of his heartbeat, the almost unbearable awareness of her warm, womanly fragrance, the hungry stirring of his body....

"Cat got your tongue?" Allegra asked, her smile even wider than before. She noticed Starke and pressed a pair of small, elaborately wrapped boxes into the butler's hands. "I hope I haven't missed all the fun!"

Fitzsimmons came up behind her. "I'm sorry for being so late, sir," he said to Griffin. "There was an inordinate amount of traffic—"

"And I wasn't quite ready when Fitzy arrived at my place," Allegra said. "Like my new dress?" She spun around, lifting the already short hem even higher. "I wore it just for you."

Griffin went hot and cold by turns. "Miss...

Allegra," he said hoarsely, "I hope you realize that this is a young lady's birthday party, not a—"

"Two-bit dance hall?" She strolled toward him, the fringes along her hemline swinging with every step. "Scared that my obviously bad breeding will send the old biddies and their offspring straight to the fainting couch?"

Griffin held himself very still. "I apologize if I've offended you."

"I'm not offended. You invited me against your better judgment, but you did it anyway." She walked around him, her heels clicking on the parquet floor. "I think *you* wanted to see me again."

Griffin had no ready retort. After a long silence he said, "Most of the guests are outside, but Starke will see that you receive everything you might require in the summer parlor."

Allegra stopped in front of him. "Convenient, isn't it? The desirable guests are outside, and I have to stay indoors."

Griffin wanted nothing more than to seize her arms and give her a good shake. "You won't be left alone. Either I or Gemma will keep you company."

"Ah. *Now* I understand." She looped her arm through the crook of his elbow. "Take me to this summer parlor of yours. I can't wait to see how the other half lives."

Together they walked through the hall and the music room to the summer parlor. Sunlight streamed through the tall windows and French doors. The guests in their airy dresses could be seen circling about the refreshment tables like flocks of gaudy butterflies. Allegra paused where the edge of the light crossed the carpet.

"Very nice," she said, gazing about the room. "I'd expected horsehair sofas and clawfoot tables."

"Even I have become aware that we live in the twentieth century."

She smiled up at him. "There's some hope for you yet." She threw herself into an antique Stickley chair. "Well? Where's the birthday girl?"

"If you'll excuse me, I'll let her know you're here." He signaled to Starke, who waited in the doorway, and then stepped out through the French doors into the garden. No one who greeted him would have guessed he was less than tranquil. As soon as he informed Gemma about Allegra's arrival, she broke off her conversation with the Pemberton boy and rushed into the house.

Griffin began circulating again, the back of his neck prickling at the thought of his sister alone with Allegra. Ten minutes passed, then fifteen. He was just about to go in and fetch Gemma when the French doors swung open wide and Allegra sauntered out onto the garden walk.

"Ah," she said, stretching her arms above her head, "what a beautiful day!"

Seldom had Griffin felt so astonished or so gripped with sheer terror. In his mind's eye he saw not smooth, pale skin but blistering flesh, red as Allegra's frock, turning sere and black in the harsh light of day. He abandoned Mrs. Higgenbotham and charged toward Allegra, ready to cover her body with his own and push her back inside the house.

Her face, cool and unmarred, turned toward him. He skidded to a halt seconds before he reached her, his legs trembling with reaction and relief.

There was nothing wrong with her—no burns on her cheeks, discolorations of her hands or peeling skin on her bare arms. She regarded him with a half smile as if to ask what the fuss was all about.

"Allegra," he said. "What—"

"When can I open my presents, Grif?" Gemma asked, emerging from the house to take Allegra's arm.

He stared at his sister, trying to make sense of her words. The party came crashing down around him like rotted timbers in an abandoned house, all chattering voices and screeching violins. The smells of human sweat and rank perfume overwhelmed his senses.

"Oh," Mrs. Dearing cooed next to his ear, "is this the entertainment, Mr. Durant? Are we to have a Vaudeville show?"

It took Griffin a moment to realize that Mrs. Dearing was referring to Allegra, who examined the curious guests as a tigress might study a herd of plump, pampered deer in a royal park. "I'd be happy to give a little performance," she said, licking her lips. "What would you like to see?"

Mrs. Dearing started, as if she hadn't expected such a creature to speak. Her daughter, Elvira, drifted to her side, staring at Allegra with open fascination. Several of the young men began to converge around the garden walk. A group of Gemma's friends whispered and exchanged looks of amazement and distaste.

Mrs. Higgenbotham approached with her neck extended like a goose about to snap up an insect. She raised her lorgnette to her faded blue eyes.

"Do I know you, dear?" she asked Allegra. "You seem very familiar...."

Griffin came back to himself. "Mrs. Higgenbotham," he said, "may I present Miss Allegra Chase?"

"I do know that name," the older woman said. "Or something very like it. It was in Huntington, wasn't it? Yes, I do believe—"

"You must be mistaken," Allegra interrupted. "I've never been out here in my life." She made a show of admiring Mrs. Higgenbotham's overly snug Vionnet tea gown. "What a lovely dress."

"Thank you." Mrs. Higgenbotham's gaze fixed on Allegra's bare knees. She made a faint choking sound, and Griffin found it advisable to lead her to one of the chairs under the awning. As soon as she was gone, others arrived to take her place. One of the boys gave a low whistle, while Jane Pomeroy looked Allegra up and down with the subtlest of sneers.

"The poor thing ran out of fabric," Jane said in a stage whisper to a pair of her favorite confidantes. "Do you think we should give her enough money so she can finish the dress?"

Gemma stepped forward, fists clenched. "There's nothing wrong with her dress," she said. "So you can keep your catty remarks to yourself, Jane Pomeroy."

Jane fell back in affront. Her mother dragged her away toward the tables. Griffin watched them go, his vision hazed with anger that seemed to have sprung up out of nowhere at all. He turned in a slow circle, his gaze traveling from face to face. The young men who'd been ogling Allegra with wolfish grins had the sudden urge to return to the punch bowl. The matrons with their cold, rigid faces beat a dignified retreat.

Griffin would have been glad to banish them all. Instead, he moved closer to Allegra, close enough to drown in her intoxicating scent.

"Gemma, go join your guests," he said.

"Did you see how they looked at Allie? I—"

"This would be a good time for you to open your gifts."

Gemma blew out her breath and stalked away. Griffin stood toe to toe with Allegra, his heart beating madly against his ribs.

"Are you mad?" he demanded.

She met his gaze with a raised brow. "They all survived the sight of me, didn't they?"

He gripped her arm. "You know what I mean. You're in full sunlight. You could have been—"

"Mr. Durant!"

Mrs. Julia Pomeroy strolled up to join them, the crepe georgette skirt and sleeves of her mauve gown fluttering about her arms and legs as if to emphasize the youth she had lost and sought so desperately to recover. She linked her arm through Griffin's and pinned Allegra with a hostile smile.

"Oh," she said, her voice honeyed with malice, "did I interrupt? Do forgive me."

Griffin bore the woman's assault with all the calm he could muster. "As a matter of fact, Mrs. Pomeroy—"

"You weren't interrupting anything important," Allegra said, returning Julia's smile with one that would have sent a less hardened woman scurrying for cover. "We were just discussing the beauty of the day."

"How nice." Julia's gaze dropped to Allegra's ankles and swept up to her knees. "There is a bit of a breeze off the Sound, though…are you certain you won't catch cold, my dear?"

Allegra smoothed her dress over her hips with an insolent shimmy. "I'm very hot blooded," she said, then looked at Griffin from under her thick black lashes. "I always find ways to keep myself warm."

Julia's lips twitched. "I don't doubt it." Her grip tightened on Griffin's arm. "You won't mind if I borrow Mr. Durant, will you, Miss Chase?"

Allegra concealed a yawn behind her hand. "Not at all, Mrs. Pomeroy. Just make sure you bring him back in one piece."

If Griffin had been in wolf-shape at that moment, neither woman would have had any doubt as to his feelings at being caught in the middle of their spiteful games. As it was, he could only give Allegra a stare promising that their discussion was far from over.

He let Mrs. Pomeroy lead him away, forcing himself to attend to her wheedling conversation.

"Where *did* you find that…young woman, Mr. Durant?" she said. "I confess that I've never seen her before…certainly not anywhere on the North Shore. She's a friend of Gemma's?"

"In a manner of speaking."

Julia laughed. "Dear, dear Gemma. She has always been so broad-minded and kind toward those less fortunate. Didn't she rescue a stray kitten this winter?" She patted Griffin's arm as if to let him in on her joke. "Where did she meet Miss Chase?"

Griffin had no desire to get into a protracted conversation about Allegra's life and origins. He certainly had no intention of informing Julia Pomeroy of Gemma's escapades in Lulu's.

"One meets with a wide variety of people in the city," he said. "As you said, Gemma has never been swayed by prejudice against those different from herself."

"So true. You must sometimes worry that her natural generosity might…lead her into awkward situations."

"I am perfectly capable of protecting my sister from any detrimental influences."

"I've no doubt of that. And it's only to be expected that an elder brother should occasionally indulge his sister when she begs him to bring one of her little pets into the house."

Griffin stopped. "You refer to Miss Chase?"

"Why, Mr. Durant, whatever put such an idea into your head?" She studied his face, her eyes narrowed like those of a cat with a bird in its sights. "Still, *you* can hardly approve of that young woman's appearance."

"Surely her appearance can do little harm to anyone, Mrs. Pomeroy."

She laughed again, brittle and harsh. "Spoken just like a man. We mothers know better. You've no idea what a negative effect these 'jazz babies' have on our children. Why, my Jane was telling me just the other day that Roberta Tidwell was caught accepting a delivery of gin at her parents' summer house and Evie Hemming has begun to smoke…. Can you imagine?"

"Gemma neither smokes nor drinks."

"Of course not. And yet…Gemma would benefit so greatly from having a more mature young lady close at hand…one who could set an example she might easily follow."

Griffin dropped his arm, forcing her to release it. "What did you have in mind, Mrs. Pomeroy?"

"You are still young, my dear Mr. Durant. Surely you've considered the advantages of a good marriage, especially in setting an example for your sister."

"And you have a bride in mind for me."

She had the sense to look abashed and dropped her gaze. "I would never presume. But Jane and Gemma have been acquainted for some time, and I can't help but feel…"

The sound of her voice continued, but Griffin no longer listened. He could not, as a gentleman, tell Mrs.

Pomeroy what he thought of her blatant scheming. In truth, it wasn't much worse than what the other matrons with eligible daughters had tried at one time or another. And he found that he was far more angry with her unsubtle gibes at Allegra.

He looked back across the lawn toward the French doors and the garden room. Allegra was nowhere to be seen. Gemma had finished opening her presents and was making her thanks to the boys and girls gathered about the gift table. As Griffin watched, she snatched up one of the opened boxes and dashed into the house, trailed by several of her young guests. Jane Pomeroy and her cronies declined to follow.

"…does so admire what you've done for the dear little orphans in Hell's Kitchen," Julia rattled on. "He has been looking for a partner in a new financial venture that holds a great deal of promise, and he feels quite certain that you…"

Griffin waited, a strange sense of anticipation building in his chest. Except for Mrs. Pomeroy's droning voice, everything seemed very quiet. The adult guests barely spoke to one another. The string quartet whispered and sighed as if the musicians had lost all interest in their work. The setting could not have been more ideal for the sudden blast of drums, horns and bass issuing from the summer parlor.

Julia Pomeroy broke off, her head snapping toward the house. Matrons gaped, and the handful of mature gentlemen in attendance muttered and shook their heads. Even the imperturbable Starke looked vaguely startled.

One by one the older guests and the few younger ones who had remained outside converged on the house like sleepwalkers under some sorcerer's spell.

Griffin left Mrs. Pomeroy and strode ahead of the others, already suspecting what he was about to find.

Every shade and curtain in the summer parlor had been drawn back to let in the sun. The oriental carpet had been rolled up and pushed against the wall, and a jazz recording was spinning on the turntable of the flat-top Victrola, while a dozen young men and women clustered around Allegra Chase, clapping in time to her gyrating body and flying feet.

Griffin stood transfixed in the doorway, held captive by the music and the woman who danced with such abandon. Francis Spaulding began to copy Allegra's movements, knobby arms and legs flailing. Elvira Dearing lifted her skirts above her knees and gave a few hesitant kicks, and then Tansy Higgenbotham threw herself into the dance with a little squeal of delight.

Allegra looked up at Griffin with a smile that he knew was meant for him and him alone. *You see?* she seemed to say. *What's the harm in a little fun?*

Gemma laughed, her face glowing with happiness. Across the summer parlor, leaning against the door-jamb, Malcolm Owen gave a wry smile. *Don't ruin it. Let them be kids a little while longer....*

"My God!" Mrs. Higgenbotham gasped in Griffin's ear. "Is my Tansy...is that one of those hor-rid jazz dances?"

"Oh, my. Oh, my," Mrs. Dearing murmured.

"Disgraceful," Julia Pomeroy hissed.

"Come out of there at once, young man!" Mr. Spaulding bellowed at his son. He plunged past Griffin and reached for Francis, knocking into Gemma, who in turn bumped into the Victrola. The needle skidded off the record with a screech that brought everything to a violent halt.

CHAPTER SIX

GRIFFIN STEPPED into the room and pulled Gemma out of the way. "Mr. Spaulding," he said sharply, "I'll ask you to watch where you're going."

"And I'll ask you, Mr. Durant, not to expose my son to this vile mongrel…" He made a sound of disgust and dragged Francis from the room. The other young people looked at each other in stunned silence.

"What are you afraid of?" Allegra said to the parents, her body like a defiant shout. "Do you really believe that a little music and high spirits will turn your children into monsters of sin and depravity?" She met Griffin's gaze. "*Do* you?"

"Well, I *never!*" someone choked.

"Disgusting!" another voice barked from the rear of the crowd.

Julia Pomeroy pushed forward, facing Allegra with a look of such hatred that it seemed her brittle face was about to crack under the strain. "You and your kind," she snarled, "are destroying this great country with your filth and immorality. If I had my way—"

"If you had your way, madam," Griffin said, "no one would be allowed to live in this great country but people exactly like you."

Her eyes nearly popped out of her head. "Mr. Durant! I—"

"You would suffer a very great shock if you were to discover the extent of your ignorance of the world, Mrs. Pomeroy. There are far worse things than jazz and lipstick."

His words shook the room like thunderclaps. For a moment no one stirred, and then everyone moved at once. Julia Pomeroy swayed as if she were about to faint. Distraught parents snatched their children from the jaws of corruption and scurried to safety. Mrs. Higgenbotham bellowed at her cringing daughter. Elvira Dearing hung back, resisting Mrs. Dearing's limp tug.

"That was simply the bee's knees, Miss Chase," she said. "If I could only—"

Mrs. Dearing found unexpected strength and hauled Elvira away. Within two minutes the room was deserted except for Allegra, Griffin and Gemma, who stared after her friends with anger and bewilderment.

"Don't they have any guts at all?" she demanded. "And you think I should marry one of *them?*"

Griffin held on to his calm by a thread. "This is hardly the time to discuss such matters, Gemma."

She wrenched out of his hold and snatched her record from the Victrola. "It's ruined," she said, as if the gift were the only casualty of the afternoon's fracas. "I only got to play it once."

Allegra glanced at Griffin, her expression almost subdued. "I'm sorry, Gemma."

"It isn't your fault." Gemma hugged the scratched disc to her chest. "It was the best present anyone could have given me."

Griffin raked his hands through his hair and looked out the window. The lawn was deserted. The guests had undoubtedly found their way to the drive and their limousines. The party was most definitely over.

"Aren't you going to go after them and apologize?" Mal asked from the hall doorway.

Griffin was in no mood for Mal's gentle mockery. "Apologize?" he snapped. "Apologize for what? This is my home, and my sister. I won't tolerate any self-righteous criticism about how Gemma conducts herself or whom she chooses to invite to her own party. If those dried-up old prunes can't bring themselves to crawl out of the nineteenth century…"

He stopped, aware that Gemma was staring at him in astonishment. Allegra watched him with an expression he couldn't interpret. Mal lifted his glass in salute.

"Do you really mean it, Grif?" Gemma said, uncertainty in her voice. "The things you said to Mrs. Pomeroy…"

Were most ill-advised, Griffin thought grimly. *Even if they are true.* "My remarks may have been somewhat intemperate," he said.

"But you aren't angry with me?"

Griffin knew he'd painted himself into a corner. Gemma must have had some idea of the disruption the dancing would cause, but she could hardly be blamed when Allegra had practically driven her to it by presenting herself in such a fashion and with such a gift in hand. Yet if he felt inclined to upbraid Allegra for her provocative dress and manner, he had only to remember the way he'd defended her to Mrs. Pomeroy.

And the moment of sheer terror when he'd seen her walk into the sunlight…

"You showed a remarkable lack of discretion, Gemma," he said, returning to the matter at hand. "But the behavior of your guests was no better. I think it might be advisable for you to spend the rest of the evening in your room."

Gemma ducked her head. "Please don't be angry with Allie, Grif. She didn't—"

"Thank you, Gemma. You may go."

With an apologetic glance at Allegra, Gemma slipped past Mal and left the room.

Griffin turned to Allegra. "Are you quite satisfied?" he said.

She held his gaze without flinching. "I never intended—"

"You're far too intelligent not to have realized what you were doing. You came here dressed in a deliberately provocative manner designed to attract comment. You provided 'entertainment' that you must have known would be unacceptable to the more conservative guests." He stalked to the window and pressed his hand to the glass. "Perhaps you found it amusing to disrupt such a dull gathering, considering the degree of contempt in which you obviously hold those who don't share your idea of amusement. Or are you simply incapable of appearing at any function in which you are not the center of attention?"

He didn't see Allegra's reaction to his accusations, but he heard her draw in a breath, felt his skin grow tight as she moved up behind him.

"Maybe I had that coming," she said. "I guess I ought to thank you for thinking I'm intelligent, anyway."

"Is that all you have to say, Miss Chase?"

"You're right that I don't have a very high opinion of the types who inhabit the North Shore," she said. "But it seems *you* don't, either."

Griffin turned to face her. "I'm well aware that I hardly behaved like a gentleman."

"You told them the truth."

"The truth is too terrible for most people to endure."

"You defended me even when it was against your best interests."

"I would defend any woman who was being abused in that manner."

"Even Mrs. Pomeroy?"

"If she were in similar circumstances, yes."

"And you still want Gemma to marry one of those boys?"

Griffin looked away. "You make it sound as if I were condemning my sister to a fate worse than death."

"You saw for yourself the kind of relatives she'd have. And it's doubly worse for a girl like Gemma."

He bowed stiffly. "I'm deeply indebted to you for your advice, Miss Chase. I feel certain that, should you ever find yourself in need of cash, you could easily make a career out of undermining the institution of marriage."

For the first time she seemed to feel the effects of his words. Her pale skin developed a very human flush, and she jerked on the locket that nestled between her breasts. "I've got nothing against the idea of marriage in general, Griffin. Only unhappiness."

They gazed at each other for an acutely uncomfortable minute. Allegra folded her arms across her chest and assumed Griffin's former position by the window. Late-afternoon sunlight cascaded over her hair and shoulders like a golden veil.

Griffin's heart turned over, though he knew he had no reason to be afraid. "Why didn't you tell me, Allegra? Or was that also part of the game?"

She glanced back at him. "What?"

"That you can't be harmed by sunlight."

She rubbed her bare arms and shivered. "I thought it would be fun to startle you," she said. "It wasn't."

Her honest answer robbed him of his retort. He sighed and clasped his hands behind his back. "Is it just a legend then, the part about vampires being allergic to sunlight?"

"Not at all. I don't even know if there are others like me."

"I see." He pinched the bridge of his nose. "I confess that I don't understand a great deal about how vampires are…created. How did you come to be different?"

Allegra turned her back to the window and stretched her arms wide. "That's something I've been trying to figure out since my Conversion. My patron, Cato, was an unusual man, a brilliant scientist. I was his first protégée in…oh, decades. He treated me like a daughter, not a piece of property."

"But he couldn't explain why you could tolerate sunlight?"

"I don't think even he knew."

"Surely such a gift would be of tremendous value to your clan."

"And a dangerous one, if anyone else found out about it. The Master, Raoul, has no idea, but he's already pressuring me to come back into the fold."

"But if I understood your earlier implications, your patron's death freed you from all obligation to the clan."

"That's right. *Strigoi* don't die very often, but there are laws to deal with the situation. No one can force me to take another patron."

Griffin mulled over the things she'd told him, piecing together the puzzle that was Allegra Chase. "Raoul doesn't approve of your independence?"

"He doesn't much care for the idea that even one vampire in the city isn't under his control, directly or otherwise."

"The pressure on you must be most unpleasant."

"I can handle it."

"One woman against the entire clan?"

She smiled lazily. "You think just because I'm female that I can't hold my own as well as you. But Raoul's the one at a disadvantage, not me. It would lead to chaos if he were to break clan law without extraordinary cause." Her smile turned into a much less pleasant expression. "He'll never have me."

So you're a rebel among humans and *vampires,* Griffin thought. *You live to defy any rule you consider too binding on your freedom. And you know damned well how dangerous it is....*

But was he any different, neither human nor wolf, suspended between two worlds and never fully a part of either?

Aloud he said, "I'm surprised you trusted me enough to reveal your unique gift."

"Why shouldn't I? I know my secret's safe with you."

They gazed at each other for an acutely uncomfortable minute. Someone cleared his throat.

"I don't mean to intrude," Mal said, "but this doorway is getting a little cramped. Mind if I come in?"

Griffin wondered how much Mal might have overheard. "Sorry, Mal," he said. "Please join us."

Mal sat on the sofa and set his empty glass down on the side table. "From the looks of things, you two weren't just discussing the weather."

"I was apologizing for the mess I made of Gemma's party," Allie said, taking a seat in a chair opposite the sofa.

"An apology?" Mal said, raising a fair brow. "That's something new."

"Another black mark on my reputation." She leaned her head against the back of the chair.

"Miss Chase is being entirely too modest," Griffin said.

"We're not back to *that* again, are we?" Allegra said. "It's Allie."

Griffin joined Mal on the sofa, pretending an ease he didn't feel. "Allegra."

"Better."

Mal made a noise in his throat, calling for their attention. "I have a small question," he said. "I know it's not sporting of me to have eavesdropped, but…um… Allie?"

"Yes, Mal?"

"Are you really a vampire?"

That answered Griffin's question about how much Mal had heard. He waited for Allie to speak. She looked not in the least uncomfortable.

"You know about vampires?" she asked.

"Griffin told me, about the same time he explained what he was. We had a lot of time to talk in the trenches."

"You believed him, of course."

"He'd given me plenty of proof that werewolves existed. It wasn't such a leap from there to believing in vampires."

Allie smiled. "Well, I guess it was only a matter of time. You're the only one of my human friends who knows, at least so far. I'd appreciate it if you'd keep it that way."

"Of course." He studied her curiously. "Someday you'll have to tell me all about your world."

"Sure. Someday."

Mal fidgeted, obviously not quite finished with his questions. "Listen, Allie," he said, "I've been meaning to ask you something ever since we met up again—something that doesn't have anything to do with your being…what you are. I should have come to you earlier, since you always know what's going on in the Village, but I haven't been thinking too clearly." He rubbed at the creases between his eyebrows. "You haven't heard anything from Margot, have you?"

If Griffin hadn't been watching Allegra, he might not have noticed the way she straightened at Mal's question, or the sudden, wary alertness in her eyes. She noticed his stare and slumped in her chair, all idle nonchalance once more.

"Margot?" she said. "I haven't seen her in weeks… around the last time I saw you at Lulu's, as a matter of fact. I just assumed you'd found other things to do than hang around with us." She smoothed a stray lock of hair. "Did you two have a fight?"

"No. That's just the point. She disappeared, and there's no explanation for it."

"Hmm." Allegra stared up at the shadowed ceiling. "Very strange. I wish I could help you, Mal."

His shoulders slumped. "Damn. I don't suppose you've learned anything, Grif?"

"Not yet."

Mal rose, his body bent like an old man's. "Thanks for trying. Listen, I won't be very good company tonight. I think I'll drive back to Manhattan and get myself drunk."

"Maybe you shouldn't be alone," Allie said.

He gave a crooked grin. "I'm used to it by now. See you later, Allie."

She lifted a hand, apparently lost in her own thoughts. Once Mal had left the room, Griffin said, "Are you sure you don't know anything about Margot?"

Allegra glanced up, seeming surprised. "Why

should I? She was just someone who used to come to the clubs with Mal."

Griffin knew she was lying. He couldn't guess why, or what she could possibly have to gain by hiding what she knew. But she wasn't nearly as ignorant as she pretended.

"Mal is devastated by this," he said. "I'm concerned about his state of mind."

"You ought to have a little more faith in him."

"I'm sure he appreciates your concern for him, as well." Griffin got to his feet. "Would you care for some light refreshment before you return to Manhattan? As I recall, vampires are capable of eating normal food."

She smiled, showing the tips of her slightly pointed incisors. "Oh, yes. We quite enjoy a good meal from time to time."

He ushered her from the room. "If you have no objection, I'll accompany you back to New York. I have some business in my office I'd like to complete."

"At night?"

"I often work better at night. That shouldn't seem so strange to you."

"Not at all. I just wish you'd let yourself have a little fun once in a while." She shot him a sly glance. "You invited me to Gemma's party. Why don't you visit *my* world next time?"

"I've already had a good look at your world."

"Only through a worried brother's eyes."

"I doubt my vision would undergo a radical change even under the most favorable conditions."

"Do all werewolves judge everything on first impressions, or is it just you?"

"Allegra...I think it's clear that you and I...we don't—"

"Belong together?"

Her question shocked him. Somehow she'd built a relationship out of a few brief meetings and wary conversations, and he had no idea how she'd reached such a conclusion. She looked up at him with those brilliant eyes and a half-teasing smile, undeniably beautiful beneath her paint and the fringe of black hair. Undeniably female. Undeniably capable of making him forget how hard he'd tried to be a gentleman…

"Perhaps…" he said stiffly, taking a deep breath, "perhaps if we'd met under different circumstances… if we had something in common…"

"And we don't? We both have to hide a part of ourselves from the human world. Neither one of us can escape what we are. The only difference is that I don't want to."

"Both our races would be extinct if we hadn't learned how to survive among humans."

"You can't really believe that survival is enough."

"There's no life to enjoy without it."

She grabbed his hand. "Then let yourself *live,* Grif. Don't hide on this island and in your office. You're a fighter, not some pencil-pusher, happy to let the world go by."

A fighter? You have no idea what I'm capable of. No idea…

He gently unwound his hand from hers. "I am what I am, and I'm not likely to change."

"Baloney. Everyone changes." She sidled closer to him, her breasts nearly touching his jacket. "You find me attractive, Grif. Don't try to deny it."

He couldn't bring himself to lie. "I don't deny it."

"Are you so shocked that the feeling's mutual?"

His body hardened to aching readiness. "I'm flattered, Allegra," he said hoarsely, "but physical attraction isn't enough."

"Enough for what? I didn't ask you to marry me."

Her words sent a jolt through his system, just as if she'd proposed they retire to his room and make love then and there.

And if she had...would it be so difficult to accept her offer? Who would be hurt? He didn't for a moment entertain the thought that Allegra was a virgin. He couldn't make her pregnant. Gemma need never know....

He backed away. "You're very generous, Miss Chase. Shall I fetch your coat?"

She shrugged, apparently conceding this battle to him. But he knew it wasn't over. Allegra Chase wanted something from him...something he surely couldn't give, even if he had any desire to enter into the kind of casual relationship she'd suggested.

He turned and walked toward the vestibule, not waiting to see if Allegra followed.

THE RIDE BACK to Manhattan was tense and awkward, at least as far as Griffin Durant was concerned. For Allie, it was merely frustrating.

There was plenty of room on the backseat of the limousine, more than enough for Griffin to make sure he and Allie never touched. He stared out the window, doing his best to avoid resuming their earlier conversation.

But Allie couldn't forget that he was there. She watched him, studying his profile with its strong chin and uncompromising brow. She remembered how he'd defended her at the party, pretending afterward that it was only the natural behavior of a gentleman. She recalled the way he'd looked at her, time and again, whenever he thought she wouldn't notice—how his gaze lingered on her figure and her legs and her lips. She thought about what it would be like to kiss him, and how much more she would have to do to break through that white knight's armor and reveal the hungry, passionate man beneath.

She'd gone to the party in the hopes of provoking a reaction from Griffin. In that she'd certainly been successful; he'd turned on the people he most wanted to impress for Gemma's sake. He'd been forced to compromise some of his beliefs in the evils of Allie's way of life. All that, in addition to scaring off the rich snobs, had been good fun.

But the amusement hadn't lasted. She'd put him in an untenable position for a man who placed so much value on dignity and honor. Gemma had been upset, and Allie was responsible—even if she did believe she'd done the girl a good turn by exposing her "friends" for the bigots they were.

Allie had found a certain emptiness within herself once the guests were gone and she was alone with Griffin. It was the emptiness of the space between her and the man who seemed so resistant to her charms. It was a feeling she hadn't experienced in two years of living just as she pleased.

Uncomfortable with that train of thought, she considered the difficult situation of Mal and Margot. She'd been caught off guard when Mal asked her about his lover, and she shouldn't have been. After all, they had been regular patrons at many of the clubs and speakeasies Allie frequented, since Margot's father, Carmine De Luca, controlled most of the booze trade in and around Greenwich Village. No one could deny that the playwright and the bootlegger's daughter were a couple.

Naturally Mal had looked for Margot when she so mysteriously "disappeared." He'd made the rounds of the clubs, asking all the usual questions; Allie had kept out of his way, but she'd known she couldn't avoid him forever. She was frankly annoyed that De Luca hadn't found a better story to put Mal off than some vague claim about Margot going overseas. Margot had lacked any say in the matter, and there wasn't a chance in hell that Mal would ever see her again. Not while Raoul was alive.

It was a damned tragedy.

Allie frowned at her reflection in the tinted window. She hadn't been to see Margot for several weeks; hard as it was to admit, she felt more than a little guilt when she visited the girl. They'd become good friends since Margot's Conversion, but whenever Allie saw Margot, she imagined what she herself could have become with a different sort of patron. And there was always a risk involved when she entered Raoul's lair.

What had she told Griffin? *"You can't really believe that survival is enough."* If there was one thing she couldn't stand, it was hypocrisy—especially in herself.

She'd just made the decision to visit Margot the next day when the limousine arrived at her building and Fitzsimmons hopped out to open her door. Griffin joined his driver, his expression closed and solemn.

"Thank you again for helping Gemma," he said formally. "Should you ever require any assistance, please call on me."

She looked into his eyes. *"Any* assistance?"

He inclined his head. She reached up with lightning speed, trapped his head between her hands and kissed him. It was a very brief kiss, and he didn't resist as his warm breath poured into her mouth. She released him before he could decide to push her away.

"You haven't seen the last of me, Griffin Durant," she said. "I'm likely to turn up where you least expect it."

He stared over her head. "Goodbye, Miss Chase."

"Good *night.*" She ran up to the door, then turned and blew him another kiss. He stood there frozen like a wolf caught in a trap, and then got into the car, his eyes reflecting yellow in the streetlamp's unforgiving light.

THE NEW TUTOR was arriving on Monday, and Gemma knew it was going to be the worst day of her life.

"She won't be anything like Miss Spires," Griffin had warned her. "She demands a great deal of her students, and you'll have little time to get into trouble."

Gemma wondered if the new tutor would be anything like the nuns at St. Lucia's. She had barely come through those months alive. Grif didn't know about that; he thought she'd been the perfect schoolgirl, disciplined and meek. That was why he'd been so shocked when he found her at Lulu's.

Of course, she hadn't really done anything bad in school. She wasn't wicked, after all, no matter what the nuns said. But Griffin hadn't seen much of her after he'd sent her to those fancy schools in France and Switzerland. He barely knew her. He didn't understand that she wasn't a child anymore. Even though he'd stood up for her and Allie at the party, that obviously hadn't changed.

As for his opinion of Allie, Gemma couldn't help but fear that the events of the party had been a negative influence. When he'd come to Lulu's, Griffin had shown more interest in a woman than Gemma could remember ever happening before, even if that interest was expressed as irritation and disapproval. Gemma could tell he secretly admired Allie in spite of his criticism of her clothing and audacious behavior. And Allie liked *him,* even though she seemed to enjoy making fun of his Victorian manners and his aggravating seriousness.

Yes, it had all looked very promising. Allie was exactly the kind of person Griffin needed to make him realize how much he'd been missing, and if he accepted her…well, he couldn't very well chastise his own sister for wanting to be just like his lady friend.

But things hadn't quite turned out as Gemma had hoped. She and Allie had gone too far. If she knew Grif at all, he would escort Allie home and do his best to put her out of his mind. He was stubborn that way. Stubborn and thickheaded—and she had every right to think so, since he was her brother and she loved him in spite of his faults.

Gemma flung herself onto her bed and put a tightly rolled piece of paper between her lips, pretending it was a cigarette. She hadn't gotten the chance to try a real one at Lulu's; Allie kept changing the subject whenever she brought it up. But Allie had brought her that wonderful record, even though it was ruined now. Allie understood her the way no one else did.

She'd never make me marry one of those awful boys, Gemma thought. She curled her lip. How could *they* ever understand someone like her? So what if she'd lived most of her life among people who had no idea what she was? That didn't mean she had to keep doing it.

And as for the pack…well, after what had happened on Thursday night, *they* hardly seemed any better. Griffin had definitely been right about one thing: they wouldn't give her any more freedom than he did, and probably a lot less. Garret Sloan and his lieutenants wanted to control every *loup-garou* in New York City, probably the whole state, if they could.

No, there had to be a better place for her than this dusty old mansion or one just like it, chained to some boring milquetoast who thought more of his polo ponies than he did of his wife.

I'm strong and smart. Not every girl has to marry. Maybe I'll be just like Allie, living my own life for myself.

She jumped up and walked to the window. The lawn stretching down to the dock was dark and silent. A perfect night for a solitary walk. Uncle Edward was probably still up, but he was only human, and Grif hadn't yet resorted to keeping his sister under lock and key.

I promised I wouldn't go back to Manhattan alone, she thought. *I could get Grif into a lot of trouble with the pack if I did. But there aren't any other werewolves on Long Island. I bet I could run all the way to Montauk and be back before dawn. Maybe I can even find a place like Lulu's….*

Something moved on the lawn, a dark, man-sized shape that pressed low to the ground as it crept toward the house. A sharp, half-familiar scent filled Gemma's nose. She strained to see through the closed window. Whoever it was had no business on Durant property, of that she was sure.

The most sensible thing to do was to call Uncle Edward, but Gemma was in no mood to be sensible.

She eased the window open by the tiniest increments, careful not to let it squeak.

The man on the lawn had disappeared, but his distinctive scent lingered. Gemma hastily donned a pair of her brother's cut-down trousers, which she had stolen from the laundry, and threw on a blouse. Barefoot, she shimmied out the window and scrambled down the ivy that clung to the wall.

Only the sound of her feet hitting the ground broke the moonlit stillness. She crouched, listening. The intruder was very quiet, indeed, but he made just enough noise for her to determine his general direction. She headed that way at a fast but cautious pace, leaving hardly a mark in the grass.

There. She saw the shape again, only a few feet from the French doors to the summer parlor. He was trying to get into the house, but he wouldn't succeed. She would catch him. Let Grif rail on about her feminine limitations then. She would—

She blinked. The man was gone. The hair stood up on the back of Gemma's neck. He couldn't have sneaked past her. Perhaps he'd turned the corner of the house. With a soft growl, she stalked toward the French doors.

A hand shot out of nowhere and covered her mouth. Before she could think of fighting, a lean and muscular arm pulled her against a hard masculine body, and she felt someone's warm breath on her cheek.

"Don't cry out," he said. "I wouldn't want to hurt you, Gemma Durant."

CHAPTER SEVEN

THE FIRST THING Gemma thought was that she was an utter fool. The second was that she'd been right all along. The man who held her wasn't human.

"Who—" she began, struggling to form words beneath the smothering hand "—who are you?"

He eased his grip a little, his chest rising and falling against her back. "Do you promise not to scream?"

"I never scream."

She thought she heard a laugh, abruptly cut short. He removed his hand from her mouth but kept his arm locked around her waist.

"You're making a big mistake," she said, catching her breath. "When my brother finds out—"

"He's not here." The intruder marched her into the shelter of some well-groomed shrubs. "I've been watching for a few hours, and I saw him drive off with the leech."

Gemma bristled. "Don't call Allie that. Who are you, and what are you doing here?"

He turned her around, and for the first time she saw his features: young, not much older than herself, with pale brown eyes and a disheveled thatch of dark blond hair. He was more than a little good-looking, tall and broad-shouldered, but not yet fully grown into his manhood. He wore no coat and his feet were bare.

She glared at him. He grinned, all strong white teeth, and her heart began to beat very fast.

"My name is Wyatt," he said. "Wyatt Dempsey. And I'm here to see you."

"What?"

"I saw you outside Lulu's the other night."

She stiffened and pulled against his hold. "You were with Ivar!"

He shook his head. "I wasn't *with* them. I only saw what happened."

"But you're a member of the pack."

"Everyone is, except you and your brother."

"Have you come to kidnap me?"

He laughed. "Kidnap you? That's a childish idea, Gemma."

"That's 'Miss Durant' to you, Mr. Dempsey."

"Well, 'Miss Durant,' I'm not here to do anything to you." His voice softened, and he gazed into her eyes with warmth she felt all the way down to her toes. "Like I said, I saw you on the street when you left the speak. I recognized your brother right away, so I knew who you had to be." He relaxed his hold on her arms. "I heard him yell at you. You weren't supposed to be there, were you?"

"I don't see what business that is of yours."

"I wasn't supposed to be out, either. Garret keeps a pretty strict curfew for anyone under twenty-one, especially us young males." He leaned closer. "I could see that you and I were just the same. We don't like all the rules they make for us. We both want to be free."

Gemma shivered with a surge of excitement. "And that's why you came all the way out to Long Island? Aren't there any others in the pack who feel like you do?"

"If there are, they never do anything about it. You *did*."

"*I* wasn't afraid. The worst that could happen to me was that Griffin would find out."

"He's a pretty formidable man." Wyatt Dempsey glanced toward the house, as if he expected Griffin to return at any moment. "That's why I didn't let either of you see me on the street. I didn't want you to think I agreed with what Ivar and his bully-boys were doing."

"You mean, threatening me and my brother?"

"It was a stupid thing to do. Garret should know by now that he can't make your brother join the pack by using force."

Gemma stared at him, amazed at the seeming normality of their conversation when there was nothing ordinary about it at all. "You grabbed me outside my own house just to tell me that?"

"No." He dropped his hands, his fingers grazing her arms all the way down. "I…I just had to see you again. I've never met anyone so…so…"

"Beautiful?" she asked, half mocking.

He held her gaze. The yellow in his eyes absorbed the softer brown. "Yes. Beautiful and fine and brave."

"Oh." Gemma swallowed and looked away. "I'm not so… I mean…"

He pressed his finger to her lips. "Isn't there somewhere else we can talk?"

Gemma knew she ought to send Wyatt away and return to her room. Griffin wouldn't approve of this at all. He would be suspicious of any member of the pack who would turn up at Oakdene in the middle of the night. He would certainly never believe that a young man might want to see Gemma just because she was "beautiful and fine and brave."

And that's why I have to snatch every opportunity I can, she thought. "Starke—our butler—is probably waiting up to make sure I don't go anywhere," she said. "I'd better go back to my room and make up my bed so it looks like someone is sleeping in it."

Wyatt frowned. "Maybe you'll change your mind. Maybe you'll tell your butler I'm here."

"If you're afraid of that, you can run away," she said. "Or you can meet me down in the boathouse. I'll be there in ten minutes."

Without waiting for his answer, Gemma climbed back up to her room and slipped through the window. She bundled up several items of clothing, stuffed them under the blanket and was back outside in five minutes, running toward the dock.

Wyatt was sitting on a sawhorse in the boathouse, his arms folded across his chest. He jumped up as she walked in.

"You came back," he said.

"I said I would, didn't I?"

He gestured to the sawhorse. "Will milady sit?"

She took the seat he offered, wishing she were wearing anything but Griffin's baggy old trousers. She couldn't think of a single intelligent or fascinating thing to say. "Aren't you…didn't you say that Garret Sloan has a curfew?"

"Yes," he said, gazing at her with disconcerting intensity.

"So won't you get into trouble when they find out you've been gone?"

"If they do find out, it'll be worth it."

"Just to sit and stare at me?"

He grinned in that heart-stopping way that would have made any girl melt into a puddle. "I could do that all night. But we don't have to sit, Gemma. We could do something else."

"Like what?"

"Run." His eyes gleamed, wolf-bright. "How many times have you Changed and run in the moonlight with another of your kind?"

She began to feel dizzy. "Only once, with my brother. I've been in America for three months, but he…he doesn't approve. He wants me to marry a human boy and live an ordinary life."

"You're kidding."

"I'm serious. He doesn't trust other werewolves." She closed her eyes. "All the time I was in Europe I never met anyone like us, and now…"

A strong, callused hand slipped into hers. "Now things will be different. Tonight we'll run until our muscles ache and our lungs burn, until we can't run anymore. Just you and me."

She opened her eyes. He was just inches away, his handsome face filled with yearning she understood so well. If she agreed to his proposal—if she Changed in front of him and watched him do the same—it would be the most intimate act of her life. She would be exposing the most secret part of herself to a virtual stranger.

Yes, he was her kind, but he would see her as she truly was, as only one other person in the world had ever done.

She stood and slowly began to unbutton her blouse. Wyatt hesitated, gaze half averted, and started on the studs at his collar. There was a moment of charged awkwardness as they stood naked before each other, but then a new excitement took hold of them. Their gazes locked.

"Now?" Wyatt asked.

In answer, Gemma let the Change take her…let her body relax until each muscle was soft and fluid, while every nerve crackled with energy. There was no pain; the feeling was indescribable, euphoric, as natural as breathing. She felt her body flow downward, arms becoming strong front legs, hands tightening into broad paws, eyes and nose and ears opening up to the world in a way no human could ever imagine.

In a minute it was done. Wyatt stretched his lean body, golden fur sleek and thick over his shoulders and hindquarters. He waved his tail and grinned, a half-human expression that invited her to play. She touched his muzzle with her own, tasting his wonderful scent. He licked her lips. They circled each other, hackles raised in mock challenge, and then Gemma wheeled and dashed from the boathouse.

Time ceased to have meaning. Only the night itself was real, pulsing with wonders painted in smells and sounds and colors none but wolf eyes could see. Gemma and Wyatt ran side by side, sometimes touching, other times ranging far apart, but always connected by their lupine awareness. The miles vanished beneath their feet. They galloped along the beach, darting in and out of the waves. They sped through the gardens and across the lawns of the unsuspecting wealthy inhabitants of the North Shore. They wove among the trees of the pine barrens, howling as they went.

The night was waning when they turned for home. Gemma's limbs ached, but she gloried in the soreness and the burning of her pads. It was hard to Change back. She kept her distance from Wyatt as she gathered up her clothing, afraid he would see the depth of her emotion. Once they were dressed, they walked back toward the house, hand in hand. The breeze dried the tears on Gemma's face.

"I have to go," Wyatt said.

"I know."

"Do you want to see me again?"

She took his other hand and squeezed it tight. "What about your family?"

"I don't have anyone but my father, and he's too busy with pack business to pay much attention to what I do."

Gemma smiled, suddenly shy after her boldness. "I do want you to come back, Wyatt. As often as you can."

"Then I will." He bent toward her, his gaze on her lips. "Gemma, I—"

She silenced him with the briefest of kisses. The sensation sent her reeling. Wyatt stepped back and shook himself from head to toe, his hair standing on end.

"Watch for me, Gemma," he said.

He left before she could draw another breath. She ran after him a little way, but soon he disappeared behind the house. His scent trailed after him like a joyful memory.

Gemma walked slowly across the lawn, kicking at the grass with her toes. A few hours ago she'd been wondering how she could make her dreams come true. Now everything had changed. Someone had come into her world…someone she never could have expected, someone she hardly knew and yet understood with all her heart.

Whatever waited in her future, Gemma knew she wouldn't be alone. Wyatt would be there. And neither her brother nor the pack would be able to hold them much longer.

RAOUL'S MANSION STOOD tall and imposing in the darkness, its anachronistic gothic ornaments and moldings making it seem like a castle transplanted whole from a mountain stronghold in some barbaric Eastern European country.

Allie smiled grimly. Raoul was the flamboyant type. He liked to make a statement, even when it went right over the heads of the humans it was meant to impress. Stoker's Dracula might well have lived in such a place. Stoker himself must have known a few real *strigoi* in his day, even if he'd chosen to exaggerate and embellish in order to make his tale all the more terrifying.

Real vampires, Allie reflected, were quite frightening enough when they wanted to be. Especially the ones like Raoul.

She walked through the gates and up to the door, with its immense Dickensian knocker. She didn't try to use it. Raoul's servants would know she was here soon enough.

Her watch had ticked off three minutes when the door swung open. It was Crispus himself who answered it. He was lean to the point of emaciation, his age indeterminable, his blue eyes hollow and hopeless with the long years of low rank and unquestioning obedience.

"Allegra Chase," he said. "May I inquire after the purpose of your visit?"

"Tell Raoul that I'm here to see Margot."

Even Crispus's dour face reflected surprise at her bald statement. "Miss Margot," he whispered, "is not to be disturbed."

"She'll see me."

He stared dolefully at her feet. "My Liege believes she requires more rest and time for reflection."

Allie set her hands on her hips. "Oh, really? What exactly is he afraid of, Crispy? I know he's obsessed with her, but is he so unsure of the blood-bond that he can't risk letting her see anyone but his own cowering servants?"

Crispus stared, too far gone to take offense. "I cannot speak for my Master," he said.

"Then remind him that Margot won't like him any better if he prevents her from visiting with her closest friend."

A little shudder ran through Crispus, the instinctive dread of a slave compelled to deliver an unpleasant message to a capricious Master. "Please wait here, Miss Chase."

She waited. Another five minutes passed before Crispus returned. Silently, he opened the door, and Allie stepped into a dark, massive great hall festooned with medieval banners and busts of great human conquerors. There was nowhere to sit, no touch of warmth to welcome any guest, invited or otherwise.

Without a word Crispus led her up the grand staircase. Baroque paintings marched up the wall, some of them undoubtedly worth a fortune in human terms. They were all invariably dark and imposing, like storms perpetually poised on the brink of disgorging their burdens of rain and lightning. A uniformed human servant girl came creeping down the stairs, her arms full of clean linens; she cringed as Crispus and Allie passed, her eyes averted. Raoul's human servants were paid extremely well, but their service was for a lifetime. There was no escape from Raoul Boucher.

The second-floor landing was hardly different from

the hall, though on a lesser scale. A row of doors stretched down a dimly lit corridor. Each of the rooms was a sizable and luxurious suite, designed for the use of Raoul's protégés and those lesser vassals who claimed a few protégés of their own. The more powerful vassals, whose service to the clan had won them the right to create the most Converts, kept their own more modest mansions nearby, semi-independent but firmly bound to Raoul by ties of law and tradition.

Just as Crispus began to ascend the second staircase, one of the doors opened and a young woman stepped out into the hallway. She was strikingly beautiful, with a cloud of pale hair and vivid aquamarine eyes. She stared at Allie, recognition slowly dawning on her face.

"Apostate," she hissed. "Have you finally come to your senses?"

Allie paused, leaning on the banister with crossed arms. "Marina," she said, "so nice to see you again."

Marina swept toward Allie, her scarlet dressing gown as bright as fresh blood. "You belong here—with us," she said in a slightly less hostile tone. "Why don't you see? Why must you live among the breeders, tainting yourself with their brutishness?"

"Maybe because I don't see any benefit to living out a few thousand years as a slave in Raoul's harem," Allie said.

Marina's eyes burned like those of a fanatic. "Is that what you think of your sisters?" she demanded. "Do you have such unnatural feelings toward your own kind?"

Allie sighed. "What's unnatural is the way you live, Marina…leaving this mansion only to feed, never getting the chance to better your situation. Maybe it was different with the previous Master, but what chance has a woman got to gain status under Raoul's dominion? You can't be part of the bootlegging operation or participate in any of the other work that lets the males move up in rank. Doesn't that bother you at all?"

"I have no ambition other than to serve My Liege," Marina said. "I am content."

And that, Allie thought, was probably no more than the truth. A vampire as powerful as Raoul had absolute control over his protégés. The blood-bond that formed between a patron and the human he Converted was virtually unbreakable. It was of far greater benefit to the patron, but even he was tied emotionally and physically to his protégés, and was thus obliged to provide every comfort to his dependents.

For some, comfort was enough. Plenty of humans would have found it so. They would be glad to give up their free will for the promise of safety and the privilege of never having to think a single thought of their own.

Just as Marina had done.

"I've enjoyed our conversation, Marina," Allie said, "but I have an appointment to keep." She began climbing again, passing Crispus. By the time they paused on the third-floor landing, Allie had acquired a train of *strigoi,* male and female, whose antagonism blazed at her back like a three-alarm fire.

"It's nice to be popular, isn't it, Crispus?" she said.

He glanced back at the others, his hangdog expression never changing. He continued along the landing to a single door that led to rooms occupying an entire wing of the third floor: Raoul's personal suite, where his most treasured protégés provided him with constant companionship. Two hard-looking men stood to either side of the door: Raoul's enforcers, highly trained fighters whose only duty was to suppress any hint of rebellion among the vassals and punish those, vampire or otherwise, who ran afoul of the Master.

Crispus exchanged a few words with the enforcers and opened the door, gesturing Allie to precede him. Allie's vampire entourage retreated, but every one of them looked as if he or she would like nothing better than to drive the mythical stake through Allie's heart.

The door gave onto a gorgeously appointed ante-room, marble-floored and furnished with Louis XIV chairs, cabinets and tables polished to a mirror finish. A man sat in one of the chairs facing the door, languid hands folded in his lap. His silk shirt was a vivid shade of azure, defying the usual *strigoi* preference for dark colors, and he wore a large silver hoop in one ear. His long black hair was knotted at the back of his neck. Allie had always thought that he looked like nothing so much as an amateur pirate.

"Allegra," he said, "I see you haven't changed."

"Hello, Sebastian. I see you're in a joking mood today."

"Someone has to counter our grim reputation, don't you think?"

Allie wandered about the room, examining the delicate porcelain figurines on display in the cabinets. "I'm doing my best," she said.

Sebastian steepled his fingers under his chin. "Raoul isn't best pleased with you, you know."

"I've noticed."

"I'm not sure he'd approve of your coming to see Margot again."

"Then why did you let me in?"

"The Master's lieutenants must have some autonomy, or what good are they?" Sebastian stretched out his long legs. "I've always liked you, Allie. I think you're a fool, but I like you. And Margot could use a bit of cheering up."

Allie turned to face him. "Still the same?"

"I'm afraid so. It hasn't been that long for her, you know. Some find it harder to make the adjustment."

"She wants out."

"Perhaps you ought not to express your opinions so forcefully, my dear."

"Margot always had a mind of her own. And she didn't choose this."

"A lot of us didn't choose it, but we make the best of what we have." He rose from the chair. "Ten minutes, Allie. That's all I can give you."

"I appreciate the risk you're taking, Sebastian."

He shrugged. "I used to be a gambler. It ruined me, but I always felt most alive when everything was on the line. I still enjoy the feeling." He gestured toward one of several doors opening from the anteroom. "Margot's waiting for you."

Allie went through the door and into another short hallway. Though there were no windows, the hall was brightly lit and painted a pale hue that gave it a sense of lightness absent in other parts of the mansion. She tapped on the door at the end of the hall, suddenly nervous.

The woman who answered her knock looked almost the same as Allie remembered from before the accident: her hair was still the color of burnished copper; her eyes as green as the hills of her Irish mother's homeland; her skin fair almost to the point of translucence. There was not a single sign of the terrible injuries that had brought her to the point of death three months ago. She resembled nothing so much as one of the porcelain figurines in Raoul's anteroom, but her fragile appearance had always belied the fierce independence of her character.

It was in her character that Allie had seen the greatest change. Margot smiled, and there was genuine pleasure in the expression. But the sorrow, the resignation, in her eyes was almost more than Allie could bear.

"Allie," Margot said, "I'm so glad you've come."

Allie took Margot's hands. "So am I, gorgeous. So am I."

Margot stepped back, ushered Allie into the room and closed the door. Like the anteroom, her suite was expensively and tastefully furnished with Louis XIV antiques, but the color scheme was all soft pastels in cool hues that lent an air of deceptive tranquility. The canopied bed was fit for a princess and jewelry replete with precious stones lay scattered across Margot's dressing table.

"Will you have something to drink, Allie?" Margot asked, pushing her hair away from her face. "I've got just about everything here."

"No, thanks. We haven't got much time to talk." Allie made Margot sit in the most comfortable-looking chair. "I'm sorry I didn't come sooner. I was…" She tripped over the flimsy explanations lined up in her mind. "I don't really have an excuse. I'm sorry."

"I know it's dangerous for you to come here. If not for Sebastian…"

"I know." Allie searched Margot's eyes. "He said you needed cheering up."

"He's a good man. Too good for this place." She shook her head and smiled. "You look wonderful, Allie. Life must be treating you well."

"I'm not here to talk about me, my friend." Allie leaned forward in her chair. "Nothing has changed, has it?"

"Always straight to the point." Margot stared down at her interlaced fingers. "What's done is done. It's just that I...I haven't quite accepted..." She closed her eyes. "It would have been better if I'd died, Allie."

Allie pulled her chair closer to Margot's and lay her hand on Margot's arm. "It's still bad, then. Is it Raoul? Is he..."

"Raoul is the soul of generosity," Margot said, her voice harsh with bitterness. "He treats me as his most prized possession. Nothing is too good for me." She rose and began to walk restlessly about the room. "He'd take me out every night if I asked. He'd love to show me off as much as possible. But I..." She lifted a diamond necklace from her dressing table and let it slide through her fingers. "When he changed me, he did something to my heart. It feels like a stone, Allie. I can barely remember what it was like to be...to love..."

Allie thought of Mal. "You can only lose things like love and compassion if you never had them to begin with," she said gently.

"You're wrong." Margot looked up, her eyes filled with emotion. "I know I've lost Mal forever. I won't love again. But I can hate, Allie. My father, who forced me to take this life...Raoul..." She caught her breath, generously leaving Allie off the list. "Oh, Allie..."

Margot slumped back into her chair, as if the brief flare of defiance had sapped her strength. Allie knew that Margot desperately wanted to weep. Allie's own throat was hard and tight with the tears she couldn't shed. She felt as helpless as when she'd been confined to her bed in those long, terrible years before Cato had come to release her, helpless to give Margot anything but empty reassurances. Margot had been saved against her will and brought into a world she could only despise; Allie had been given a new chance and glorious freedom.

She knelt before Margot and took the young woman in her arms. "I know there's nothing I can do," she said. "But if you ever need me, Margot—for anything, no matter how odd or foolish it may seem—get a message to me, and I'll come."

"Oh, Allie…"

"I mean it, beautiful." She tipped up Margot's chin. "We youngbloods have to stick together."

Margot rubbed at her eyes. "Is he… Is Mal well, Allie? Have you spoken to him?"

Allie looked away. "I haven't seen him."

"He doesn't go out anymore…to the places we used to go?"

"No. I'm sorry, Margot."

Margot straightened, pushing Allie away as surely as if she'd struck out with her fists. "Maybe he's forgotten me. That would be best. Yes, that would be best for everyone." Her lips curved in an empty smile. "It was another life, after all."

Allie struggled with the conscience she'd thought she discarded long ago. If Margot knew the man she loved hadn't given up on her, surely it would only add to her pain. She could never be with Mal again. Unless Raoul were to meet with an untimely death, Margot would be blood-bound to him until his power withered with great age or he suffered the loss of potency that inevitably led to a Master's downfall. No, it would do her no good to learn of Mal's suffering.

Damn Raoul. Damn Carmine De Luca. And damn Allegra Chase....

Someone knocked on the door, and then Sebastian looked in, his face drawn with apology.

"It's time," he said, and left them alone again.

Allie rose, and Margot walked her to the door. "Thank you for coming," she said. "I know it's not easy, with Raoul pressuring you to give in."

"Maybe," Allie said slowly, "maybe it would be better for you if I did."

"No!" Margot seized Allie's hand and squeezed hard. "Knowing you're out there...sometimes that thought alone keeps me sane." Her words caught on a dry sob. "Keep fighting, Allie. Fight for both of us. That way I can pretend that part of me is free."

She led Allie back to the anteroom, giving Sebastian a smile that still held a trace of her old warmth.

"Thank you, Sebastian," she said. "Will you see Allie to the front door?"

He inclined his head. Margot hugged Allie, her desperate strength great enough to snap a human's spine.

"Keep safe," she whispered. "If I don't see you again..."

"Don't be ridiculous. I'll be back."

Allie broke away and strode for the door of the suite, afraid her own emotions would betray her. She kept her face impassive as Sebastian accompanied her out to the hall. The enforcers still stood guard like cruel, beautiful statues, but the resentful *strigoi* mob had dispersed.

Sebastian stopped her as they reached the front door. "Rumor has it that you've been seen with dogs, Allie. If it's true, it might give Raoul the final excuse he needs to violate tradition and use force to bind you."

"I never heard there was any law against associating with werewolves."

"Don't play stupid, Allie. You know perfectly well it isn't a matter of law." He narrowed his eyes. "It's true, then."

"I helped a kid who was in over her head, that's all."

"You're too softhearted for one of us, Allie."

"Look who's talking." She hesitated. "I have a question for *you*. Have you heard anything about someone trying to break into my place?"

Sebastian raised a brow. "Break in? No, I hadn't heard. Are you sure it was *strigoi?*"

Allie kept her face expressionless. Sebastian was lying. He knew something he wasn't telling, and it wouldn't do any good to press him.

She put her hand on the doorknob. "It's too bad *you're* not the Master, Sebastian."

He glanced over his shoulder. "I'd appreciate a little more discretion in your opinions, especially when my future might be at stake."

"Your future? Or your life?"

"I don't understand you."

"I may be only two years old, but I've heard that more than one vampire has permanently disappeared since Raoul took over."

"It's better not to dwell on such rumors, Allie."

"I've just been wondering if my patron's recent demise was really the delayed result of the influenza."

Sebastian started, his pale skin even more ghostly with shock. "Cato? Why would anyone want him dead?"

"That's what I'd like to know."

"He was important to Raoul. You know that. He was the one who invented the elixir."

"You mean, the stuff that keeps us all sterile, unless Raoul condescends to bestow his grand dispensation?"

"It's saved us from dangerous overpopulation, Allie. If everyone went around Converting humans whenever they felt the urge, the humans would begin to notice. Raoul brought order to the clan after years of chaos."

Some might disagree with that idea, Allie thought. She'd heard more than a few rumors that not every vassal approved of the changes Raoul had instituted since the previous Master's fall. "Whatever he did for Raoul," she said, "Cato was devoted to his science. He couldn't have been a threat to anyone."

"Exactly. Your imagination is running away with you. It would be wise for you to desist with this pointless speculation."

"Thanks for the advice." She stepped out into the pleasantly cool night air. "Look after Margot, will you?"

"I'll do what I can." He withdrew behind the door. "Watch your back, Allie."

The door closed, and Allie stood on the steps, considering what Sebastian had said about her association with "dogs." She'd laughed off Bendik's threats when she'd met him in the alley, but it would be very unwise to ignore Sebastian's warnings. He knew Raoul better than almost anyone else. He could guess what Raoul was planning. If Sebastian believed that her dealings with werewolves would provoke Raoul into action, it might be dangerous for her. But what about Gemma and Griffin?

Allie frowned. Raoul was perfectly capable of ordering the assassination of any *strigoi* who threatened his rule. Just as he might have killed Cato, for reasons Allie couldn't as yet imagine. But he wouldn't be any danger to Griffin or Gemma; if he were to harm a werewolf, the political repercussions would be dire.

No, the Durants weren't in any danger just for keeping company with her. She, on the other hand, could be on the verge of losing her freedom permanently. If Raoul gained the support of the elder vassals—if he convinced them that Allie was a threat to the clan—they wouldn't protest if he bound her against her will.

She shivered. There was only one thing she truly feared, and that was the loss of her freedom. She was intrigued by Griffin Durant… No, much more than intrigued. She would have enjoyed the challenge of getting under his skin, learning what made him tick, seeing how far she could push him to abandon those prehistoric attitudes he clung to with such determination. To feel his arms around her, his mouth on hers, their bodies tangled in the sheets…

She began to walk away from the mansion, her strides long and frantic. Griffin would be just as happy if he never saw her again. Maybe he was right. They were both better off apart, safe in their separate worlds.

Maybe in a few weeks or months, she could even forget she'd ever seen his face.

CHAPTER EIGHT

THE PHONE WAS RINGING when Allie walked into her apartment. Louise had already answered it by the time Allie deposited her coat and clutch on the nearest chair. She watched as Lou listened intently, nodded to herself, then set the receiver facedown on the telephone table.

"Who is it, Lou?" Allie asked, walking into the kitchen.

Louise followed her, leaning against the kitchen table while Allie poured herself a glass of tomato juice. "It's Mr. Durant," Lou said. "It's the second time he's called since midnight. Do you want me to tell him you aren't available?"

Allie saw the reproachful look in Lou's eyes and averted her gaze. "That would be a little hard to do, wouldn't it, since he probably knows I'm home?"

"I don't think it's right for you to avoid him like this, Allie. He's a good man. You seemed to like him well enough two weeks ago."

That's right, Allie thought, *but that was before my little talk with Sebastian.* She took her glass into the living room, kicked off her pumps and sank into the couch. Two weeks. Was that all the time that had passed since the party? It seemed ten times as long.

"I can tell him you're entertaining someone else,"

Louise offered, her expression still disapproving. "But he did say it was important. Something about a mutual friend."

Allie stared at the thick red liquid in her glass. Curse it all. Why couldn't Griffin have left well enough alone? He'd obviously taken her casual kiss all too seriously.

She hadn't. When it came right down to it, Griffin Durant was just another guy to take or leave alone as she chose. Yes, she decided, two weeks had given her a better perspective on the whole situation, and she could meet Griffin again with complete disinterest.

"I know you won't listen to my advice," Lou said, "but if you want my opinion—"

Allie flung up her hands. "All right. I'll talk to him, if that will satisfy you." She set her glass on the table and went to the telephone, snatching up the receiver. "Hello? Griffin?"

"Allegra?"

A charge of electricity shot up Allie's spine at the sound of his voice. "That's me."

"I haven't heard from you since the party."

"Gee. I didn't know I was supposed to make regular reports."

She could almost feel him stiffen at the other end of the line. "I apologize for disturbing your busy life, Miss Chase, but I am obliged to request your assistance in a matter regarding a mutual friend."

Allie bit her lip, regretting her rudeness. "Look, I'm sorry, Griffin. I've just been...otherwise engaged."

"I've no doubt."

His sarcasm cut her to the quick. "Just because *you* don't have a real—" She stopped and took a deep breath. "How is Gemma?"

"She's fine. She's asked after you several times."

"Well…tell her I've thought about her, too."

An awkward silence fell. "I wouldn't have called if the matter weren't urgent."

Now, isn't that flattering? Allie thought, well aware of her own contradictory emotions. "I'm sure you've been very busy yourself."

"Yes." He cleared his throat. "Allegra…"

"What is this about a mutual friend?"

She thought she heard him sigh. "It's Mal. He's disappeared."

"Disappeared? Since the party?"

"Since last Saturday. I haven't been able to reach him at his apartment for the past seven days."

"Why does that make you think he's disappeared? There's nothing strange about a guy leaving town for a little vacation."

"He would have said something to me if he were going away."

"Why? You're not his big brother."

He made a sound of impatience. "He's my brother in everything but blood. He may be an artist and a dreamer, but he wouldn't run off without telling someone, and none of his other friends have heard from him, either."

Allie picked up a pencil and tapped it against the table. "He's never done this kind of thing before?"

"Never since I've known him. And there's more—he had a meeting scheduled with a very wealthy theatrical backer last Thursday. I know he didn't keep that appointment. Considering how important his plays are to him, he would never have missed the meeting unless he was physically incapable of keeping it."

Allie chewed on the pencil. "You're right about that.

He's passionate about his plays. He could hardly stop talking about them when he was with Margot. She hung on every word." She fought off a wave of sadness. "I guess you called to see if I'd heard from him?"

"Obviously you haven't."

"No. But he hasn't been coming to the clubs, so it wasn't very likely that our paths would have crossed again."

"Yes." The sound of Griffin's breathing grew slightly more distant as he shifted his receiver. "I'd like to compare my list of his friends to yours. Perhaps…if it's not inconvenient…we could visit some of his old haunts."

Allie felt her pulse begin to speed up. "You really are worried about him, aren't you?"

"He's been despondent over Margot, more than I've ever seen him about anything. Men of his character sometimes go to extremes."

Allie snapped the pencil in half. "When do you want to begin the search?"

"I'll meet you at your apartment at eight tonight."

"I'll be waiting."

She hung up, her body tense with worry and excitement. Despite Griffin's fears, she didn't for a moment believe that Mal had killed himself. Still, she wouldn't put it past the kid to have done something stupid in his grief over losing Margot—like making himself a pest with Carmine De Luca. The bootlegger could be pushed too far, and he was as dangerous as any human boss in the city. Still, if Mal was in New York—and alive—Allie was sure that she would be able to track him down.

And as for Griffin… She paced over to the couch, began to sit, then bounced back onto her feet. Nothing had really changed since two weeks ago when she'd decided not to get tangled up with him again. But she'd had a little time to think, and she was beginning to believe that she'd badly overreacted when she'd worried that Raoul might exploit her association with the werewolves. It was only the visit to the mansion and seeing Margot that had made her so paranoid. If she started living in a constant state of suspicion and fear, Raoul had already won. And he would know it.

This was an excellent opportunity to prove once again that she wouldn't play the mouse to Raoul's cat. Anyway, it would be just this one time, for Mal's sake. And for Margot's.

"Well?" Louise said, breaking into Allie's thoughts as she walked into the room. "How is Mr. Durant?"

"Same as ever," Allie said lightly. "He'll be coming around at eight tonight."

Lou's dark eyes twinkled. "It'll do you a world of good to be with a real gentleman for once."

Allie laughed. "A good man to reform a lost soul."

"A good man for a good woman," Lou said.

"I think you need spectacles, Louise."

"Maybe. But I'm not the one who's blind."

GRIFFIN SET DOWN the telephone, surprised to see that his hands were shaking. Part of it he could attribute to his real fears for Mal, but the rest…

He hadn't expected that after two weeks apart Allie Chase could still affect his heart.

It's not your heart she's affecting, he thought. *Don't get the two confused, Durant.*

But he had always tried to be honest with himself, and he had to admit that he'd thought about Allie every day since the party. Every day…hell, every hour. Her kiss had been anything but platonic, and her words and audacious manner had given him every reason to believe she intended to pursue him. He'd been thinking of ways to fend her off at the same time that he was anticipating their next meeting.

But she hadn't called. She'd apparently forgotten about him as easily as she doubtless did her other lovers, and he should have been relieved.

Griffin circled the library, his gaze roaming over the titles of the books in their neat rows reaching up to the ceiling. There wasn't anything ever written that could advise him on how to deal with Allegra Chase; not even Shakespeare had the answers. But it didn't really matter now. Allegra had agreed to help him find Mal. Their rendezvous would be strictly business, and that was the sum of it.

He returned to his desk and picked up the telephone. A call to Ross Kavanagh enlisted the detective's help in looking for Mal. Ross was doubtful that Mal would have taken his own life, but he agreed to keep an eye on the morgue just in case.

"I sure as hell hope it doesn't come to that," Ross said.

"So do I," Griffin said. "No news on Margot?"

"Not a thing. I've still got my ear to the ground."

"Thanks, Ross. I owe you yet another debt."

Ross gave a short laugh. "I'll remember."

He hung up, and Griffin returned to his circuit of the room. Somehow he got through the day without dwelling too much on his coming reunion with Allie, and by seven he was in his Rolls-Royce on the way to Manhattan. Allie came down to meet him dressed in a surprisingly modest frock and a coat that covered her from ears to ankles.

They stood stock-still, staring like a pair of street dogs sizing each other up and debating whether to run or fight. Allie made the first move, her vivid red lips parting in a smile.

"Look what the cat dragged in," she said. "Hello, Griffin."

"Allie. You look well."

"I'm not complaining."

He looked into her eyes, amazed that they were so much brighter than he remembered. Even in the darkness her face seemed to glow. And her mouth…

"I haven't developed a wart on my nose, have I?" she asked.

Griffin shook himself. "Sorry. I've been thinking about Mal."

"So where do you want to go first?"

"If you've no objection, I'd like to visit his apartment. There may be some clue there as to where he's gone, and why."

"Do you have a key?"

"Mal gave me one, but I haven't had the occasion to use it until now."

"Okay, then. Let's go."

Griffin held the car door open and waited until she was comfortably settled, then took his seat behind the wheel. The streets were moderately congested with New Yorkers out for the usual nightlife, but he made good time to Greenwich Village.

They climbed the stairs up to the third floor of the restored tenement building, surrounded by the smells of stale cooking and the shouts of children on the landings. Someone was playing a violin with surprising skill, and a couple was quarreling enthusiastically in Italian.

Mal's apartment was at the end of the hall. Griffin had just fitted the key into the lock when the door swung open, hinges creaking.

"Unlocked," he said. "Stay here, Allie. I'll go in first."

Allie shuddered in mock fear. "Ooh, the big bad werewolf will protect the weak little vampire."

Griffin looked askance at her. "Indulge me."

She pulled a face but remained behind while he entered the apartment. At first glance it appeared that nothing had been disturbed, but it would have been difficult to tell; papers covered almost every available surface, and piles of books were scattered about the pitted floor. A single window, grimy with dirt, looked out on an alley. A patched leather chair sat behind a battered desk bearing a primitive typewriter. The sunken bed was draped with a faded quilt. An open doorway led to a tiny kitchen, where a stack of chipped plates stood beside the stained sink.

"It's so small," Allie said at Griffin's shoulder. "He sure didn't believe in personal luxuries."

"He spent all his money on Margot," Griffin said.

"Masculine pride," Allie said. "Wouldn't let her pay for anything."

Griffin let her comment pass and sniffed the air. "I don't smell anything unusual. No recent cooking. Mal's scent is on everything, of course, but I'd say he hasn't been here in a week."

"Which tallies with when he stopped answering your calls."

"Someone else has been here, however. I'm catching two different scents I can't identify."

"Whoever broke the lock?"

"I don't know. The smells in this building are overwhelming."

Allie waved at the air. "Sometimes I'm glad my nose is still relatively human. What next?"

"I'll take the left side of the room and you take the right. Look for anything out of place."

"I hope we won't have to look through all those papers," Allie said.

Griffin shared her sentiment, but he kept his thoughts to himself as he began to comb his half of the apartment. He found a great many half-finished plays, scribbled notes, newspaper clippings and a dozen chewed pencil stubs. Aside from a pad of paper scrawled over and over again with Margot's name, he found nothing to indicate trouble or a reason for Mal's sudden disappearance.

"At least there's no suicide note," Allie said. "No dirty dishes in the kitchen and the bed's made. It doesn't look as if he left in a hurry, or under any kind of duress, but there's a clean square over here on this table, as if someone removed something. A thief, maybe?"

"Mal doesn't have much worth stealing. Could be a book or a manuscript." He glanced inside the scratched armoire that stood opposite the bed. It was empty.

"His clothes are gone," Griffin said.

"Which suggests he planned to leave," Allie said. "Either that, or a thief stole all his clothes. I just can't see it. No self-respecting burglar would bother looking for loot in apartments like these. So—" she raised a finger "—someone had some other reason for breaking in. Could they have been after Mal?"

"I can't think of anyone who'd want to hurt Mal, except possibly De Luca, and only if Mal became a real liability with his questions. De Luca isn't known for pointless killings."

"He wouldn't stay in business long if he went around murdering every bystander who asked questions." Allie wagged her third finger. "Mal probably left of his own free will, for reasons unknown."

Griffin smoothed back his hair. "I think it's time to start visiting his local haunts. If he has any friends I don't know about, you can introduce me to them."

"Then you'll have to accept my guidance," Allie said. "It's *my* world you're about to enter."

"That's why I asked for your help."

"Then let's ankle it."

They left Mal's apartment and headed for the nearest speakeasy. It was a grimmer, darker place than Lulu's; Allie thought that Mal had only been there a few times, and no one had seen or heard from the young playwright in months.

The next stop was a little better, blessed with a tinny piano and a slightly higher quality of clientele, but the results were the same. Mal hadn't visited the place since around the time Margot had vanished.

So it went for the rest of the evening. Not a soul had heard from Mal in weeks, nor did any of his acquaintances have the vaguest idea of where he might have gone.

Griffin and Allie ended up at Lulu's, where she accepted the accolades of the regulars with the ease of a reigning queen. None of her closest companions were present that night, but she took her regular table and insisted that Griffin have a drink.

"You need it," she said. "Worrying yourself sick won't help Mal."

Griffin glared at the tabletop. "I don't drink."

"Is that a werewolf thing, or a personal quirk?"

"Alcohol is too strong for most of us," he said. "I prefer to keep my head clear."

Allie flagged down a waiter and ordered two drinks. "It won't hurt you once in a while," she said.

It was a measure of Griffin's disquiet that he took a sip of the drink the waiter set before him. The taste was almost overpowering, but he emptied the glass before he could give himself time to think.

"There, now," Allie said, resting her hand on his arm. "That wasn't so bad, was it?"

"Do you think there's something admirable in inebriation?"

"Not as a rule. It's almost impossible to get me drunk."

Griffin blew out his breath, already aware of a slight buzzing in his head. He took a second drink without pausing to question his lack of control. "I don't know where else to look," he said. "Maybe I should see De Luca."

"It's only been a week," Allie said. "Maybe we should wait a little longer. If he's still gone two weeks from now, then you can talk to De Luca."

"He's no danger to me."

"No, but your visiting him wouldn't make the pack any happier about you and Gemma running loose, would it? I mean, hobnobbing with the biggest human syndicate boss in New York…"

"You're right. Only Garret Sloan is supposed to deal directly with De Luca."

"Then it's better to be cautious for the time being."

Griffin looked up in disbelief. "Allegra Chase, counseling discretion?"

"I still have a few tricks up my sleeve." She traced her fingertips down his arm. "Tell me more about how you met Mal. It was during the Great War, wasn't it?"

"I don't… I prefer not to talk about it."

"The War, you mean."

He contemplated his third drink and picked up the glass. The buzzing in his skull was growing louder and his limbs felt heavy. It was not an altogether unpleasant feeling.

"Mal was a decorated hero," he said. "Saved a lot of men. Saved my life more than once."

"A human saving a werewolf's life?"

"Even we can be killed."

She swirled the liquor in her glass. "When did you join up?"

"At the beginning."

"You couldn't have been more than eighteen."

"Seventeen. Mal was only sixteen when he came over in '17."

Allie rested her chin in her palm. "What made you go? I mean, it was a human war. *We* had nothing to do with starting it."

"I'm an American. Americans didn't start the Great War, but we saw the need to help our allies."

"Maybe. But that wasn't the real reason, was it? It was something much more personal."

He stared at her, knowing she'd seen through him. He almost didn't care. The painful memories of childhood were dulled to the point that he could actually speak of them without shaking like a buck private facing his first Hun.

"My parents died when I was fourteen," he said. "They left me and Gemma a generous inheritance, but…I didn't…a lot of things weren't very clear to me then. I left school as soon as the War started."

Allie's eyes darkened with sympathy. "I'm sorry. About your parents, I mean."

She didn't ask how they'd died, and he was grateful. "Gemma was…very young. I shouldn't have left her.

But Starke…he was like a second father to us. Gemma had the best nurses and tutors, went to the best schools in Europe. I wasn't much good for her."

"But you still feel guilty."

"I ran away. I thought I'd—"

He stopped himself, unprepared to admit his deepest regrets to a woman he had only begun to know. "I can't undo the past," he said. "But as long as I live, I'll never let Gemma see the kinds of things I saw."

Allie was silent for a long while, gazing into her glass. "What will you do when she's twenty-one and free to make her own decisions?"

"She won't defy me."

"Oh, Griffin. How little you understand the opposite sex."

He pushed his empty glasses aside and leaned across the table. "Explain it to me, then."

"For one thing, this is the modern world. Women expect to make their own decisions."

"Even if they're wrong?"

"We want the right to be wrong."

"When have you been wrong, Allie?"

"I didn't have much chance to be wrong about anything before my Conversion."

"Why?"

She gave him a brittle smile. "You know how you don't like to talk about the War? That's how I feel about my human years."

"So you want *me* to talk, but you won't tell me about yourself."

"You wouldn't find it very interesting."

"Try me."

Her eyes turned cold. "I swore I'd never go back. That's all you need to know."

He tapped his glass. "*This* isn't the way to escape your pain."

"And your way is better?"

"Maybe there's a better way for both of us."

She half rose. "If you want to hear a sob story, find some other girl."

He grabbed her wrist. "What if someone…wanted to help you?"

Her chair scraped as she wrenched free and pushed away from the table. "Help me do what? Abandon my wicked ways?"

"You're not wicked, Allegra."

"Yes, I am. I'm selfish and conceited and don't give a damn about anyone but myself."

"What about Miss Moreau and Gemma? Was helping save them an act of selfishness?"

"I didn't have anything to lose."

"Lying to yourself only works for so long." He rose to face her. "What is this anger, Allie? How long can you live with it before it strangles you?"

She laughed. "My God. You *are* drunk." Suddenly her expression changed, turning from hellcat to seductress in an instant. "Ah, Grif," she said softly. "Why are we fighting when we could be doing something a lot more fun?"

Her words conjured up astonishingly erotic imagery in Griffin's mind, and he swayed over the table. All his arguments dissolved in a rush of sheer, raging lust. Hardly aware of his own actions, he lunged for Allegra and pulled her into his arms. And he kissed her, hard, the way he hadn't kissed a woman since the Great War.

At first she pushed against him, her palms spread flat on his chest; then all at once she relented. Her mouth opened to welcome him. Her teeth scraped his lower lip and her nails curved into his waistcoat. It was as if they were standing alone in a darkened corner instead of a wild, loud speakeasy filled with observers.

When it was over and Allie took him by the hand, he knew he would have followed her into the very pit of Hell itself.

CHAPTER NINE

THIS WASN'T HOW it was supposed to be.

Oh, she'd wanted him almost from the beginning. She'd wanted to prove that he would fall just like every other male who'd laid eyes on her, that she could hook him and throw him back whenever she wanted.

Now she had him. But it wasn't on her terms. He'd changed the rules of the game, demanding too much, presuming he knew her when he didn't really know her at all.

If she'd followed her instincts and stayed away, this never would have happened. If she'd refused to help him find Mal, he would have accepted the fact that her flirtation at the party was no more than an empty gesture, that she really *didn't* care about anything or anyone but herself.

There was only one thing left to do. She led Griffin out to his Rolls, dumped him into the passenger seat and took the wheel. She would take him home, give him the ride of his life and then discard him in such a way that he would never doubt she'd been in complete control all along.

Not a few outraged males cursed the "lady driver" as she sped back to her apartment, careening around corners and hurtling past more-leisurely motorists. She pulled up at the curb of her building, set the brake and met Griffin on the sidewalk as he was shutting the passenger door.

The look in his eyes was well beyond the bounds of rationality, and if it hadn't been for her slightly superior strength, he might have kissed her again right on the sidewalk.

"Not here," she whispered.

He cast her a strange, dark look, more wolf than human, and kept a tight grip on her arm as they walked to the elevator. In spite of her anger, Allie felt as she did after the best feedings—supremely alive, powerful, more drunk than she could ever become on mere alcohol. She *did* want this man—wanted him badly—and once she'd had him, she could finally let him go.

Only the boy running the elevator kept them from coming together again, and Griffin seized another kiss the moment they reached Allie's door. Allie fumbled with the key and managed to get it in the lock. She pulled away as the door swung open.

"I have to… Let me see if…" She caught her breath. "Lou? Are you here?"

There was no answer. Louise usually slept like a log, accustomed as she was to Allie's comings and goings, and her bedroom was at the opposite end of the flat from Allie's. But it was usually Allie's practice to inform Lou when she intended to entertain male guests in the apartment. She didn't want to embarrass her friend with an unexpected tryst.

"My room's at the end of the hall," she told Griffin. "Wait for me there."

His eyes were nearly pure yellow now, and she wasn't at all certain she could make him leave her. But he did, with several hot backward glances, and went into her room. Nearly shaking with the ferment of her tangled thoughts, Allie strode past the kitchen to Lou's door and knocked softly. No one answered. She pushed the door open as gently as she could.

Lou appeared to be sleeping, the blankets tucked up about her shoulders. Allie went out to the telephone table, wrote a quick note and returned to Lou's room. She was just leaving the note on Lou's bureau when the figure in the bed stirred.

"Allie? Is that you?" Lou sat up, rubbing at her eyes. "Is something wrong?"

"No, Lou. Go back to sleep."

"What's that in your hand?"

Allie remembered the note and crumpled it in her fist. "I…I was just letting you know that I have a guest who may stay the night."

"A guest?" Lou smiled, her half-lidded eyes concealing her interest. "Anyone I know?"

"If you don't mind, Lou, I'd rather discuss it later."

"Whoever he is, he sure has you riled up."

Allie reached for the doorknob. "Good night, Lou. I'll see you in the morning."

"Will the gentleman want breakfast?"

"I can manage." She shut the door, surprised at her own self-consciousness. Lou didn't judge her life; she'd known Allie since they were children. She understood what drove Allie and what she did in order to survive. But Allie didn't bring many men to the apartment, and Lou had guessed that this one was more than just a night's casual fling.

But that's exactly what he is, Allie thought, smoothing her emotions as she would a wrinkled frock. A fling, a one-night stand, a fevered interlude that would end whatever trifling connection had formed between them.

She walked back through the living room and down the hall, measuring her steps to the beat of her heart. *You must stay in control. Don't let him think he can rule you. Don't let him think for a minute that you give a damn for anything beyond the pleasure of the moment. Because you don't. You don't....*

She took a deep breath and opened the door. Griffin was sprawled across the bed, his coat flung over a chair and his vest unbuttoned. He was smiling. And he was sleeping like the dead.

Allie laughed. Griffin didn't wake. He groaned, muttered a word that sounded very much like her name and rolled onto his chest, his arm draping over the side of the bed.

Never in all the time she'd known him had Griffin Durant looked so ridiculous. Or so utterly endearing.

Her legs suddenly unsteady, Allie sat on the chair at her dressing table and watched him. His face was so relaxed in sleep, all the tension and almost military discipline softened into a memory of the boy he must have been before tragedy claimed him. His hair was tumbled over his forehead, his mouth half-open, his long legs gangly as a newborn foal's.

Allie closed her eyes. She didn't want to be a witness to this fleeting innocence, this terrible honesty. It would have been so much easier to deal with the wolf she'd seen in his gaze such a short time ago. Naked lust was something she dealt with nearly every day. But this…this vulnerable person, this man who wanted to save her…how was she to handle him now?

You've lost your way, Allie Chase. You can't convince him you don't give a damn if you can't convince yourself.

She rose from the chair, unfolded the quilt from the

foot of the bed and spread it carefully over Griffin, making sure not to disturb his sleep.

"Goodbye," she whispered.

GRIFFIN WOKE with a splitting headache and a sour taste in his mouth that gave him every reason never to touch a drop of alcohol again.

He sat up in the bed, blinked at the unfamiliar surroundings and pushed the blanket from his chest. Memory washed over him like a deluge of nightmares. He looked at the empty place beside him, saw the unwrinkled bedspread and pristine pillow and began to understand.

Allie wasn't there. She'd never been in bed with him, and he had a pretty good idea why. The liquor had done its work, and whatever he'd intended the night before had been swallowed up in the soporific effects of gin.

He rubbed his face, trying to piece together the events of the previous night. He and Allie had gone to Lulu's after the fruitless search for Mal. They'd talked. Allie had taken offense at something he'd said. She'd started to walk away, and he…

He'd seized her like a savage and forced himself on her, right there in the speakeasy. And she'd responded. God, how she'd responded. And somehow they'd wound up back here, in a place that smelled of Allie through and through.

But Allie was gone. And his body still ached with wanting her.

Griffin swung his legs over the side of the bed, buttoned his waistcoat and grabbed his jacket from the back of the chair. He opened the bedroom door. A short hall led to an open room, awash with morning sunlight.

"Allie?"

The clinking of dishes was coming from somewhere at the opposite end of the apartment. He followed the sound. The handsome living room was as bright as the summer parlor at Oakdene was dull and dark, furnished with the most modern sofa and chairs, and hung with Expressionist paintings. The colors were as vivid as Allie herself.

"Mr. Durant?"

Griffin looked up to see Miss Louise Moreau, dressed in a smart blue frock and white apron, a breakfast tray in her hands.

"Miss Moreau," he said, stumbling over his words. "How pleasant to see you again."

She smiled kindly, as if she recognized his consternation. "Would you like a bit of breakfast, Mr. Durant?"

He scrubbed at his day's growth of beard. "I… Is Miss Chase at home?"

The clumsiness of his question appalled him, but Miss Moreau didn't bat an eyelash. "She has left on an unexpected trip, Mr. Durant. She asked me to make you comfortable and see that you have anything you require."

"An unexpected trip?"

"Yes, Mr. Durant. If you'll come into the kitchen…"

"Where has she gone?"

Miss Moreau set the tray on a nearby table and folded her hands. "She didn't tell me. I believe she'll be gone for several weeks."

Griffin turned toward the window, wincing at the light. Allie had left without a goodbye, and he could guess why. He'd let himself get dismally drunk. His clumsy attempts to understand her had backfired, and when she'd tried to lighten the mood, he'd failed to deliver. Contempt might be an accurate description of her feelings. He felt plenty of contempt for himself, but not for the same reasons.

"Are you sure you won't have something to eat, Mr. Durant?"

He straightened, facing her like a man instead of a bewildered boy. "Forgive me, Miss Moreau. I'm not at my best this morning."

"Miss Chase told me about your friend. I'm sorry you haven't found him."

He blessed the woman's tact even as he berated himself for his stupidity. "Miss Chase was…very helpful in my search. I would have liked to thank her."

"I think she knows how you feel." She picked up the tray again. "Come into the kitchen. It's a much more pleasant place to talk."

She walked away, and he followed. He did want to talk, to make sense of what had happened last night. Louise Moreau was the sort of woman who naturally attracted confidences. Allie Chase wouldn't reveal anything significant about herself or her past, but Griffin had the feeling that her friend might be more forthcoming.

Miss Moreau pulled out a chair at the kitchen table and gestured for Griffin to sit. She poured out a generous glass of orange juice and set it before him.

"Drink this," she commanded. "You'll feel much better."

Griffin picked up the glass and set it down again. "Why did she go, Miss Moreau?"

"Louise. Or Lou, if you prefer." She bustled about the kitchen, retrieving a bowl of eggs from the icebox. "She didn't tell me that, either, Mr. Durant."

"Griffin."

She paused and met his gaze. "Griffin. She didn't tell me why she left, but I have my suspicions."

He braced himself for the worst. "I'd appreciate it if you'd share them with me, Louise."

She sighed and took the seat opposite him at the table. "I'd never betray Miss Allie, but I think you deserve the truth—not only because of what you did for me that day on Forty-second Street, but because I've seen what's happened to Allie since she met you."

"Please, go on."

"You think she left because she was mad at you for some reason. That's probably how she would have made it seem if she'd stayed long enough to talk to you. She'd have to have some excuse for just going off like that, and it's a lot easier to pretend you're upset than to admit there's something very different going on."

Griffin's heart thrummed like a hive of angry bees. "I admit that I don't understand what goes on in Allegra's mind," he said. "I've never met a woman so…"

"So contrary?" Louise smiled. "Don't I know it. But there's a reason for that, too." She spread her hands on the table. "Did she ever tell you anything about her childhood, Griffin?"

"She did everything possible to avoid the subject."

"That doesn't surprise me. She'd rather forget she ever had a life before she changed."

"I'd gathered that it wasn't pleasant."

"That's right. You see, I've known her since we were children. My mother, rest her soul, was the last servant to stay on with theCharleses after Allie's mother spent her way through the inheritance left by Mr.Charles when he died. Mother took care of Allie when Mrs.Charles all but abandoned her. I saw how evil that woman was." She caught herself and pressed her hand to her cheek. "I'm sorry. It's wrong to speak ill of the dead."

"Allie's mother passed away?"

"Just last year. But Allie hadn't spoken to her since she was Converted. Mrs.Charles hated Allie from the moment Allie got sick."

Griffin snatched at the one piece of information that stood out from the rest. "Allie was sick?"

"Oh, you don't know how sick. A few years after Mr.Charles died—he was a good man, that one, a scholarly man for one so wealthy—just after Allie's seventeenth birthday, Allie started having problems walking. Her muscles got weak, and she'd fall all the time." She twisted her fingers together, taken by some strong emotion. "Allie had been a beautiful child, the kindest, sweetest girl you could imagine. Everyone loved her. Mrs.Charles seemed to dote on her because she was so perfect, and she had so many friends... I never saw so many beautiful people in one place. By the time she was sixteen, one particular young man seemed very serious about her. He came to the house almost every day with flowers and presents. But when Allie started having the trouble, when she wasn't so perfect anymore, her mother was the first to turn her back."

Sick at the image Lou's words created in his mind, Griffin stared at the table. "What was wrong with her?"

"The doctors never could say—or if they did, they never told Allie. She just kept getting worse, you see. First it was her legs, so she could hardly go anywhere. Then it was her arms that got weak. Pretty soon she couldn't get out of bed. Her pretty friends stopped coming to see her. Then her young man drifted away, pretending it had nothing to do with her sickness, and started seeing another girl. It was as if Allie was dead to them. And Mrs.Charles wanted the money for her amusements, so she fired all the servants and left my mother to care for Allie.

"For five years her whole life was in that one room of the big house…that big, empty house with just me and my mother. She couldn't go out to see the flowers and the blue sky. Her bright mind was trapped in a useless body. After a while Mrs.Charles never came back at all, and the checks dried up. We scraped by as best we could, but—" she touched the corner of her eye "—Allie was dying. The doctors couldn't do anything for her."

"But she didn't die."

"No. In those last days a man came to see her, a man who promised he could cure her of the disease."

"A vampire," Griffin said.

Lou nodded solemnly. "Of course, in those days I didn't know anything about vampires. I would have said such things couldn't exist in God's world. I didn't find out that Mr. Cato was one of them until after Allie came back from Manhattan, walking and laughing like she'd never been sick a day in her life. That's when she told me everything. And once my mother died, she asked me to stay with her."

Griffin remembered what Allie had said about her patron. "Do you know why Cato came to her?"

"Allie said he'd known her father. Mr.Charles and Mr. Cato were both scientists. I don't think Mr.Charles knew anything about vampires, either, but Mr. Cato seemed to feel he owed his old friend a debt of some kind. Why he didn't come to Allie earlier, I don't know. I just know that he saved her."

Griffin's stomach knotted with anger and pity.

"That's what she meant when she didn't have much chance to be wrong before her Conversion," he murmured. "Why she says she wants to live only for herself…"

"She had no pleasure in life, only pain and loneliness. No dances, no parties, nothing but that room day after day. She saw everyone and everything she cared about taken away from her. Her mother rejected her. Her friends deserted her. The boy she loved betrayed her. Why should she trust anyone?"

"Except you. You stood by her."

"She was always good to me and my mother. Once Mr. Cato fixed her up, he treated her just like a daughter. He gave her money, and she shared it with me and Mama. She paid for Mama's funeral. She would have set me up in a fine apartment if I'd wanted, but I knew she still needed me."

Griffin covered Louise's hand. "You're a good friend, Louise. Thank you for confiding in me."

"I thought you deserved to know, seeing as how you—" Her light-brown skin flushed. "She wants to pretend she doesn't care, but it's a lie. She thinks being a vampire makes it easier to be free and think only of herself. Maybe most of them are like that, but not Allie."

Griffin got up from the table and paced a tight circle around the kitchen. He didn't have to ask Louise why she thought Allie had run away. It was clear in everything Louise had told him.

It wasn't contempt. It was fear. Fear that she might actually come to care…

Griffin dutifully ate the toast and eggs Louise put before him. Then he washed up in the bathroom, thanked Louise again and made for the door.

A crowd of half-familiar faces met him on the landing.

"Who are you?" one of the young men blurted, his square face blotched with the effects of strong drink. "Where's Allie?"

"You're silly, Jimmy," the red-haired woman said. "Can't you see she has comp'ny?"

The biggest man in the group—the one Griffin remembered as Bruce—looked Griffin over as if he were examining a particularly ugly toad. "I remember you. You're the one who stormed into Lulu's looking for your sister."

"Of course," the redhead said. "I do recall. Don't you, Kolya?"

The dark-haired melancholic shrugged. Bruce continued to stare at Griffin. "What are you doing here?" he demanded.

Griffin lowered his head. "That's none of your business."

"Oh, my," the redhead drawled. She drifted closer to Griffin and smiled into his face. "Did she invite you up for a good time?"

Bruce snorted. "Him?"

"Don't you see? He's exactly the type she'd find interestin'. Not like her usual lovers at all. You're a hard nut to crack, aren't you, darlin'?"

"Kakaya merzost," the Russian said. "She would spit him out and throw him away, like the others."

The others. Griffin clenched his fists. "I'm sure you don't intend to insult Miss Chase."

The redhead laughed gaily. "Insult her? Just because she has every man wrapped around her little finger? Sugar, I can see she's gotten to you, but you'd better not get too attached, you know what I mean?" She traced a red nail across Griffin's chin. "She just has a natural way of makin' every fella think he's special, especially in bed. That's just part of the game."

Griffin pushed her hand away, his mind filled with images of Allie with those other men, limbs entwined, lips on lips, bodies heaving. Hadn't he judged her to be exactly that sort of woman from the moment they'd met? But she'd endured a terrible youth, and perhaps she had every right in the world to make up for it in any way she chose.

He shoved his way through the wall of Allie's friends. "You won't find Miss Chase at home," he said coldly. "I believe she's left town."

"Oh," the redhead pouted. "Didn't you live up to her high standards?"

Bruce glowered. "If you did anything to upset her…"

"How could *I,* one among so many, have the power to upset Miss Chase?" Griffin asked with a mocking smile. He tipped his hat to the redhead. "Good day to you, miss."

He left them standing outside Allegra's door, relieved to know that he was quit of her at last.

CHAPTER TEN

ALLIE STEPPED OUT of the taxi, handing the cabbie an extravagant tip and a smile that left him melting in his seat.

Home.

She looked up at her building with an uncomfortable mixture of relief and apprehension. She should have been glad to be back; Atlantic City was amusing enough for a couple of weeks, and the hunting had been good, but she found she missed her friends. She'd spent half her time away wondering how she'd become so soft.

Wondering if she could put Griffin Durant entirely out of her mind.

In that she'd almost been successful. Whole hours had passed without her thinking about him. She'd come very close to taking a lover to speed the process, but in the end she'd left the would-be suitor sulking outside her hotel-room door. On closer inspection, he hadn't held up to comparison with a certain brooding werewolf.

Damn.

She tossed her coat over one shoulder and took the stairs to her floor, unwilling to make polite noises at the elevator attendant. She hoped that Lou wasn't in the mood for talking. It was just barely dark, so she would have to wait a few hours before Pepper and

Kolya and the others would begin making the rounds. Until then, she would simply pretend that she'd never invited Griffin into her apartment.

I wonder if he's found Mal....

With a hard shake of her head, she opened the door. Instantly her senses were on the alert, humming with the recognition of danger. Someone was in her apartment—someone she definitely hadn't invited.

"What are you doing here?" she demanded.

The two men seated on her living-room sofa, dressed alike in black suits and grim expressions, got to their feet. "Allegra Chase?" one of them said.

"Since you're in my apartment, I assume you know my name. Who the hell are you?"

The gray-eyed enforcer inclined his head. "I am Dorian," he said, "and this is Javier."

Allie dropped her coat onto a chair. "Where's Lou?"

"Your human servant is unharmed," Dorian said. "We asked her to remain in her room."

"I see. You don't mind if I check for myself?" She strode for Lou's bedroom before the enforcers could object. Lou answered, opening the door wide when she recognized Allie.

"Are you all right?" Allie asked.

"I'm fine," Lou said. She peered past Allie's shoulder. "I tried to keep them out, but—"

"Don't be foolish. You couldn't have stopped them." Allie gripped the edge of the door. "How long have they been here?"

"Since sunset. They've been showing up every evening for the past four days. All they've done is sit there, waiting for you." She gripped Allie's arm. "What do they want?"

"I've no idea." She squeezed Lou's hand. "Whatever it is, you aren't to become involved. They won't harm you as long as you stay out of the way."

Lou was no fool. She nodded reluctantly. "I understand. But—"

"I can handle them. Try not to worry."

"That I can't promise you." Lou shivered. "Be careful."

Allie closed the door and returned to the living room. The enforcers stood by the sofa, watching her with their cold killer's eyes. She sauntered toward them, swinging her hips with deliberate insolence.

"To what do I owe the dubious pleasure of this visit, gentlemen?" she asked.

Dorian's eyes revealed a hint of emotion. Allie wondered if it might be anger. "You've been away," he said.

"So? I have every right to go where I please."

"Your timing was unfortunate. Raoul has been looking for you."

"Oh? What a pity I inconvenienced him." She sat on a chair, crossing her legs to reveal several inches of thigh. "What does he want this time?"

Javier started toward her, fingers curled, but Dorian stopped him. "It won't do you any good to flaunt your insubordination," he said. "Your independence ends when you become a liability to the clan."

Allie stretched with a sensuous arch of her back. "I didn't know a trip to Atlantic City threatened the clan."

Dorian moved to stand over her, his muscular energy barely contained in his neatly pressed suit. "We won't bandy words with you, Allegra. When was the last time you saw Margot De Luca?"

A dozen competing thoughts raced through Allie's mind, none of them in the least comforting. She kept her expression relaxed. "Margot? I visited her at the mansion a few weeks ago. Why?"

"Are you quite sure you haven't seen her since?" Dorian asked, his voice heavy with warning.

Allie sat up, genuinely alarmed. "What's happened to her?"

The enforcers exchanged glances, reaching some silent agreement.

"She's gone," Javier said.

"Gone? What the hell does that mean?"

"She vanished from the mansion six days ago," Dorian said.

"You mean, she ran away?"

Dorian leaned down, holding her gaze. "What do you know about it?"

"Nothing. But it was pretty obvious to me that she wasn't happy with Raoul."

Dorian straightened, his steel-gray eyes limned with red. "That is matter for speculation beyond our purview," he said. "We're only interested in learning where she's gone."

"Then you've come to the wrong place. It's true that Margot and I are friends, but she never told me anything about trying to escape."

"What *did* she tell you?"

"Just the usual girl talk. I'm sure it wouldn't interest you."

"You said she spoke out against Raoul."

"No, I didn't. I said she didn't look happy."

"Did she mention anyone else? Anyone who might have helped her leave?"

"Don't be ridiculous. Raoul is crazy for Margot. Who would dare to walk away with his most precious possession, even if she could bear the separation?"

She could see that neither enforcer was prepared to answer that question. If Margot really was gone, Raoul would be in a rage…not only because he'd lost his most favored protégée, but because her escape would reflect very badly on his leadership. A Master's blood-bond was supposed to be inviolable.

"I can't believe that Raoul is worried that she won't come back," she said, hiding her dangerous thoughts. "How can she stay away when she's bonded to him?"

Dorian took a step back, his eyes shuttered. "She can't. Not for long."

"Then I'd advise you to be patient. Raoul can live without her for a few days."

Javier lowered his head between his shoulders. "She knows more than she's telling," he said to his partner. "Let me question her. She'll—"

"No." Dorian stared at Allie as if he could hear exactly what she was thinking. "There's no need for that. Not yet." He turned for the door, Javier at his heels, and paused on the threshold.

"Take my warning, Allegra," he said. "Don't push Raoul too far. If you're concealing anything, no matter how small, you may hurt others besides yourself."

Allie lunged up, her blood running cold. "Are you threatening my friends?"

"Many humans were acquainted with Miss Margot in her previous life. Even if they know nothing, you have made them vulnerable by your association with them. Don't let your companions pay the price for misplaced loyalties."

Allie crossed the room with a swiftness no human could match. "Let me warn *you,* Dorian. I'll kill anyone who harms my friends. Feel free to share that message with your Master."

Javier laughed, but Dorian only regarded her with icy dispassion. "I'll tell him," he said. In an instant he and Javier were gone, leaving Allie trembling in their wake.

She wanted nothing then so much as a drink, little comfort though it might bring, but she set her weakness aside and hurried to Lou's bedroom.

"They're gone," she said when Lou opened the door. "I want you to pack your things. You're going on a little vacation."

"What are you talking about?"

Allie pushed past her, knelt beside the bed and pulled out Lou's suitcase. "You're leaving tonight. No arguments."

"Is it because of them?"

"I won't have you getting hurt because Raoul thinks I know something about Margot that he doesn't."

Lou gazed at her steadily. "Do you?"

"No. But this isn't the end of it." She lay her hands on Lou's shoulders. "You've stuck by me all this time, and I'll never forget it. But now you have to do as I say, just until this is over."

"But what—"

"Trust me. Please." She opened the doors of Lou's closet and gathered up an armful of dresses. Lou stared at the open suitcase.

"I'll go, if my being here will make it harder for you," she said. "But you have to promise me one thing. You won't face this—whatever it is—alone."

"I have to, Lou. If it comes to a real fight, no human can stand up to a vampire."

"I wasn't thinking about a human."

"Lou…"

"Maybe you two parted on bad terms. Maybe it

doesn't seem as if you have anything in common except not being human. But I believe he cares for you, and you for him. He'll stand by you, Allie."

Allie didn't try to argue. She left Lou to her packing and poured herself a glass of whiskey, then left the glass untouched as she turned her fears around and around in her head.

It wasn't any of his business. Margot wasn't *his* friend. She wasn't obliged to ask for help just because Lou insisted on it.

Damn, damn, damn.

It was well past midnight when she picked up the telephone.

"Hello?"

His voice curled through her veins like a drug. She lost the thread of her thoughts, and her tongue refused to move.

"Allie?"

"Yes. It's me."

His silence was thick with the awkwardness of a stranger. "How are you?"

"Fine. And you?"

"Very well. Did you enjoy your trip?"

His voice held not a trace of censure or curiosity. *So he did get over me. Just as I'm over him.*

"It was wonderful," she said.

"Why are you calling, Allegra?"

She twisted the telephone cord around her fingers. "It's… Uh… Oh, hell."

"What's wrong?"

The alarm in his question destroyed any hope of dispassion between them. "It's not me. At least not at the moment."

"Tell me."

"You haven't heard from Mal, have you?"

"No. I went back to his apartment and searched more thoroughly. I found notes about a summer cabin in the Adirondacks. He never told me about it, but apparently he sometimes goes there to write."

"You think he really might be there?"

He sighed. "No, but I have to go."

Allie gathered her thoughts. "I asked about Mal because I've just learned something about Margot."

"You know where she is?"

She hesitated. "I've known for some time, but I couldn't tell Mal, and I didn't tell you, because Mal might have found out. It was for his own protection."

"Where is she?"

Now he was angry, but there was nothing to do but plunge ahead. "Margot is a vampire," she said. "She's been one for over three months now, and I was there when she was Converted."

Griffin's astonishment was almost palpable. "How did it happen?"

"She didn't intend it. She wouldn't have left Mal of her own free will, but she didn't have a choice."

"Who did it to her? Why?"

"It was done with her father's consent, to save her life. She was in a terrible automobile accident. She was taken to the hospital, so badly hurt that she wasn't going to live out the night. De Luca was with her, crying out for someone to save her. And then he thought of Raoul Boucher."

She quickly told Griffin that De Luca was fully aware of his rival, Raoul Boucher's, true nature. Margot's father was one of the few influential humans who knew that the city harbored inhuman residents. By unspoken truce he kept the secret, preventing the inevitable bloodshed that would result if he ever revealed what he'd learned. De Luca knew that a vampire's bite could not only create another vampire, but that it could heal the most deadly injuries.

"Raoul had seen Margot several times," she said. "He wasn't immune to her beauty, so he agreed to De Luca's proposal. They took Margot to Raoul's mansion. Cato asked me to be there, because I was a recent Convert and had known Margot from her clubbing days with Mal.

"De Luca knew that Margot would become Raoul's property if he successfully Converted her, and also that there was a chance she would die in the process. Margot was conscious enough to know that she'd lose Mal forever once she became Raoul's protégée. She said she'd rather die. De Luca begged her to agree. I argued with her. I tried to make her see that it was always better to live, and I knew more than anyone that—"

She stopped, unwilling to reopen the subject of her past. "She finally accepted our arguments."

"But something went wrong," Griffin said.

"No. It worked. But I made a terrible mistake that day. *I* had freedom with Cato as my patron. Margot would never…" She swallowed. "Raoul Converted her and made her whole again. She went to live in his mansion with his other protégés, and De Luca told Mal that she'd gone away."

"Why are you telling me this now?"

"Because Margot has also disappeared, and Raoul is in a rage. He sent his enforcers to question me tonight. It shouldn't even be possible for Margot to leave Raoul. A blood-bond between patron and protégé is virtually unbreakable. Prolonged separation is unpleasant enough for the patron, but Margot would find it agonizing. I can think of only one thing that would make her do something so desperate."

"Mal."

"She still loves him. She was miserable with Raoul, but she could have borne it if not for Mal. And since Mal disappeared just two weeks before Margot…"

"Good Lord. You think Mal helped her escape."

"I don't know. It seems crazy. Mal didn't even know Margot was a vampire. He wouldn't be able to get into Raoul's mansion, so she'd have had to go to him. But even if it isn't true, the timing is just too damning. Raoul has agents all over the city, and one of them has surely heard that Mal is missing. Raoul knows that Margot and Mal were a couple before her Conversion. If he has even the tiniest suspicion that Mal might have had a part in Margot's disappearance…"

"Mal would be in terrible danger."

"They'd kill him," Allie said. "That's why we have to find him before they do."

Griffin fell silent. "Thank you for sharing this information, Allegra," he said at last. "I'll leave for Mal's cottage in the morning."

"Make it evening and I'll come with you," Allie said before she could think better of it.

"I…don't think that would be a good idea."

"Why? Because you can't stand the sight of me?"

"There's no need for you to get further involved."

"But I *am* involved. I don't take kindly to threats. And I'm more than strong enough to help you in a fight, if it comes to that."

"Are you sure you wouldn't just rather leave town again?"

The coldness in his voice told her that he hadn't let

her departure go, after all. Did he think she'd played him for a fool? She couldn't blame him. But she wasn't about to crawl.

"Look," she said, "what happened that night was a mistake for both of us. Let's leave it at that."

"An excellent suggestion, Miss Chase."

"Okay, then." She released the telephone cord. "You'll need to give me a few hours to get to the island. I have to warn my friends that they might be in danger."

She braced herself for a caustic comment about her much-vaunted selfishness, but he only sighed.

"Try to get here before midnight."

"That shouldn't be a problem."

"Good night, Miss Chase."

"Good night." She hung up, resisting the urge to throw the telephone across the room.

She saw to it that Lou finished packing, spent several minutes prowling about the apartment building, on the lookout for possible spies, and decided that Raoul's men had more pressing business at hand than following her around. She drove Lou to Grand Central Station and put her on a train to her aunt's house in North Carolina.

"I'll send for you when it's safe," Allie promised. "Enjoy your visit."

Lou frowned. "I still think—"

The porter indicated that the train was about to leave. Allie stepped back and waved, turning away so she wouldn't see Lou's worried face peering out the window.

"ROSS, IT'S GRIFFIN."

"Hey. What's up?"

"I have new information regarding Margot De Luca's disappearance."

"Oh, yeah?" Griffin heard rattling at the other end of the line as Ross picked up a pencil and paper. "I haven't dug up anything more about Mal, but I'm still working on it."

"So am I. What I've just learned may strongly affect the investigation."

"Go ahead."

Griffin repeated what Allegra had told him, pausing as Ross swore in amazement.

"You mean, De Luca's daughter is a leech?"

"Yes. And now Margot has vanished from Boucher's mansion. His enforcers are searching for her. It seems possible that Mal's disappearance and hers might in some way be connected."

Ross grunted. "How did you find this out?"

Bringing Allegra's name to the attention of the police, even to as trusted a friend as Ross, hadn't been part of Griffin's plan, but he saw the necessity in sharing all the information he had. He told Ross about Allegra, briefly explaining how they'd met and how she related to the other vampires in the city.

"The enforcers knew she was Margot's friend and questioned her first. Miss Chase could be in some danger herself."

"But she doesn't know where Margot is."

"She says she doesn't, and I believe her."

"You think Mal's mixed up in this?"

"He was in a bad state the last time I saw him, but for a single human to go up against the clan..."

"Yeah." Ross clicked his tongue. "I'll keep doing what I can, but my connections to the clan are tenuous at best."

"I have a few leads to follow myself."

"You're only one man, Grif. Be careful."

"I will."

"Grif, about this Allegra Chase…you're not stuck on her, are you?"

"I beg your pardon?"

"Don't go all hoity-toity on me, pal. I'm not deaf. The way you talk about her…it strikes me as a little personal, if you know what I mean."

"We both want to see Margot and Mal safe," Griffin said stiffly.

"You sure that's all it is?"

Griffin took a deep breath. "I would ask…if she ever needs help, and I'm not here…" He cleared his throat. "She has enemies, and she's alone. I'd appreciate it if you'd look after her, make sure she's safe."

"Safe from what? The clan?"

"Yes."

Ross laughed. "You do know you're crazy."

"Maybe I am. Maybe it's too much to ask—"

"Hell, no. I ain't scared of no leeches." He dropped his deliberately rough speech. "I sure hope you know what you're doing, Grif."

I do, too, Griffin thought. "I can't turn back now."

"Yeah. Well, keep me informed."

"I will. Thanks, old friend."

Ross hung up. Griffin set the receiver down and settled himself to wait for midnight.

THEY WERE ALL AT LULU'S, just as Allie had hoped. Kolya was already well into his usual state of inebriation, jotting down crooked lines of poetry as the mood struck him. Pepper was flitting from table to table, the fringe on her dress bouncing with every step. Sibella had her nose in her sketch pad, while Jimmy was making a terrible racket on one of the trumpet player's horns.

Allie joined Kolya at the table. With an effort, he focused on her face.

"Alliushka!" he said. "Where have you been? I have written nothing—*nothing*—since I last saw your face."

"I know, Kolya. There's something very important I have to—"

"Allie, darlin'!" Pepper flounced up, beaming beneath her cloud of red hair. "Jimmy, come on over here. Our little lost lamb has returned to the fold!"

"I'll be damned. Where the hell you been?" Jimmy pulled a chair around and sat astride it, drumming his hands on the back.

"That isn't important now," Allie said, gathering them in with her gaze. "There's something I need to tell all of you. Where are Bruce and Nathan?"

"Now, that's mighty strange," Pepper said. "They were supposed to come at the usual time tonight. Nathan, the little dear, is always so punctual."

Allie's chest tightened. "I think we'd all better go to their place."

"Why?" Jimmy asked. "They're probably just… you know…"

"I want you to come with me," Allie said. "Now."

They looked at her as if she'd just lost her mind. "What's so urgent, sugar?" Pepper asked.

"You'll know soon enough." She took Sibella's sketchbook out of her hands. "Come on."

With shrugs and puzzled looks, they followed her out of the speakeasy, Jimmy riding in Pepper's car, while Kolya and Sibella joined Allie in hers.

No one answered the door to Bruce and Nathan's flat at Allie's first knock. She waited a minute and then began to pound on the door with her fist.

"Bruce! Nathan! It's Allie. Open the door!"

The bolt snicked, and the door opened a crack to reveal Bruce's face. One of his eyes was black, and his lower lip was split in two places. His angry, bewildered gaze was as dark as Allie had ever seen it.

"My Lord!" Pepper exclaimed. "Whatever happened to you, darlin'?"

Allie's stomach plunged to her toes. She knew. Oh, yes, she knew all too well.

"Are you all right?" she asked. "How is Nathan?"

Bruce didn't answer. He stepped back to allow the crowd into the parlor. Sibella sat quietly in a corner, while Jimmy stood uneasily, hands shoved in his pockets, and Kolya rubbed at his unshaven jaw.

"Two men came," Bruce said in a flat voice. "They said they were looking for Margot De Luca."

Allie felt for a chair. Pepper gingerly touched Bruce's discolored cheek. "Margot De Luca? She's been away for months, hasn't she? I heard she was in Europe. Did somethin' happen to her?"

"I remember when Mal Owen came around asking about her," Jimmy said. "But that was weeks ago."

Bruce jerked away from Pepper's touch. "Whoever these guys were, they wanted very badly to know where she is."

"Why in hell would they think you'd know, anyway?" Jimmy asked.

"I don't know." He turned to Allie. "You spent more time with her than any of us. What the hell is going on?"

Allie closed her eyes and breathed deeply. "I don't think they believed you knew anything, Bruce," she said. "They came here because of me."

Everyone stared at her. She forced herself to sit very still and meet their gazes one by one.

"The things I have to tell you are going to seem beyond belief," she said. "But every word is the truth. And your safety may depend on your acceptance." She clenched her hands together. "Bruce, can you get Nathan?"

"He's resting," he said, his eyes full of a new hostility. "I can tell him whatever you have to say."

"All right." She looked at each of them again to make sure she had their complete attention. "The first thing you've got to know is that vampires are real. And I'm one of them."

She didn't wait for the nervous titters and sounds of disbelief to die down. "I can prove it. I will, if you still need proof when I'm done. But the fact is that one of the major syndicates in this city is run by vampires. Raoul Boucher is Master of the clan and has been for thirty years. He has a truce with the other gangs, human and…" She hesitated, wondering if mentioning werewolves would be too much, and decided to leave that part out. She explained how vampires made other vampires, and about her own Conversion. "Margot… Raoul bit her just before she supposedly went to Europe. She's been living with him ever since, as his protégée."

Incredulous silence followed her monologue. "What the hell?" Bruce said. "You're trying to make us believe that blood-sucking monsters are running around New York?"

"It's true whether you believe or not. And we don't really suck blood. The old stories are exaggerations. We don't kill…not any more than humans kill each other. And we aren't undead. I'm as alive as you are."

Pepper bit hard on her lip. "You…you really mean it, don't you?"

"I'm deadly serious. Bruce, didn't you notice that the gunsels who came here were stronger than other men?"

Bruce stared at the worn carpet. "Yeah. I didn't stand a chance."

"And you're stronger, too," Pepper said to Allie. "We've all seen how she put Jake Greco in his place."

"How many are there?" Sibella asked unexpectedly, pushing untidy brown hair from her face.

"I've never counted. Enough to run a syndicate and then some."

Jimmy uttered a crude expletive. "If that's true, why haven't we all been bitten?"

"You might have been, but you'd never know it. That's how it works."

"Did you…bite us?" Pepper asked.

"I don't use my friends."

"This is insane!" Bruce exploded. "You're saying the men who came here were vampires?"

"Yes. And they're after Margot because Raoul is obsessed with her, and she's disappeared from his mansion. They think someone helped her escape. They came to me first, but when I couldn't tell them anything…" She lowered her voice, afraid that her rage would overwhelm her. "They threatened my friends. That's why I came right out to warn you."

"Warn us?" Bruce laughed. "You're a little late."

"I know. But I'm here now to tell you that none of you are safe as long as Raoul and his enforcers think I'm hiding something."

"You mean, we have to leave?" Pepper asked.

"For a little while. I don't think they'll waste any time looking for you if you get out of town. Once they find Margot, they'll forget about you."

Bruce swung his fist against the wall, cracking the paint. "So this is all because of you. Because you didn't tell your *friends* the truth."

"How could she?" Kolya said, rising from his seat. "We Russians know that such things exist in the world, but would you have believed her?"

No one spoke. Allie could see that they were still struggling with their disbelief. She got up, evaluated the heavy coffee table with its marble top, then lifted it with no effort at all. She held it in the air with one hand.

"I don't age," she said. "I can see in the dark. But there isn't any time for that now." She lowered the coffee table back to the carpet. "Bruce, what about Nathan?"

His face had gone white, and for a moment he looked near tears. "Get out of here. We don't need your help."

"I want to see him."

All at once Bruce seemed to collapse, his broad shoulders hunching, as if he expected another beating. "Let me talk to him first," he said, and turned for the bedroom door. Ten minutes later, after the others had exchanged many glances and ruminated on the impossible, Bruce reappeared.

"You can go in now," he said, standing aside.

Allie strode into the room and shut the door behind her. Nathan lay on the bed, wrapped in makeshift bandages stained with blood. He held one arm at an awkward angle. His face was almost unrecognizable.

Allie knelt beside the bed. "Nathan…God, I'm so sorry."

He cracked open one swollen lid and tried to smile. "Allie…wasn't your fault." He moved his good hand restlessly across his chest. "Is it true, what Bruce said?"

"All true." She pressed her cheek to Nathan's hand. "Has Bruce sent for a doctor?"

"We don't…" He licked his lips. "We can't."

"I'll handle the bills. As soon as you've seen a doctor, you and Bruce are to leave New York."

Bruce walked into the room and stood in the doorway, his eyes welling with tears. "I'd kill them if I could. If I'd had a gun…"

"It wouldn't have worked," Allie said, half turning. "It's very hard to kill a vampire."

"Then we're helpless."

"No." She rose to face him. "I won't let this pass. I promise you, the ones who did this won't get away with it again."

"How can you stop them?"

"I have an advantage over the rest of them. My patron is dead, and that makes me a free agent. I'll find a way." She returned to the bed, pulling a chair up beside it. "Make him see reason, Nathan."

"I'll try." The younger man breathed in, wincing at the pain of cracked ribs. "There's something I have to tell you. I…didn't know anything about the vampire stuff then, but it all fits." He coughed weakly and lowered his voice so that only Allie could hear. "Mal swore me to silence. After he disappeared, I just assumed… and now with Margot gone, as well…"

"What about Mal and Margot?"

He gave her an unhappy glance. "Just a day before Mal vanished, he told me that he'd found Margot, that he'd just begun corresponding with her. He…said she was a prisoner, and that he intended to set her free."

Allie hid her shock. "Did he say where he found her?"

"No. But he was excited. And scared." Nathan passed his hand over his damp forehead. "I guess…I figured that Mal had run off with Margot when he disappeared, and then those men came…."

"Yes," Allie said slowly. "It all makes sense. I don't know how Mal found out about Margot being a vampire. *I* didn't tell him." *And Griffin didn't know about Margot at the time.* "Maybe Margot managed to bribe some lower-ranked protégé to help her reach him."

Still, assuming they did manage to get away together…why didn't Mal tell his best friend about his plans? Griffin would never have betrayed him.

After a moment's thought, she answered her own question. *He knew that Grif would never let him go up against the clan, not even for the woman who was the love of his life.*

Allie stood and gently touched Nathan's good arm. "Thanks for telling me this, Nathan. It may help."

"I didn't tell those hatchet men, Allie. No matter what they did."

"You were very brave, Nathan. It'll be safest if you keep this information from anyone else, even Bruce, until we find out what's really going on."

Nathan nodded and subsided back against his pillows. Allie returned to the parlor, followed by Bruce. Once she'd satisfied herself that her friends believed her story, however reluctantly, she forced them to take enough money to help them get out of town for a couple of weeks.

It was with bewildered, frightened faces that they scattered to their various rooms and apartments, mute with the shock of the night's revelations. Allie drove back to her flat and changed her clothes, shaking with the anger she had held inside since the enforcers had shown up at her door. There was nothing more she could do for now; she wouldn't gain anything by confronting Raoul when she was too furious to think straight. Drawing his attention to the humans he despised would only bring more trouble down on them.

Your day will come, Raoul. And when it does, I'll be the first one in line for the celebration.

CHAPTER ELEVEN

ALLEGRA PULLED INTO THE DRIVE behind Griffin's touring car and hopped out of her roadster, her hair tucked beneath a close-fitting cloche hat and her legs encased in full trousers that had not the least hint of masculinity about them.

"Hello, Griffin," she said, her face unusually solemn.

"Allegra," he said, walking over to meet her. He stopped at what he felt was a safe distance, enveloped by the natural perfume of her body and a faint whiff of lavender. The darkness didn't inhibit his vision; he drank in the familiar tilt of her high cheekbones, the slight arch of her dark brows, the bow of her lips colored by the most modest tint of rouge. Her body was strong and lissome under the unconventional clothing. Two weeks had done nothing to settle his unwelcome response to her presence.

Remember what she is. Remember all those others....

He stuffed his hands in his trouser pockets. "We'll take my car, if you've no objection."

"Don't tell me you're afraid of lady drivers?"

He didn't answer, letting her reach her own conclusions. "If you're ready…"

She walked a circle around his car. "Nice," she said, trailing her fingers across the tourer's glossy finish. "How fast can she go?"

"Fast enough." He opened the passenger door. Allegra slid into the seat, settling into the smooth leather.

"Very nice," she said, stroking the dashboard.

Griffin climbed in beside her and started the engine. "Did you bring a coat?" he asked.

"I don't need it. I like to feel the air on my skin, don't you?"

He set his jaw and pulled out of the drive. She *couldn't* be flirting with him. *She* was the one who'd said what had happened that night had been a mistake for both of them.

Whatever her latest game, he was proof against it now. His senses might challenge his mastery, but he could control them. Her going upstate with him was the best possible test of his resolve.

They drove out of the metropolitan area with hardly a word spoken between them. The touring car rode smoothly and swiftly along the Hudson, and they made Albany by four in the morning. Griffin topped off the tank at a filling station, and they continued north and west into Hamilton County. Soon they were driving on narrow dirt roads through rolling, forested hills, crossing countless creeks and looping around lakes as still as glass. Houses were few and far between.

"This really is the wilderness," Allie remarked.

"That's apparently why Mal liked it," Griffin said, as he pulled a folded sheet of paper from his pocket and read the scrawled directions. Though road signs were as rare as buildings, he found his way with only a few wrong turns and drove up to the porch of a ramshackle cabin, complete with peeling paint and an ancient canoe leaning against the sagging wall.

Allie wrinkled her nose. "He could work in a place like this?"

"Mal never needed much." He raised his hand for

silence and listened. Not a sound came from the cabin. Small animals rustled in the underbrush and waking birds stirred in the woods. The scents of undomesticated animals and clean soil and growing things excited a part of him he'd pushed far to the back of his mind. He could almost feel the wind in his fur, the welcoming earth giving way beneath his paws....

"What is it?" Allie whispered.

He remembered that she, as a vampire, had senses superior to those of humans but not quite as keen as a *loup-garou*'s. He opened his door and stepped out, head up, hands loose at his sides.

Allie joined him, scanning the waning darkness. "Is he here?" she asked.

"I can't hear anything." He studied the ground and crouched beside the car. "Tire tracks. It was raining just before someone parked here—see the ruts?"

"Mal's car?"

"They look to be the right size, but they aren't recent." He looked past the ruts. "A man's footprints, leading to the veranda."

Allie wiped a streak of dirt from her right pump. "Don't you think we should go inside?"

He nodded and led the way up the low steps to the porch. Loose boards creaked beneath their feet. The front windows were half open. The door was unlocked and opened onto a single large room, furnished with primitive chairs and a vast oak table. A desk sat in one corner by a cracked window. Another doorway led to a second room graced by a rickety bed.

Allie sneezed. "One thing's for sure. Mal isn't much of a housekeeper."

Her observation was apt enough. Dust and a litter of leaves covered floor and furnishings alike, dulling

Griffin's sense of smell. It was obvious that Mal hadn't been working at the cabin in days, probably not in weeks.

But someone had been here. The prints of a man's shoes continued into the cabin and crisscrossed the room, covered lightly with more recent layers of dust. Hands had wiped away the litter from the center of the desk. The visitor had begun to sweep a corner of the small kitchen, but the swept area ended abruptly, as if he had lost interest in his work.

"Any human scents that might have been here are too old for me to read," Griffin said. "But it must have been Mal. No one else would have a reason to come to this place."

"He came, but he left again pretty quickly," Allie said. "But where did he go from here?"

Discouraged, Griffin followed the dust-covered prints into the bedroom. A third door, showing a thin sliver of dawn light, led outside to the rear of the cabin. The broad window on the far wall had been thrown wide-open, and on the floor…

He froze, staring in consternation. Under the recent debris was a wild crisscrossing of tracks, both human and animal, skittering here and there as if engaged in a frantic struggle. The four feet that had made the animal prints were broad and tipped with strong, curved claws.

"What have you found?" Allie asked, coming up behind him.

He pointed to the floor. She sucked in her breath.

"Is that what I think it is?" she said.

He knelt, ran his fingers across several of the wolf tracks and held his hand up to his face. "This was no ordinary wolf. Look at the size of the paws. It came through the window, landed here and…" He glanced at the bed, noting the disordered blankets. "Someone was in that bed when the intruder appeared. There was some kind of scuffle. And then…"

Keeping low, he pointed out another set of very different tracks. "Look."

Allie followed his gaze. "Bare feet!"

"And the owner of those feet dragged something heavy right to that back door. Something human." He straightened. "If we go outside, we'll find more tracks, shod and bare."

"Mal and a werewolf? But what can it mean?"

"I've no idea. From the looks of things, Mal didn't go willingly. He has no acquaintance with the pack. They'd have no reason to hurt him—"

"Unless they wanted to get at you?"

He grunted. "It's possible a lone wolf was responsible, but what could the motive possibly be? *Loups-garous* don't hunt humans for sport. And if Garret was behind this…"

"At least we know that Mal hasn't just run off," Allie said.

Griffin glared at the door. "Garret keeps tabs on every werewolf in the state, pack or loner. If he had something to do with this abduction, I'll find out. If he didn't…"

"You think someone could have done this without the pack leader's permission?"

"If that's the case, Garret will be forced to investigate."

He made a last circuit of the cabin; then he and Allie went out the back door, following bare footprints and drag marks into the woods. After a short distance both sets of tracks vanished, replaced by more tire ruts cut into the soft soil.

"There must have been more than one kidnapper," he said. "Mal's car is gone."

"Unless it was stolen later."

"Whoever approached the house came from the woods and left the same way. An accomplice could have taken the car, and if we hadn't gone in to investigate, we most likely wouldn't have seen the tracks. Without the weight of a man to impede him, a werewolf seldom leaves any tracks at all."

"Not unlike a vampire." Allie stretched, her supple body momentarily drawing Griffin's thoughts away from his worries. "What now?"

"Back to New York. I'll see Garret first thing tomorrow."

"Won't that be dangerous?"

"Would you let that stop you if Miss Moreau were involved?"

"Not on your life." She looked up at him and took a deep breath. "There's something I need to tell you."

He listened in growing amazement as she related what had happened to her friends and what Nathan had shared with her.

"So you do think Mal took Margot?" he asked.

"I don't see how it's possible, given what we've seen here."

"Unless he was setting things up for Margot's escape and was interrupted in the process." He scrubbed at his chin. "I'd say these tracks are about three weeks old, so whatever happened here occurred around the time I lost contact with Mal. If he never had the chance to help Margot leave Raoul…"

"It begs the question of what *did* happen to her."

"Indeed. It appears we have an even deeper mystery to solve."

She grinned, showing the slightly pointed tips of her incisors. "I'm with you all the way."

Griffin fought the powerful sense of camaraderie that brought him so very close to taking her in his arms. "It's not my habit to put women in danger," he said.

"Oh, God. Not that again." She rolled her eyes. "Dip your toes into the modern world. It might not be as bad as you think."

"I never was much of a swimmer."

"Maybe I'll teach you someday."

Griffin wiped the image of Allie in the water from his mind. "There's something you need to know. I've brought someone else in on this investigation."

"And who would that be?"

"His name is Ross Kavanagh." Griffin pulled a card from his jacket and handed it to her. "He's a homicide detective. He's also a werewolf."

"You're kidding. A werewolf cop?"

"It gives him certain advantages. And he's not with the pack. They consider him an outcast."

"Do tell. I guess he can join the club."

"You can trust him, Allie. Don't hesitate to call him if…if ever I'm not available."

Allie pocketed the card. "I'll keep it in mind."

"Good." He took a last long look at the area around the cabin. "If it's acceptable to you, I'll drop you off at your apartment and send Fitzsimmons to deliver your roadster."

"Why don't I just come back to Long Island with you?"

"I'd like to spend a little time alone with Gemma."

She touched his arm. "You want to see her before you go to the pack, just in case."

"Nothing will happen."

Allie released his arm and started back for the car. "For *their* sakes, I hope you're right."

GRIFFIN SMELLED the stranger as soon as he stepped onto the drive. He stiffened, ears pricked for any unusual sound. The urge to Change and run the outer perimeter of the estate was overwhelming, but he ignored instinct and went into the house.

"Starke?"

His voice echoed in the vestibule. After a tense moment he remembered that the butler had probably gone with Demetria on an early morning drive into town to buy staples and kitchen supplies. As for Gemma's new teacher, she ought to be in the kitchen having her usual cup of tea.

He strode to the breakfast room. It was deserted. He raced up the stairs three at a time and rapped on Miss Arnold's door.

She opened it a crack, peering at Griffin in vague surprise.

"Mr. Durant?"

He noted her rumpled hair and hastily tied dressing gown. "Where is Gemma?" he asked.

She blinked. "In her room. We were up very late last night, reading *The Odyssey*. I agreed to let her sleep in this morning. I didn't think you'd object, Mr. Durant."

Griffin turned away and hurried to Gemma's room before the woman could ask what he wanted.

"Gemma?" he called.

Silence. He knocked on the door. It didn't take more than that to wake a *loup-garou*, but Gemma didn't answer. He opened the door. A quiet lump lay in Gemma's bed, smelling of musty wool and feathers.

Griffin pulled back the bedspread, exposing thread-bare down pillows and a bundled, hole-ridden wool blanket. Where Gemma had found such rubbish was the least of Griffin's questions, but it was evident that she had hoped to deceive her human guardians into be-lieving she was safe in her bed.

He checked Gemma's window, opened it and stared down onto the lawn. The scent of Gemma's skin still clung to the windowsill and the wall immediately be-neath it. She'd climbed down in order to avoid using her door, and she'd been out for at least an hour.

Furious at her defiance and sick with worry, Griffin ran back down the stairs. He stripped out of his clothes with no concern for the state of his shirt and suit, leaving the garments in a heap on the floor. He flung open the front door, sucked in a lungful of morning air and Changed, forcing the transformation so hard that his muscles screamed and his bones popped.

Sensation hit his wolf's ears and nose with the vi-olence of a sledgehammer. He trembled, seeking the unfamiliar smell. It mingled with Gemma's, caught like wisps of hair in the shrubs and grass.

Like a greyhound, he leaped into motion. He skimmed across the lawn, paws barely touching the ground, his nostrils flared wide as he tracked the scent to its source.

They were sitting in the shelter of a pair of old wil-lows, Gemma and a lanky young man who couldn't have been much older than she was. Gemma wore an old pair of trousers and a shirt that fell almost to her knees. The boy was bare-chested, the lean muscles of his arms and shoulders flexing under fair, freckled skin.

Griffin never altered his pace. He charged the stranger, teeth bared, and bowled the boy over.

"Griffin!"

Gemma's shout rang like the clanging of bells. It slowed him only for an instant, and then Griffin straddled the young man's chest, jaws inches from his throat.

Desperate hands grasped at his fur. "No, Griffin! It's not what you think! Wyatt doesn't mean any harm." She tugged harder. "You have to believe me!"

The boy she'd called Wyatt averted his gaze. "Mr. Durant," he said in a slightly shaky voice, "I know I've trespassed on your property. I'm sorry about that. If you'll just let me explain…"

Griffin's instincts told him that Wyatt's submission was sincere, but something in the boy's scent kept his hackles standing on end. He retreated with only the greatest reluctance. Wyatt remained flat on his back.

"Thank you, Grif," Gemma breathed.

Griffin shook himself and Changed. "Gemma, go into the house."

"But—"

He snarled, his voice only half human, and she crept away. Griffin faced Wyatt with narrowed eyes.

"Who are you?" he demanded.

"Can I sit up?"

Griffin grunted permission. Wyatt pushed himself up to his elbows. "I'm sorry to have disturbed you, sir. I only came to see Gemma."

"That hardly endears you to me. You're a member of the pack?"

"Yes."

"Then why have you strayed so far from your territory to see my sister?"

Wyatt was careful to look anywhere but into Griffin's eyes. "It's like this, sir. I saw her on Fifty-second Street the night…the night you were with her and Ivar tried to make trouble. I, uh…I just had to see her again, and the only way to do that was to come out here. I didn't mean any harm…."

"You think some transient attraction gives you the excuse to trespass on my territory?"

"It wasn't like that. I—"

"You have no business visiting Gemma. I decide whom she sees—"

"And you keep her away from her own kind," Wyatt said with a sudden burst of defiance.

"That's none of your concern, boy." Griffin leaned forward, sifting Wyatt's scent, comparing it against his memory of a hundred other smells. There was a wrongness in it he couldn't identify.

"Do your kin know you're here?" he asked.

"No. They wouldn't like it any more than you do… sir."

"And what were you doing with my sister?"

Wyatt squirmed, all gangly arms and legs. "Talking. Just talking."

"Are you sure you want to stick by that story?"

"We…we ran together. That's all."

"You Changed?"

"I never touched her. It was all proper."

"Proper? You were both unclothed."

"If Gemma doesn't mind—"

"Gemma is too young to make rational decisions, especially not where young men are concerned." He got to his feet. "Put on your shirt and leave."

Wyatt rose, his head lowered. "I want to see Gemma again."

"You'll never set foot on my land again if you want to keep yourself in one piece."

In spite of his bravado, the boy knew better than to offer an open challenge. He grabbed his shirt and pulled it on with angry jerks. "You can't always keep her locked up here," he said.

I've heard that before, Griffin thought bitterly. "You'd be wise to understand that Gemma is beyond your reach. I'm letting you go. Be grateful for the favor."

Wyatt bunched his fists and strode off in the direction of the small wood bordering the estate. Griffin watched him until he was out of sight and returned to the house at a run.

Starke was waiting in the vestibule, Griffin's clothes lying neatly across his arm. "I heard some disturbance," he said.

Griffin stepped into his trousers. "Don't worry, Uncle Edward. It's over now." He eased into his shirt. "I thought you were going out with Demetria this morning?"

"The Packard wouldn't start. After I failed to correct the problem, I was obliged to call a mechanic." He peered at Griffin with concern. "Perhaps you'd like something to eat. Demetria is out of sorts, but I can still manage a tolerable scrambled egg."

"Thanks, but I'm not very hungry this morning." He glanced toward the stairs. "Is Gemma in her room?"

"Yes. She was weeping."

"She's misbehaved again."

"I'm sorry I wasn't here to prevent her transgression."

"It's hardly your responsibility."

Edward looked at Griffin the way he remembered from his childhood, the old man's expression a mixture of affection, exasperation and hidden sorrow. "Much has been troubling you of late, Griffin," he said. "You haven't let me help you in a long while."

Griffin winced. "I'm sorry, Edward. I haven't shown

much appreciation for all you've done since you and Gemma returned from Europe."

"I did it most willingly."

"With virtually no assistance from me."

"You had the business to rebuild, and after the War…"

"That's no excuse for my neglect." Griffin met his gaze. "You've been a second father to us. I've been a very poor son."

"You would have made your father proud, as you make me proud."

Griffin felt a shameful tightness in his throat. "I never intended for you to continue on as butler. I'd still like you to come in with me as full partner in the company—"

"I prefer things just as they are, if you have no objection," Edward said, falling back on his butler's practiced dignity. "I understand that Gemma is not a child anymore, and that you alone must determine what is best for her."

"But you don't agree with my plans for her."

"I only wish to see both of you happy." Starke's mouth quirked in the slightest of smiles. "I like that young woman of yours, Griffin."

"My young…" Griffin's face grew hot. "Miss Chase is not *mine* in any sense of the word. We have mutual interests for the time being, but there's nothing…we have nothing in common."

Edward inclined his head. "As you wish, sir." But there was a twinkle in his eye as he said it. "Is there anything else I can do?"

"Not at the moment, thanks." Griffin stared at his dusty shoes. "Edward…"

"Go to your sister. She needs you." Starke turned smoothly and walked away.

Griffin felt as inadequate as the fourteen-year-old

he'd been so long ago. It wasn't that Starke had given even a hint of reprimand, but Griffin took no pleasure in thinking of those early years when his grief and anger had overruled his sense. The period after the War had been little better.

Is Gemma paying the price for my failures?

Unsettled by his thoughts, Griffin climbed the stairs to Gemma's room. She answered his knock, her face red and her eyes swollen.

"Have you come to yell at me?" she asked.

"May I come in?"

She stepped away from the door and sat on her bed, legs curled beneath her. "It wasn't what you thought. Wyatt and I...we never—"

"I know." He took the chair in the corner of the room. "How long ago did you meet him? This isn't the first time you've been with him, is it?"

She picked up her pillow and hugged it to her chest. "It's only the second time. You shouldn't blame him. I said he could come."

"And you believe what he said about why he came here?"

"Is there a reason why I shouldn't? Am I so ugly that a young man wouldn't find me attractive?"

"It isn't that at all, and you know it. I don't know anything about this boy, and neither do you."

"But he—"

"Hear me out, Gemma. He's a member of the pack. The pack doesn't allow its youngsters to wander about at will, however free they may seem to you."

"So he snuck away. Maybe they can't control him so easily."

"It's possible. But it's also possible that he was sent here deliberately."

She stared at him. "Sent here? Why would they do that?"

"For the same reason Ivar confronted us in the street outside Lulu's. They want to control us and our fortune."

"And you think Wyatt's a spy? That he…used me…" She buried her face in the pillow.

Griffin cursed himself roundly. He couldn't articulate his feeling that there was something wrong with the boy, something dangerous to both him and Gemma.

"I may be wrong," he said. "It may be exactly as he claims, but I don't dare assume he's telling the truth. You must see that."

She tossed the pillow onto the floor. "You wouldn't want me to see him even if he's not a spy. If I like him, you have to hate him."

"I don't hate him, Gemma. But you must choose your friends carefully."

"What friends? You think I still have any after the party?"

Griffin sat down beside her and stroked her hair. "I wish I could make it easier for you. I'd give my life to make you happy. But I won't risk your future for temporary pleasure."

Gemma shook him off and flung herself facedown on the bed.

Griffin left her, knowing that she had to accept what he'd told her in her own good time. He went downstairs and found Starke in the kitchen.

"Would you like some breakfast after all?" the butler asked.

"I have a favor to ask of you, Uncle Edward."

"Of course."

"I'm going to see Garret Sloan, and I need you and

Miss Arnold to watch Gemma carefully while I'm gone."

Edward put down the silver he'd been polishing. "Garret Sloan? Why?"

"I have a few questions to ask him about what Miss Chase and I found last night." He explained briefly what they'd discovered. Edward's face tightened.

"It sounds most unpleasant," he said. "Must you go alone?"

"I'll call Ross Kavanagh before I leave and tell him what I'm doing, so if anything goes wrong…"

"God forbid." Edward twisted the polishing cloth between his hands.

Indeed. God might very well forbid, but Griffin was once again left without a choice. To beard the wolf in his den, he might very well have to become the wolf himself, no matter how much he dreaded the prospect.

"When might we expect you home?" Edward said, his voice subdued.

"I don't know. If you don't hear from me by six o'clock…"

"We shall hold dinner for you, Mr. Durant."

Griffin smiled. "Thanks, old friend."

Griffin retreated to his library and made a quick call to Ross, then had Fitzsimmons bring the roadster around to the drive. It was eleven o'clock when he parked on the curb beside a row of neat houses—too small to be mansions, too large for the budgets of average New Yorkers—that gave the deceptive appearance of a prosperous but very ordinary neighborhood.

Griffin got out of the car and continued along the sidewalk until he reached a house that seemed very much like the others, calling no attention to itself with bright colors or embellishments of any kind. The tiny lawn was neatly trimmed, the hedges clipped to perfection. He walked up to the porch and knocked on the door.

A woman dressed in a maid's uniform answered, her pleasantly bland face cast in an expression of polite inquiry. The moment she got a good look at Griffin her demeanor subtly changed from that of a dutiful servant to wary gatekeeper.

"Griffin Durant," she said, her eyes slightly averted.

"Marianne," he said, tipping his hat.

She looked surprised that he remembered her name. Her air of guarded hostility gave way to curiosity. "Why are you here, Mr. Durant?"

Her formality made clear that he was not welcome, since he was not of the pack. He was not in the least troubled by the subtle warning.

"I've come to see Garret," he said. "If you'd be so kind as to tell him I'm here."

Her nostrils flared, sifting his scent for his true feelings. She wouldn't be surprised to find that his polite words covered unshakable determination. He was ready for a fight, and nothing would discourage him into leaving unsatisfied.

Marianne drew back from the doorway. "You can come in, but you'll have to wait to see Garret until Ivar gives permission."

"Ivar? Since when has he become the pack leader's voice?"

She squirmed, unwilling to be caught between Griffin and his enemies. "If you'll wait in the reception room, I'll find Ivar," she said, and disappeared through a doorway.

Griffin looked about at the staid, conservatively furnished parlor. The antique display cases were filled with faded photos and Victorian figurines; it might have been the province of some elderly lady who had no interest in twentieth-century fashion. No human entering this house would ever guess what it contained.

He tasted the air, counting perhaps four *loups-garous* in the immediate vicinity, not including Marianne. There was no trace of the boy, Wyatt, but he more than likely resided in some other part of the den. Each house around the block was connected to the next by an underground passage, creating one continuous space that could lodge many families. Though a few werewolves lived in separate domiciles, this was the center of pack activity and power.

Ivar broadcast his arrival with an acrid wave of scent that shouted challenge. He strode into the room, his eyes immediately seeking Griffin's. They stood facing each other, neither giving way, until Ivar grew tired of the game.

"What do you want?" he snarled.

Griffin bared his teeth. "Such a pleasant welcome. Does Garret know how charmingly you greet visitors?"

"I'm not here to make nice with you, Durant. As far as I'm concerned, Garret should have killed you as soon as you refused to join us."

"Your opinion on that matter is well known. By the way, congratulations on your promotion. How much licking up did you have to do to get it?"

Ivar bristled. "What do you want?" he repeated.

"A chat with Garret. I think he'll find it mutually beneficial."

Ivar narrowed his eyes. "You coming around, Durant?"

"That's between me and Sloan."

"Maybe he won't want to see you."

"I think he will." He advanced on Ivar one step at a time. "I don't think he'd appreciate it if you and I were to fight it out here in the reception room. But if that's what you prefer…"

Ivar trembled with rage. "I'll tell him. I hope you get what you deserve." He spun on his heel and charged out of the room.

CHAPTER TWELVE

IT WAS A FULL TWENTY MINUTES before another were-wolf, a youngster with a nervous gaze, came to escort Griffin to Garret's lair. The boy led Griffin to the rear of the house, through a door and down a staircase ending at the underground passage. The concrete tunnel was dimly lit, since any *loup-garou* would easily be able to find his way in the dark. Every so often, at the point where a house was located above-ground, a steel door opened onto another set of stairs.

Garret's rooms were in the second-to-last house, a suite also inhabited by his mate and younger children. The rest of the house provided living quarters for other members of the pack leader's extended family.

Griffin maintained an air of confidence as his guide paused to speak with several older *loups-garous* ranged about the large living room on the ground floor. Unlike the hall and reception area in the central house, this room was furnished in a way most humans would have found eccentric: a skylight let the sun shine on a whole jungle of potted plants; a stone fountain splashed in the center of the floor; and every inch was scattered with large floor pillows and low tables.

A half-dozen eyes fixed on Griffin. One of the young men got to his feet, dismissed the guide and circled Griffin slowly.

"Griffin Durant," he said. "I'm Joseph, Garret's son by Leila. I'm to take you to my father."

Griffin remembered that Leila had been Garret's first mate, killed in an accident some dozen years before. The young man was well grown and muscular, and though he was wary, he showed no signs of overt antagonism.

Joseph led Griffin to the back of the room, entered a hallway, climbed a broad staircase and stopped before wooden double doors carved with scenes of thick woods and running wolves, so expertly devised that they seemed to leap out from the richly grained surface.

"A reminder of our origins," Joseph commented. He scratched at the door. A young woman opened it.

"Joseph," she said. "Mr. Durant. My father is expecting you."

She ushered them into the room, where Joseph took up a post near the door. A vast desk dominated the wide space, backed by a window that looked out on the miniature wooded park. Garret sat behind the desk like a king on his throne, a pair of young children on his lap. A handsome woman in her late thirties, her long blond hair threaded with silver, stood beside the desk and regarded Griffin with wise green eyes.

Garret seemed not to notice Griffin's presence. He whispered to the children, who giggled and squirmed. There was no doubt of his affection for them, or of the love and pride that shone on his hard face when he looked up at his green-eyed mate.

"Rayna," the woman said to the girl who'd answered the door. "Please take Jocelyne and Jeroen to the nursery."

The girl smiled and opened her arms. The children

ran to her and took her hands, and the three of them left by an unobtrusive side door.

Even then Garret didn't look up. He shuffled a pile of papers on his desk, seemingly lost in thought.

"Why are you here, Durant?" he asked abruptly, his eyes still scanning the paper in his hands.

Griffin planted his legs apart and stood very still. "I'm here on a matter of some urgency, Mr. Sloan," he said.

Garret flung down the papers and stared at Griffin. "You haven't decided to join us?"

"Not at this time." Griffin held Garret's gaze, refusing to concede the pack leader's authority over him but careful not to make any move that might be misconstrued as challenge. It was a delicate balancing act. "Something has happened that I feel you should know," he said. "A matter that involves the possible kidnapping of a human by *loups-garous*."

Garret's body came to full alert, his lips curling back from his teeth. "What in hell are you talking about?"

His mate lay her hand on his shoulder. His muscles relaxed. "Will you excuse us, Ingrid?" he asked softly.

She smiled at the top of his head, nodded to Griffin and left the room. Garret leaned heavily on the table. "You have a lot of nerve coming here like this," he said. "You and your sister have caused enough—"

"Will you hear me out, Sloan, or aren't you interested in what goes on outside this house?"

Sloan growled low in his throat. "All right. Talk."

Griffin looked around, found a chair and drew it toward the desk. He had no intention of standing before Garret like a delinquent awaiting judgment. Garret's eyes flickered with annoyance, but he didn't object when Griffin sat down.

"A human friend of mine disappeared a little over three weeks ago," Griffin began without preamble. He described Mal, the circumstances of his disappearance—leaving out all reference to Margot—and what he himself had discovered at the upstate cabin.

"Mal doesn't know any werewolves but me," he finished. "They didn't come to his cabin for a friendly chat."

Garret laughed. "That's quite a story. Why would any *loup-garou* want to kidnap a human?"

"You tell me."

Garret surged up from his chair and circled the desk, his head held low between his shoulders. "You're not stupid enough to lie to me, Durant. Isn't this Malcolm Owen the man who used to pant after Margot De Luca?"

"He was seeing her at one time."

"I know she was Converted by Raoul a few months ago. Her father was in on the deal. Now she's gone missing from Raoul's headquarters, and the leeches are looking for her."

"I'm not interested in the whereabouts of Margot De Luca."

"No? Then why have you been keeping company with a female leech who's been asking questions about the De Luca bitch all over town?"

Griffin let no trace of surprise cross his face. He had made the mistake of underestimating the reach of Garret's elaborate spy network. Allie must have been very busy since she returned to Manhattan.

"Miss Chase," he said coldly, "was Margot's friend and has been concerned about her. My acquaintance with Miss Chase does no harm to the pack."

"Even when the leech is known to be a rogue among her own kind? Even though Raoul has a keen interest in her and might resent interference from one of us?"

"I'm not one of you."

"Do you think Raoul knows the difference?" Garret stopped before Griffin's chair, leaning forward in a posture of open aggression. "What do you want, Durant?"

"I want to know if you or any of your underlings had something to do with what happened to Mal."

"You're treading on very dangerous ground, boy."

Griffin stood, the toes of his shoes nearly touching Garret's. "I won't stop asking questions, Sloan, even if you set the whole pack against me."

Garret shifted from one foot to the other, his muscles bulging with the urge to fight. "Your senses must have deceived you, Durant. No one here kidnapped your human friend."

"Then you know nothing about this."

The tendons of Garret's neck stood out beneath his skin. "I tell you again, Durant. You're mistaken. I suggest you look somewhere else for the human. And don't show your face here again."

Griffin smiled. "You've made yourself very clear, Sloan." He walked to the double doors. "One more thing…I suggest you rein Ivar in. I won't tolerate any more threats from him, against myself or anyone under my protection."

"*I* could kill you here and now."

"But you won't. That's Ivar's way, not yours." He opened the door. "You might want to watch your own back. Ivar's exactly the type to weaken your grip on the pack with subterfuge, then challenge you when you least expect it."

He didn't wait for Garret's reply but left without a backward glance.

No one followed him as he retraced his steps through the tunnel and back up the stairs to the "public" entrance. His thoughts were a whirlpool of dangerous speculation. Garret had claimed not to know anything of Mal's disappearance, and denied the involvement of the pack and, by extension, any *loup-garou* in New York. But he hadn't been telling the full truth. His hostility had masked a very real alarm at Griffin's revelation. Either he had an inexplicable motive for wanting Mal, or there were *loups-garous* operating independently of his control.

If the latter were true, it was a mark of impending trouble within the pack and the sign of a deeper conspiracy than Griffin had ever imagined.

THE MASTER STUDIED the hand laid out on his table and selected a new card.

"Well?" he said. "What is it?"

Ivar cringed, as he always did in the Master's presence. "I have news about the lone wolf."

"Indeed?" The Master gathered up the cards and tapped them into a neat stack. "What is our rebellious lycanthrope doing now?"

"Asking more questions, but this time of Sloan."

"Don't be obscure, Ivar."

The werewolf all but hopped from foot to foot. "He went to the cabin and figured out that the human was kidnapped by werewolves. He came to ask Sloan if he knew anything about it."

The Master rose from his chair, hardly noticing when Ivar slunk out of his way. "What did Sloan tell him?"

"He denied it."

"Did Durant believe him?"

"I don't know."

"And Sloan? Was he suspicious?"

"I don't…" Ivar swallowed. "He told Durant to get out and not come back."

The Master paused beside the boarded window. "That's fortunate. But it's evident that some of your men bungled badly, Ivar."

"That's not my fault."

"It is when you're in command."

"Dempsey must have screwed up. I'll see to him, sir. I'll—"

"It's a little too late to undo the damage now," the Master said. "What of Allegra Chase?"

"She's sticking by Durant, but she's not getting any more answers than he is. She's made herself very unpopular with certain parties in the clan."

"Then one might even call her an unwitting ally—as long as she continues to provide a distraction." The Master turned to the empty fireplace and gazed at ashes undisturbed since the last owner of the place had abandoned it to time and the elements. "You'll return and continue to make certain that our enemies are led in the right direction. It may yet be possible for you to redeem yourself."

Ivar moved in the shadows like a jackal circling a lion, waiting for it to abandon its kill. "It won't happen again."

The Master waved him away, considering the consequences of trusting a creature like Ivar. He was not in a position to dispense with any reasonable ally. But once he was finished, he would find a more competent dog to hold the position Ivar so coveted—assuming any dogs were left alive.

The time of restoration was close at hand, and it would be glorious, indeed.

ALLIE ANSWERED THE PHONE on the first ring.

"Griffin?"

"Are you all right?"

"Why shouldn't I be?"

"I understand you've been out asking about Margot."

She frowned and gazed out the window at the darkening sky. "How did you know?"

"Sloan informed me. He has a very efficient network of confidential agents."

"Why does he care what I do?"

"You may remember that Ivar didn't approve of my association with a vampire. Anything you do may affect me and thus the pack, as well."

"I was careful." She exhaled, trying to unwind the knot of concern that had been building in her chest since Griffin had gone to see Sloan. "How did it go with your little visit?"

"Garret wouldn't admit anything, but I didn't expect he would." Griffin paused, subsiding into some worrisome thought. "I'm not convinced he knew anything about the kidnapping until I told him. No *loup-garou* in this state ties his shoes unless Garret gives permission. If he didn't give the orders for what happened in the Adirondacks…"

"Then we're back to square one." Allie sat on the arm of the couch. "You've seen Garret, and I've had my little tête-a-tête with Raoul's enforcers. Maybe it's time to visit the third point in the triangle."

"De Luca."

"If he knows Margot's missing, which he surely does, he's bound to be upset. He won't be happy with Raoul, and he'll have his own men looking for her."

"You're assuming he didn't take Margot himself."

"I doubt she told him how unhappy she was with Raoul. Still, he's probably the first suspect Raoul's enforcers questioned."

Griffin grunted agreement. "Would he be concerned about Mal?"

"I don't think he'd give Mal enough thought to consider him as a possible conspirator in Margot's disappearance. But I can't shake the feeling that there is a direct connection between Margot and what happened to Mal."

"Will De Luca talk to us?"

"I was there with Margot when Raoul Converted her. If De Luca's willing to talk to anyone, it's me."

Griffin sighed. "Allie, I'd prefer—"

"Forget it, boyo." She twisted her jet earring. "In fact, I ought to go alone."

"No."

"De Luca has no reason to trust a werewolf any more than he trusts Raoul."

"Forget it." Something scraped against wood, as if Griffin were moving a heavy object on his desk. "What if Raoul's men follow you and suspect you of colluding with De Luca?"

"That's a risk we'll have to take." She glanced at her watch. "De Luca holds court at Cherubino's most evenings. Can you meet me there at nine o'clock?"

"Yes. Don't do anything without me."

"Aye aye, Captain." She hung up, annoyed and unsettled. Wasn't this partnership supposed to be strictly a matter of convenience and mutual goals? Why in hell was he still hovering over her like a hen with one chick, clucking on about her safety?

And why did her heart beat so fast when he did it?

With a snort of self-derision, Allie dressed in a crepe satin evening gown with a handkerchief hem and a floating cape back that dipped almost to her waist. She fastened a string of pearls around her neck, combed her hair and began to pace the room, waiting for full dark.

She arrived at Cherubino's well before nine o'clock, paid an attendant a generous tip to park her car and strolled into the restaurant.

To the inexperienced eye, Cherubino's resembled a typical Italian eatery, family run, with an interior of warm reds and yellows. Booths lined the walls, and individual tables filled the remaining space. The area once reserved for the bar stood empty, but that by no means meant that Cherubino's was dry. The new bar was located in one of the storerooms behind the private dining room. For all its humble origins, the restaurant had become a favorite of the smart set—and of Carmine De Luca, his partisans and certain corrupt politicians.

Griffin arrived a few minutes before nine, dressed impeccably in a tuxedo cut to enhance his lean, muscular frame. He was almost imposing in his elegance, and when he smiled at Allie, she was in danger of forgetting why they were there.

"You look lovely tonight, Allegra," he said.

"So do you."

A slight flush darkened his cheeks. "Are you ready?"

She nodded and approached the maître d'. He offered them one of his best tables, but Allie slipped him a twenty and told him that she and Mr. Durant had come to see Mr. De Luca. After a moment's hesitation, the maître d' sent a waiter into the back rooms, apologizing for the delay.

The waiter returned and whispered a message in his

superior's ear. The maître d' smiled at Allie. "If you and the gentleman will follow me, madam," he said.

Griffin offered his arm. Allie took it, ignoring the admiring stares of a number of young men lounging in the booths. The maître d' passed through the back door and down a short hallway leading to a second door. It opened onto a private dining room, luxuriously furnished with gilded ornamentation and velvet-upholstered chairs and couches. A half-dozen men sat around a long table, each of them soberly dressed and with eyes as cold as any vampire's. They rose as Allie entered, and the man at the head of the table inclined his head.

"Miss Allegra Chase," he said with deceptive mildness. "How nice to see you again."

Allie gave him her most dazzling smile. "Mr. De Luca," she said. "I hope we're not disturbing you."

De Luca returned her smile with all the warmth of a shark. "Not at all, Miss Chase. Our gathering has been sadly lacking in feminine charm." His gaze settled on Griffin, and Allie took the hint.

"Mr. De Luca," she said, "this is Griffin Durant."

De Luca's men, who had resumed their seats, half rose again. De Luca waved them down.

"Mr. Durant," he said. "This is an unexpected pleasure."

"How do you do?" Griffin said, his body loose and relaxed. "Miss Chase asked me to escort her tonight. I hope you don't find it inconvenient."

"Not in the least." De Luca spread his hands on the table. "I wasn't aware that you'd become one of Sloan's lieutenants."

"I'm not," Griffin said, "I don't belong to the pack."

One of De Luca's men spoke to his boss in a low

voice, and De Luca nodded. "Of course. A lone wolf." He settled back into his chair, his slight frame and pleasant manner obscuring his true nature. "You'll grant that it's unusual to see a werewolf with a vampire."

Allie signaled to the waiter standing in the back of the room. "Whiskey straight," she said, and turned again to De Luca. "Mr. Durant and I have similar interests," she said. "Interests you also share."

De Luca raised a dark brow. "Indeed?"

"Your daughter, Mr. De Luca."

The gangster straightened, his eyes turning as black as obsidian. "What about my daughter?"

"I've just learned that she's disappeared from Raoul's mansion," Allie said. She paused to watch for De Luca's reaction, but his expression remained impassive. "Raoul's enforcers came to interrogate me, to see if I had any idea where Margot might have gone."

"And what did you tell Raoul's enforcers?"

"The truth. That I didn't know anything."

De Luca's tension eased slightly. "As it happens," he said, "Raoul's men also came to see me. I didn't much care for their line of questioning."

Allie imagined the encounter and wondered how anyone had come out of it alive. "They thought you took Margot," she said.

Once again De Luca's henchmen stirred, but none moved from his chair. De Luca picked up his glass and took a sip of liquor. "You have a very direct manner of speaking, Miss Chase."

"You found that quality useful enough when you wanted me to convince Margot to Convert."

"And you've come here tonight out of concern for her."

"That's right."

De Luca emptied his glass and set it down. "I have no idea what's become of my daughter. I haven't seen her since her Conversion."

"And the last time I saw her," Allie said, "she said nothing that would explain what might have happened."

The waiter brought De Luca a fresh glass. He pushed it aside. "She was well?"

"Physically, yes."

De Luca brooded over his folded hands. "She was unhappy."

Allie thought it best not to offer an opinion. De Luca clenched his fist and flexed it as if he were imagining someone's painful death. "I will hold Raoul personally responsible if any harm comes to Margot," he said. Suddenly he stared at Griffin. "What is Mr. Durant's part in this?"

Griffin stepped forward. "You may remember, Mr. De Luca," he said, "that your daughter had been seeing a young man named Malcolm Owen."

"I seem to recall the name."

Griffin explained his and Allie's speculation that there was a possible link between Mal's and Margot's disappearances. De Luca rose, knocking his glass over in his haste. "You mean, this kid took my daughter?"

Margot shrugged and accepted her whiskey from the waiter. "He couldn't exactly walk into Raoul's mansion and sweep Margot away."

"Then stop wasting my time. If you have any idea—"

"Kindly remember that you're speaking to a lady," Griffin said icily.

Two of De Luca's men reached inside their jackets. "This is my territory, Durant," De Luca said. "I suggest you keep that in mind."

"You might keep in mind that Miss Chase came here to help."

The two men stared at each other. Allie stepped between them.

"We ought to be allies, not enemies," she said. "Look, if Mal really did intend to take Margot, she was in on it. But the evidence suggests that they never went through with the plan."

De Luca's jaw flexed. "Well?"

"I have reason to believe that Mal may be in some danger himself," Griffin said. "If and when I find him, he'll be under my protection."

The gunsel nearest Griffin lunged from his seat, revolver in hand. Griffin moved with almost imperceptible speed, grabbing his attacker's hand and twisting the gun from his grip a second after the man left his chair.

"As Miss Chase suggested," Griffin said, "we should be allies, Mr. De Luca. Let me deal with Mal, if and when we find him."

For several long moments the room fairly vibrated with hostility. Allie looked at each man at the table, sending the intangible signals that worked both to calm potential donors and rouse their sexual interest. Breathing slowed. Muscles went slack. Aggressive energy that had been focused on Griffin changed to a very different sort, and every male in the room, including the injured gunsel, stared at Allie with fascinated desire.

Griffin took Allie's arm. "Perhaps it would be a good time to leave," he said.

But De Luca raised his hand as they turned to go. "Wait," he said, "you have my personal apology for Cesare's behavior, Mr. Durant." He met Allie's gaze. "I'm not prepared for open war between my people and the clan. This matter must be handled with discretion."

"I agree," Allie said. "I have a feeling this is going to get a lot more complicated before we have the answers."

"Then we'll keep each other informed of any progress."

"Agreed."

Allie gave way to Griffin's insistence and let herself be pulled from the room.

Griffin's face was grim and pale. "That didn't go well," he said.

"No? I thought it went just fine." She frowned. "Are you upset that De Luca's man went after you?"

Griffin shook his head. "Something is very wrong, Allegra. The truce between the humans, the clan and the pack is like a pile of dry tinder waiting for a match."

"Then it's up to us to make sure that match never gets lit."

He took her hand, led her outside and planted her in the shadows of the adjoining alley. "Promise me that you won't go near Raoul or his followers," he said.

"I never said—"

"You don't have to."

"It was okay for *you* to see Garret—"

"There's no need to be reckless. You and I have to trust each other."

"So you trust me?"

"Yes."

Allie shivered with unexpected emotion and pulled away. "Okay, then."

They were still staring at each other when one of De Luca's hatchet men emerged from the restaurant, followed by his boss, De Luca's lieutenants and several more guards. De Luca threw Allie and Griffin a seemingly indifferent glance and got into his waiting limousine.

"Let's walk," Griffin suggested.

Allie almost demurred. There was a very physical hunger in her that could only be filled one way, and Griffin certainly wouldn't be of any help in finding what she needed. Suddenly she felt very much alone—isolated from her friends, her own kind, anyone who belonged to something greater than herself.

Anyone but the single creature who might understand.

"What's changed, Allegra?" Griffin asked, startling her out of her thoughts.

"Excuse me?"

"What made you decide that the world deserves your efforts to save it?"

She began walking, her heels beating an angry tattoo on the sidewalk. "Who said I wanted to save the world?"

"You said it was up to us to see that the tinder smoldering in this city doesn't ignite."

"A figure of speech."

"I don't think so." He caught up to her, matching his stride to hers. "It's more than just Margot now, isn't it?"

"So what if it is?"

"Those aren't the sentiments of the Allegra Chase who said she didn't give a damn about anyone but herself."

"A gang war would tend to interfere with my pleasures, don't you think?"

"You could just as easily move to another city, find a new circle of like-minded Bohemians to trot along at your heels. No, Allie…I think you're in great danger of becoming an idealist."

"Is this Griffin Durant talking? The man who was

so unwilling to venture out of the safe little world he'd created for himself and his sister?"

Griffin was silent for several blocks. "You're right," he said. "Maybe both of us have changed since this began. We—"

The bark of gunshots cracked the air. Griffin froze, his head going up like a hound on the scent.

"Blood," he said. "I think it's coming from the next street over."

CHAPTER THIRTEEN

THE SCENE WAS strangely quiet when Griffin and Allegra arrived.

A limousine and coupe were parked aslant in the middle of the street, acting as barricades for the armed men crouched behind them. On the pavement between the vehicles and sidewalk lay another man, facedown in a pool of blood. A single streetlamp cast the tableau in eerie shadow.

"That's De Luca and his men," Griffin said, his nostrils stinging with the scent of violence.

Allegra stopped beside him in the shelter of a battered truck parked along the sidewalk. "That's De Luca, all right," she said. "Looks like he ran into an ambush."

Griffin pulled her down when she would have straightened for a better view. "Who would be attacking De Luca?"

"No one's dared in a long time," she said. "He's too powerful. But there's always someone who wants a bigger piece of the action…former hatchet men, defeated rivals, lieutenants who—"

A thin wail reached Griffin's ears, and he held up his hand for silence. His hackles rose.

"Was that a kid I just heard?" Allie asked.

"Yes. And a woman crying." He shifted, peering up

into the tenements on the other side of De Luca's make-shift fortifications. "Whoever attacked De Luca is in that building."

"No woman or kid would be involved in a shoot-out."

"Unless they happened to get in the way. Would De Luca hesitate to endanger innocent bystanders if he had a good shot at an enemy?"

Allegra's expression was answer enough. "What's your plan?"

He allowed himself a moment of amazement at how remarkably easy it was for her to read his thoughts. "I'm going to ask De Luca to hold his fire while I look for whoever laid this ambush and dis-arm them if I can. You'll stay with De Luca and make sure he doesn't do anything foolish while I'm in the building."

"No. I'm coming with you."

"This won't be some speakeasy brawl, Allegra. These men are armed and dangerous."

"So were Raoul's enforcers."

"Vampires can be killed by gunfire."

"Only if the bullet hits directly in the heart or the brain."

He felt a chill at the image her words evoked. "You've never been in a real fight."

"Who says I have to fight? I'm fast on my feet. I can be a distraction, draw their attention while you sneak up from behind."

"Such plans are very seldom successful in the heat of battle. I don't want you in the middle of this."

Her face showed not a hint of surrender. "I wouldn't miss it for the world."

He fought the urge to become the wolf, pin her

down by the throat and snarl in her face, asserting his dominance. It wouldn't do any good. They'd had this discussion before, and he'd always lost.

He started out into the street, shielding Allegra with his body. They were halfway to De Luca when a spray of bullets pelted the ground beside them. Griffin pushed Allegra ahead of him and dropped down beside her in the midst of De Luca's startled men. In an instant he and Allie were faced with the muzzles of a half-dozen tommy guns.

"What the hell are you doing here, Durant?" De Luca asked from the shadows.

"We heard the gunfire."

"So naturally you ran right into it."

Suspicion came as naturally to De Luca as breathing. Griffin kept his voice calm and level. "Do you know who attacked you?"

"Whoever did is gonna pay," a triggerman snapped.

De Luca ignored him. "I don't know," he said, "but I assure you they'll suffer the consequences of this unprovoked assault." He signaled to his men, who lowered their weapons. "What do you want?"

"To stop this before innocent people are hurt."

"Stop it?" He laughed. "It's my man lying dead out there."

"And there are children in that tenement."

"It was a kid who led us into this ambush," another voice said.

"That may be true," Allegra said, "but does that mean every child in there is guilty?"

"What do you want me to do about it?" De Luca asked.

Griffin leaned forward. "Let me go in and root out your enemies."

"What do a bunch of human kids mean to a werewolf?"

"The future," Griffin said. "Hope. A chance that they might build a better world than this one."

One of De Luca's men laughed. De Luca silenced him. "There might be twenty men in that building," he said. "They could be holed up anywhere. What do you expect to do if you find them?"

"What does a wolf do when it finds its prey?" Allie asked with a grin.

Griffin shuddered. "I'll disarm or disable them. All I ask is that you hold your fire and let the police handle the prisoners when it's over."

De Luca's men muttered in protest. "That ain't the way we do—"

"*Silenzio!*" De Luca snapped. He held Griffin's gaze. "Why should I trust you, Durant?"

"All I want is a chance to keep this from turning into a bloodbath."

De Luca weighed Griffin's words. "Okay. I'll give you fifteen minutes, and then I can't be responsible for what happens." He held out a tommy gun. "Take this."

Griffin recoiled. "No guns," he said. "I don't need them."

"Neither do I," Allie said dryly, "but thanks for the offer."

Griffin turned to Allie. "Please. Stay here."

"Not in a million years."

"Allie…"

"Look, you go right and I'll go left. I'll meet you at the stairwell."

She was off before he could summon up another useless protest, flying across the street, as swift as a gazelle. Griffin swerved the other way, deliberately slowing to call the enemy's attention to himself. Bullets lanced the air. He drew up in the stairwell, breath coming hard.

"Allie?"

She wasn't there. He knew without a moment's thought that she'd already entered the building.

He took the stairs two at a time and plunged into the dingy hallway. His nose told him where she had gone. He raced up the interior staircase, leaping over loose boards and straining his ears for the sounds of running feet. The doors in the hall off the second-floor landing were firmly closed, though he could smell the cowering inhabitants behind them.

Allie had continued up, and so did he. The third floor was saturated with the smells of fear and discharged weapons. Griffin heard the human intruder before he had taken two steps into the hallway, turning to meet the mobster's gun with a swipe of his hand. The weapon clattered and spun across the pitted floor. The gunsel pulled a knife. Griffin's fist connected with the man's face before the blade had moved another inch. It took another blow to render the human incapable of doing anyone further harm.

Griffin paused to examine the man's face. There was nothing to indicate his origins or affiliations. His clothing was nondescript and well-worn, suggesting a definite lack of prosperity.

The sound of a child's cry reached Griffin's ears again, followed by a gasp and whimper. Praying that Allie would be safe, he charged to the second door down the hall.

It gave under his weight and crashed open. A pair of armed men were standing by a grimy, broken window in the small apartment's living room. A child lay still in his weeping mother's arms.

The men fired at almost the same instant. Griffin ducked and rolled, skimming across the bare wood floor. He plowed into one of the gunsels, knocking him into his companion. Both men stumbled and fell, the bullets from their guns peppering the cracked ceiling.

Griffin seized mother and child, covering them with his body as he rushed them to the door. The gunmen recovered and dashed out after him. A fresh spate of bullets whizzed over Griffin's head, several coming so close that they nearly creased his skull.

Machine-gun fire raked the trench as the doughboys made a desperate stand. Griffin breathed in the stink of terror as soldiers loosed their bowels and vomited with fear. A young man, hardly more than a boy, fell across his feet. The top of his skull had been blown away....

Griffin pulled the woman and child down the hall and pounded on the next door. When no one answered, he leaned against it and snapped the flimsy lock.

An elderly man backed away from the door, a kitchen knife in his hand. He rushed to stand guard over an equally aged woman huddled in a corner.

"Don't...don't try anything," the old man gasped, "or I'll—" His gaze flickered to the mother and child. "My God. What—"

"This woman needs help," Griffin said. "Take care of her."

"But—"

Griffin carried the young woman to the sprung sofa and laid her down, the child still nestled in her arms. "Stay here," he told her silent, grieving face. "Don't leave this room."

The old man crept closer. "Who are you?"

But Griffin had no time to answer. He got to the door and closed it behind him just as the gunmen opened fire from the top of the stairs.

Griffin ran, zigzagging toward the men. A bullet shaved an inch of skin off his left arm. Another burned his cheek.

He plunged forward with the others, exhorting his soldiers in the only way he could. One by one, they fell around him. He felt little pain, even when bullets gouged the flesh of his leg and passed through his shoulder....

He had almost reached the gunsels when one of them got lucky. A hot spear of agony thrust into Griffin's gut, and his vision went dark. Somehow he kept on his feet. His legs carried him to the foot of the stairs and up to the enemy in a few long strides. Griffin grabbed the barrel of a tommy gun, yanked it from the man's hands and slammed the butt against the gunsel's startled face. The second human was too close to get in another shot. Griffin seized both men by their shirt fronts, shook them like rats and threw them over the broken banister.

Then he fell to his knees on the stairs, his breath sawing in his throat. There was no longer any danger from the gunmen, but he could feel the damage in his body, the severed blood vessels and the torn organs too badly mangled to benefit from a *loup-garou*'s ordinarily swift healing.

He gazed up the stairs. He hadn't heard the sound of gunplay elsewhere in the building, but Allie was on the floor above, laying a trap—or walking into one. He tried to stand, but his legs gave way and blood spilled from underneath his shirt and waistcoat.

There was only one thing to be done, one desperate measure that would make him fit to fight again. He would lose precious moments, and he would be vulnerable for most of them. But if he waited, he would be dead from blood loss before he could look into Allie's eyes again.

With trembling hands, he tore off his clothing, filling his thoughts with the Change and the transformation that would save him.

His leg was shattered. It could no longer bear his weight, yet his men continued toward the enemy, falling right and left like grass mown by a scythe. Griffin threw aside his rifle and stripped off his uniform. The Change came upon him like a storm. The pain of it threw him to the ground; he writhed in silent torment as flesh and bone reshaped themselves, knitting together in a new conformation.

The agony of the forced healing spiraled to heights of pain Griffin had known only once before. Somehow he clung to consciousness as tissue regrew and the gaping tears in his belly closed, driving infection away with fresh, cleansing blood.

He scrambled to four broad paws, shaking in the aftermath of his body's extraordinary effort. He heard the scraping of footsteps on the floor above, smelled the acrid odor of his own life's fluid pooled under his feet.

Dazed and still weak, he lifted his muzzle to the choking air. He knew he couldn't stay as he was, for he had kept his secret safe and would not add to his men's fear with this alien shape. He Changed again, compelling his body to perform one last labor.

Griffin grabbed the banister and pulled himself to his feet, human once again. Nausea coiled under his ribs, but it was no more than he had expected. He ignored his ruined clothes and started for the fourth floor.

He'd taken only a few steps when the air exploded with gunfire. It came from the street below and the floor above, rattling the walls with a frenzy of violence.

De Luca's fifteen minutes were up.

Griffin bounded up the stairs, ears ringing and sweat slicking his skin.

The noise of the artillery had grown so loud and constant that the sound had imprinted itself on his soul, jarring his bones and filling his head with a whine like a hive of frantic bees. It drove out all thought, all emotion but rage and fear; it drowned the screams and groans of dying men whose limbs had been torn from their bodies. Mud sucked at Griffin's bare legs, and yet he continued, deafened and crazed with a madness no force on earth could cure.

The world shifted before Griffin's eyes, twisting and spinning in time to the thunder of his heart. He reached the fourth floor and paused, listening, scanning the dark hallway.

Another body fell, the shattered torso crashing at his feet. A boy screamed for his mother. A man Griffin's age stood, bewildered, with his entrails falling out of his belly, and singing "My Belgian Rose" in a thin, sweet tenor.

A new round of gunfire spat from the end of the hall. Griffin ran.

Rage kept Griffin moving when his skull was no more than a boiling cauldron of fire and chaos. He reached the edge of the enemy trench. Startled, dirt-smeared faces stared up from under dark helmets. Rifles lifted. He fell among them like the Angel of Death, laying about with his fists and anything that came to hand, snapping limbs and necks like match-sticks. Blood coated his fingers, but he didn't notice.

He didn't feel the bayonets stabbing into his legs or the scrape of broken nails clawing at his arms. He thought only of his men lying dead on the muddy, sterile field, dead because he had no power to save them...and of the handful of soldiers who might yet survive.

He reached the gunman and beat the weapon aside with his clenched fist, leaving the mobster's arm smashed and useless. A woman's shrieks echoed in the sudden silence. Another gunsel appeared, crouched in the shelter of an apartment doorway. Without stopping, Griffin routed him out and crushed the human's hand beneath his foot. He continued toward the smell of the one he had been seeking.

Allie waited in an empty apartment, standing amongst a heap of bodies. One shoulder strap of her gown was torn, dangling down at her side; the hem was ripped to the top of her thigh. The silk was spattered with blood. Her black hair hung over her face, and her mouth...

Her mouth was red.

She stared at Griffin, her aqua eyes all pupil. Griffin felt reality fall into place around him, the horror of the past few minutes rolling over him like a black wave.

Allie wiped her mouth. "Griffin?"

She sounded dazed, yet when she looked down at the bodies, her expression didn't change. He turned his head away.

"Are you...are you hurt?" he croaked.

"No." She took a deep breath, then let it out again, as if she were struggling to form ordinary words. "You...you're bleeding."

"It's nothing." He gazed at the fallen men, at the blood smearing their bared necks. "Are they... did you..."

He couldn't complete the question. All at once he was drawn back to the first time he'd seen Allegra's face, mocking and proud, in the alley outside Madame Aimery's dress shop. He'd known even then what she might be capable of, but since that evening she'd treated her vampire nature so casually that he'd come very close to forgetting what she was. He'd accepted her intemperate past and overcome his own doubts, certain that she was and always would be free of a killer's taint.

Now he saw how he'd been deceived. Allie looked like the perfect predator, her carnivore's teeth painted scarlet, her hands curled into claws made to rend and tear.

It was like staring into a mirror.

Griffin leaned against the wall, his legs trembling with shock. The gunfire had ceased. There were no men left in the tenement capable of holding a weapon. Some would never hold anything again.

But the war was far from over.

"Griffin?"

Allie came toward him, her hand outstretched. He backed away, the distant wail of a siren vibrating in his ears. He swallowed bile. "Get out," he said. "Get out before the police arrive."

She clenched and unclenched her hands as if she didn't know what to do with them. "You...I—"

"Get out!" Griffin banged his shoulder against the doorjamb as he stumbled from the room.

The gunman with the crushed hand lay propped against the corridor wall, incapable of doing further harm to anyone; the second mobster had vanished, leaving a bloody trail down the stairs. On the third floor Griffin found the three other mobsters as he'd left them, one dead, the others immobilized with broken legs and arms. He gathered up the remnants of his clothing and dressed as best he could, then returned to the old man's apartment.

"Who is it?" a thin voice demanded through the door.

"I'm the one who brought the woman," Griffin called, half surprised he was capable of ordinary speech. "How is the child?"

The old man opened the door. "He's alive." He peered up and down the hallway. "Is it…those men…"

"You're safe now." Griffin dragged his hand across his face. "Can you call a doctor?"

"Sure." The old man squinted at Griffin through clouded eyes. "Are you a cop?"

Griffin shook his head. "Look after them."

"Yeah. Say, you don't look so good yourself. Sure you don't want to—"

But Griffin wasn't listening. He was already making his way to the first floor, where a pair of De Luca's hatchet men were entering the building, guns in hand.

"Durant?" one of them said.

"It's over." Griffin blocked their way. "There's no one left who can fight. Let the police take care of them."

"If they ain't dead—"

"Take my advice and walk out."

The men looked at Griffin's blood-stained clothing, exchanged glances and retreated. The sirens grew louder. Griffin sat down on the stairs to wait. He knew De Luca wouldn't be around when the police arrived.

But he would. Because even though his senses told him that Allie was gone, there were surely tenants who'd seen her here, perhaps even a few who'd witnessed how ruthlessly she'd dealt with the human mobsters. If Griffin stayed to meet the police, he could ask for Ross, and deflect any investigation away from Allie and onto himself.

If he was lucky, Ross would suggest an explanation for the carnage that placed the blame on warring mobsters, exactly where it belonged. The likelihood that a pair of bystanders could wreak such havoc would seem wildly improbable to any but the most well-informed officials.

But if they called Griffin a murderer, if they refused to believe he had acted in self-defense—it was not so very far from the truth—but at least Griffin would face his accusers knowing that Allegra was free.

And that he would never have to see her terrible face again.

IT WAS THE LOOK in Griffin's eyes that broke Allie's stupor.

She knew she wasn't thinking straight even as she fled the building, the taste of blood still on her tongue. Her mind was full of a predator's thoughts, dismissing the dog she'd left behind as she might brush an ant from her shoulder; her body was a live wire acutely sensitive to every sound, smell and sight with which she came in contact.

This was what it was to be *strigoi*...this powerful, this strong, this swift. This invincible.

She let her emotions take her, running through the darkness in her torn gown and red-stained hands. Her bare feet hardly touched the pavement; her eyes teased out the secrets behind every shadow, the shames and sorrows humans so feared to acknowledge. The few people she passed flinched in instinctive terror; a priest crossed himself, as if his faith could save him.

They were as insects. She laughed at the pathetic creatures that believed they ruled the world. She laughed at Raoul, who controlled *strigoi* procreation because he feared drawing too much human attention and placing the clan at risk. How could he not see that *they* were the chosen people, humanity perfected, the very culmination of a million years of evolution?

Allie slowed, her toes brushing through soft grass. Trees rose about her, and she realized she walking in the grove in Central Park where she had cast Cato's ashes to the wind not so long ago. Bitter memory sent her plunging from the heights of ecstasy, weighting her like chains. Her legs buckled. She knelt beneath the trees, earthbound once again, and the images of victory that had seemed so thrilling crumbled into abomination.

I have killed.

She remembered every detail: how she had found the gunmen abusing a girl several years younger than Gemma, how she'd given them the chance to surrender, how they'd laughed. It had been so easy to evade their weapons, to counter their clumsy attacks and reach vulnerable flesh. At first she had held back, restrained by the threads of her former humanity. But then one of the men had grabbed the child to use as a shield, and all thoughts of mercy had fled.

After it was over, a raging thirst had come upon her, and she had thought only of feeding. She had not been enough in her right mind to recognize the compulsion that bade her take the blood of the vanquished; she had never experienced such a savage encounter before. But now her thoughts were clear, and she understood what Cato had once tried to explain.

"Not all blood is alike," he had told her. *"For sus-*

tenance alone it is enough to take from a passive donor, as we do throughout most of our lives. This does no harm to those who provide our essential sustenance, and so balance is maintained.

"But in every age of history, there have been strigoi *who are drawn to conflict...who either seek it out or create it themselves. Humans caught up in violence and heightened emotion produce chemicals in the blood that are like the elixir of the gods to our kind... substances that act upon us like the most potent drug. It is an addiction, more terrible than any human could ever imagine...."*

Allie dropped her head into her stained hands. She knew well enough the pleasure that came from taking blood from a donor who was sexually aroused. But now she'd tasted the blood of violence...violence in which she herself had participated. For a few heady moments she had believed that she could rule the world.

"They are false, the emotions that come from such feeding," Cato had said. *"And taking the blood of violence exacts a terrible price. For the* strigoi *who succumbs will find little nourishment in what he has stolen. He will suffer such pain that he will be driven again and again to acquire more of his drug."*

Shaking as if with fever, Allie got to her feet and wandered aimlessly through the park. The effects of her feeding had not quite worn off; she could still feel the lingering euphoria even as her stomach began to cramp with unappeased hunger.

She'd been so sure, so very sure that becoming a vampire was the best thing that had ever happened in her life. Her disease was gone. She enjoyed perfect health, strength, beauty—all the things she needed to make an independent life she alone could control. If other *strigoi* gloried in the evil reputation of legend, what was that to her? *She* was in it for herself, and only for herself....

Until she had wakened from a dream of ecstasy and realized that she had become a thing she couldn't have imagined in her wildest nightmares.

Allie staggered to the nearest tree and heaved, but the sickness of memory could not be expunged so easily. Memory of the bodies sprawled around her, limbs splayed and faces slack. Memory she would carry with her every time she took what she must have to live.

With a cry of anguish, Allie turned from the accusing silence of the park, racing for the safety of her apartment on Fifth Avenue. The cramping in her stomach had become something worse, as if the gunmen's blood had not only failed to nourish her but had increased her normal hunger a hundredfold.

This was more than hunger. This was a foretaste of the blood starvation that could kill a *strigoi* in a matter of days or even hours.

Stumbling to the bathroom, she ripped off her gown and scrubbed at her skin until it was almost raw. No amount of washing could make her feel clean again. She smeared lipstick across her mouth, put on a short dress loaded with fringe and beads, and slid on a pair of red patent pumps that practically shouted sex.

The dive she chose was too humble to have its own band. A barely competent pianist banged away at the keys while ill-shaven men danced with floozies who wore more paint than a circus clown. Allie grabbed a whiskey at the bar and struck a blatantly seductive pose.

It didn't take long for someone to take the bait. The man was coarse, brawny and completely lacking in the slightest trace of chivalry. Still, in spite of his worn clothes, he exuded good health; he would serve Allie's needs with no fuss or consequences to haunt her when it was over.

She went with him to his tiny apartment. The sheer ugliness of the place matched her mood exactly. She let him paw and fondle her, accepting the punishment as her just due. She endured his obscene attempts to excite himself with crude references to her anatomy and lay passively on his bed, feeling nothing as she waited to steal his blood.

But then something changed. She began to hate the sight of his empty eyes and his casual brutality. When he crawled on top of her, it was as if her entire being revolted, rejecting him as if her vampire flesh were trying to cast off some nasty human disease. When he seized her hair and tried to throw her back on the bed, she grabbed him by the throat and came within an inch of breaking his neck.

If she killed him now, his blood would give her everything she so desperately craved. All she had to do was strangle him, slowly, and drink while he died.

So easy. So very, very easy.

Then she remembered Griffin's expression when he'd found her—the shock and revulsion, the horror of watching a tame tigress become a man-eater before his very eyes.

Allie threw the man to the ground and stumbled from the apartment. She walked the streets for the rest of the night, her thoughts growing more cold and clear as her body grew increasingly weak.

What had Griffin been doing while she was dealing

with her prey? What had happened to him after he'd ordered her to run? She'd fled the building, so lost in her ecstatic dreams that his welfare had held no more meaning for her than that of a cockroach in the sewers. Had he escaped, or remained behind to deal with the police?

He would have been crazy to stay. She remembered seeing blood on his hands, and he'd been naked; he hadn't come out of the fight unscathed. The cops could charge him with murder. His friend Ross Kavanagh might pull a few strings to protect him, but they could still hold him, put him in a cell, interrogate him....

Allie gathered her strength and made her way back to her apartment, ignoring the stabs of pain beneath her ribs. Dawn was breaking when she dialed Oakdene.

Griffin's butler answered. Allie asked for Griffin without giving her name. The edge of worry in Starke's voice when he replied that Griffin wasn't there told Allie all she needed to know. Ross Kavanagh was next on her list. She had to go through several subordinates to get to him, and when he answered, he was anything but cordial.

"Kavanagh."

"I'm calling about Griffin Durant. Is he there?"

"Who is this?"

"A friend. I heard he might have been in some sort of dustup."

"What friend?"

She released her breath, fighting her growing lassitude. "Allegra Chase."

"Oh, yeah. The mysterious lady vampire Griffin's so reluctant to talk about."

"Is he all right?"

She could practically hear the suspicion at the other end of the line. "Were you involved in this business?"

"I was with him last night." Kavanagh's silence accused her more surely than any words. "Is Griffin there?"

"Yes."

"What did he say about the fight?"

"Enough to suggest he had legitimate reasons for getting himself mixed up in it."

Allie collapsed onto the sofa, no longer able to stand. "He's not under arrest?"

"Not at the moment. He wasn't armed, and several people in the building came forward to testify that he'd defended them from the men who attacked De Luca." Kavanagh's voice took on a cynical edge. "De Luca's paying his debts. He's laying some pressure on certain higher-ups to ignore Grif's involvement. In any case, no one's going to believe that one man managed to overcome a whole squad of triggermen."

"No one found out…they didn't see…"

"No one said anything about you, including Grif."

"But Griffin must have Changed."

"If anyone saw it happen, they aren't talking."

Thank God, if He's still listening. "How many… how many died?"

"All of them."

She nearly dropped the receiver. "But Griffin…he would never—"

"*He* wouldn't, unless he had no other choice. What about you, Miss Chase?"

Allie's fingers went numb. "I never meant—"

"Whatever you meant, several of the men had injuries severe enough to cause their deaths. The others died suddenly when we brought them in. The coroner thinks it was some kind of poison."

"Poison?" She rested her forehead against the telephone table. "Do you know who the men were?"

"Don't you?"

"I'd never seen them before."

"You must have noticed the tattoos."

Allie focused again on what she'd seen during and after the fight. "Yes. They were crude, not like any I've ever seen."

"The kind vampires use to mark their human servants."

Allie couldn't deny it, but she was only now thinking straight enough to realize how bizarre the entire situation was.

"Why would vampires send humans to ambush De Luca?" she asked.

"You tell me."

"Raoul would have to be crazy to try it." She massaged her forehead, forcing herself to talk through the pain. "You know about the situation with Margot?"

"A nice little can of worms. Still, it seems excessive for Raoul to go after De Luca with no evidence that Carmine had anything to do with Margot's disappearance."

Excessive? It was insane. "Does De Luca know about the tattoos and how the men died?"

"No. And I don't intend to tell him. Very few in the department beside myself know what's really at stake."

"Then as far as he knows, it could be a rival human syndicate who attacked him."

"Unless De Luca's got some connections I don't know about."

Allie closed her eyes. "You're a good friend to Griffin. Thank you."

"Right now he needs his friends. What he doesn't need is more trouble."

"Do you mean me, Mr. Kavanagh?"

"Good guess."

"Because I'm not your kind?"

"I don't give a damn about that. I know something strange is going on. Grif's up to his neck in it, and you're a wild card I can't account for."

"I'd never do him any harm, Mr. Kavanagh."

"Then maybe you should leave him alone. You're a bad influence. Whatever those stupid legends say, werewolves don't enjoy killing."

"It isn't exactly natural for *us* to enjoy—" She caught herself. *What the hell do I know about what's natural for vampires anymore?*

"I know Griffin hates violence," she said wearily.

"He had to do some pretty terrible things in the War. He was decorated for his courage, and he saved a lot of lives, but it made him a little crazy, especially after what happened to his family."

Allie wrapped her arms around herself to ward off a sudden chill. "What happened?"

Kavanagh hesitated. "If it'll make you understand…Grif's family lived in San Francisco when he was a kid. His mom and dad were only loosely affiliated with the dominant pack there. The situation wasn't easy for them, but they held on to their independence—until someone came after them. Griffin was away when someone trapped his parents and older brother inside the house and set it on fire. He was only able to save his little sister."

"Oh, God. Other werewolves did it?"

"Who else would have a motive?" Kavanagh covered his receiver and spoke to someone in his office. "I have business to attend to, Miss Chase. At least maybe now you understand what Griffin's been through, what last night was like for him. And why you should leave him alone."

And why should I understand? Allie thought bitterly. *I'm a vampire. What do mortal lives mean to us?*

"Thank you, Mr. Kavanagh," she said coldly. "I'll keep your advice in mind."

She hung up, slowly unclenching her fingers from around the receiver. Griffin was safe and in the clear; there was no danger that the police would hold him responsible for the carnage in the tenement.

And now she had another piece in the puzzle that was Griffin Durant. No wonder he distrusted the New York pack, if his own kind had killed his family. Then there was the Great War. *He had to do some terrible things.* Was that why he couldn't abide the wolf, even in himself?

How can I ever accept what I'm *capable of?*

How Raoul would laugh to see her so anguished over something he would hardly consider worth a moment's thought. She could almost hear him now. *Now you see where you belong. Stop fighting it, Allie. Rejoice in what you are. Live as you were meant to live. Come to me....*

She sank down on the sofa and crossed her arms against her ribs. Hunger had begun to demand all her attention, and yet she couldn't bring herself to go out in search of what she must have to survive. Even the idea of hunting seemed an obscenity.

I'm going to die, she thought. The idea brought little regret. A few people might miss her. No one else would mourn.

And Griffin would never have to see her again.

"Oh, hell." She got up, wobbled across the room and poured herself a huge glass of whiskey. If she had to go, she might as well enjoy her last few hours.

She lifted the glass. "To you, Griffin Durant. May you find your peace."

CHAPTER FOURTEEN

"WHAT'S WRONG WITH HIM, Uncle Edward?" Gemma whispered.

The butler gazed up the stairs, pinching his chin between his thumb and forefinger. "I wish I could tell you, Miss Gemma," he said. "He has refused to eat or leave his rooms since he returned from Manhattan early this morning."

Gemma hugged herself. "I saw him when he came in. I haven't seen him look that way since—" She shivered. "I'm afraid something awful has happened."

Edward got that stubborn look on his face that Gemma remembered from her earliest childhood. "Whatever it may be, Miss Gemma, your brother is sure to emerge in his own good time. And if he does not put in an appearance at dinner, I shall take it upon myself to inquire after his health."

"Will you, Uncle Edward? I'd do it myself, but I don't think he really wants to see me."

"Nonsense. Griffin has had a great deal on his mind."

A great deal including me, Gemma thought, escaping the tomblike stillness of the house with one of Demetria's egg-salad sandwiches. She took the hasty lunch with her more out of habit than any desire to eat; worry always made her stomach knot up, and she couldn't stop worrying about Griffin.

Yesterday she'd been terribly angry with him. The humiliation of watching him run Wyatt off and chastise her again was almost more than she could bear. It was obvious he would never understand her, that he couldn't remember what it was like to be young. She'd started to wonder if Griffin had ever been young at all.

But then she thought of the family she'd never known—Father and Mother and Will, all lost to the fire—and knew Griffin couldn't always have been this way. She even had to admit that she'd caught glimpses of a different Griffin sometimes, especially when Allie had come to her party.

Gemma crossed the lawn and started away from the house on the tree-lined gravel drive that wound toward the village and the main road. She took a thoughtful bite of her sandwich. She hadn't spoken to Allie since the party; she knew that Griffin had been angry with Allie, but at the same time, she was convinced that something was going on between them. Maybe Griffin had been out seeing her, and they'd had another argument.

One thing was for certain: Griffin never confided in his sister. If only he would let her help, he would see that she was mature enough to set the course for her own life.

The sound of wheels grinding on the drive diverted Gemma's attention from her worries. A boy on a bicycle was approaching at a reckless speed, his cap pulled low over his eyes and his arms extended to either side, as if he were deliberately hoping to crash into the nearest tree.

Gemma stepped out of the way, watching curiously. Abruptly the boy caught the handles, braked and planted his high-top sneakers in the gravel. He tipped up the brim of his cap.

"You Gemma Durant?" he asked.

"Who wants to know?"

He grinned. "Yeah, you're her, all right."

She sniffed and narrowed her eyes. "I remember you. Robbie Kinsale, from the village."

"Yeah." He looked her up and down. "You've grown up nice, Durant. Very nice."

"And you haven't changed, Kinsale."

He shrugged. "You got a new boyfriend, Durant?"

"What's it to you?"

He fished inside his jacket pocket. "I have a letter from some guy who paid me to deliver it to you. Fella named Wyatt Demp—"

She was on him before he could finish the sentence, snatching the crumpled paper from his hand. "When did he give it to you?"

He raised both hands as if to ward her off. "Whoa there, Nellie. He showed up last night."

"Is he still in the village?"

"How should I know? He *said* he'd come back to-morrow morning to see if you had an answer for him."

It was all Gemma could do not to shout questions at Robbie, demanding to know how Wyatt had looked, how he'd acted, what he'd said. She assumed an air of quiet dignity and tucked the letter in the pocket of her skirt.

"I'll have an answer for Mr. Dempsey ready by to-night. Can you meet me here around nine? I'll make it worth your while."

"Dempsey paid me two bucks."

"I'll double that."

"Done."

"Good. And whatever you do, don't let my brother see you."

"That's what Dempsey said." He rolled his eyes. "Romeo and Juliet. How rom*an*tic."

"Just wait until you leave childhood, Kinsale."

He snorted, jerked the bike around and pushed off in a spray of gravel. Gemma waited until he was out of sight around the bend before she found shelter beneath an elm, sat with her back to the trunk and pulled the letter from her pocket.

She read through the two scribbled pages in breathless haste, lower lip between her teeth, and then read them again more slowly. When she was finished, she laid the sheets in her lap and stared at nothing, her thoughts awhirl with everything Wyatt had told her.

Apparently Mal had disappeared. He'd vanished from the face of the earth, and Griffin had been trying to find him for weeks. Not only that, but Griffin had gone to see Garret Sloan and accused him or someone in the pack of kidnapping Mal for unknown reasons, and now the pack leader was in a fury.

All this Wyatt had learned when he'd overheard some of the elder *loups-garous* discussing Griffin's visit, and he'd felt it was necessary to find out if Gemma knew what her brother was doing. He was worried about her, about the trouble Griffin might get not only himself but her into by goading Garret with wild accusations.

"No one here had anything to do with this guy's disappearance," Wyatt had assured her. "Maybe you can make your brother see that."

Gemma gave a bitter laugh. *How can I make him see anything, especially once he has an idea in his head?*

She refolded the letter, tucked it away and returned to the house by a circuitous path, weighing the possible consequences of her next decision. Griffin had to be very upset to do what he'd done…upset enough to risk drawing the pack's ire when he'd been so careful to maintain his neutrality. And that meant he must believe that Mal really was in danger.

He wouldn't have gone to Garret unless he'd exhausted every other possible explanation for Mal's disappearance, but he wasn't perfect. He could have missed something vitally important just because he was so personally involved.

What he needs is a fresh perspective, she thought, *but he'll never accept it willingly.*

She continued into the house and looked for Uncle Edward, who was talking in low tones with Demetria in the kitchen. "Miss Gemma?" he said, when he saw her hovering in the doorway.

"Can I speak with you, Uncle Edward?"

"Of course." He followed her into the summer parlor and waited while she took a seat on the sofa. "Is something troubling you, my dear?"

"Has Griffin come out of his room?"

"Not yet, Miss Gemma. We must give him a little more time."

"Of course. It's just…" She scuffed at the carpet with the toe of her shoe. "I've been thinking about what you said…Griffin having so much on his mind these days. I know I've been a burden to him lately—"

"Now, Miss Gemma—"

"It's true. He can't stop worrying about me as long as I'm around. I know he said he wanted me back from England, but…" She sighed. "Uncle Edward, I think I should go away for a little while. Susannah Spiegel invited me to spend the summer with her and her family in the Catskills. I could be ready to leave as soon as she gives the word."

Uncle Edward frowned. "Don't you think this is a bit sudden, Gemma? You haven't even spoken to your brother. I'm sure when you've seen him—"

"I know it would be a relief to him, Uncle. I'd like some time away. And I like Susannah, even though we haven't known each other long. She's not like most of the other girls on Long Island." She smiled winningly. "Would you speak to Griffin for me? Please?"

He gave her a long, considering look and slowly nodded. "Very well. I'll approach him this evening."

She jumped up from the sofa. "Thank you, Uncle Edward." She rushed up to him, kissed his cheek and hurried away before he could detect the incongruous level of her excitement. Once in her room, she shut the door, pulled several pieces of stationery from her writing desk and gently smoothed the fine-milled paper with the palm of her hand.

There were a great many things to arrange, of course, before she could begin her own investigation. First she had to make sure that Wyatt was willing to help, and that she could arrange a place to meet with him in Manhattan. Then she had to secure Susannah's aid…which shouldn't be any problem at all, since Susannah shared her yearning for adventure and her disdain for the prehistoric attitudes of the older generation.

After that, the most difficult part would be over. And if she could find one clue, one single piece of information that Griffin had overlooked…why, he would never be able to dismiss her as a helpless child again.

THE HOURS PASSED in a blur. Allie found that the longer she went without feeding and the more she drank, the better she felt. It was as if just giving up had brought her a measure of peace. Her body had stopped fighting. It didn't hurt so much now; she was even able to get up and open another bottle of whiskey.

The only thing she still regretted was not being able to call Griffin and say goodbye.

She was lying on the bed, letting herself drift into a strangely pleasant state of indifference, when she heard banging on the front door. She would have ignored the racket if it hadn't been for the sound of someone actually breaking down the door. Footsteps whispered in the hallway, following a rush of cool night air.

"Griffin," Allie whispered.

He stopped in the doorway, face flushed, hair awry, hands gripping the door frame as if he might pull the building down around their ears. Allie knew at once that he'd been running as a wolf; his coat and vest were missing, his shirt hung open and collarless at the neck, and his feet were bare. His eyes still blazed with a feral light, as if his course had finally brought him to the prey he had been seeking.

"What was it like?" he demanded hoarsely.

Allie got up, as dizzy as if she'd been struck. "Griffin, are you—"

"What was it like when you killed those men? Did you enjoy it?"

She remembered to breathe only when she realized how much she craved another shot of whiskey. "Would you like a drink?" she asked.

Griffin followed her into the living room, his heat burning into her back. "I asked you a question."

Allie stopped at the sideboard and poured herself a glass. "What would you like me to say? Are you here to condemn me or absolve me of my sins?"

He clenched and unclenched his fists, lips stretched over his teeth like a beast fighting its instinct to spring. "The blood…you fed…"

She dropped the empty glass. It bounced across the carpet, unbroken.

"What a novel idea," she said with a shaky laugh. "Imagine a vampire who drinks blood."

Griffin's chest rose and fell as he gulped great lungfuls of air. "Tell me. Tell me you didn't…it wasn't—" He dragged his hands over his face. "Oh, God."

The sense of false well-being that had cradled her minutes before melted away. It should have been easy to mock him, to hurt him as she was hurting. But the anguish in his eyes filled her heart with the bitter taste of poison.

"No," she said, her voice deliberately devoid of emotion. "I've never done anything like that before. Yes, I enjoyed it."

Griffin covered his mouth with a trembling hand and looked around the room as if he'd forgotten how he'd come to be there. "I don't believe you," he said hoarsely. "You couldn't have—" his expression hardened "—you couldn't have enjoyed it."

"How can you be so sure?"

"Because I know you. I *know* you."

"You thought you knew me. Now that you've seen what I really am, you don't have to pretend anymore."

"God, Allie…" The haze of anger and confusion faded from his eyes. "You weren't in your right mind."

It would be so easy to take the escape he offered, accept that what had happened was a fluke, never to be repeated.

"You'd better go," she said, despair giving her a last burst of strength.

"I can't. Not until I know you're all right."

"Something tells me I'm better off than you."

Griffin gazed at her, disbelief in his eyes. "If I could help…if I could make this easier…"

She shrugged, wanting him gone, wanting him to take her in his arms. "I can't change what I am," she said. "All I can do is make sure it never happens again."

Griffin flinched as if she'd showered him with curses. "I beg your pardon," he said. "I shouldn't have come." He backed away toward the door. "I'll have a locksmith here first thing in the morning."

Allie almost laughed aloud. He didn't know there would be no morning for her. She pried herself from the chair, caught her balance and stopped Griffin halfway to the door. She dug her fingers into the sleeves of his shirt, tearing at the buttons, and seized his mouth with hers.

The kiss wasn't meant to be friendly. Allie clutched the back of Griffin's neck, scratching his skin with her nails, and nipped his lower lip as if she would draw blood. He responded instantly, pulling her against him as he lifted her off her feet. He thrust with his tongue, as hard and as ruthless as she in his desire; she wrapped her legs around his hips, feeling the hardness beneath the thin wool of his trousers. He threaded his fingers through her hair, pulling her head back to expose her neck, and licked her skin from jaw to collarbone. She pulled his shirt apart and spread her fingers across his chest, her palms vibrating with the frantic beating of his heart.

He turned so that her back was against the door, his hands stroking up her bare thighs and beneath the hem of her dress. Beads rattled and fringe trembled. She was already warm and wet; she'd deliberately done without underthings, and as Griffin forced her thighs apart, she worked at the buttons of his trousers. He slid hot and heavy into her hand.

It was happening at last, the thing she'd been thinking about from the moment she'd met him. Finally it would be over and done with, fast and furious, without the burdens of sentiment or implied commitment. No pretense, no morality, just sheer, unadulterated lust between two people who knew exactly what they wanted.

One last, glorious fling.

"Now, Griffin," Allie panted, her face pressed into his shoulder. "Now. *Now*—"

Everything stopped. Griffin reared back, his eyes dark with something very like horror. He released Allie, letting her slide to the floor as he smoothed her dress down over her hips.

"I'm not an animal," he whispered. He fumbled at the buttons of his trousers and turned away, shaking like a man in the grip of the influenza. "No. I'm worse than an animal. *I* know what I'm doing." He swung about, his face contorted into a mask of loathing and self-contempt. "Don't you see? It's not you, Allie. It's me. *I* am the monster."

GRIFFIN CUPPED THE GLASS between his hands and stared down into the honey-colored liquid, his sense of smell overwhelmed by the liquor's fragrance. Until a few weeks ago, when he and Allie had gone looking for Mal, he hadn't touched the stuff for nearly nine years. Tonight he was tempted to throw sobriety to the winds once more.

Allie sat across from him on an oversized chair, her legs tucked under her, a silk wrap drawn around her shoulders. She didn't look like a woman who'd nearly been ravaged by a man lost to all reason; except for a few glossy black hairs out of place and the bruising on her lips, she might have been enjoying a quiet evening at home. Her expression was calm, her eyes untroubled. It was as if nothing could touch her.

That was the only thing that made it possible for Griffin to speak at all.

"I blamed you," he said. "For a few hours I allowed myself to believe that you might be something worse than I ever was…a creature I might despise as more worthy of contempt than myself. But the thought tormented me, Allie." He met her gaze, almost yearning for her condemnation. "It drove me mad to know that I—"

"That you were wrong about me," Allie said quietly. "You never thought you and I would be in a position where I'd have to show what one of my kind can do. You had an idea about me…maybe it wasn't such a great idea at the beginning, but at least my flaws seemed human."

Griffin set down his glass untouched, bile thick in his throat. "Nothing in the world will convince me that you're a murderer."

"You saw what I did."

He almost went to her then, but nothing in her attitude suggested that she would welcome any comfort from him. "It was an aberration. I *know*."

They stared at each other in silence. Gradually the stiffness went out of Allie's shoulders. She sagged in her chair, her posture unutterably weary.

"You were right," she said. "I didn't know what I was doing. But I'm still to blame."

Griffin looked down at the carpet, unable to bear the bleak mirror of her face. "If you are, then I'm even more so."

"Because you saved a kid and kept more innocent people from being hurt? That hardly makes you a monster."

"I've said enough." He rose from the sofa and started again for the door. "I hope in time you'll forgive me."

"I know about the War," she said.

Her voice stopped him like a hail of bullets. He turned to gaze out the window at the lights of the buildings on the other side of Central Park. The smells of early summer flowed into the room: pavement still radiating heat after a sweltering day, grass and leaves and earth from the park, a faint whiff of sour water from the East River.

"Who told you?" he asked.

"Don't blame Kavanagh. He was trying to convince me to stay away from you." The beads on her dress clinked and rustled as she poured herself another drink. "That's why you hate violence. Why you hate yourself."

She spoke gently, as if she knew he hadn't spoken of the War to anyone but Ross, Mal and Edward since the Armistice. The things he had seen and done in the heat of battle could not be explained to anyone who didn't know what he was.

Allie knew. She'd seen what he could become when control was lost, when lust and rage consumed reason and restraint.

He would have said she could never understand what it meant to be a soldier, to live with disease and mayhem and death every hour of every day. But in this very room Miss Moreau had told him of Allie's miserable past, how she had fought against impossible odds of rejection, constant pain and impending extinction.

And she had fallen victim to the dark side of herself. Perhaps no one could understand better than she.

"Don't think I suffered," he said. "Not like the others, the common doughboys who died in the trenches by the thousands. I was privileged in so many ways. I had wealth, an officer's rank, and I wasn't human." He closed his eyes. "Do you know what a battlefield is like, Allie? You can't escape the smell of rot…rotting food, vegetation, flesh. Then there's the odor of sewage that has nowhere to go, the effluvia of sickness, the stench of gangrene…"

He paused, aware that he'd already forgotten to whom he was speaking. "I'm sorry. I shouldn't speak of such things."

Allie's face was a shade paler than it had been. "I asked," she said.

"There's no reason for you to endure this."

"Let me be the judge of that. Go on."

He faced the window again, seeing in the distant lights the tiny cook-fires of a desperate enemy. So much of it had been tedium…the breaks in the fighting, when soldiers snatched precious minutes to catch their breaths and smoke and share grim jokes, never knowing when the next order to advance would come down from on high.

In some ways the waiting was the worst. Then there was the sickness that wore down so many brave men and stole their courage or their lives. The poison gas that destroyed their lungs. The bleakness of miles of mud where everything living had been trampled into a indistinguishable mess.

"At least I had a way of escaping the trenches," he said. "A wolf can travel silently where men can't. I spent the better part of every night patrolling the lines because I couldn't stand the stink of my own men."

Allie's voice came from a great distance. "You must have suffered twice as much as the humans."

But she was wrong. Terribly wrong. When disease cut down young boys in the prime of youth, it didn't touch him. He had a *loup-garou*'s immunity, his ability to heal counteracting the grinding illnesses that jumped from man to man in their filthy bunkers. He'd watched boys choke on their own vomit and burn up with fever, going blind and coughing out their lungs under clouds of chlorine gas.

"There was nothing I could do," he said. "Nothing. Nothing."

"How old were you when you joined up? Seventeen? Eighteen?"

Oh, yes. He'd been raw and foolish, but he was old enough to send young men to their deaths because incompetent generals considered common soldiers no better than cannon fodder. He'd tried not to abandon them, even when there was no hope. But the risk for him had never been what it was for them.

He charged onto the battlefield, and it was as if an invisible shield had fallen around him. Instinct saved him a hundred times, his senses and swiftness sparing him the attacks of enemy soldiers and the impact of grenades and mortars.

When the orders came down to advance, he had tried to lead them. But they died. The shrapnel took their arms and legs and faces. They screamed and wept as he held them in his arms. And when the retreat sounded, dozens would be left on the field while he limped back to the trenches with his minor wounds, only to heal in hours or days.

The men had laughed and said his "luck" was proof that they would get home alive.

"The one time I came close to dying," he said, "Mal saved me. He was brave and reckless and utterly loyal to his mates. His good cheer kept the men from despair when things were at their worst.

He would have fought the devil himself to save a single fellow soldier."

"And you never did anything like that…you, who went into a tenement crawling with gunmen to save a child you didn't know?"

"I didn't save that child," Griffin whispered. "He died on the way to the hospital."

Allie lifted her hand as if she might touch him and let it fall again. "You did everything you could."

"I did what I swore I'd never do again." He shivered, ears ringing with the pounding of artillery and whining of bullets…and the screams. Always the screams.

The first time had been at the Battle of the Somme. He'd faced the enemy and remembered every man he couldn't save, every boy who'd died when he'd lived. On that day he'd chosen to forget the rules by which humans waged their wars. He'd gone behind enemy lines after dark…

He braced his arms against the sofa, fighting dry heaves. "I was out of my mind, but no court of law would exonerate me for what I did. One morning just before dawn I found myself lying naked in a pool of blood, and I knew what I'd become. I crawled back to our trench. The men hadn't seen what I'd become. They thought I'd been killed. They laughed and crowded around me…" He sucked air through clenched teeth. It had taken him years to wash off that blood. Years of trying to make an ordinary life as a productive member of society. As a civilized being.

"As an ordinary human," Allie said.

"No," he said. He sat down heavily, every muscle trembling. "I knew I could never be a real part of society. But Gemma…I knew she must never discover that side of herself, that thing—"

"That part that exists in all of us." Allie sighed and sank deeper into her chair. She'd grown even paler, her cheekbones standing out in harsh relief, her eyes deeply shadowed.

Griffin took a step toward her. "You're not well."

"I'm better than you are. Sit down."

"I should have known better—"

"Than to tell me the truth?" She met his gaze. "I know why you did what you did during the War, why you went into that tenement. It was because of the fire."

He froze as if she'd thrown a grenade into his path. "Kavanagh."

"Yes." She shivered and drew her wrap more tightly about her shoulders. "You watched your family die, and there was nothing you could do to stop it."

He stared past her. The screams. He could still hear them calling from inside the house, dying, beyond his reach. Gemma had wailed in his arms, pounding her little fists against his chest and crying out for her mama; when the neighbors came to take her, he plunged back into the fire. Twice he tried, but the smoke and the heat of the flames stopped him, searing his flesh until it blackened.

They told him later that he'd refused to eat or drink for days afterward, that the doctors who cared for him and Gemma feared for his sanity. All he'd said, over and over, was "I should have been with them. I should have been with them.…"

"I'd had some kind of argument with my father that morning," he said, part of him still standing outside the house on Nob Hill. "I went down to the waterfront to watch the boats. The servants had the day off. No one was in the house but my parents, Gemma and William. If I'd been there—"

"Do you really think you could have made a difference?" She leaned forward and fell back again, catching her breath. "You did everything you could to save them. Everything a man could do."

"But why was I spared? I should have been with them."

"If you had, Gemma would be dead."

Her bald words sliced into his gut like the blade of a bayonet. "If she hadn't been in her bed near the window where I could reach her…"

"But she was." Allie stood, bracing her hands on the arms of the chair. "You asked why you were spared. How many lives did you save in the War?"

"I was useless to them. I lived while they died."

"You were a decorated hero credited with saving dozens of men."

"Not enough," he said, shaking his head back and forth. "Never enough."

"So you've spent your life living the day of that fire over and over again, blaming yourself for the deaths of your family. Volunteering for the War gave you the perfect opportunity to get yourself killed. But it didn't turn out that way." She leaned against the wall, breathing deeply. "You became responsible for others weaker than yourself. You had to save them as you hadn't been able to save your parents and brother—however you had to do it."

She spoke with such dispassion, as if it were nothing at all to expose his innermost soul with a few simple phrases. She had seen through him as if he were made of glass, ready to shatter.

"There's a beast in all of us," she said. "Most of the time it stays in its cage. But you and me…" She paused, pressing both palms on the wall behind her.

"When it does come out it's like someone's been holding a finger in the dike and suddenly lets go."

Griffin raised his head, his senses so attuned to her that he smelled her tears before he saw them.

Allegra Chase was weeping. And *strigoi* didn't cry.

All at once the confusion and torment of his memories crumbled and were forgotten. Allie turned her back as he reached for her. He put his arms around her, pulling her against his chest, pressing his cheek to her hair.

"Allie," he whispered. "Forgive me. Forgive me for failing you."

She stood rigid in his embrace, her face averted. "You didn't fail me. You're not responsible."

"I was worse than stupid. I was so blinded by what happened in the tenement that I didn't let myself see how deeply you would be affected. You were lost, and I abandoned you."

She tried to shake him off, but he refused to let her go. "The fight with those men," he said. "You said nothing like that ever happened to you before."

"No," she said in a small voice. "Never like that."

"Then is it any wonder that you didn't know how to deal with your power and the instincts that live inside you?" He gripped her shoulders. "Maybe I was trying to keep you away from danger because I feared what would happen if you ever had to fight for survival. I never wanted…" He brushed his lips across her hair. "Forgive me, Allie."

She bent her head so that her chin touched his arms. "I can't forgive myself."

"I can't believe you did what you did without reason."

"There…there was a girl…they were hurting her."

"Then you didn't act without some cause. They

were bad men, Allie." He turned her around and cupped her face between his hands. "You mustn't continue to torment yourself. Today you've made me see what was hidden from me for fifteen years. Maybe we were meant to help each other, Allie. Not only today, but for the rest of our lives."

She went still, her heart suspended between beats as if time itself had come to a halt. He couldn't have meant what he'd just said. If he were any other man, she would have considered it a joke.

His eyes told her that he wasn't joking. His expression had changed to a kind of half-bewildered wonderment, as if even he hadn't expected to say something so utterly fantastic.

She managed to work her way out of his arms and walked unsteadily to the other side of the room. "What time is it?" she asked, her thoughts beginning to blur. "My mother always told me I should never have men in my room after 2:00 a.m."

Griffin didn't laugh. "I'm in earnest, Allie. As much in earnest as I've ever been about anything in my life."

"And I'm…very flattered," she said thickly, making a wide and clumsy circle toward the sideboard. "I just never saw myself as anyone's mistress."

Griffin's face flushed and then went white. "Mistress? Is that what you think I—" He caught himself. "I care about you, Allie. I want you to be my wife."

The bottle of whiskey shook in Allie's hand. "For God's sake, Griffin. Think what you're saying." She poured with difficulty and clutched the glass, fearing it might slip from her fingers. "It's the middle of the night. You should go home and rest."

His stare was direct and unflinching. "I haven't lost

my reason. I'm finally seeing myself clearly. You made that possible. I want to make things possible for you."

"You don't owe me anything, let alone the rest of your life."

"Is the idea so repugnant to you, Allie?"

She tossed off the whiskey and swayed with sudden weakness. "Did it ever occur to you that you're saying all this because you think you took advantage of me tonight?"

"That has nothing to do with—"

"I knew exactly what I was doing." She blew out her breath. "It's not that I don't think you're a nice guy. But just look at me." She set down her glass and stood facing him, hands on hips, shoulders cocked back. "Do I look like somebody's wife?"

"You look beautiful, as always."

"No. *Look* at me. Can you see me strolling arm in arm with Mrs. Higgenbotham or Miss Pomeroy at some North Shore regatta? Giving genteel little teas for the local matrons? Listening to opera singers at dull evening parties? It's not the way I live, Griffin. It never will be."

"Are you so sure it's the way *I* want to live?"

"It's what you want for Gemma. You wouldn't insist that she submit to it if *you* couldn't."

His expression was grave. "You make a compelling argument, Allegra. But you've left out one very important point. Do you…feel anything for me?"

At that moment Allie would have given anything to be able to run from the room, just as she'd run after that first night she'd brought Griffin home. She stood where she was, ignoring the nausea and dizziness that threatened to knock her off her feet.

"I like you, Griffin," she said slowly. "I like you very

much. I admire you. I want you. But…" She looked away. "What you're asking—I'm not capable of that. Not anymore."

His steady gaze pounded against her like a storm. Her stomach felt as if she'd swallowed a bowlful of nails.

"Please," she whispered. "I—"

Her muscles gave way. Griffin caught her before her body hit the floor.

"Allie?" He cradled her head in his arms, his voice rough with anxiety. "Can you hear me?"

She opened her eyes, trying to focus. "Not…very well."

"You're ill!"

She struggled to stand, but he lifted her and carried her to the sofa, arranging her wrap over her chest and shoulders. He knelt beside the sofa, combing her hair away from her face.

"What's wrong, sweetheart? Tell me how I can help."

The pain in her head was so severe that she couldn't summon up an answer. Griffin pressed his palm to her forehead.

"You're icy cold," he said. "I should call for a doctor.…"

She croaked a laugh. "You know you can't."

"Then tell me what to do."

"It's…it's a vampire sickness. I…haven't fed…"

He leaned closer, his breath warm on her lips. "What have you been doing to yourself?"

"I…it's been almost a week. I meant to do it, but I…"

"The men in the tenement—"

"It…only made things worse." A violent spasm racked her body. Griffin held her until it passed.

"For God's sake, Allie…"

She tried to smile. "My own fault." She broke into a fit of coughing. Griffin wiped at her mouth with a handkerchief and massaged her numb hand between his.

"If it's blood you need," he said, "take mine."

CHAPTER FIFTEEN

GRIFFIN'S OFFER set off an almost uncontrollable hunger in Allie, bidding her to seize him as she had seized De Luca's enemies. She fought off the compulsion and gripped his hand.

"I've…I've never taken werewolf blood. I don't know…"

"Surely my blood isn't so different from a human's. I doubt you could Convert me."

"I doubt it."

"Then there's no reason not to attempt it."

She tried to shake her head, but it was too heavy to lift. She found she wasn't ready to die after all.

"Where?" he asked. "Is the neck best, or is there some other place?"

"The wrist," she whispered.

Griffin raised her and tucked pillows around her to support her body. He sat beside her, rolled his shirt-sleeve up to the elbow and held out his arm.

"Is there something else I should do?" he asked.

In answer she lifted hands like lead weights, clasping his hand and elbow. "You may feel…strange," she said. "There is a chemical in our saliva…it—"

"Don't talk," he said. "Do it."

He didn't move when she pierced his skin. For humans the pain was almost imperceptible and quickly gone. If werewolves were more sensitive to such sensations, Griffin didn't show it. A quiver ran through him as the blood began to flow freely; he was beginning to feel the sensual euphoria that was the *strigoi's* payment to their human prey.

And something was happening to Allie, as well… something more than the relief and growing strength that came in the wake of the feeding. There was nothing easy and impersonal about this exchange, as there would have been with the humans she chose as donors. It was as if Griffin's very blood contained some element that acted on her with a thousand times more potency than the blood of the men taken in violence. Warmth exploded through her body, gathering between her thighs. She moaned, and Griffin echoed the sound with a rough, deep growl. As his blood became part of her, so did his being: his strength, his virility, his soul.

It was too much. Even as she tried to disengage, her body demanded more. Griffin's fingers clasped the back of her neck, willing her to continue. Elation turned to ecstasy. She was one with Griffin—one with him in a way no sexual joining could ever match—yet she knew she could not live another hour unless she felt him moving inside her.

With supreme effort she pulled free, licking the blood from his skin. Almost instantly the small wound on Griffin's wrist began to heal. His lips were slightly parted, his eyes hazed with the same pleasure and hunger she still felt playing along her nerves. Before she could let her rational mind intrude, she kissed him.

He set her back among the pillows before she could draw another breath.

"Allie," he said, her name rumbling in his throat as if he'd searched far to find it. "Are you all right?"

She took his hand and kissed his palm. "Better. Better than all right."

And she realized it was true—in every sense of the word. The influence of the mobsters' blood was gone and wouldn't return. Griffin had truly healed her.

"You have everything you need?" Griffin asked.

"No." She guided his hand to her breast. "I still need you, Griffin. All of you."

She could see the struggle in his eyes as he shook off the influence of her bite. "Is it always like this for you?"

The heat of desire made it impossible for her to think. "What?"

"Do you initiate sex with every man whose blood you take?"

The very calmness of his question cleared her mind like a slap. "I'm not your wife, remember?"

He grabbed her arm as she moved to rise. "It *was* different, wasn't it?"

"What if it was? You obviously don't want to find out what it could be like if we—"

"Rutted like animals in the wilderness?" The wolf's ferocity crouched behind his quiet words. "I won't take you halfway. If I'm to have you, Allie, I want all of you."

She jerked away, threw her legs over the side of the sofa and stalked across the room, every muscle bursting with energy, her heart pumping like a piston. "Thank you, Griffin," she said. "You saved my life tonight. I'm very grateful."

"It's not your gratitude I want." He rolled down his sleeve. "May I call one of your friends to stay with you?"

"No. I've told them to keep away until…until things

are normal again." She rubbed her arms and stared out the window. "Really, I'm fine."

"Then promise me you'll never let anything like this happen again."

"I'll do my best."

He began to speak again, thought better of it and went to the telephone table. "I intend to keep looking for Mal. It would be better if you—"

"Stayed out of this? Forget it. As far as I'm concerned, nothing has changed."

He accepted her lie with calm resignation. "I'm going to the office today. I've neglected my work for the past week, and others depend on the decisions I make." He found a pencil and paper on the table and wrote out a number in a bold, neat hand. "You can reach me at this number should you need anything at all. In the meantime, I strongly suggest you rest."

She followed him to the door. "You've been through hell. Shouldn't you rest, too?"

He met her gaze with terrible honesty. "'A time for war and a time for peace,'" he quoted softly. "I'll talk to Ross and call you when we've determined what to do next."

"And if I think of anything, I'll let you know."

He paused on the threshold, every last trace of vulnerability gone from his face. "Be careful, Allie."

"Same to you. And…thanks again."

"You're welcome. Good night."

"Good night."

He closed the door quietly behind him. Allie listened to his footsteps echoing down the corridor until they were drowned by the hum of the elevator. She went to the window and waited until he appeared in front of the building, a long, dark figure in the waning moonlight. When he'd driven away, she collapsed on the sofa and buried her face in the pillows, muffling her sobs.

Vampires don't cry. They can't.

And they didn't walk in sunlight, or count humans and werewolves among their friends. They didn't have friends at all.

She sat up abruptly, scrubbed at her eyes and stared at the abstract painting on the opposite wall. The energy she'd taken from Griffin's blood continued to course through her like lightning in a lightning rod, searing her nerves. She felt strong enough to lift a truck or scale the Woolworth Building. The desire she'd tried to hold in check threatened to send her climbing the walls instead. And her emotions…

It was the feeding, she told herself. *It affected us both more than I ever could have expected. He wouldn't have proposed if he hadn't fallen under the influence of my bite. It made him a little crazy.*

And *his* blood had done the same to her. That was the only explanation for how she felt now, bawling like some spoiled brat who had put her hand in the cookie jar once too often.

She banged on the back of the sofa with such force that the frame cracked under the blow. *He actually asked me to marry him. As if we'd had a regular court-ship. As if…*

As if he loved me.

She snatched one of her discarded pumps from the floor and threw it at the painting. The canvas clattered to the table below, then landed facedown on the carpet. *Love a girl he's known for a month? Not Griffin Durant. He's far too sensible.*

And he'd never said anything about love, anyway,

had he? He'd said he "cared about her." Such a neat little turn of phrase. She'd let down her guard a little too much, gotten a little too vulnerable, and he'd felt sorry for her.

He thinks I've suffered like he has. But I don't like pain. I'll do anything I can to avoid pain...even his.

But, oh, the anguish in his eyes when he talked about the War, about the fire—as if it were happening all over again and would keep happening until the day he died.

She got up, threw on her coat and left the flat. She crossed the street to Central Park and wandered along the nearest path, hearing Griffin's words repeat in her mind like a broken record. *I won't take you halfway. If I'm to have you, Allie, I want all of you.*

All of her—as if she would ever agree to *belong* to anyone. She'd worked hard to keep herself free of Raoul or any ties that would bind her as her illness had done for those last few years of her human existence.

She must have made *that* point plain enough. Griffin had given up in the end. And if he'd been persistent, she could have presented a dozen more arguments without half trying.

Vampires and werewolves don't marry each other. Both sides would oppose it. Raoul would go crazy with rage, and the pack would consider you an outright threat. Then there's the little matter of age. Would you want someone around who doesn't seem to get any older and is still young when your hair is white? How will you feel when your wife goes out every other night to find suitable donors, most of whom are men? And what about the tenement fight? You may accept what I did, but are you ever going to be able to forget it? Will you spend your life wondering when I might lose control again?

Oh, yes. A dozen arguments, easy. And the biggest argument of all was the one she couldn't tell him.

I've known what it's like to love, Griffin Durant. I got exactly nothing for my trouble. I respect you too much to let you accept an unequal partnership. Because I can't give you what you want.

She looked up at the sky. The moon had sunk below the skyline, and the trees whispered fairy tales that always ended with happily-ever-after. Allie turned back the way she had come and was about to cross the street when a black coupe pulled up at the curb.

Instinct told her who the men were before they got out of the car. She hesitated only a moment and then went to meet them.

"Dorian," she said. "Javier."

"Miss Chase," Dorian said with cool courtesy.

"Would you like to come up with me now, or would you prefer to break in afterward?"

Javier scowled, but Dorian offered the slightest of smiles. "We have no wish to disturb your evening."

"So you're here to take a stroll in the park?"

"Please go on about your business, Miss Chase, and we'll take care of ours."

"Which is watching me." She held Dorian's gaze. "This doesn't have anything to do with the ambush on De Luca a few nights ago?"

Dorian's eyes narrowed. "Raoul doesn't confide the reasons for his orders to us."

"Of course not. No word about Margot?"

"We might ask you the same question."

"Not a thing."

"No help from your canine suitor?" Javier sneered.

"Positively useless. Durant's been good for a few laughs, that's all."

Dorian pushed Javier out of Allie's path. "We won't keep you any longer, Miss Durant."

She grinned and tossed off a mocking salute. "As you were, boys."

She felt them watching as she returned to her apartment and closed the curtains. Whether or not Raoul had instigated the ambush on De Luca, he would certainly have learned all the details of her involvement by now. So far he hadn't chosen to act against her. And as long as his enforcers were out in the open, they weren't likely to try anything.

She retreated to the bedroom, stripped out of her dress and lay naked on the sheets. It was really a pointless ritual; she might walk in sunlight, she might even bawl like a baby, but there wasn't a chance in hell she would fall asleep, let alone dream.

For that she was profoundly grateful.

GEMMA STOOD by the entrance of the speakeasy, hiding her nervousness behind a bored expression and a glass of gin she'd left untouched. The joint was nothing like Lulu's; it was smaller, grimier, and patronized by frowsy women and grizzled men who looked as though they'd each killed several times in the last hour. But Gemma knew this was the right place; Wyatt's scent still lingered in the air, not quite lost beneath the stench of cigarette smoke, sweat and spilled liquor.

"Don't like the taste of our booze, honey?" the bartender asked, leering at her from behind the stained and pitted bar. "Maybe you're used to something better?"

Gemma leaned away, wreathed in the garlic fumes of his breath. "Did you send for Mr. Dempsey as I asked?"

He began to polish a glass on a none-too-clean rag.

"Sure, lady, but he don't live here. You're just gonna have to be patient."

"He told you he was expecting me."

"Yeah. He's quite a man for the dames."

Gemma thought about drinking the gin but decided against it, remembering how easy it would be for her to lose her head. So far she'd been lucky. It hadn't been difficult to get back to New York once Susannah had agreed to help her; Susannah's father had been called away on business, and her mother had decided to accompany her husband to the city, leaving Gemma and Susannah with the run of the Spiegels' summer house in the Catskills. Then it had only been a matter of manipulating or bribing various servants before Gemma was on her way to meet Wyatt at the rendez-vous he'd suggested.

Little as she liked the looks of his chosen meeting place, Gemma couldn't deny that this was just the sort of adventure she'd been longing to have since her initiation at Lulu's. It was a little scary, to be sure, but Wyatt had proven to be a real friend; he'd agreed to go with her to Mal's apartment to look for clues, even though he was risking the displeasure of his kin by neglecting his work for the pack. She couldn't hold it against him if he'd kept her waiting a couple of hours.

She was contemplating asking the bartender for a soda when she looked up to find Wyatt approaching from the back door.

"Gemma!" he said, holding out his hands. "Sorry I'm late. I couldn't get away any sooner."

Gemma smiled shyly. "It's nothing. I understand."

His admiring gaze took her in from head to toe. "You're beautiful," he said.

So are you, she thought. It wasn't that he was wearing anything special; he looked like any man of the working class, dressed in a simple shirt and trousers, and carrying a leather bag over his shoulder, but to her he was far more handsome than the slick and polished male denizens of the Gold Coast.

She felt as though she and Wyatt had known each other forever.

"Are you sure you won't get into too much trouble?" she asked.

"Even if I did, it'd be worth it." He glanced at the bartender. "Thanks for looking after her, Joe."

"Yeah. It's been enchantin'." The man pocketed the coins Wyatt laid on the counter and went back to his polishing.

"No one knows you're here?" Wyatt asked as he escorted her out to the street.

"No one but Susannah, and she won't talk. I just need to be back by dawn tomorrow."

"I think we can manage that." He flagged down a passing taxi and helped Gemma into the backseat.

"You've been to Owen's place before?" Wyatt asked as the cab sped toward Washington Square.

"Only once," Gemma said. "I think he's a little ashamed of it because he never has much money. Not that Grif and I ever cared about that."

"But you think your brother has already looked there."

"That's the first place he would have gone when Mal disappeared."

"So you hope you can find something he didn't."

She picked at a loose thread on the hem of her blouse. "Maybe there's not much chance of it, but if I could, Griffin would see that I'm good for something besides marrying some stuck-up boy who's never had to do anything more difficult than tie his shoelaces."

Wyatt grinned. "You prefer someone with a little more punch."

"Yes." She gazed into his eyes. "If I—"

The taxi slammed to a stop. Wyatt steadied Gemma and handed her out to the curb, refusing her request to pay the fare. "This might not be much of a date, but I can still take care of my girl."

Gemma's legs trembled. "Am I your girl?"

"Do you want to be?"

She glanced hastily up at the building before them. "I... We'd better get going."

He nodded, suddenly serious, and preceded her into the vestibule. The stairwell stank of cabbage and mildew. Together they climbed the three flights of stairs to Mal's floor.

"I don't have a key," Gemma said, "but I don't want it to look like anyone broke in."

"Don't worry about that," Wyatt said, lifting his leather bag. "I'll be careful." They stopped before the door, and Wyatt gave it a slight push. "Not much of a lock," he said. He pulled something that looked like a kind of pin from his bag and pushed it into the keyhole, jiggling it back and forth until the lock opened with a soft click.

The first thing Gemma noticed was that the room smelled as if someone had been in it not very long ago; the scent was undeniably human, but it definitely wasn't Mal's.

"Yeah," Wyatt said when she started to speak. "Whoever was in here must have had a key, since the lock was intact."

"One of Mal's artist friends?" she speculated.

"Or maybe the landlord. Could be he's thinking of renting it out, since your friend is gone."

"That's ridiculous. It's not as if Mal is—" She bit her lip. "Let's start looking."

She and Wyatt began combing the front room, examining the desk, shelves and the piles of paper scattered over the floor. After half an hour, Gemma had begun to believe that the idea of finding something Griffin had missed was the purest foolishness. Surely he'd been through every piece of paper, every drawer, every—

"Gemma!"

She shimmied out from beneath the desk and hurried to Wyatt's side. "What is it?"

He held out a stained and badly wrinkled sheet of paper, fragrant with perfume and crisscrossed with writing in a delicate hand. "It was in the kitchen behind the range. It must have fallen there some time ago."

"What does it say?"

Wyatt moved to the small window and held the sheet up to the light. "It's a letter," he said, and read it aloud.

"My Dearest Mal,
It seems impossible that we shall soon be together again. Though I know how much you risk to help me escape this place, I shall let you take that risk, because I have known since we first met that we were destined to share our lives.

I will be waiting for you at the appointed place and time.
Yours alone…"

"Margot," Gemma whispered. She gave a whoop of triumph and quickly covered her mouth. "Do you know what this means, Wyatt? Grif thought maybe her father was trying to keep her away from Mal because he didn't approve of their affair."

"And?"

"Don't you see? It's obvious from the letter that Margot was being held captive somewhere. Somehow Mal must have found out where she was and why she hadn't been in contact with him. They made a secret plan for him to rescue her."

Wyatt nodded slowly. "I get it. That's why he disappeared."

She sniffed the paper, but it gave up nothing except the perfume smell, with a tinge of bread crumbs and mouse droppings. "What if De Luca *did* have her? What if Mal tried to rescue Margot and failed, so De Luca had him…"

"If he was killed, it wasn't in this apartment," Wyatt said. "No trace of blood."

Gemma hugged herself. "Oh, God. We have to show this to Griffin right away."

"What can he do? He's already accused the pack of being involved in Owen's disappearance."

"I don't know what he'll do, but he has to know." She folded the paper and tucked it in the pocket of her skirt. "Let's search a little longer. If Griffin didn't find this, there may be other things he overlooked."

THE ENFORCERS CAME in broad daylight, muffled in dark overcoats, scarves and wide-brimmed hats even in the heat of early summer. The fact that they had ventured out at so inconvenient an hour was proof that their business with her was urgent, and Allie made no attempt to keep them out of the flat.

As usual, Dorian was at least minimally courteous, though his expression as he removed his hat was certainly grim enough. Javier didn't bother with the niceties.

"What do you know about Malcolm Owen?" he snarled, pushing her down onto the sofa.

Allie bounced back up, arms extended, and hurled the startled enforcer across the room. Dorian smoothly set himself between them.

"Please sit, Miss Chase," he said. Allie cast a warning look at Javier and perched on the edge of an armchair, ready to spring up again at the first sign of threat.

"We know about Owen and Margot," Dorian said. "It would be wise for you to cooperate."

"If you know so much, why do you need my cooperation?" she asked coldly.

"Because I feel certain that you wouldn't want any harm to come to Miss Moreau."

"What?" Allie dug her fingernails into the brocade of the chair, struggling to contain her fear. "What have you done to Lou?"

"No lasting damage, I assure you." He sat opposite her, ignoring his partner. "It took some time for us to find your servant. She is admirably loyal to you, Miss Chase, but she is only human. It wasn't unduly difficult to extract the necessary information from her."

"If you've touched a hair on her head…"

"As I said, she is presently in good health. Let us hope she remains so."

"You bastard. She doesn't know anything."

"To the contrary. She overheard a certain conversation with Griffin Durant, in which you connected Malcolm Owen with the Master's protégée and implied that they had run off together."

"I never—"

"'She still loves him. She was miserable with

Raoul.' Those were your words, Miss Chase. And, as you pointed out to your werewolf friend, Owen disappeared just two weeks before Margot. Most convenient, wouldn't you agree?"

"It was just wild speculation. We've found no indication that Mal took Margot."

"Nor have we. In fact, Raoul had dismissed Owen as a possible accomplice, but he has since revised his opinion."

Her thoughts strung as taut as a bowstring, Allie considered telling Dorian about the werewolf presence at Mal's summer cottage. Mentioning Griffin's suspicions that the pack had been responsible for Mal's disappearance might take the heat off the young human, but it could also ignite the very war she and Griffin were determined to prevent.

"I don't know a damned thing more than you do," she said. "I've been trying to find Margot for days, but I don't have the resources Raoul does. What do you expect me to say?"

Javier advanced on her. "Are you claiming Margot hasn't contacted you?"

"Yes. And you'd have to be pretty incompetent not to know if I'd seen her—or Mal, for that matter."

Dorian sighed. "You place us in a difficult situation, Miss Chase. I'm afraid Raoul won't be satisfied with your answers."

"Sorry. I can't change them, even to please your Master."

Javier snickered. "You'd better think twice if you want your little human to stay alive."

Allie took a swing at his smug face. Dorian caught her arm and held her back, his strength just superior to hers. She turned and grabbed the lapels of his coat.

"Don't let them hurt Lou. She has nothing to do with this. I'll come to Raoul, if that's what will satisfy him."

Dorian gently disengaged her hands. "I think that would, indeed, be best, Miss Chase. Perhaps the sight of your friend will encourage you to be more forthcoming."

"Damn it, Dorian, I—" The telephone rang, cutting off her plea. Dorian exchanged glances with Javier, then indicated that Allie should answer. She picked up the receiver.

"Hello?"

The voice that asked for Dorian was sharp and unfamiliar, but Allie couldn't mistake the urgency in his tone. "I guess everyone knows you're here," she said to Dorian, handing him the phone.

Dorian listened to the caller, his frown deepening. "It seems we have another engagement, Miss Chase," he said, returning the receiver to its cradle. "I would be most appreciative if you'd accompany us."

Allie didn't argue. Not with Lou's life hanging in the balance. She put on a pair of dark hose, selected her longest coat and pulled a cloche hat with an attached veil over her hair. Dorian and Javier hustled her out to their car around the corner. Javier took the wheel, driving like a madman and leaving a trail of blaring horns and furious drivers behind him.

They pulled up in front of a building Allie remembered very well. Her first wild thought was that Mal had returned to his apartment and Raoul had learned of it. But the enforcers, though alert and obviously ready for action, didn't look as though they expected a major coup.

"Wait here, Miss Chase," Dorian said, his tone warning her not to take liberties with his trust.

"What is it?" she asked. "Why are you here?"

Dorian didn't answer. He and Javier got out of the car and started at a brisk pace toward the building. They were inside perhaps five minutes before they returned, escorting a pair of white-faced young people Allie recognized with a sinking heart.

CHAPTER SIXTEEN

"ALLIE?" GEMMA SAID, surprise and hope mingling in her eyes.

"What's the meaning of this, Dorian?" Allie demanded as the enforcer herded Gemma and the young man into the backseat. "What the hell do you think you're doing?"

Dorian took his seat and shut the door. "We received a tip, Miss Chase. A tip that these two young shifters were searching Owen's apartment."

"A tip? Who from?"

"We don't know. But apparently whoever it was has some valuable knowledge." He raised his hand, displaying a wrinkled sheet of paper. "Durant's sister found this—a 'love letter' arranging an assignation between Owen and Margot."

Allie looked askance at the boy, then turned to Gemma. "What were you doing here? I thought Griffin told you not to come back to Manhattan alone?"

Gemma lifted her chin. "I'm not alone. Wyatt was with me." She swallowed. "Who are these men, Allie?"

"They're Raoul's enforcers, and they've been looking for something to tie Mal to Margot's disappearance. It seems you've given it to them."

Gemma's eyes widened. "The clan leader? What does he have to do with Margot?"

"I guess Griffin never saw the need to tell you that she'd become one of Raoul's protégées."

"You mean, she's a vampire?"

"That's right. And you haven't done her or Mal any favors by sticking your nose into this."

Wyatt growled. "Gemma was only trying to help her brother find out what happened to his friend."

"And you thought you'd scrounge around for evidence in Mal's apartment, even though Griffin and I had already searched it thoroughly."

"Obviously you missed something," Gemma said.

So it would seem, Allie thought. She almost asked Gemma how she'd met the young werewolf, but the current situation wasn't conducive to casual conversation. "You're really in it now, honey."

"How was she supposed to know how dangerous it was?" Wyatt demanded.

"You'd do well to keep your mouth shut," Allie said. "We're headed to a place that isn't exactly friendly to dogs."

"But we don't know anything else," Gemma protested.

Allie shot a quick glance at the enforcers in the front seat and leaned close to Gemma. "Who else knew you were coming here?" she whispered.

"No one."

"For God's sake, don't let *them* know that."

The car continued across town to Park Avenue, and the mansions of Raoul and his chief lieutenants. Javier pulled up in front of Raoul's Gothic monstrosity, grinning maliciously. He and Dorian escorted Allie, Gemma and Wyatt into the great hall.

As they had during Allie's last visit, the mansion's residents emerged from their rooms to observe the visitors, but their hostility was even more palpable when they saw the werewolves. Gemma shrank under their stares, but Wyatt put up a brave front, wrapping his arm around Gemma's shoulders.

Raoul was waiting in his palatial suite, holding court like an emperor on his antique Russian throne. His latest favorites sat at his feet, both male and female; they hissed and rustled like serpents when Allie and the others walked through the door.

"So, Allegra," Raoul said, smiling faintly, "you've come to me at last."

She stopped in the middle of the room. "Not willingly, Raoul." She struck an insolent pose. "I understand you have my human in your care."

"Ah, yes. Miss Moreau. A credit to her species." He looked past Allie to Gemma and Wyatt. "Dogs in the house, Dorian?"

Dorian advanced, his body slightly bent in submission. "We found them at Owen's quarters. The tipster didn't specify who was in the apartment, but considering what these two found, I thought it best to bring them." He produced the letter. "Further proof that Owen was conspiring to take Miss De Luca."

Raoul held out his hand. Dorian passed him the paper and retreated while the Master read. The only sign of Raoul's rage was the way he crumpled the letter in his hand.

"So," he said. "How long have you known of this, Allegra?"

"Like I told your gunsels, I didn't."

"And Griffin Durant?"

"He doesn't know any more than I do. His concern has been for Owen all along."

Raoul leaned back in his chair, his fingers steepled

beneath his chin. "You've played a dangerous game, Allie. I'm almost prepared do away with both custom and law where you're concerned."

"Fine. You can do what you want with me, but let the kids and Miss Moreau go free."

Raoul contemplated Gemma and Wyatt through narrowed eyes. "Perhaps."

"You're already on the brink of war with De Luca. You don't need the dogs against you, too."

He straightened, anger red in his eyes. "I had nothing to do with the attack on De Luca, which I made very clear to him through our subordinates."

"Did he believe you?"

"Careful, Allegra."

"Who did it, then?"

Raoul brooded, obviously unable to answer the question. To admit other *strigoi* had been behind the attack would call his authority into question, but he was no fool to court outright war without a powerful advantage.

He rose and descended from his dais. His favorites surrounded him like a living wall, their eyes fixed on Allie.

"There is something I'd like you to see, Allegra," Raoul said, his voice deceptively mild. "Bring the children along. They may learn something, as well."

Filled with foreboding, Allie stuck close to Gemma and Wyatt as Dorian and Javier fell into step behind them. Led by Raoul, they descended the stairs to the first floor and continued down another flight into the underground rooms Raoul reserved for those who invoked his displeasure. They paused at a heavy metal door, where a lone enforcer stood guard.

"How is our guest?" Raoul asked him.

The enforcer smiled. "Uncomfortable, My Liege."

Raoul signaled the guard to open the door. Allie hung back.

"Leave the kids out of this," she said.

Raoul ignored her and stepped into the room. Javier gave Allie a push. Only her concern for Gemma and Wyatt kept her from pushing back.

A prisoner was hanging from chains in the center of the room. His face was pale and gaunt, and saliva ran from the corners of his cracked lips.

"Sebastian," Allie whispered.

"Yes." Raoul walked around his former lieutenant, studying him with interest. "When Margot disappeared, I invited all my vassals for private interviews, particularly those who'd had direct contact with her. Sebastian spent a great deal of time in her company. Margot was fond of him, and he displayed a certain partiality toward her, an affinity I chose to disregard—until my protégée vanished."

Allie stood before Sebastian, sickened by what Raoul had done. There was no doubt that the lieutenant was in the final stages of blood starvation; he had gone well past the weakness and nausea Allie had experienced, beyond the phase of convulsions and psychosis. Deprived of the substance every *strigoi* needed to survive, Sebastian's mind and body had shut down. Even a blood transfusion wouldn't save him now.

I'm sorry, Allie thought. *You never deserved this, my friend.*

"It took some time to obtain his confession," Raoul said, "but Sebastian finally admitted that he'd passed letters between Malcolm Owen and Margot. He never did acknowledge helping her to escape."

Allie turned on Raoul, fists clenched. "Maybe he didn't do it."

Raoul shook his head with the strained patience of one indulging an eccentric relative. "My dear Allegra…if you know anything at all, now would be the time to confess."

"Or you'll do *that* to me?"

"Only as a last resort. I do have two dogs here who are apparently of some value to you, and there is Miss Moreau—"

"I'll kill you if you touch any of them."

"I always did admire your spirit." He gestured Dorian and Javier to escort his prisoners from the room. "I'll give you a little time to think things over."

The enforcers ushered Allie and the werewolves down the dark hallway. Gemma was wan and silent; Wyatt's jaw was set in incipient rebellion. Allie hoped he was capable of controlling his impulses.

Dorian and Javier paused at another metal door. "You'll wait here," Dorian told Allie.

"What about the kids?"

"They'll be in the next room."

"No. We stay together."

"That isn't possible, Miss Chase."

Allie weighed her chances and decided that outright resistance would be highly unlikely to succeed. "At least let me see Miss Moreau," she said.

"I'll see what I can arrange."

Allie looked past him to Gemma. "Keep your chin up, kid."

Dorian shut the door. Allie heard the click of the heavy lock. She tested the metal, but the door had been made vampireproof. She paced the small room, her thoughts inevitably flying to Griffin.

Thank God you don't know what's going on, she thought. If he were to find out, he would undoubtedly do something crazy to save Gemma. And that would be a very bad idea.

Still, a treacherous little part of Allie's mind desperately wanted Griffin to come to their rescue.

To hell with that. I'll get us out of this, one way or another.

Even if it meant giving herself to Raoul in exchange for Gemma, Wyatt and Lou. And losing Griffin forever.

She laughed at her own absurdity. *You can't lose him, Allie Chase. You've already let him go.*

"IT'S REALLY THAT BAD." Ross stretched his long legs out on his desk, regarding Griffin with sympathetic pity. "You really are in love with her."

Griffin stopped in midstride, struggling to keep his expression a perfect blank. "No," he said stiffly. "It's not…it's not that simple, Ross."

"Not simple? You asked her to marry you."

"You don't understand."

Ross sighed. "If it was just sex…hell, she was willing enough, from what you've said. Except when it came to settling down with one guy."

"She'd just been through a traumatic experience."

"Yeah." Ross lowered his legs to the floor with a thump. "She's not the marrying kind, Grif. You must see that."

Griffin glanced across the room, reassuring himself that none of the human officers were listening in on the conversation. "You don't know her as I do, Ross. She's not what she appears to be on the surface. There's so much more to her."

"She's still a vampire. I never heard that they were capable of relationships outside their own kind."

"Allie's free, not like the others who—"

Ross's telephone rang. He raised his finger, signaling for Griffin to wait, and answered.

"He's here," he said to the person on the other end. He held the receiver out to Griffin. "It's for you. I think it's your butler."

Griffin took the phone. "Starke?"

"Mr. Durant. Thank God I've found you."

"What is it, Edward? What's wrong?"

"I've received a call from the Spiegels. They tell me that Susannah assisted Gemma in leaving the house and boarding a train bound for Manhattan. She has not as yet returned."

Griffin cursed under his breath. "Did Susannah know what she planned?"

"Something about meeting a young man."

Of course. "Very well. Don't worry, Edward. I'll find her."

"I'm sorry, Griffin."

"It isn't your fault. I'm entirely to blame."

He passed the phone back to Ross to hang up. "Gemma's run off again," he said grimly.

"Need some help?"

"If you're free."

"Sure. I—" The phone rang again. Ross picked it up and listened, his expression growing more troubled as the seconds passed.

"Okay," he said. "Good job, Mike. I'll take care of it."

He hung up and met Griffin's gaze. "I know where your sister is," he said. "When you told me about that kid, Wyatt, and your concern about his motives in coming to Oakdene, I had a man keep an eye on him. He saw the boy meet a young woman who matches Gemma's description."

"Where were they?"

"They went to Mal's apartment. But that's not all of it, Grif. A pair of vampire enforcers showed up about an hour later, and they had Allie with them."

"What?"

"They nabbed Gemma and the kid, and drove off with all three of them. My man followed. They ended up at Raoul's mansion."

A chill raced up Griffin's spine. "Have you got a gun I can borrow, Ross?"

"I'll do better than that. I'm coming with you."

IT WASN'T PARTICULARLY DIFFICULT getting into Raoul's mansion. A pair of enforcers stood just outside the vestibule, wrapped in black clothing and dark glasses. By the time they recognized Ross, he was already climbing the stairs, badge prominently displayed. While their attention was focused on him, Griffin jumped up from the side and jammed the muzzle of his gun against the shorter enforcer's skull. Ross neatly removed the guns from beneath the guards' overcoats.

"We want to see Raoul," Griffin said.

The taller enforcer laughed. "Forget it, dog. He doesn't let animals into the house."

"Oh, yeah?" Ross said, his own gun aimed at the second vampire's heart. "I know you've got two in there already, and kidnapping is still a crime in New York."

"You don't know what you're dealing with, dog."

"You want to bet your life on that?"

The enforcer looked down at the gun. "You've only got a fifty percent chance of succeeding."

"That's a fifty percent chance of your dying, and Raoul's already under investigation. You kill me or my friend, and every cop in the city will be on top of you. You want more humans to find out what you're hiding?"

The enforcer glanced at his companion, who gave an almost imperceptible shake of his head. As one, they turned for the door, Ross and Griffin on their heels.

"How much of that was bluff?" Griffin whispered.

"It worked, didn't it?"

The mansion was cool and dark. Griffin paused in the vestibule to smell the air. It stank of vampires and blood.

Ross wrinkled his nose. "God," he said. "I could have done without ever smelling this place."

"You're the one who stinks, dog," the tall enforcer said.

"Too bad for you." Ross moved closer to Griffin. "Gemma?"

"She's been here very recently. So have Wyatt and Allie." He began to move slowly, shoving the enforcer ahead of him. The most recent tracery of scents led to a staircase descending to a basement; Ross gestured for the enforcers to precede him and Griffin down the steps.

"What does Raoul keep down here?" Ross asked the vampires. "No, don't answer. It's obvious."

Griffin didn't have to ask what he meant. The stench of sickness and rot permeated the unlit corridor at the foot of the staircase. He ran down the corridor, following the scent to a broad metal door.

"Open it," he demanded.

"We can't," the taller one said. "Only Raoul has the key."

"Whoever's in there isn't a werewolf," Ross said.

Griffin pressed his palms to the metal. "Allie." He moved with ferocious swiftness, grabbing the enforcer by the collar. "Where is my sister?"

The enforcer hesitated and glanced down the hall. Griffin moved from door to door, pausing at each one to sniff the air until he smelled fear and Gemma's unmistakable scent.

"Gemma!" he called, pounding on the door.

"Griffin?"

Her voice was muffled, but it sounded strong enough.

"Gemma, are you hurt?" he asked.

"No." A faint banging came from the other side of the door. "Griffin, the door is locked!"

Griffin leaned his weight against the door. It didn't so much as creak. "Don't worry, Gemma. We'll get you out."

"Wyatt and Allie are in the next rooms, and they have Allie's friend Lou. I'm afraid Raoul will hurt Allie."

Griffin shivered with the old battle-fever. "He won't. Be brave, Gemma. We'll be back for you."

He returned to Ross and his prisoners, his heart roaring like a machine gun. "Raoul," he said to the enforcers. "Now."

"Were you looking for me, gentlemen?"

Raoul was standing at the top of the stairs, a dozen vampires crowded at his back. In his hands he held what could only be described as a collar, jewel-encrusted and closed with a tiny golden lock.

"What an unexpected pleasure," he said, strolling toward them. He glanced at the captive enforcers with a look that didn't bode well for their futures. "You've arrived just in time."

Griffin's hand twitched on his gun. "In time for what, Raoul?"

"To witness Allegra's surrender."

"Huh," Ross said, aiming his own weapon carefully

at Raoul's forehead. "Whatever you've got on your mind, Raoul, it ain't gonna work."

"No?" Raoul lifted a languid hand. "I am currently in possession of Miss Gemma Durant, Miss Louise Moreau and a young man by the name of Wyatt Dempsey. I've long been desiring Miss Chase's companionship, and now I believe that she will be glad to exchange her troublesome freedom for their release."

Griffin lunged for Raoul, but Ross held him back.

"You're nuts," Ross said. "You don't have any leverage. Harm any one of them, and you're dead meat."

Raoul's eyes flickered red, and Griffin knew that he was bluffing every bit as much as Ross was. "You assume a great deal, dog."

"I assume you don't want every cop in the city against you now that you've started a war with Carmine De Luca."

"I started nothing," Raoul said, his feigned affability dissolving in anger. "I've been set up, Kavanagh, and you know it."

"I know nothing of the kind, and I'm not alone in my thinking."

The vampires behind Raoul stirred, and several moved down the stairs with hostile intent. Raoul waved them back.

"Your threats are meaningless," Raoul said. "I may, however, permit you to leave with your heads still on your shoulders."

Griffin held on to his control by a thread. "Was this your plan all along, Raoul? To get Allegra by kidnapping the people she cares about?"

"Allegra has an unfortunate flaw. She has clung to the breeder habit of affection for humans, and that makes her vulnerable. But I didn't take your sister for such a purpose. She and the boy found a letter implicating your friend Malcolm Owen in the disappearance of my protégée, and I offered them my… hospitality."

"You're about to be a gracious host and send them on their way," Ross said.

"I don't believe I will, Detective. I—"

"You," Ross interrupted, calling to someone behind Raoul. "Christof. What do you think of this circumvention of vampire law?"

Griffin followed Ross's gaze. He didn't recognize the fair-haired vampire, but it was clear from Christof's bearing that he held some authority. He stood very still, but his expression was grave.

"The rest of you," Ross said, "you who are patrons in your own right, will you let this tyrant set a precedent you'll live to regret? Consider what will come next. He'll steal your protégés from you one by one. He'll force you to accept his bite. You'll lose any independence you once claimed."

No one spoke. The vassals shifted uneasily.

Raoul bared his incisors. "Liar," he snarled. "I take Allegra only because her indiscretions are a threat to us all."

"So *he* says," Ross said.

"Raoul," Christof said slowly, "the law does forbid such compulsion, no matter what form it takes."

"Do you wish to lose your position, Christof? It can easily be arranged."

Christof leaned closer to Raoul, speaking in a low voice. Raoul lost what little color he had. He would clearly have attacked the man if two other lieutenants hadn't moved to back their colleague.

"You think you've won," Raoul said with deadly calm, "but this isn't over. Allegra will come to me of her own free will." He reached inside his velvet coat and pulled out a set of keys, tossing them to Griffin. "Take your bitch. Enjoy her while you can."

Griffin backed away, stopping at Allie's cell. He unlocked it, and Allie all but fell into his arms.

"Griffin!" She raised her head, taking in Raoul and his vassals with a sweep of her gaze. "Oh, damn."

"It's all right," Griffin said, examining her intently. She appeared unharmed. "Stay right here."

He moved down the hall, opening more doors while Ross kept his revolver aimed at Raoul. He released Gemma first. She crumpled against him.

"Are you all right?" Griffin asked, holding her close.

"Yes." She glanced at Allie. "They didn't… I was so afraid…"

"Go to Allie," he said, giving her a gentle push. He opened the next door. "Miss Moreau?"

The woman looked up from her place in the corner of the cell, her eyes rimmed with red. "Mr. Durant?"

"Yes. We're here to take you out of this place."

"Thank God. How is Allie? Is she—"

"She's fine."

Louise covered her face. "When they came for me…I tried to hold out, but they—"

"Never mind," Griffin said, offering his hand. "All Allie cares about is that you're safe."

He half carried Lou from the room, where Allie met her with a hug.

"I'm so sorry, Allie," Lou whispered. "I should never have—"

"Be quiet," Allie said, touching her cheek. "We'll talk about it when you're feeling better."

Griffin moved to the last door, and a moment later Wyatt Dempsey burst from the room.

"Gemma?" he cried, looking around wildly. He rushed to her and seized her hands. "Gemma!"

"They didn't hurt me," she said. "Griffin came for us, Wyatt. I knew he would."

"And now I suggest we leave," Ross said. He waved his gun at Raoul, who moved to the side with barely concealed hatred in his eyes. Tucking Gemma in the crook of his arm, Griffin led the others up the stairs, hurrying them out of the mansion and into the waning afternoon sunlight. Allie paused on the threshold to don her hat and sunglasses.

No one followed as they made their way to Ross's patrol car. Just as Gemma, Allie and Lou were sliding into the backseat, Wyatt bolted, running as if the entire clan were after him.

Ross watched him go with drawn brows. "Either he's spooked or he has something to hide," he said.

"Let him go," Griffin said. "We need to get the women to a safe place."

"They'll be safe at the precinct. Even Raoul won't bother them there." Ross took the wheel, turning on his siren as they sped to police headquarters. Almost as soon as they entered the building, a uniformed patrolmen met Ross and delivered a whispered message only Griffin was close enough to hear. He tensed but quickly forced himself to relax again. Ross continued through the maze of corridors without revealing his thoughts.

Allie drew alongside Griffin, staring straight ahead as she loosened her coat.

"You took a terrible risk," she said.

He resisted the powerful need to take her in his

arms. "Did you know what Raoul intended to do with you?"

"I had an idea."

"Would you have gone through with it?"

"If there was no other way to get them out of there."

Griffin took Allie's arm and stopped. "If Raoul had taken you…"

She shrugged. "I would have survived."

He gestured her ahead of him, his thoughts in turmoil. She might have survived in body, but her soul would have been as good as dead. Her beloved freedom would have been lost…the freedom she'd refused to compromise even in marriage.

Gemma and Miss Moreau were gone when they reached Ross's office, already in the custody of one of Ross's trusted officers. Ross stood beside his desk, tapping a pen on the scratched wood.

"This has been one helluva day," he said. "Wouldn't you like to rest, Miss Chase? We have a bed you can use."

She glanced at him sharply. "What's going on, Mr. Kavanagh?"

"I didn't think I could put anything past you." He met Griffin's gaze. "We've found Mal."

CHAPTER SEVENTEEN

GRIFFIN, WHO'D OBVIOUSLY been keeping something to himself since Ross had talked to the patrolman, finally let his concern and worry show on his face. Allie knew he'd been hoping to keep the information from her, even though she was more intimately involved in the business than ever.

God knew she'd felt a treacherous relief when Griffin and Kavanagh had saved her from the necessity of surrendering to Raoul. Yet a strange, dull sort of fatalism had overcome her during those desperate hours of waiting. She'd begun to believe that it was only a matter of time before Raoul claimed her. Sooner or later he'd find a way to circumvent *strigoi* law. Sooner or later the close relationships she'd sworn never to risk again would bring about her downfall.

And she didn't want to take anyone with her.

"Did you find Margot, Mr. Kavanagh?" she asked.

"Call me Ross," he said, with the first warmth he'd shown her since their telephone conversation. "There's been no sign of Miss De Luca. We conducted a raid on a speakeasy, a routine operation. Our men discovered a hidden room in the back, expecting to find cases of booze. Instead they found a man badly beaten and shackled to a chair. He couldn't talk, but someone recognized him from the picture I circulated when Mal first disappeared. They took him straight to the hospital."

"How badly is he hurt?" Griffin asked.

"He'll live, but he'll be in the hospital for a few days."

Griffin paced the small office, his hands locked behind his back. "Who had him, Ross? Who did this?"

"We don't know yet. My men are collecting evidence on the scene, but it doesn't look as if the kidnappers left much behind."

Allie laughed hoarsely. "Raoul would be very interested in this information."

"Do you think he'd finally believe that Mal wasn't involved in Margot's escape?" Griffin asked.

"Not until he'd questioned Mal himself."

"And killed him, just by accident," Ross said. "I doubt Raoul knows what's happened yet, but I've got a couple of officers on guard outside Mal's room at the hospital. If Raoul or the kidnappers come after him, they'll meet with some resistance."

Griffin came to a halt before Ross's desk. "I want to see him."

"The doctors gave him something to help him rest. He may still be asleep."

"Then I'll stay with him until he wakes up." Griffin met Allie's gaze. "I wish you'd remain here and rest."

"There's nothing wrong with me. Mal may know something about Margot, even if he wasn't involved in her disappearance."

"I'll give you an escort to the hospital, just in case," Ross said.

As soon as the escort was arranged, a patrol car carried Allie and Griffin to the hospital. The white-capped nurse who showed them to Mal's room admonished

Griffin not to disturb the patient, reminding him that he was only allowed to see Mal as a special favor to the police.

Mal's room was plain and sterile, furnished with a single cot, two chairs and an unadorned table. A small window looked down at the street. Mal lay on the bed, swathed in blankets and bandages, the uncovered portion of his face gray with bruises. He didn't stir as they entered. Allie retreated to the far end of the room, arms folded across her chest.

Griffin pulled a chair up beside the bed. "Mal? Can you hear me?"

Mal opened his swollen eyelids, his lips moving stiffly. "Griffin?"

"I'm here."

The younger man let out a deep breath. "I didn't think…anyone would ever find me."

"You're safe now," Griffin said gently.

Mal tried to raise his hand to his face, but Griffin pushed his arm down again. "Don't try to move. Is there anything you need?"

"No." He coughed. "I'm just so tired."

"Can you tell me who did this, Mal?"

"There's a lot…I don't remember. Men came to my cottage right after I arrived. But they…weren't men."

"Loups-garous," Griffin said.

"Yes. They forced me to go with them…blindfolded me. Didn't see where we went. Then they held me, without…telling me why."

Griffin nodded to Allie. "We were at the cottage," he said. "I knew werewolves had been there, but I couldn't imagine what they had to gain from your disappearance."

Mal laughed weakly. "Whatever it was, they…

made it very clear that they would just as soon kill me as keep me alive."

Griffin clenched his teeth. "I went to Sloan after Allie and I returned from the cottage, but he insisted he knew nothing about it." He leaned over the bed. "Mal…do you know what happened to Margot?"

For a moment Mal only stared, as if Griffin had said something nonsensical. "You know I don't, Grif. I've been…looking for her, but she—"

"You don't have to lie to us," Allie said. "You discovered that she'd become a vampire, didn't you?"

Mal's surprise turned to wariness. "You…you knew?"

"Yes. But I couldn't tell you because of the circumstances, and because of the risks involved for both you and her."

"And you, Grif? Did you know, too?"

"Don't blame him," Allie said before Griffin could answer. "I didn't tell him until after you disappeared." She moved to stand beside Griffin. "How did you find out, Mal?"

He subsided back among the pillows. "Margot wrote to me a few days after Gemma's party. I couldn't believe it at first. It all seemed crazy, and yet it made sense. It was the only thing that did. That's why I went up to the cottage…to think, and to figure out what to do."

"Without telling anyone," Griffin said.

"I couldn't, Grif. Not even you."

Griffin rose and walked to the window. "Obviously Margot judged it worth the risk to contact you."

"She said it had taken some time before she found someone in…in Raoul's house willing to smuggle a letter out." He choked and turned his face away. "She said she still loved me. When I think of what she must have gone through…what she suffered…"

"Margot only sent you the one letter?" Griffin asked.

Mal shook his head. "I was able to answer using the same man who'd delivered her letter to me. I told her it was too dangerous to communicate when Raoul had such a hold over her. But she wrote back and said she would arrange to…run away with me, if I was willing." He laughed. "Willing! If it weren't for the danger to her, I—"

"You didn't make any such plans?" Allie interrupted.

"Even if I'd wanted to, I… Why do you ask?" He sat up in the bed. "What is it?"

Griffin returned to the bed. "You didn't hear anything about Margot when you were with the werewolves?"

"Damn it, Grif…tell me!"

Allie put her hand on Mal's chest and pushed him back down. "Margot went missing two weeks after you did," she said. "Raoul has been looking for her ever since. He just found out about the letters, and since the timing was so suspicious—"

"She's gone? Margot's gone?"

"We haven't been able to locate her, and neither has Raoul," Griffin said. "I'm sorry, Mal. We considered that you might have been involved, but the odds against your pulling it off seemed very high. And then there were the werewolves—"

"I didn't know," Mal whispered. Then his face went white. "Oh, God. I remember now. They talked about someone being abducted. A woman."

"If that woman was Margot," Allie said to Griffin,

"why would werewolves be involved in taking her, as well as Mal?"

"I've no idea," Griffin said. "It would seem extremely foolish for the pack, let alone unaffiliated *loups-garous,* to steal Raoul's most valued property. And we don't know it was Margot they were speaking of." He set his hand on Mal's shoulder. "Do you remember anything else? Anything at all?"

"No. Damn it, no." He shivered. "You said that Raoul has our letters?"

"Someone found a letter in your apartment that suggested you had finalized plans to run away with Margot," Allie said. "Raoul was tipped off about it, and he uncovered Margot's hidden ally in the clan. He forced Sebastian to confess his part in the exchange." She stared at the far wall, the taste of stale blood on her tongue. "I'm afraid he won't survive."

"But we made no such plans," Mal protested.

"Then the letter was a forgery, planted to implicate you," Griffin said.

"It was too easy, too convenient," Allie said. "Gemma just happened to find the letter after we'd thoroughly searched Mal's apartment, and some mysterious caller informed Raoul just in time for his enforcers to pick up the kids." She focused on Mal again. "Someone really wanted Raoul to believe you took Margot."

"Someone who is either a werewolf or an ally of werewolves," Griffin said.

Allie paced away from the bed, pausing in the middle of the room. "Wyatt ran off as soon as we freed him from Raoul."

"Wyatt who was with Gemma all the time." Griffin bared his teeth. "I never trusted him. If he's a part of this…this conspiracy…"

"But who *would* take Margot?" Mal exclaimed, his fists working among the sheets. "What would anyone have to gain? Margot said that Raoul was obsessed with her. If the pack was ever implicated in kidnapping her, there'd be hell to pay—vampires against werewolves—"

"All-out war," Griffin said quietly.

"As there would be if Raoul really had attacked De Luca in the streets," Allie said.

"Raoul attacked De Luca?" Mal asked.

"So it would appear at first glance," Griffin said. "Raoul denies it, and I'm inclined to believe him. He has nothing to gain by such an act." He walked again to the window. "It almost seems as if someone is deliberately trying to create havoc. A sustained, violent conflict between the races might let some in lesser positions rise to power, or it might wipe out everyone involved."

"Raoul got rid of any vampire who might conceivably challenge him," Allie said. "I can't think of anyone in the clan who'd try such a mad scheme in hopes that Raoul might fall from power."

"And I can't imagine how Sloan doesn't know about this. If he doesn't, if he's got freelance werewolves operating right under his nose, he's in serious danger of losing his leadership."

"I only understand half of what you're saying," Mal said, "but what about Margot? Who has her? I've got to find her, Grif."

"If you find out *why* someone would want her, you'll find out who," Allie said.

"We still don't have enough information," Griffin said. "We—" He broke off, pressing against the window.

"What is it?" Allie asked.

"A car just pulled up to the curb." He hissed through his teeth. "*Loups-garous.* I don't recognize them."

Allie looked over his shoulder. "What do you suppose they want?"

"I'm going to find out." He started for the door. Allie caught up with him.

"I'm going with you."

He turned, catching her arms and holding her so close that his breath warmed her face. "No. Stay with Mal, in case something happens here."

Reluctantly, she let him go, her arms still tingling with the aftereffects of his touch. She strode to the window, staying well back from the glass, and watched the trench-coated figures standing in the shadows. A few minutes after Griffin left the room, the werewolves suddenly dashed for their car and drove away.

Griffin returned with a scowl on his face. "They saw me," he said. "I'm sure they recognized me, but I still couldn't place them."

"Do you think they wanted to get at Mal?" Allie asked.

"I wouldn't doubt it, but they'd be reckless, indeed, to pit themselves against Ross's men and the hospital staff." He looked sternly at Mal. "It's absolutely necessary for you to remain here until we can decide how to protect you."

"You can't expect me to sit here while Margot's in danger."

"We expect exactly that," Ross Kavanagh said, walking into the room. "You'll stay here under guard until we figure out what the hell is going on. And as for you two—" His gaze swept from Griffin to Allie and back again "—I want you to take a breather while I work on this case."

"Surely we can—" Griffin began.

"You'll only get in the way. Trust me on this. And anyway, you'll need to look after Miss Chase. I can't spare any more men to guard her from Raoul."

Allie thought of protesting, but she knew she wouldn't win the argument with both werewolves standing against her. If she went along quietly now, it would be a lot easier to slip away from Griffin before he got it into his head to propose again.

"I'll take care of it," Griffin said. "I'll ask Starke to escort Gemma back to the Spiegels, where she'll be out of the way. Allie will come with me to Oakdene."

"What about Lou?" Allie asked.

"She'll come, too, naturally."

"Then I'll need to get some things at my apartment before we pick her up. Can we stop there on the way?"

"Of course," Griffin said, obviously relieved that she'd given in so easily. "We'll go first thing in the morning. I want to stay here for the night, Ross. There were *loups-garous* loitering outside the hospital."

"I saw them leaving," Ross said. "I promise you, my men are ready to take them on if they come into the hospital."

"I'd prefer to remain just the same."

"All right. Even if they don't return, we'll find them sooner or later. And now, Mr. Owen, I'd like to ask you a few questions, if you're up to it."

Mal agreed, so Allie and Griffin went down to the cafeteria for weak coffee and stale sandwiches. Ross came to find them after an hour, telling them that Mal was fast asleep. Griffin arranged to stay the rest of the night, and he and Allie settled in. Their silence might have been companionable if not for the bleak thoughts running through her head.

"Are you sure you're all right?" Griffin asked, a certain diffidence in his voice. "You've had so little time to recover from your ordeal."

Allie leaned back in her stiff, uncomfortable chair. "We don't cling to unpleasant memories the way humans do."

"Don't you?"

The last thing she wanted was another deep, earnest conversation, so she was grateful when Mal stirred again and beckoned Griffin to his bedside. Allie closed her eyes and dozed in the shallow manner of her kind.

THE MORNING CAME with surprising swiftness. Mal was asleep again; the police guard outside the door had changed; and Griffin decided there was nothing they could do until Ross pursued every lead from the speakeasy raid. Dawn was just breaking when they left the hospital and caught a taxi for Fifth Avenue.

Once they arrived at Allie's building, she stood on the curb, head raised and a frown on her face as she stared toward the park.

"What is it?" Griffin asked.

"I don't know. Something's wrong." Without waiting for Griffin to respond, she stepped into the street.

The trees still had a somewhat misty appearance in the dim morning light, and the grass was slightly wet, making little sound under Griffin's feet. He let Allie wander a little ahead, knowing that his senses would detect an intruder long before a potential antagonist could reach her.

He smelled the bodies just as Allie turned a corner on the path and vanished out of sight.

Griffin set off at a dead run, his heart pumping fire through his veins. Allie waited in a small clearing, her attention fixed on a half-dozen bodies sprawled in various awkward positions across the lawn and benches to either side of the path. She looked up as Griffin approached.

"Vampires," she whispered. "One of Raoul's lieutenants, and several of his enforcers."

Griffin nearly choked at the smell of blood, vast quantities of it painting the ground in great swathes of maroon and scarlet. The men had obviously fought death. Some lay in contorted positions with arms outflung; others still wore expressions of violent hatred. Most had been shot in the head, a relatively quick way of dying for *strigoi,* but some had suffered additional mutilations: missing limbs, torn throats and severe burns that could only suggest the killers had considered the murders more than a simple job. Now that the sun was rising, the bodies were beginning to blister, flesh turning red and then black.

"Who would do this?" Griffin asked, fighting off queasiness at the carnage. "Who would dare massacre so many of Raoul's men?"

Allie sat down on a bench, her hands knotted in her lap. "I can think of only one explanation," she said. "This is De Luca's revenge."

As calm as her voice sounded, Griffin knew she wasn't nearly as sanguine as she appeared. "Raoul suggested they'd reached some sort of understanding," he said.

"Obviously not as clear an understanding as he thought. De Luca must not have believed his denials."

"With no evidence to the contrary…" Griffin circled the corpses again, bending close to sift the various scents beneath the burned flesh, powder residue and ever-present blood. "Humans were here, but I can't identify them. None of the men we met at Cherubino's."

"De Luca wouldn't have sent them to do something like this. He has plenty of thugs to handle his dirtiest work." She rose again, accepting Griffin's offered hand. "It isn't easy to kill one of us. The murderers knew exactly what they were doing, and they intended to leave a message."

"Which Raoul is bound to receive very soon, even without our help."

Allie met his eyes in silent understanding. "We might delay the war a little longer if we could get Ross's men to clean this up quickly."

"He's got his hands full right now, but I'll telephone him from your apartment." He took Allie's arm. "There's nothing we can do for the moment. Let's get out of here."

Allie went along, lost in her own thoughts, and soon they were in her apartment. She went into her bedroom to pack for herself and Louise, while Griffin made the call to Ross's office. The detective wasn't there, but just as Allie was finishing her preparations, the telephone rang again.

"Grif," Ross said, "I've got some news that might interest you."

"So have I," Griffin said. He explained quickly what he and Allie had discovered in the park.

"You're sure De Luca did it?"

"Humans were there. An internal struggle within the clan, carried to such violent lengths, would be insane when relations between the races are already strained."

"Agreed. I'll send a few men down to examine the crime scene and retrieve the bodies." Ross hesitated. "Most of the guys don't know anything about vampires, but I don't see that as a problem unless one of the victims suddenly comes back to life."

"Unlikely," Griffin said dryly. "The assassins knew their work."

"I'll advise my men to use discretion." Ross moved away from the phone and returned, papers crackling. "I've got something from the forensics investigation of the speakeasy crime scene…some new evidence I thought you might like to examine."

Griffin's hair began to bristle. "What is it?"

"Like I said, nothing much. But maybe you can shed new light on things. You and Allie need to get down here as soon as you can."

Griffin hung up, speculation running rampant through his mind, and waited a few more minutes until Allie emerged with two small suitcases. They took her car to police headquarters, where Ross met them near the door.

"Your butler is here," he told Griffin. "He's just returned from driving Gemma to the Catskills. He's anxious to see you."

"I'll speak to him," Griffin said.

"Lou?" Allie asked.

"Resting. She seems in good spirits."

"That's Lou," Allie said. "Can you get someone to take her suitcase to her?"

Ross flagged down a passing patrolman and directed him to take the suitcase to their guest.

"What's this new evidence you've found?" Griffin asked as they began to walk again.

"It might not mean anything. I can't get any useful information out of it, but you've spent more time with the pack than I have."

He entered his office and closed the door behind

him. Starke was waiting there, his posture erect, his suit as impeccable as always.

"Mr. Durant," he said. "Miss Chase."

"Starke," Griffin acknowledged. "How is Gemma?"

"Very well, sir, and safely in the hands of the elder Spiegels. They tender their apologies for their negligence in supervising Gemma and their daughter, and promise the young people will not escape their scrutiny again."

"Very good." He noticed Starke's troubled gaze. "Is there something else?"

"Only that I have been concerned for your well-being, Mr. Durant."

"There's no need. As you can see, Miss Chase and I are well and whole."

"Thank God for that, sir." He retreated to the back of the room and made himself invisible, as he had always been so good at doing.

Ross accepted his presence without demur and opened a drawer in his desk, from which he pulled a large envelope, which contained folded squares of tissue. He opened the smaller square to reveal a pair of long reddish hairs. The other held a scrap of cloth, slightly stained with blood.

"This cloth was caught on a discarded piece of metal in the alley outside the speak. We're pretty sure it was torn off the shirt of one of the kidnappers when he fled the raid. The hair was stuck on the—"

Griffin stopped listening, his senses focused on the scrap of cloth. Though the scent that lingered on it was faint, he knew it instantly. It had been burned into his consciousness on the day his parents and brother had died.

"I know him," Griffin whispered. "He was one of the animals who murdered my parents."

CHAPTER EIGHTEEN

ROSS STARED. Allie went over to Griffin, her hands fluttering in the air in a gesture of helpless concern.

"You know who this is?" Ross asked.

Trembling, Griffin felt for the nearest chair and sat down. "I know the smell," he said. "I could never forget it. There were three strange *loups-garous* at the house that night. I never saw anything, but I—" He closed his eyes. "At least one of them is here in New York."

"But that's incredible," Allie said, pulling up a chair beside him. "Could it just be coincidence?"

"Is it coincidence that a *loup-garou* who carries traces of the same scent has been pursuing my sister?"

"Wyatt?" Ross asked in amazement.

"I've been suspicious of him from the first time I found him with Gemma at Oakdene," Griffin said grimly. "I just never placed his scent. Until now."

"But surely he's too young to have been one of the killers," Allie said.

Ross pushed a pencil in his mouth and chewed on the end with intense concentration. "It's been almost sixteen years. Wyatt can't be more than nineteen or twenty."

"Yet there is a connection," Griffin said. "Damn it. If only I'd realized…"

"You never had an idea who committed the crime?" Ross said.

"No. But I know there had to be a reason for what happened. *Loups-garous* don't generally murder each other in secret."

"Did your parents have enemies?" Allie asked.

"Not that I knew of. They lived on the fringes of the San Francisco pack, but they never caused trouble."

"The attack had all the earmarks of an assassination," Ross said. The pencil crunched between his teeth. "Given the serious nature of the crime, it's possible that the arsonists left San Francisco and ended up here, just as you did. It's no surprise that they'd get mixed up in kidnapping, as well as murder."

"Hired gunmen," Allie murmured.

"Who just happened to turn up in New York," Griffin said. "And Wyatt is directly linked to at least one of them."

The three fell silent, considering the possibilities. After several long moments Ross said, "Whatever the connection, it looks like someone wants Mal blamed for Margot's disappearance."

"Or whoever had Griffin's parents murdered found out where he'd settled and have been trying to get to him through Mal," Allie said.

"But if these werewolves killed Grif's parents and wanted to trap him by using Mal," Ross said, "wouldn't they have contacted him by now? Wouldn't they have had ample opportunities to grab Gemma, as well?"

"I doubt they would make the attempt," Starke said, stepping away from the wall. "The conflict that led to the deaths of the Durants is no longer important, at least not to those who ordered the assassination."

Griffin turned to his old friend, the beginnings of a dreadful fear stealing his breath. "Edward?"

"I've known for some time," the butler said, meeting his gaze. "Your father confided in me a few weeks before his death. He didn't want you to know anything about it, and I..." He cleared his throat. "You know that your father, despite being somewhat removed from the pack, was very proud of his race and the traditions of the werewolf kind. So when he discovered that certain members of the pack were working for the local vampire clan, he was horrified."

Griffin cleared his mind of all emotion. "*Loups-garous* working for vampires?"

"To put it colloquially, attending to their 'dirty laundry'—performing those unpleasant and illegal tasks the vampires felt were beneath them." Starke's mouth twisted in disgust. "They not only undermined werewolf influence throughout the city, but also helped to upset the balance of power in the clan, undoubtedly for the benefit of some lieutenant who coveted mastery."

Ross threw his pencil down on the desk. "That's crazy. You'd have to be a belly scraper to work for leeches. Beg pardon, Miss Chase."

"The elder Mr. Durant speculated that these hooligans had been promised leadership of the pack once the clan had sufficiently weakened the position of the current leader," Starke said. "There are many who will surrender their pride for such power."

"How was my father involved, Starke?" Griffin asked.

"In some way he never confided to me, he learned of this clandestine activity. It was his intention to go to the pack leader and expose the traitors. It would have meant great shame to the pack and certain death for the renegades."

"And someone found out he was about to spill the beans," Ross said quietly.

"They silenced him," Griffin said, forcing out the words. "They not only murdered him but my mother and brother, just in case he'd said something to them."

"And you'd be dead, too, if you hadn't been out at the time," Ross said.

Hardly aware of what he did, Griffin lunged at Starke, blinded by tears. "For God's sake, why didn't you tell me?" he demanded.

"Easy," Allie said. "Let him explain."

Griffin gave himself a hard shake. "I'm sorry, Edward."

"I perfectly understand." Starke straightened his tie and sighed. "You may very well blame me for failing to tell you all these years, but I believed I had good cause. At first you were too young and too angry, not entirely in your right mind. My primary concern was to get you and Miss Gemma out of San Francisco. I feared you would run away and seek the killers if you had even the slightest idea who they might be, and you weren't strong enough then to take on such a burden. Your health, and Gemma's, was my responsibility, and I knew your father would have wanted me to protect you at all costs."

Griffin stared at the opposite wall. "I'm not so young anymore."

"Yes." Starke rubbed at his forehead. "After you and Gemma were settled in Europe, I made it my business to ascertain the current situation with the pack. I had a few connections I was able to employ, but it took me some time to learn that there had been a purge of pack members after a near-successful coup. The original leader, with whom your father had an amicable agreement, remained in power. Since there was clearly no lingering danger that your parents' killers would pursue you, I let the matter lie. And when you grew to manhood and returned from the War, I could not bring myself to destroy your fragile peace, or watch you ruin your life in a search for revenge against men you might never find." His voice grew tight. "I cannot regret my actions, Griffin. Your parents were dead, and nothing would bring them back. I wanted you to live and find some measure of happiness."

How could you believe I'd ever find happiness, Griffin thought, *knowing my parents' murderers were still alive?* But he kept silent, swiftly calculating what could be done. "We'll have all the answers when we find the kidnappers," he said. "And Wyatt will tell me who and where they are."

"If you can find him," Ross said. "They probably know we're on to them by now."

"Perhaps. But Wyatt *was* with the pack. He may have gone to ground there, particularly if Sloan is involved."

Ross shook his head. "You've got to be patient, Grif. Don't try to take the law into your own hands."

"Ross is right," Allie said. "You can't go up against the pack alone."

Griffin touched her cool cheek. He should have been grateful that she'd emerged from the bleak detachment she'd shown since they'd escaped from Raoul, but he felt only sorrow. It would be so much better for her if she didn't give a damn.

"I promise I won't do anything rash," he said, lying as smoothly as any criminal. "But I think it would be wise for you and Miss Moreau to leave town as planned. Starke," he said, turning to the butler, "you'll fetch Gemma from the Spiegels' summer home and take her to a safe place outside the state. Miss Chase and Miss Moreau will join you."

"Just a minute," Allie said. "I make my own decisions about where I go."

"It's only a precaution, Allegra. Nothing will happen to me."

She stared at him with open disbelief, her lips stretched into a thin line. "Griffin…"

"When did you become such a worrier?" he asked lightly. "What happened to the old carefree Allegra Chase?"

Her expression shifted to one of cynical mockery. "You want the old Allie?" she asked. "That can be arranged." She strode for the office door. "You'll find me at Lulu's…that is, if you manage to survive the night." She slammed the door behind her, shaking the walls.

Griffin released his breath. Ross chuckled without a trace of humor.

"Don't be too concerned," Ross said. "She may be a vampire, but she's still a woman. She'll get over this mood and realize how stupid it would be for her to wander around town alone."

"I want her out of New York, Ross."

"Why don't you take her yourself?"

"You know why."

"Consider what you're doing. Consider Gemma. Consider the woman you love."

Ross's words hit hard, but Griffin maintained his composure. "I won't be any good to anyone if I let this go," he said.

"And you'll be even less useful if you're dead."

"I won't judge Gemma safe until I've had it out with Garret once and for all. This isn't only about revenge,

Ross. I can't let Sloan or his followers trifle with me and those I care for, or they'll see it as a sign of weakness."

"What about your dislike of violence?"

What, indeed. Griffin knew that the risk of losing control to the wolf would be greater than ever.

"My family is involved," he said, subduing his fear. "No one will hurt them while I'm alive."

Ross growled. "I joined the police for a reason, Grif. I wish you'd let me do my job."

"You have enough to deal with now."

"At least let me go with you to see Sloan."

"No. You're in bad odor with the pack as it is. I don't want you any more involved."

"You're crazy."

"I've been crazy for a long time. Maybe this is my last chance at sanity."

Ross made no further arguments, but he seemed to withdraw as if he, like Allie, were protecting himself against an imminent loss.

After calling his bank to release unlimited funds for Starke's use, Griffin went to see Louise Moreau. Allie was with her. They had been talking in low tones but stopped as he entered.

Allie picked up her coat and stood facing Griffin like a bull about to charge. "Excuse me," she said coldly. "I was just on my way out."

Griffin glanced away. "Miss Moreau... Louise... would you mind if Allegra and I speak alone?"

Lou, her eyes full of sadness, gathered up her things and left the room. Allie made a move toward the door.

"Allie," Griffin said softly.

"I think we've said everything that needed saying."

"Have we?" He walked up behind her and lay his

hands on her shoulders. "Allie, I don't mean to hurt you. I don't want you to think that what I have to do means you're any less important to me."

She shrugged. "I never gave it much thought."

"If you had, you'd be justified in your anger." He dropped his hands. "Do you have any idea how much I admire you?"

"Why? For being such a sucker?"

"You're many things, Allie, but never that. If you were any other woman—an ordinary woman—I'd never ask you to endure so much. But you're far from ordinary. You're stronger than anyone I know, except maybe Ross and Mal. Stronger than me. You understand how things are."

"Do I?"

"You're a survivor. No matter what happens, you'll go on. You'll stay free of Raoul, because it's not in your nature to surrender."

"That's right."

He turned her to face him, fighting the stiffness of her body. "There is something more I need to say to you. I should have said it a long time ago."

"If you're going to propose again—"

"I love you, Allegra Chase."

She lifted her eyes to his. "Isn't that just fine," she said hoarsely. "What am I supposed to do now, swoon with gratitude?"

"I know it's a bad time to tell you.…"

"You said it."

"I don't expect you to return the sentiment. I know how you feel about emotional entanglements. I only hope you realize you mean more to me than anyone but Gemma—"

"And revenge."

"If it were only that…" He hesitated, realizing how hollow his explanations would sound to her now. "There's so much more at stake, Allie."

"You don't have to justify yourself to me. I'd do the same thing in your place if I found out who killed Cato, and you wouldn't be able to stop me."

"I know."

"I guess we're both too stubborn for our own good."

"I never should have gotten you mixed up in my concerns," he said.

"You didn't have any say in it. I intended to cause you trouble from the first time I laid eyes on that pretty face."

Griffin tried to smile. "I guessed as much." His smile faded. "You opened up a new world to me, Allie. I was only half-alive before that night in Lulu's."

"But the past still holds you." She looked up with a sad smile. "Even a vampire isn't strong enough to break those chains."

"Allie…"

"It's a damned shame that we didn't get the chance to make love."

"My mistake."

"Maybe some other time." She adjusted her coat and glanced toward the door. "I've talked to Lou. She's agreed to accompany Gemma and Starke."

"I'm glad to hear it." He raised his hand toward her and let it fall again. "Go with them, Allie."

"They don't need me."

He held her gaze. "I have no right to ask this of you, but aside from Starke, there's no one I trust more with my sister's life. Look after her. Protect her as best you can. She needs a firm hand, and she admires you."

"Me, a firm hand? That's a first." She looked away quickly. "Wouldn't Ross be a better choice?"

"He'd do it gladly, but he's on the pack's blacklist. And you're the one…the one who might have been—" He cleared his throat. "Will you do this for me?"

"I guess I already took on the job when she walked into Lulu's." Her expression softened. "I won't let anything happen to the kid. That I promise."

"Thank you, Allie."

"Yeah." Her jaw set, the fine bones standing out under her delicate skin. "Just remember one thing when you're duking it out with Sloan…if you do get yourself killed, I'll never forgive you."

"I wouldn't expect it."

"And don't think I'll forget the ones who did it, either. Vampires live a long time. Gemma won't always be a kid. And I'll still be waiting."

"Whatever I've done…don't live for vengeance, Allie."

"That's up to you." She seized his face between her hands. "Stay alive, damn you. Stay alive."

She turned on her heel, fleeing for the door.

Griffin caught her, pulled her close and kissed her. He poured his heart into the kiss, everything he felt, everything he feared, the desire he had never fully expressed. She responded with the sort of ferocity he expected and welcomed, teasing his tongue with hers, grazing his lower lip with her sharp incisors. When it was finished, she left without a word. He knew he wouldn't see her again until his business with Sloan was complete.

Maybe then she would forgive him.

He exchanged a final word with Ross and took a taxi to his office, where he signed certain papers and took meetings with his most trusted employees. Then he visited his bank, making arrangements to supply

Starke with the funds he would require to establish himself, Gemma and Lou in a safe location out of state.

It was late afternoon when he caught another taxi to pack headquarters. Several young *loups-garous* were loading unmarked crates into a truck in the drive between two of the houses; they stared as Griffin walked up the stairs of the main house. He strode past the startled sentinels who met him in the vestibule and entered the great room, where werewolves at leisure—the very young, very old and pregnant females—leaped up from their cushions and tried to block his way. He pushed them aside and descended the steps into the tunnels, following the path that had been marked for him on his last visit. He reached Garret Sloan's quarters before the alarm could be raised and walked through the door.

Sloan was standing at his desk, nostrils flared and eyes narrowed in threat. "Durant," he said. "I thought I smelled you coming."

Griffin came to a stop before the desk. "A pity your best men weren't here to spare you the inconvenience of granting me an interview," he said.

Sloan sat down again, his body relaxed. "I don't have anything to fear from you, Durant."

"Not if you tell me the truth."

"The truth? About what?"

"About the men who killed my parents."

Sloan picked up a decanter on his desk and poured himself a drink. "Quite a ways out of my jurisdiction, and long before my time."

"At least one of the werewolves responsible is here in New York. I want to know if he's working for you."

"I don't know what you're talking about."

"We found Malcolm Owen. *Loups-garous* were

holding him hostage in a speakeasy's back room. You wouldn't happen to know anything about that, would you?"

Sloan frowned in what seemed to be genuine puzzlement. "We've been through this before. Why in hell should I want to kidnap some human I barely know?"

"What do you know about Wyatt Dempsey?"

"Dempsey? I—" He paused, his gaze flickering toward the door. Griffin heard them coming before they burst into the room—a contingent of the young men he'd seen loading the truck. He lunged across the desk, grabbed Sloan by the lapels and rolled with him to the carpet.

"Stay where you are," he told the youngsters, his fingers biting deep into Sloan's neck.

The young men paused, every face burning with hostility.

"You're badly outnumbered, Durant," Sloan croaked. "You won't get out of here alive."

"That remains to be seen." He dug into his pocket, pulled out the scrap of carefully wrapped bloodstained cloth and threw it on the desk. "Take a smell of that and tell me who it is."

Sloan stared at the cloth. His body stiffened, though his expression didn't change.

"He's a member of your pack, Sloan." Griffin glanced at the young men. "You recognize it, too," he said. "Did you know whoever wore this helped kidnap a human, bringing the attention of the police down on the whole pack? Did you know he was among those who served vampires in San Francisco and slaughtered the *loup-garou* who would have exposed him?"

The youngsters exchanged glances. "Garret?" one of them said.

Sloan bared his teeth. "I didn't send anyone after Owen."

"Then you don't know what your own subordinates have been doing," Griffin said. "That's a dangerous flaw in a pack leader. I'd think you'd want to expose any traitors in your midst."

One of the young men, the biggest of the lot, stepped forward. His eyes glittered with speculation. Like the others, he had begun to sense weakness in his chief, and his wolfish instincts were rising to the surface.

"His name is Conlan Dempsey," he said to Griffin. "He joined the pack a year ago."

Griffin forced Sloan into his chair. "How is he related to Wyatt Dempsey?"

"He's Wyatt's father."

"Are they here now?" Griffin asked Sloan.

The pack leader glanced at the big youth. "Jorunn, find Dempsey. Bring him to me."

The boy backed away and walked out the door, leaving his companions to wait in indecision. The minutes stretched interminably. Griffin felt his hand begin to go numb on Sloan's neck, and he cursed himself for not having brought a gun.

This isn't a time for guns, he reminded himself. *This is a more ancient way.*

A way he would have given almost anything to avoid. Deliberately he concentrated on his breathing until it steadied and slowed. He was prepared when Jorunn returned. The boy was alone.

"They're gone," he said. "Both of them."

Sloan shivered almost imperceptibly. "Send for Ivar."

"He's not here, either."

"Then you hunt them down. Take all the men you need, but return them alive. We know how to deal with renegades."

"Renegades who operated under your very nose," Griffin said.

"I have only your word for that, Durant. The word of one who despises his own kind."

The young men turned their attention to Griffin, drawing together as any pack would against any outside threat. They couldn't conceal their confusion, unused as they were to facing such a volatile situation.

Griffin gave Sloan a shake. "If Dempsey was one of the men who killed my family in San Francisco," he said, "he's already had experience serving the leeches. He—"

The shock of blinding revelation washed over Griffin. He pushed his face close to Sloan's ear. "What if one of Raoul's lieutenants is plotting to topple him from his throne? What if such a traitor kidnapped Margot to undermine Raoul's position as Master of the clan? What if this vampire arranged Mal's disappearance to make it look as if a human took Margot, deflecting suspicion from himself?" He lowered his voice to a whisper. "What if he used werewolves to do his dirty work, and you knew all about it?"

"You're insane," Sloan said, his eyes dark with genuine horror.

For a minute Griffin thought Sloan was right. It *was* insane. Complete and utter surmise of the wildest kind. Yet it all made a bizarre kind of sense.

Whatever Sloan's part in the matter, Griffin didn't dare let him go. He'd challenged the pack leader's power openly. If Sloan had his way, there would be a fight to the death. Sloan's young men might permit it, allowing him the chance to redeem himself in their eyes. Or they might choose to attack Griffin to punish him for defying a thousand years of pack law and tradition. They could bring him down in seconds, and that was not the way he intended to die.

Griffin hauled Sloan to his feet and marched him toward the door. "The days of the pack are numbered if vampires suborn *loups-garous* to their own ambitions," he said. "I'm going to walk out this door, Sloan, and you're going with me."

Sloan walked rigidly, his eyes seeking those of his subordinates. His fate was in their hands now; if they chose to aid Sloan, Griffin would never escape. But if they let Griffin leave, they would declare by their indifference that they'd judged Sloan and found him wanting. In this moment they held absolute power over two men's fates.

"Don't you see?" Sloan cried. "His loyalty was never to us. He doesn't care what happens to the pack. He's the one who's allied himself with vampires and humans, spitting on our most sacred traditions."

"Maybe it's time for traditions to change," Jorunn said.

"And what," Sloan snarled, "will you do when you become leader, and the young men come for you in the night like the leeches who tear their fallen leaders apart and eat their flesh? What will protect you then?"

Jorunn moved to block Griffin's path. "What do you want, Durant?"

"Justice."

"Ask him about his leech lover," Sloan hissed. "Ask him how he can touch one of those abominations as if it were anything more than an animal."

"Miss Chase has nothing to do with this," Griffin

said, his voice flat with rage. "This is a matter for *loups-garous* alone. Ask yourselves if Sloan really wants to find Dempsey, or if he's the one who told them to run?"

One of Jorunn's companions moved away from his companions. "This should be decided by the council," he said.

"By all means, Faolan, call the council," Sloan said. "Let them judge this renegade for what he truly is, and then I will kill him."

Faolan and Jorunn glanced at each other. With a slight nod, Jorunn sent the younger man out of the room.

"Let Garret go," Jorunn told Griffin.

"That would be extremely foolish of me," Griffin said.

"Do you think you can fight all of us?"

"I'll wait for the council. It might not be so simple as Sloan supposes."

The mood among the boys shifted as abruptly as a capricious wind. "Garret's right," a sandy-haired boy said. "You're not really one of us. You're a leech lover. You don't care what happens as long as you get what you want."

One by one the young men drifted apart, forming a loose circle around Griffin and his captive. Griffin expected the attack, but there were simply too many of them. They wrestled Sloan from his grip, and he barely sprang free in time.

CHAPTER NINETEEN

THERE WAS NO OPPORTUNITY to think or form a rational plan. Griffin flung off his jacket, tore at his collar and shirtfront, shedding buttons, and kicked off his trousers and shoes with practiced speed. He changed at almost the same instant Sloan ripped free of his own clothing.

No one else moved. Jorunn and his companions had been caught up in the most primitive of rituals, losing their ambivalence in the rush of impending violence. They watched, bodies tense and heads lowered, as Sloan hurled himself at Griffin. Griffin took the impact against his chest and staggered under the heavier wolf's weight, quickly recovering to slice at Sloan's legs with razor fangs.

The fight was brutal, passing as a blur in Griffin's mind. There were no human rules, no bids or offers for mercy. Sloan made the most of his greater size, bearing Griffin to the carpet again and again, snapping at Griffin's neck in an effort to sever the veins in his throat. But Griffin was the swifter, dancing out of Sloan's path and darting in to snap at Sloan's most vulnerable flesh. Soon Sloan's muzzle was torn and dripping blood, while Griffin's neck was scored with a dozen deep cuts and punctures. It seemed that neither would gain the upper hand.

But Griffin had one more advantage; he was twenty years younger than Sloan. The struggle began to tell on the older wolf; his attacks began to lose their force, and Griffin's grew more and more effective. Sloan paused to catch his breath; Griffin lunged and closed his jaws around Sloan's foreleg, crunching bone. Sloan fell with a howl of rage. Griffin spun away and plunged in again, throwing Sloan to the ground and grinding through the thick ruff of fur around Sloan's neck.

His teeth found flesh. Blood filled his mouth. Sloan's curved claws scraped at the carpet, and then went still. The office door crashed open, a half dozen older *loups-garous* scattering the younger observers with cries of alarm and anger.

Griffin sprang back, panting and snarling. The older men and women stared at Sloan, who lay unmoving, and turned on Griffin as one.

Griffin cowered, pretending fear and submission. The elders advanced. Griffin gathered his hindquarters and waited until the first of the werewolves was within reach. Then he leaped straight up and bounded over the *loups-garous*. He landed hard and cut through the others like a bullet, racing out into the hall.

Blood pounded in his chest, and pain dogged every step. He charged into the tunnel, scrambled up the stairs and emerged into the great room so abruptly that none of the gathered pack members had a chance to stop him.

Hot summer sunlight scorched his fur as he ran from the house. He knew the pack would be on him within minutes. His only consolation was that Allie had agreed to go with Gemma, Lou and Starke.

Only a last, terrifying doubt sent him running for Allie's apartment. What if she had lied?

THE TRAIN TO LONG ISLAND was already moving when Allie jumped off, leaving Lou and Starke staring after her. She gave them a brief wave as the train sped away, turned on her heel and caught a taxi to take her back to her apartment.

The sun was low when she met the burly policeman stationed in front of her building. He introduced himself as Officer Burney, and Allie knew he'd been sent by Ross Kavanagh. The detective hadn't been deceived by her apparent willingness to leave town. He'd probably been watching her all along.

She walked in the park until sunset, hardly aware of the cop trailing behind her. Her thoughts were still seething with anger and the memory of the last few moments with Griffin. She'd never hated him as much as she had when she'd returned his kiss, had never felt so much terror for another living creature.

The rest had all been an act. She'd pretended indifference until the very end, knowing she wasn't convincing Griffin and certainly not herself. And it was her own damned fault. She'd made the mistake of succumbing to human sentiment, and this was the inevitable price.

Griffin can take care of himself. That was the mantra she repeated with every step along the path. It didn't help in the least. She imagined him beaten down by the pack, bloodied and dying, all because he'd never quite let go of that helpless, angry little boy who'd watched his parents die.

"You're stronger than anyone I know," he'd said. "Stronger than me. You understand how things are."

Oh, yeah. Sure she understood. She was the worldly one, the one who didn't give a damn. Except that wasn't true anymore. It would never be true again.

He'd said, *"You're a survivor. No matter what happens, you'll go on. You'll stay free of Raoul, because it's not in your nature to surrender."*

And with those words he'd dispelled the resignation she'd felt when she'd emerged from Raoul's lair, convinced that submission to him was inevitable. Griffin *believed* in her. She couldn't let him down, couldn't go back to her old ways, even if he left her.

With a sharp shake of her head, Allie turned back toward Fifth Avenue. Officer Burney caught up with her as she reached her apartment. She opened the door and stepped inside, closing her eyes as the memories overwhelmed her once again.

"I love you," he'd said.

She could no longer untangle Griffin's declaration from the ache in her own heart. The words could not be unspoken, the feelings recalled. They would haunt her to the end of her days.

Damn you, Griffin Durant. Damn you to—

"Miss Chase?"

She opened her eyes to the sound of the familiar voice and found herself staring down the barrel of a gun. Burney surged up behind her, ready to throw himself at the slender man who clutched the weapon in unsteady fingers.

"Stay where you are," Elisha Hatch said, his voice high-pitched with fear. "I don't want to hurt anyone, but I will if you get in the way."

The cop subsided, his face a stony mask. "Who are you?" he demanded.

"Elisha," Allie said. "Nice to see you again."

Hatch swallowed, his Adam's apple bobbing beneath his fair skin. "I'm sorry it's come to this," he said. "I wouldn't have bothered you again if I'd been able to find the notes, but I've looked everywhere else. They must be here."

Allie tossed her coat and hat on the sofa, and sat down, ignoring Elisha's squawk of protest. The cop moved in the doorway, and Elisha's gun jerked back to cover him.

"I thought we went through all this before," Allie said, attempting to soothe him with the calm tone of her words.

Elisha licked his lips. "You have to have them, even if you don't know it."

"Those mysterious papers." She examined her nails. "You know I won't hurt you, Elisha. Why don't you put that thing away?"

He shook his head. "I've come too far to stop now."

"Okay. Why don't you start from the beginning?"

His gaze shifted to the cop and back again. "You haven't forgotten. The work from his research. The work Raoul killed him for."

Allie sat up. "Raoul killed Cato? You have proof?"

Hatch flinched at her icy tone and backed against the far wall. "I…I don't need proof. I *know.*"

"And why didn't you tell me this when we met at the funeral?"

"Too dangerous. Raoul was there. What he would have done to me if he'd found me…"

Allie fingered the chain of the pendant that hung just beneath the neckline of her dress. She could have crushed it with the slightest pressure of her fingers.

"Raoul is after you?"

"He wants the research."

"Why?"

"It's too…too difficult to explain."

Allie relaxed again, feigning indifference. "If that's the way you want it. I still don't have these papers."

"But they could be hidden in something Cato gave you."

"I doubt it. He gave me some jewelry and a few other things like that, nothing important. You can take them if it will make you feel any better. It's not like I'm hurting for money."

"You'll let me search the apartment?"

"Sure."

"And just as soon as my back is turned, you'll get me."

"Don't you think I could have done that already if I'd wanted to?"

Elisha's gun wavered. "If I get you in the heart…"

She rose and strolled toward him. "I'm betting your aim isn't that good. You're not a killer, Elisha."

"Stop!"

Allie kept going. Elisha nearly dropped the gun, and Burney didn't hesitate when he saw his opening.

But Elisha was really as desperate as he seemed. He turned on the cop and shot blindly, catching the man in the shoulder. Burney went spinning against the sofa, clutching his arm, and knocked his head against the marble coffee table. He collapsed to the carpet, unconscious.

By then Allie had Elisha's wrist in an implacable grip. He shrieked and let the gun fall from nerveless fingers. Allie pushed him to his knees, kicking the gun across the room.

"If you move," she said, "I *will* kill you." She strode to the cop and knelt beside him, feeling his pulse and checking the wound. It wasn't as bad as she'd feared; the bullet had passed right through and had obviously missed any major arteries. She suppressed the natural hunger that rose at the sight of blood, and quickly removed the sheets from her bed and tore them into strips, binding Burney's shoulder before she laid him down on the sofa.

Elisha remained where he was, nursing his wrist. "Are you going to call the cops?" he whined.

She ignored him, went to the telephone and placed a call to the nearest hospital. "An ambulance will be here in ten minutes," she said. "You have that long to explain exactly what's going on."

Elisha cringed against the wall, suddenly eager to cooperate. "It's a formula," he said. "Cato was…looking for a cure for the influenza, in case it ever came back again." He smiled nervously. "Cato was a scientific genius, even before his Conversion. He was the previous Master's protégé. Raoul inherited him when he took power."

"Tell me something I don't know," Allie said impatiently.

"Maybe you don't know that he'd been given free rein to do any research he chose, as long as Raoul saw some use for it."

"You said he was working on a cure for the influenza."

Hatch began to warm to his story. "He didn't have any luck, but he found something else during his work."

"Something bad, I take it."

"Something revolutionary. He created a vaccine. A vaccine that could restore the potency of any *strigoi* who'd lost the ability to Convert."

He told her how Cato's new formula could do the seemingly impossible: allow a Master to stay in power even after he would normally have lost his ability to

Convert. Those Masters who had become too old to procreate were inevitably unseated and their power usurped by the strongest of their vassals.

"My God," Allie said, beginning to grasp the full impact of Hatch's explanations. "This vaccine would put tremendous power in the hands of the one who controlled it. A Master could dominate a clan—"

"Virtually forever."

Allie sat down abruptly. "That's why Raoul wants to control the formula."

"It's why he wanted Cato dead. Cato never was much good at thinking through the consequences of what he discovered. He told Raoul about the formula because he couldn't keep his achievement to himself." Elisha sat a little straighter, his voice gaining strength. "But it soon became apparent, even to Cato, that once Raoul made use of the vaccine, he would see its continued existence as a threat."

"Raoul took the vaccine himself."

"Yes."

"Then he must have been—"

"Raoul hadn't created a new protégé in a dozen years, and his vassals were becoming restless. They were about to issue a challenge, to force him to prove he could still Convert. The vaccine changed all that."

"And Raoul made Margot," Allie said, dazed. "She was his first after the vaccine, wasn't she? No wonder she's so precious to him. She's proof that he's still in command."

"And will continue to be…as long as the rest of the clan doesn't realize how he cheated to keep his place."

Allie gripped the arms of the sofa. Centuries of tradition, and Raoul had crushed it beneath his heel. No vampire would stand for such arrogance, especially when it would prevent any movement in rank among the lieutenants and vassals.

They would kill him if they found out.

"Cato began to understand that Raoul would sacrifice him to protect his secret. He knew his days were numbered." Elisha's face went strangely blank. "Cato decided to make sure that Raoul wouldn't profit from his death, or from the vaccine. He made contact with someone outside the clan. Someone who could use the same vaccine to overthrow Raoul."

Allie racked her brain and found a name…a name she'd only heard spoken in whispers since her Conversion.

"The former Master," she said. "Klaus Aurelien."

Elisha rose carefully, watching Allie all the while. "I was only a kid when Raoul cast him out, but I know the history. Aurelien was popular in his day. He didn't impose the blood celibacy. More humans were Converted during his reign than in any time for the past thousand years."

"And the clan faced exposure because of it," Allie said.

"To his supporters, that didn't matter. And when the clan was compelled to unseat him—when Raoul exposed Aurelien's inability to create new protégés—more than a few of Aurelien's subjects resented the new Master. Some didn't stop resenting him even after they accepted vassalage."

"What happened to Aurelien?"

"He survived the coup and went into hiding. Even after thirty years, he still has his loyal followers in the clan. That's how Cato was able to find him."

Allie heard this information with inner dread. "And Cato was supposed to deliver the formula to Aurelien."

"He died before he could do it. That's why I have to finish what he started."

"How did Raoul know there were any notes for the vaccine in the first place?"

"It was...it was an accident. But he would have suspected anyway."

"Then why didn't Cato just tell you where he'd hidden the notes? Didn't he trust you?"

Elisha craned his neck as if it pained him. "He did trust me. He just ran out of time."

"So now you're here." She got up, searching her memory for anything odd Cato might have given her. "Even if I knew where to find the papers, I don't see why I should just hand the formula over to you and Aurelien."

"You hate Raoul."

"Sure, but maybe I'm not ready to see a nasty war break out between two Masters, especially when it's bound to affect me."

"There's something more you should know. Klaus wasn't willing to wait to get hold of the formula to start reversing his own sterility. Once he found out that Margot was the product of the vaccine, he arranged to kidnap her."

Allie's heart stopped. "*He* has Margot?"

"Yes. He already has human scientists working for him in their own lab, trying to duplicate the formula by using Margot's blood."

"Oh, my God." Allie swallowed her horror. "How did he get her away from Raoul?"

"He bribed one of Raoul's chief lieutenants...a man who had his own reasons for hating Raoul. The man who facilitated the exchange of letters between Margot and Malcolm Owen, so that Margot could be taken once she attempted to leave the mansion."

"Sebastian," Allie whispered.

"He was also the one who suggested kidnapping Owen first, so that when Margot disappeared, it would seem as if Owen had run off with her."

All the facts fell into place. It made sense: not only Mal's seemingly pointless kidnapping and ignorance of Margot's second "disappearance," but also the attacks on De Luca's men. They'd been meant to destabilize Raoul's position by focusing blame on him.

"Raoul tortured Sebastian," she said, "but Sebastian only admitted his part in passing letters between Margot and Mal."

"Then Raoul may still not know about Klaus. But it's only a matter of time. I have to get those notes to him immediately."

"Or what? This isn't all revenge for Cato's death, is it? Maybe Klaus promised you something of value you can't pass up."

Elisha didn't answer, confirming her suspicions. But if Aurelien were expecting the delivery of the formula, Elisha wouldn't be in a position to refuse the man, even if he had changed his mind.

"You don't have to believe me," he said at last. "Without the formula, Klaus will continue to use Margot to duplicate the vaccine. They could drain her dry, leave her permanently impaired."

"Then Aurelien is evil."

"No more than Raoul." Elisha took a step toward her. "Look, once he has the vaccine, he won't need Margot."

"And why should he let her go if keeping her damages Raoul's standing in the clan?"

"I can convince him."

"You?" Allie wandered to the window, looking out

at the darkening sky. "As I recall the stories, Aurelien despised humans even more than Raoul does."

"But—"

"Don't worry, Elisha. If those papers are here, I'll find them. But *I'll* decide what to do with them."

Elisha shivered. "Klaus will kill me if—"

"Maybe I can arrange protective custody for you, once I explain things to a certain cop I know."

"Why should he help me?"

"He doesn't want a clan war any more than I do." She glanced at her watch. "The ambulance should be here by now. I'll call him and—"

Elisha lunged, desperation making him faster than Allie anticipated. But not fast enough. She punched him in the face, and he fell like a stone, out cold. She went into the kitchen, washed the blood from her hands and strode to her bedroom. Where the hell would a man like Cato hide such important information?

With some reluctance, she broke several expensive vases and curios, looking for false bottoms. Nothing. Her drawers had no secret compartments, nor did the kitchen cupboards contain anything but the staples and canned goods Louise kept stocked for herself and Allie's rare meals at home.

Then Allie remembered the boxes of winter clothing she'd stored away on the closet shelves. She emptied the boxes on her bed and sifted through them. One particular item, a fur-lined silk and satin coat with elaborate embroidery in the oriental style, was padded enough to hide a sheaf of papers. She checked the pockets, then turned the coat inside out and ran her fingers over the seams.

Her fingers found a length of seam, thick and poorly sewn, in the skirt of the coat. Suppressing her excitement, she used a pair of small scissors to pick out the stitching.

Just beneath was a tiny silk pouch. When she opened it, she found sheets of paper creased into small squares. The paper crackled as she unfolded it; each sheet was crisscrossed with lines of fine writing, including equations and numbers that would make sense only to someone of Cato's background.

One sheet was different. She saw her name and was just beginning to read when she heard the front door squeal and shatter like rotten wood. She threw the heavy coat into the back of the closet, snatched up a lighter one and shoved the notes into the pocket. She'd just finished when Dorian turned up at her bedroom door.

"Miss Chase," he said, "will you please come with me?"

She pulled on the coat and went with him. Waiting in the living room were Javier and a pair of unfamiliar enforcers, who lifted Elisha from the floor and dragged him out the ruined door. They left Officer Burney where he lay. Allie hoped the ambulance would arrive soon.

A pair of black coupes waited at the curb. "Where are we going?" Allie asked, as if the answer were a matter of complete indifference to her.

"We've been following your friend Elisha," Javier said with a nasty smile. "We let the human think he was safe, and now he's led us right to your door."

"It was just a social visit. He did work for my patron."

"I advise you not to prevaricate, Miss Chase," Dorian said. "We know Elisha was looking for something that rightfully belongs to Raoul."

"I don't know anything about it."

"Raoul would prefer to determine that for himself."

"Maybe I have a few objections to going back to his dungeon."

"That's too bad," Javier said. "You're—"

He came to an abrupt halt. So did Dorian. A dozen armed men had appeared on the street, rushing from concealment with tommy guns raised and faces grim with murderous intent. They belonged to De Luca, and they were clearly out for revenge.

Javier uttered a foul curse and pulled his own gun. Elisha's escorts threw the human into one of the cars and took cover behind it.

Allie waited in the street, possessed by a strange sense of invulnerability. "Looks like I might not be going to see Raoul after all," she said.

Dorian drew his revolver from his coat and pressed the muzzle to her temple. "De Luca likes you," he said. "He might not be so ready to sacrifice your life."

"I guess it depends on his gunsels," she said. "And anyway, I don't think you'll kill me."

"I do my duty."

"For a murderer like Raoul? A man who'd kill a loyal vassal to protect an illicit secret? Or don't you know exactly what he's looking for?"

Dorian shifted his grip on the revolver. "What are you talking about?"

"Cato. He knew something about Raoul, something that would destroy him if the clan ever found out."

Hesitation and doubt were clear on the enforcer's face. De Luca's men still hadn't opened fire. In the midst of the peculiar standoff, no one seemed to notice the huge brown and gray wolf who raced into the street and knocked Dorian down with a body blow not even a *strigoi* could resist.

Allie's knees threatened to buckle with relief, but somehow she kept on her feet. Javier aimed his weapon at Griffin, but Allie chopped his wrist with the side of her hand, and he lost his hold. She dove for the weapon, engaged the safety and threw it toward the nearest of De Luca's men. Griffin crouched over Dorian, his bared teeth inches from the enforcer's neck.

"I see you survived after all," Allie said, her voice shaking as she spoke to Griffin over her shoulder. "If you don't mind, I'd rather you didn't kill Dorian. He really isn't a bad sort."

Griffin Changed and leaped away from Dorian, still ready to fight. He risked a glance in Allie's direction. "You promised to leave New York."

"No, I didn't. I only said I'd take care of Gemma if something happened to you." She glimpsed the blood spattered on the pavement. "You're hurt."

"Not anymore. The Change healed my wounds." He rolled his shoulders. Muscles rippled under unblemished skin. "Are you all right?"

"So far."

"What the hell's going on?"

"That's a long story. I'll give you the juicy details as soon as we're out of this mess."

Questions boiled behind his eyes. "Why are *they* here?" he asked, jerking his head toward De Luca's men.

"Revenge."

"On Raoul."

"Yeah. But things have just gotten a lot more complicated." She backed away from Javier. "You watch the enforcers. I'll talk to De Luca."

She turned and walked quickly toward the ragged line of humans. Guns lifted.

"Hold your fire," she said. "There are a few interesting facts your boss ought to know before he starts shooting."

An expensively suited man with slick black hair came to meet her. "De Luca doesn't want you or the animal," he said. "He's here for the leeches."

"Even if they weren't responsible for the attacks on his men?"

De Luca's lieutenant met her eyes with an icy stare. "Who else would be?"

"A certain vampire who wants to topple Raoul from mastery of the clan."

The men behind him muttered, clearly unmollified. The lieutenant retreated under cover of his escort and melted into the shadows.

A few tense minutes later the lieutenant reappeared, followed by De Luca himself.

"What's this about another vampire?" the boss demanded.

Quickly Allie explained what Elisha had told her about Klaus Aurelien, omitting any mention of the formula. "Elisha was my patron's assistant. He had certain reasons to hate Raoul and was secretly working for Aurelien. He came to ask me to join him, but Raoul's men followed him to my place."

"Do you know where this Aurelien is?"

"Elisha didn't have the chance to tell me, but I'm sure Aurelien had those hatchet men attack your guys to distract Raoul and cause him as much trouble as possible. If he were engaged in a war with you, half his resources would be stuck fighting a useless battle, giving Aurelien an excellent opportunity to stage a coup."

De Luca digested this in silence, frowning. "Why didn't Raoul have his predecessor killed when he took over the clan?"

"Somehow Aurelien escaped. That's all I know."

"And why should I care which leech runs the clan?"

"Klaus has Margot."

"What?"

Allie considered telling De Luca the full truth about the vaccine, then realized it would open a can of worms that might make the situation a hundred times worse than it already was. She didn't dare tip the balance of power when matters were so precarious.

"Aurelien took her as another way of hurting Raoul," she said. "You can be sure he doesn't intend anything good for her."

De Luca's face went white, then red, with rage. "We have to find Aurelien."

"Precisely." Raoul strolled from the shadows, Javier and Dorian at his heels like whipped curs. "You want Margot safe, and so do I. Aurelien killed your men. There's no reason why we can't work together for our mutual benefit."

De Luca laughed. "*Certo.* Although I have only the word of Miss Chase and your human servant that this other vampire was behind the attacks."

"Not *my* servant," Raoul said. "Hatch was a traitor to the clan." He caught Allie's eye with unmistakable warning. "I've suspected for several days that he was serving as an agent for another vampire. He obviously hoped that Allegra would assist him."

"She wouldn't do anything of the kind," Griffin said as he came to join them, defiantly unashamed of his unclad state. "She knows what a struggle for vampire leadership would mean—utter chaos in the city." He put a possessive hand on Allie's arm. "We also know that certain werewolves have been working for vampires in the city."

"Werewolves working for vampires?" Raoul repeated, incredulous. "What would they have to gain?"

"Power over the pack, with the new Master's backing."

Raoul's eyes narrowed. "And what of you, Durant?"

"I've been trying to expose them," he said. "Now we know *who* they were working for, and why they kidnapped Mal."

"Sloan approved this?"

"Ordinarily he would be strongly opposed to such activities." Griffin glanced at Allie. "At the moment he's not in any condition to assist us with information."

Allie nodded slightly, understanding. Griffin was hardly out of danger yet. None of them were.

"Shall we call a truce?" Raoul suggested. "At least until we've confirmed the facts of this business?"

De Luca's face showed no expression. "A truce," he agreed. "Until we have answers. But if you try anything, Raoul, you'll suffer the consequences."

"You're still only human."

"And every one of my men knows how to shoot a man in the head or the heart."

They stared at each other. To Allie's private amazement, Raoul was the first to retreat. He went directly to his enforcers' car, opened the door and slid in beside Elisha. The human was just beginning to stir.

As Allie started after Raoul, Javier lunged for her. Griffin turned on the enforcer with a snarl.

"Peace," Dorian said, brushing off his trousers. "Raoul said truce. We wait."

Sick with the thought of what Raoul would do to

Elisha, Allie listened while Griffin held her close. She heard little of the distant conversation, but several times Raoul's voice rose in threat, and once Elisha shrieked in pain. De Luca and his men observed with wary interest but did nothing to interfere. A few minutes later Raoul flung open the door and hurled Elisha's body into the street.

CHAPTER TWENTY

"Murderer," Allie whispered. "I'll make him pay—"

"Not yet," Griffin said, his breath warm against her ear. "Be patient."

"The way you were patient going after Sloan?" She felt for his hand and gripped it hard. "Is he dead?"

"I think he survived, but the Pack is after me. I came to warn you, in case—"

"In case I didn't go with Gemma and Lou."

"Damn it, Allie, if only you'd—" He broke off as Raoul sauntered toward them, stepping over Elisha's body as if it were so much discarded refuse.

"I know where Margot is," Raoul said.

"Where?" De Luca demanded.

Raoul gave him an icy glance. "Somewhere to the north."

De Luca turned and strode back to his men. Griffin stepped in front of Allie. "Then you also know where to find your rival," he said.

"Unless he's been warned." Raoul stared at Allie with such hostility that Griffin bared his teeth.

Raoul ignored him. "You know what the human was looking for," he said to Allie.

"I have an idea."

"Did Hatch find them?"

"Didn't he tell you?"

"Oddly enough, he did not. Where are they?"

"I don't know."

Raoul smiled. "I don't think I'll take your word for that, Allie. Not this time."

"You'll keep your filthy hands off her," Griffin said.

"You'd best silence your dog's barking, Allegra, or I might have to put him down."

"You underestimate him, Raoul," Allie said. "Just as you overestimate yourself."

"Shall we put it to the test?" Raoul asked. He moved at lightning speed toward Griffin, who shifted his weight and caught Raoul by the arm. Dorian watched impassively. Javier seized his fellow enforcer's gun and was about to use it when a flurry of shapes, gray and black and brown, burst through the loose barrier of De Luca's men and surrounded Raoul and Griffin. The humans raised their weapons, but De Luca stopped them with a gesture.

Almost at once the foremost wolf Changed, his gray-pelted form distorting faster than the eye could follow. He rose to confront Griffin, his silver-streaked hair nearly standing on end.

"Renegade," he growled. "What a surprise to find you hiding among leeches and humans."

Raoul raised a brow. "Cassius, isn't it?" he drawled. "One of Sloan's fine young men. I trust you're here to relieve me of this canine impediment."

Cassius glanced at the vampire with utter contempt. "We aren't here for any purpose of yours, blood drinker. Stay out of our way."

"Your kind are very free with your threats. All bark and no bite, as they say."

Cassius turned back to Griffin as if Raoul hadn't

spoken. "You're coming with us to face the judgment of the elders."

"On what charge?" Allie demanded.

"For breaking pack law," Cassius said, as if he were reciting formal charges from an arrest warrant. "For encouraging open rebellion. For attacking the leader without due challenge."

"Did he kill Sloan?"

"Allie…" Griffin said softly, warningly, pushing her aside. "I regret the fight," he said to Cassius, "but I can't go with you. Not until the traitors have been exposed and those under my protection are safe."

"They'll never be safe as long as you run," Cassius said.

"You may do what you like with others of your breed and the humans they regard as their equals," Raoul said. "Miss Chase is under my authority."

"Like hell I am," Allie said. "And you aren't taking Griffin anywhere," she said to Cassius. "If he hurt Sloan, it couldn't have been unprovoked."

"Leech," Cassius snarled, "you'll pay for this."

"And you'll die if you touch her or any of my kin," Griffin said.

Allie laughed. "I don't know which are the worse blowhards, vampires or werewolves."

"We'll get him," Cassius said. "Sooner or later he'll be alone, and we'll be waiting."

In answer Allie grabbed Griffin's hand and dragged his resisting body toward De Luca, who stood well out of harm's way. "Mr. De Luca," she said, "I have a great favor to ask of you."

De Luca glanced toward the bristling werewolves. "This has something to do with those animals, I take it."

"Yes."

"Allie, don't get involved," Griffin said. "I got myself into this. It's my—"

"Oh, please." She returned her attention to De Luca. "All I ask is that you give Griffin sanctuary until this situation has blown over."

"'This situation,'" De Luca repeated. "That's a mild way of putting it." He stroked the silk of his tie. "I have no reason to help a werewolf who's been condemned by his own kind."

"Griffin helped expose the werewolves who aided the vampire responsible for the slaughter of your men. He's worth more to you as an ally than Sloan ever was."

De Luca studied Griffin carefully. "Was it your intention to take over the pack by killing Sloan?"

"No. It was my intention to get at the truth. Sloan attacked me because others had seen his weakness in failing to discover and expose the traitors."

"Allora," De Luca murmured. He addressed Allie. "If I do this for you, Miss Chase, there is something I ask in return. You have cared for Margot as a friend."

"I still do."

"Then you will gladly assist me in taking Margot back from Raoul once she's found."

"You can't expect—" Griffin began.

"It's not that simple," Allie interrupted. "Margot is bound to Raoul, as he is to her. Even though she left him willingly, it must have been—is—excruciating for her to be parted from him for any length of time."

"Which only shows her desperation," De Luca said, the muscles in his jaw taut with anger. "Is it not true that such bonds are broken by the death of the patron?"

"Yes."

"And now that Aurelien has been exposed, is it not likely that he and Raoul will attempt to destroy each other?"

"It's inevitable. Raoul can't let Aurelien live and still maintain his position."

"Then you will help me kill Raoul if he survives the fight."

Allie hesitated, pinned like a collector's specimen beneath De Luca's piercing stare. As much as she despised Raoul and longed for his downfall, she could hardly promise his death. He was still powerful, with many protégés and vassals, while she claimed no loyalty from any *strigoi* in the clan.

But she'd believed Cassius when he'd said he would be waiting for the moment when Griffin was alone and vulnerable. And she had no more faith in werewolf mercy than she did in vampire compassion.

Still, she had something Raoul badly wanted… something that might give her an advantage. Aurelien also desired the formula—perhaps, as Elisha had implied, enough to trade Margot for it. And he might be able to kill Raoul. Somehow she had to buy time to read the notes and decide how best to use them.

"I agree," she said.

"You will follow any plan I propose?"

"Yes."

"I won't accept sanctuary under these conditions," Griffin said.

"Don't be a fool, Durant," De Luca said. He signaled to the men behind him. "Go with them while you still can."

"Not without Allie." He leaned forward, catching De Luca's eye. "There's one major flaw in your plan to use her against Raoul. He's always wanted her, because he can't abide knowing that even a single vampire remains free of his control. He'll use the current conflict as an excuse to flout vampire law and claim her. You can't have it both ways. You can either protect Allie for your own benefit or kowtow to Raoul."

The gang boss looked as if he would gladly have shot Griffin point-blank, but he controlled his anger. "Very well," he said. "Join my men, both of you."

Griffin took Allie's arm, but she pulled free. "I have to talk to Raoul first."

"I can't protect you if you put yourself in his hands," De Luca said.

"I'll be fine." She took off her coat and pushed it into Griffin's arms. "Keep this for me. I'll be right back."

She walked away before Griffin could hold her, willing him to stay where he was. The werewolves were pacing in angry circles, eyeing the tommy guns trained on them from across the street. Raoul watched Allie approach with a mocking smile.

"Bargaining for your lover's life, or your own?" he asked.

She stood before him, her fist planted on one outthrust hip. "Is my life in danger?"

"It isn't yourself you should be worried about."

She clucked her tongue. "You're as bad as the dogs, always making threats."

"They aren't threats, Allegra. I can get to your friends anytime I wish, no matter where you've hidden them."

"How do you know they're hidden?"

"Come, now. You can't believe I am so ignorant of what goes on in my own city."

"Okay. So you know. But you'd better consider what

I might do to you if you bother those under my protection."

Raoul lowered his head. "You do have the notes."

"I don't need them. Elisha told me a few interesting facts before you killed him. About a formula and a Master who is ruling under false pretenses."

"Do you think anyone would take a human's word against mine?"

"There are already some with doubts about you, Raoul. You've killed Cato and Sebastian. Maybe it wouldn't take much to start an avalanche that brings you down."

"You won't get a chance to speak."

"You're outnumbered here. Sure, you could send enforcers to attack De Luca, but that would hardly strengthen your position. And you aren't ready to make a pact with the dogs when some of them are working for your enemy."

"De Luca knows Aurelien is the greater danger to him. He won't protect you forever."

"He doesn't trust you. He's the kind of man who weighs all his options before he acts."

Raoul's face tightened with fury. "Do you truly think you've escaped me?" he asked. "This is only a temporary reprieve, Allegra. Either you give yourself to me, or your friends will suffer."

"We'll see. Maybe Aurelien will get to you first. Goodbye, Raoul."

She strolled back to De Luca as if she hadn't a care in the world, but it was all she could do to hold her legs steady. Every word she'd spoken had been sheer bravado, nothing more. Raoul was a killer, and he still had control of the clan. He was like a vicious animal trapped in a corner; he wouldn't stop until he'd gotten rid of anyone who stood in his way or posed even the mildest threat. Lou and Starke and Gemma would never be safe as long as he lived.

Griffin came to meet her as she walked into De Luca's circle of hatchet men. He embraced her, his heart beating so rapidly that she could feel it through her own skin.

"God, Allie," he said. "What did you say to him?"

She drew back. "That I have certain new information that might do him considerable harm in the clan."

"He seemed very eager to get his hands on something Hatch was looking for. Does that have something to do with your 'information'?"

"Yes. Hatch told me quite a bit before he died. He gave me a very incriminating account of Raoul's highly unorthodox activities. I'll explain more as soon as it's safe." She looked toward the street where she'd left Raoul, but he and his enforcers had already gone. "Raoul knows we've sent Gemma and Lou out of town. I had to make it clear that I'd use what I'd learned against him if he goes after them for any reason."

"And now he wants you more than ever."

"With Aurelien on the loose, he can't afford to let anyone defy him. I've become a personal affront. Still, he won't try anything as long as he needs all his enforcers and vassals to counter Aurelien's threat. We have a little time."

Griffin looked away. "This is as much my doing as Raoul's. My stubbornness, my stupidity."

"We wouldn't be—" She shook her head. "I almost said we wouldn't be human if we didn't make mistakes."

"I can't protect you or my family as long as the pack is after me."

"You couldn't protect them from Raoul in any case. There's only one permanent solution. Raoul has to die."

Griffin's teeth flashed. "Leave it to me. I'll find a way."

She bit back her reply. She knew damned well he would never get close enough to hurt Raoul.

De Luca was right. It was all up to her.

Up to her to save the people she loved.

"Raoul will be forced to confront Aurelien very soon," she said. "There's a reasonable chance that he won't survive the encounter."

"Or he may be victorious," Griffin said. "We can't rely on—"

"Enough talk," De Luca said, joining them. "Go with Garibaldi. He'll get you to my hotel."

"I left a wounded man in my apartment," Allie said. "The ambulance is late. I have to make sure he's still okay."

"I'll send one of my men to do it," De Luca said. "I want you out of here."

Reluctantly Allie and Griffin went with the lieutenant, while Cassius and his companions snarled in helpless frustration. Just as Garibaldi's car pulled away, several sirens broke the night's stillness: the ambulance, finally arriving for Officer Burney, and a pair of patrol cars. Allie caught a glimpse of Ross Kavanagh before Garibaldi's coupe turned the corner.

Griffin stared out the rear window. "I'll have to tell Ross what's happening."

"De Luca may not want the police involved."

"Ross will be on his side if it comes to a gang war," he said. "De Luca must realize that."

"Let's hope you're right."

It was only a few minutes to the expensive hotel where De Luca kept his headquarters. A quartet of hatchet men escorted Allie and Griffin to a suite down the corridor from De Luca's private quarters. Once the door was closed, Griffin grabbed Allie and kissed her as if it were for the last time. For a few precious moments she allowed herself to lean on him, reveling in his strength, glad to let him hold her.

He steered her to the brocaded sofa, found a decanter of ice water and poured her a glass. She took it gratefully.

"What happened with Sloan?" she asked.

"Since the pack is after me," he concluded his explanation a few minutes later, "I must assume that Sloan still has control." He sat beside her, draining his own glass of water in one swallow. "Tell me everything you learned from Hatch before he died."

She repeated what she'd told De Luca. "But I didn't tell him the one thing that could topple Raoul if the clan ever became aware of it."

Griffin listened intently while she told him about Cato's vaccine and how Raoul had illicitly made use of it to maintain his power.

"Do you have some proof besides Hatch's word on this?" he asked.

Allie considered her answer. Until she'd read through the notes herself, she didn't want anyone to know about them. Not even Griffin.

"Raoul made sure that Elisha could never testify against him," she said, "but I may be able to locate evidence that supports his confession."

"At some risk to yourself, of course."

"All of us are at risk."

For once he didn't lecture her. "I trust your judgment, Allie," he said, his voice rough with emotion.

"Thank you. I know what that's worth."

He rose to refill their glasses. "Why *did* Hatch come to your apartment?"

"He was trying to recruit me, knowing that Raoul and I don't exactly see eye to eye."

"He thought you'd prefer Aurelien without knowing anything about him?"

"He told me that Raoul killed Cato to make sure he could never talk about the vaccine. That would have been enough."

"Did you consider it?"

She set her glass down on the coffee table with a bang. "I thought you trusted my judgment."

"I'm sorry. It's my judgment that's entirely at fault."

With a sharp sigh she relented and reached for his hand. "Stop blaming yourself, Grif. What's done is done."

He lifted her hand to his lips and kissed her palm. "How is it that you've become my greatest strength, Allegra Chase?"

She searched her mind for some airy retort, but the time for denials was past. She couldn't escape the warmth in his eyes or the effect of his nearness on her body. Every instinct told her that he wanted her...the blood pulsing beneath the tanned skin of his neck, the rhythm of his breathing, the intensity of his stare. They were bound by adversity and need, closer than ever before.

All it would take was one more kiss and he would be carrying her to the ornate bed visible through the doorway to the adjoining room. But she'd hardly forgotten his reaction the last time she'd tried to seduce him. It was his turn to make the first move.

The sofa creaked as he got to his feet. "I have to

speak to De Luca about calling Ross," he said briskly, as if his desire had existed only in her imagination. "I won't be long."

She settled back among the cushions, tracing the brocade pattern with her fingertip. "Sure."

He paused in the doorway to the suite, on the verge of saying something else, but at last he walked out, closing the door behind him.

Allie waited a few minutes and went to fetch her coat, which Griffin had returned to her on the way to the hotel. She pulled the crumpled notes from the pocket, carried them into the bedroom and stretched across the mattress to read them.

They hadn't made much sense the first time she'd seen them, and they didn't make much more now. The equations and symbols were those of a scientist, written in a code she couldn't possibly decipher. But there was a single sheet of paper covered with handwriting so small that even Allie's sharp eyes could barely make it out:

My dear Allegra,
I have taken a great risk in concealing my formulae in your apartment, and in believing that you will find them before they fall into the hands of my enemy. I have left another letter with Sebastian, whom I trust, to give to you in the event of my death. If you hold this letter in your hand, it means that Sebastian has delivered the first missive, and you have followed the clues and instructions therein.

Allie let the papers drop into her lap. Sebastian had never hinted that he had something for her, though he'd had a clear opportunity to pass her a letter when she'd visited Margot in the mansion. Surely he'd known the contents of such a letter…but if he'd realized that the "clues and instructions" led to notes that could bring about Raoul's downfall and assist his new Master, why hadn't he tried to claim the notes himself and expose Raoul?

Sebastian was beyond answering such questions, poor devil. In any case, he apparently hadn't confessed any knowledge of the notes in spite of the dreadful torture to which he'd been subjected. His hatred of Raoul must have been powerful, indeed.

Allie picked up the paper again, her heart thudding almost painfully beneath her ribs.

By now you know that Raoul has greatly benefitted from the vaccine I have produced. It reversed the sterility which old age had brought upon him, the sterility which put him in extreme danger of losing his mastery of the clan.

I have known for some time that Raoul has been plotting to kill me so that I can never speak of what these formulae contain and how they have been utilized by him. In his arrogance, he will doubtless believe that I could not utterly destroy my own work, as indeed, I have not. Now that you are in possession of the only copy of my working notes, you must at all costs keep them from Raoul. This is why I have provided you with another means of thwarting Raoul, should he force you to submit to him.

I have created a toxin which is inevitably fatal to any *strigoi* who ingests it in the blood of the one who drinks it. You will find this poison in a

vial I have given to Louise Moreau for safekeeping, though she does not know what it contains.
I have also hidden the antidote in the pendant I
asked you to wear at all times.

Allie's fingers trembled as she felt for the silver
bauble that hung around her neck. Cato had asked so
little of her; it had seemed nothing at all to promise that
she would never take the locket off.

Now she knew why he'd given it to her. Wise, pre-
scient Cato.

Allie closed her eyes, her stomach heaving. She
folded the letter, shoved it back in the pocket of her
coat and headed straight for the small sideboard where
Griffin had found the water. Someone had conve-
niently left a bottle of fine brandy in the cupboard, and
she helped herself to a generous glass.

Fortified by several drinks, which took the edge off
the turbulence of her emotions, Allie felt for the tiny
catch at the back of the locket. Inside was a tiny packet
containing some sort of powder. Taking great care, she
closed the locket firmly. She didn't dare risk losing any
of the antidote now.

She was just about to finish the letter when Griffin
returned.

"I've spoken to Ross," he began. "He said—" He
paused, looking carefully at Allie's face. "What's
wrong?"

She smiled, tilting her empty glass. "Nothing. Just
nerves. It hasn't exactly been a barrel of laughs these
days."

"No, it hasn't. My poor darling."

Once she would have balked at such sentimental
hogwash, but when Griffin embraced her, she com-

pletely forgot to be cynical. "So," she said, casually stepping away, "what did Ross have to say?"

At once his expression turned grim. "Mal has escaped from the hospital."

"What? Wasn't he under guard?"

"Ross doesn't know how he managed it, either. But it was more than just an escape. He got to one of the other patients—a man who was badly wounded trying to leave the speakeasy where they found Mal."

"You mean, one of the werewolves who took Mal? He was in the same hospital?"

"Ross didn't tell me he'd caught one of them. The man was in very bad shape, unable to speak, and Ross was afraid of what I might do before he had a chance to question him." Griffin flexed his fingers. "Maybe he was right to keep it a secret."

"Evidently not secret enough."

"Ross still hadn't been able to interrogate the man before Mal got to him. Now he'll never get the chance."

Allie sat down slowly. "You mean, Mal killed this guy?"

"I don't think so. The kidnapper was in critical condition. Even the stress of facing Mal could have killed him."

"Is that what the doctors say?"

Rubbing at the crease between his brows, Griffin gazed at the half-empty bottle of brandy. "They say he was strangled. Ross is questioning the staff, but if another intruder got into the room, he couldn't sort that scent from among all the others."

"Aurelien can't have been happy that his werewolf servants failed him," Allie said. "He sent his men to attack De Luca. He may have had others able to infiltrate the hospital."

"That's what Ross is trying to find out." Griffin sighed and picked up a glass from the sideboard. "Whatever happened, it seems likely that Mal knows where Aurelien is keeping Margot, and he's on his way there as we speak."

CHAPTER TWENTY-ONE

GRIFFIN KNEW he'd said too much when he saw the quiet despair on Allie's face. He set the glass back down and sat beside her, taking her hand between his.

"I shouldn't have burdened you with this," he said. "You have enough to deal with, and there's nothing you can do about Mal."

Allie held herself too straight, as if she feared she might fall apart if she relaxed a single muscle. "Mal knows where to find Aurelien and Margot," she said, "and so does Raoul. The rest of us are still in the dark." She smiled without humor. "I never thought I'd have to feel so uncertain again."

Griffin cupped her face in his hands, forcing her to meet his eyes. "Of one thing you can be certain," he said, and kissed her tenderly. Allie was hesitant in her response, but when it came, he felt the spark of her old fire returning, and he knew without question that the time for waiting was past. Allie needed him now, more than ever before. And he needed her. No more scruples, no antiquated codes about marriage before sexual intimacy. He and Allie had both faced death several times over, and he knew—oh, how well he knew—that the soul demanded the most fundamental promise of life when it stood on the precipice of oblivion.

Her body was supple in his arms, all sweet curves

and sinuous lines. "Don't leave me," she whispered into his shoulder.

He answered with a deeper kiss, drawing her hard against him. The tension in her body changed, and her breath quickened. His did the same. He ran his hands over her frock, molding the thin material to her waist and hips. She wore almost nothing underneath.

He could have taken her then and there on the sofa, but even in such desperate times, he could maintain some vestige of decency. He lifted her in his arms and walked to the door, turning the key in the lock. The bedroom was only a few steps away. He set Allie on her feet and flung back the bedcovers.

For once Allie was the one who hung back. Her color was high, her eyes almost hectic in their brightness.

"Are you sure?" she said.

"Yes." He stroked her cheek with the back of his hand. "Doubts, Allie?"

"No, it's not that at all." She clung to him in a way she never had before, her fingers digging into the muscle of his shoulders. "I just…I'm still…"

"I know. No thinking beyond this moment."

The silky skin of her throat trembled. "I was never with Cato," she said in a rush, as if she felt a powerful need to confess. "He never wanted me that way."

"It doesn't matter."

"Those other men…I didn't care about them."

"Allie…"

"I care for you, Griffin. Sometimes it scares me."

He traced her dark eyebrows with his thumbs. "No need for fear. I won't ask anything you can't give."

She continued to search his eyes, an unfamiliar hesitation in her own. Then she began to work at his tie, loosening the knot, slipping his collar off the studs. He tried to take command, but she stopped him, unbuttoning his shirt until she could place her palms against his chest.

"You're beautiful," she said.

It was his turn to flush. "Shouldn't that be my line?"

"I've heard it a million times. I'll bet you haven't." She pressed her cheek to his chest and wrapped her arms around his waist. "Your heart is beating very fast," she murmured.

"So is yours. I hear it."

She drew back and traced the small scar along his chin. "What's this? I thought werewolves didn't have scars."

"I was…badly wounded at the time, and couldn't Change immediately. Shrapnel hit me in the face."

"God."

"But I did heal. The same can't be said for many others."

"I'm sorry." She traced a circle around his nipple with her fingertip. "It's been a long time for you, hasn't it?"

"Years. I don't regret the wait."

"Then I'll have to make up for it." She ran her tongue over his nipple and began unbuttoning his trousers. He thought he would lose control when she took his cock in her hand and massaged him with just the right combination of pressure and gentleness.

"You'd better stop," he said, "if you want this to last more than a few minutes."

She chuckled. "Oh, I think it will." She turned her back on him. "Help me, will you?"

With awkward, eager fingers, he put his hands on her shoulders. Her frock was the slip-over kind, a straight sheath with a row of fringe around the low waist. She stretched as he lifted the dress over her head, raising her arms so that nothing impeded the flow of fabric across her body.

Beneath she wore only the sheerest of bandeau brassieres, hardly more than a scrap of lace across her breasts, and a pair of step-in panties that a strong look could have torn. The combination was made even more erotic by the stockings rolled just below her knees and the pumps she still wore.

Griffin's mouth went dry. She turned again to face him, her eyes heavy-lidded.

"Well?" she said. "Are you going to say I'm beautiful?"

"That would…never be enough."

"Good." She leaned up and kissed him, her tongue darting between her lips. He seized her, lifting her light body up, and met her tongue with his own.

By the time the kiss ended, he had already undone the hooks of her bandeau, and a moment later her small but perfectly formed breasts were pressed to him. He felt the shape of her pendant, cool against his hot skin.

"Don't you ever take that off?" he murmured as he kissed the base of her throat.

"Never." She tilted back her head. "Does it… bother you?"

"Not at all." He lifted her onto the bed and gently pushed her back onto the sheets. He knelt beside the bed. She let out a soft gasp as he ran his fingers under her step-ins, tracing the shape of her inner thigh. He easily slipped the panties off, letting them fall to the carpet.

Allie squirmed, and suddenly Griffin realized that she was unused to being in the vulnerable position; she was accustomed to taking command in any sexual situation. He wouldn't make it so easy for her to claim that dominance. The sight of her, naked except for the stockings and pumps, made it very difficult for him to take his time.

But take his time he did. And Allie knew then that this would be unlike any experience she'd ever known. His gaze was like a fevered touch; she hadn't felt so hungry and sensual since…since she had taken Griffin's blood in her apartment.

She was almost unprepared when his tongue stroked along the inside of her thigh and touched the center of her heat, dipping and tasting with lingering appreciation. Allie felt like a virgin with her first man, her body so achingly alive that she almost couldn't bear the pleasure.

"Are you…are you sure you…haven't done this in years?" she gasped.

He didn't answer. She wasn't interested in pursuing the question. He continued to lick and caress until she was on the very brink of completion, and then abruptly he withdrew. She caught her breath. He eased himself over her and drew her nipple in his mouth, circling it with his tongue until it reached a hard, sensitive peak. He suckled. Allie groaned.

Griffin gave equal attention to the other breast and then kissed his way up to her neck, nuzzling the hollow of her throat. He lowered himself between her thighs, and she felt the heavy hardness of him sliding along the inside of her thigh, seeking, finding.

He entered her gently, as if she truly were a virgin. She wrapped her legs around him and urged him with her body, but he refused to be hurried. He eased in and out of her slowly, so slowly, emphasizing each movement, gazing into her eyes. She felt taken as she'd never been taken before, possessed, naked in soul, as well as body. When she would have spoken, he closed her mouth with his lips.

"Hush," he said, in time to his thrusts. "Hush."

He penetrated more deeply. Allie arched her back, pulling him in. The speed and strength of his thrusts increased, and she felt herself falling, falling, her senses dazzled by light as she tumbled into the sun.

Breathing hard, Griffin kissed her damp forehead. He was still hard and full. She grabbed his hips.

"You're not finished," she said faintly.

"I don't want to hurt you."

She grinned, hooked her leg around his and flipped him onto his back. He didn't resist. She straddled him, her thighs to either side of his, her locket brushing his chest.

"You think I'm afraid of being hurt?" she asked, drawing a line down the center of his torso with one polished nail. "If you think we're done, you have another think coming."

The look in his eyes was so filled with emotion that she found it difficult to meet his gaze. She slid down his torso, stopping when she met an obvious obstruction. He made a low sound as she took him in her mouth and began rolling her tongue over the smooth, firm flesh. He filled her mouth as he had filled her body, awakening a new pleasure in *her* as she pleasured *him*. He tangled his fingers in her hair, head thrown back, eyes closed. The muscles in his stomach began to knot. Immediately she withdrew, slid up his thighs and straddled him again.

She braced her hands against his shoulders and eased down on top of him, welcoming him back. Then she began to move as slowly and deliberately as he had earlier. She pressed herself to his chest, bending her head so that her lips brushed his neck. She bit him, not entirely gently, and he shuddered.

The blood flowed hot and sweet. The euphoria of feeding joined with the erotic sensations of her nipples teasing the wiry hair sprinkling his chest, and his hardness inside her. She continued to move, feeling the tension build in his body, the rapture claiming him even as he stiffened and jerked with his release.

She remained joined to him for several minutes, listening to his heartbeat gradually slow. He ran his hands up and down her back. She rolled off and settled into the crook of his arm, her head on his shoulder.

"Wow," she said.

"Yes." He nuzzled her ear. "Stay with me, Allie."

"I'm not going anywhere. We've got all night."

"Never leave me. Stay with me forever."

She burrowed her face into his chest. His sigh stirred her damp hair. After a while Griffin kissed her again, more urgently. And for a little while they both forgot about forever.

DAWN BROKE like a revelation. Allie climbed out of bed with a vampire's soundless grace, pulled on a dressing gown left by some thoughtful maid and settled into a chair beneath the window, savoring a moment that might never come again.

The last time she had watched Griffin sleep had been in her apartment just after her first, failed attempt to get him into her bed. Then he'd been in a drunken stupor, his body unused to consuming the quantities of alcohol she was accustomed to.

Now he was sober, his legs flung across the bed in an exhausted sprawl. His hair was getting long, falling across his face; several days' growth of beard shadowed his jaw. The sleek, powerful muscles of his arms and chest were relaxed now, but she remembered the feeling of them flexing against her bare skin, the passion with which he'd used that magnificent physique to bring her pleasure.

He had fought so long to be a proper gentleman, restrained and dignified. That gentleman was gone, lost to grim necessity, and in his place the werewolf rested, a chilling instant away from deadly action.

"Leave it to me," he'd said when she'd told him that Raoul had to die. And he'd meant it. He was willing to sacrifice his principles, his future, his very life, to take Raoul down, and count it worth the cost.

Allie knew he could never succeed. Too many stood against him, and he had no entrée into the *strigoi* world. His sacrifice would be all for nothing. She wouldn't let him make it.

Only one person had the means to end the greatest threat to him and those he loved.

She rose, paced across the room on bare feet, struggling with her fear. The poison had an antidote; there was no reason why she would have to die. She would be tied to Raoul only for a short period. And as for Aurelien…she would simply have to take her chances with him.

Shivering, Allie tried to keep her mind focused. The first thing she had to do was get out of the suite without waking Griffin. De Luca would let her go if she told him she had found a way to get Margot free of Aurelien, and that she had to do it alone. Once she'd convinced him, though, she would have to evade whoever had been set to watch the hotel, whether vampire or werewolf.

As dangerous as it was to return to her flat, that was the first place she would have to go.

She strode to the generous closet in the bedroom and opened the doors. Several men's suits, and a selection of dresses and coats, hung inside; evidently De Luca was used to having guests of both sexes and considered it part of his duty as host to provide them with changes of clothing should circumstances require it.

A simple black frock was close to Allie's size. She slipped it on over her bandeau and step-ins, then chose a fur-collared coat with ample pockets. Raoul wasn't likely to think she had the notes on her person, and if things went as she hoped, she might use them as a bargaining chip with Aurelien. She found her pumps halfway under the bed and carried them out of the bedroom, listening for the sound of any movement.

Hastily, she transferred the notes from the pocket of her own coat to the borrowed garment, then turned the new coat inside out and pinched the end of the pocket so it formed an inner pouch. She found a needle and several spools of thread in one of the cabinets of the bathroom and sewed the pouch shut. Then she put on the coat and hurried to the door. One of De Luca's men was standing outside.

"Can I help you, Miss Chase?" he asked.

"Yes. Take me to De Luca."

"I'll have to see if he's available."

"It concerns his daughter."

The gunsel came alert and asked her to follow him down the hall to De Luca's suite, which was guarded by two hatchet men. After a brief conference, one of the men entered the suite, then returned a few minutes later to invite Allie inside.

She gave De Luca a vague story about having learned something from Raoul about Margot's location, telling him that she had to pursue the lead alone but would let him know what she discovered.

"Keep Griffin here, no matter what you have to do," she said. "One way or another, I'll fulfill my part of the bargain."

De Luca frowned. "Sloan's and Raoul's men might very well be outside waiting for you to leave."

"I'll handle it. Just don't let Griffin come after me or there'll be hell to pay."

"He won't get away." De Luca sent a pair of underlings to watch the door of the guest suite and continued to regard Allie with a piercing stare. "At least my people can distract any observers while you make your break."

"Done." She offered her hand and matched him grip for grip.

"I hope you know what you're doing, Allegra."

So do I, Allie thought, but she gave De Luca a confident reply and waited impatiently while he gave instructions to several young hotheads eager to prove their worth.

As the men scattered on the street and Allie waited for a taxi, she reflected on the lies she'd just told a very dangerous man. It was entirely possible that she wouldn't be able to inform De Luca of her plan after she'd set it in motion; she would have to hope he trusted her enough to hold Griffin until it was too late for him to interfere.

The whole plan rested on the location of the vial and the hope that Raoul hadn't already gone after Aurelien. For the first time in many years, Allie was tempted to pray.

GEMMA HAD EXPLORED every inch of the lawn and gardens at the Spiegels' summer house. Her feet had already memorized the path through the adjoining woods, the only area beyond the immediate grounds that she was allowed to visit alone.

The Spiegels, making up for their previous lapse in chaperoning their daughter's guest, had been very firm about keeping Gemma in their sights since Starke had dropped her off the day before yesterday in the wee hours of the morning. Susannah had been her constant companion from breakfast to bedtime, chattering incessantly about trivial subjects. Gemma had thought she would lose her mind. Only now, in the hour just before dawn, did she have a chance to think.

How could you do it, Grif? she thought, as she followed the winding trail among the pines. *How could you send me away when we were getting so close to the truth?*

Of course, she knew the answer. It would have been remarkable if he hadn't made her leave. She certainly hadn't proven that she could be useful in helping him solve the mystery of Mal's disappearance; to the contrary, she'd only made things worse by letting herself fall into Raoul's hands.

There was no denying that she'd been scared— scared for herself and Wyatt and Allie. But at the same time, she'd known in her heart that Griffin would learn what had happened and come for them.

And that was the problem. She should have figured out a way to escape without his help. She'd behaved like a frightened child, and that was why she was wasting away in exile now, while Griffin and Allie did all the dangerous work.

"I can do better," she muttered aloud, briefly silencing the dawn chorus of the birds overhead. "If only you'd give me another chance...."

"Gemma."

She started at the sound of her name and swung

to face the intruder, crouched and ready. But the eyes that met hers were familiar, and it was all she could do not to fling herself into his arms.

"Wyatt!"

He paused in the narrow space between two trees, shoulders hunched. "Hello, Gemma."

"How did you know where to find me?"

Pine needles and old leaves crackled under his shuffling feet. "I figured your brother might want you out of the city after what happened. You told me about the Spiegels. It wasn't that hard to find out where they lived."

"Of course." She took a step toward him. "What's happening in New York? Do you have news for me?"

His face twisted in something very like shame. "I…I, uh…"

"Don't worry," she said impatiently. "I know why you ran away after Griffin found us. He might have given you a thrashing just for helping me. I would have done the—"

"That isn't why," Wyatt said. The pale, filtered light picked out the hectic color in his cheeks. "Listen, Gemma, you have to come with me. We'll go away together. We'll find a place where nobody can interfere with our lives or…make us do what we don't want." He paused to suck in a breath. "We can't trust anyone, not even our families. We don't need them. If you come with me now, everything will be all right."

Gemma stared at him in disbelief. "What are you talking about? What's wrong?"

"He knows I've betrayed him," a man said, slipping out of the woods like a ghost.

Wyatt didn't turn, but Gemma had no doubt that he and the man knew each other. In a few seconds she understood why. They had similar scents, and the family resemblance was unmistakable: same sandy hair, same lanky build, same eyes. The man was just old enough to be Wyatt's father.

But Wyatt had never spoken of his father, and this was the last place she would have expected either one of them to turn up.

"Mr. Dempsey?" she asked.

He nodded, the deep lines in his face shifting into an expression of terrible sorrow. "I'm sorry to bother you like this, Miss Chase. I never intended for you to be hurt."

A thrill of alarm shook Gemma like a cold, hard wind. "What is he talking about, Wyatt? Why is your father here? What does he mean about betraying you?"

Wyatt kept his back to his father, eyes fixed on some point above Gemma's head. "I didn't come to Oakdene that first time because I'd seen you at the speakeasy and wanted to meet you."

Her heart tripped over itself. "Why *did* you come?" she asked with deceptive calm.

"My father and I only arrived in New York a year ago. We joined the pack, but when Dad found out that Griffin Durant lived here…" He swallowed and started again. "My father sent me to watch you and gain your trust, because your brother was his enemy years ago, in San Francisco. He said he had to find some way of protecting himself in case Griffin came to kill him."

"What?" She stared at the elder Dempsey, legs tensed to run. "Who *are* you? Why should my brother be your enemy?"

Dempsey folded his arms tightly across his chest. "Your brother has reason to hate me," he said. "I've done some terrible things, things I'll regret for the rest of my life. And now my son is paying for them."

"He lied," Wyatt said, as if his father weren't standing behind him. "He told me his life was in danger, but not why. Or who he was really working for…"

Gemma backed away. "Griffin always said you were a spy for the pack. I should have listened to him."

"It wasn't for the pack, or even just for my father. It was for the werewolves who kidnapped Mal, only I didn't know it."

"You mean, my brother was right in his suspicions when he went to see Sloan?"

"Yes," Dempsey said quietly.

"My father was trying to keep both Sloan and Griffin from finding out that renegade—" Wyatt choked on the word "—that certain werewolves in the pack were helping vampires without Sloan's knowledge."

"What does that mean?" Gemma demanded. "Are you saying that werewolves kidnapped Mal for vampires?"

"That's how it started. But it's gone bad, Gemma. My father was one of the men who took Mal. It's not your brother who's after Dad now." He shoved his hands in his pockets. "Aurelien will kill us, if the pack doesn't find us first."

He began to speak in low tones of Klaus Aurelien and his ambition to reclaim power over the Manhattan clan—and about how Aurelien had discovered a secret that could aid him in his quest, a secret that involved Margot De Luca.

"He wanted Raoul to believe it was Mal who took her," Gemma whispered. A jolt of realization stole her breath. "Did *you* put that letter in Mal's apartment?"

"No," Dempsey said. "I encouraged Wyatt to continue offering you his help to keep your trust, but I didn't tell him that we had planted the letter for you to find. We called Raoul anonymously to alert him to your presence at the apartment. Wyatt didn't know anything about Aurelien's plot until it became necessary for us to leave the city."

"Then, you put him in terrible danger."

"Yes." Dempsey's eyes had gone flat and empty. "I didn't think Raoul would hurt either one of you once he realized you were simply bystanders, but…" He shuddered like a man in the grip of a fever. "You can't despise me more than I despise myself."

Gemma's stomach began to ache. "If you didn't know what your father was really doing," she asked Wyatt, "why did you run away from us when we escaped Raoul's?"

"I was—" he swallowed "—I was ashamed because I wasn't able to protect you from Raoul and his enforcers." He closed his eyes. "I went back to my father to tell him what had happened, and that's when…when he told me everything about Mal and Aurelien. The cops had just found where they were hiding Owen, and Owen told your brother that werewolves were involved. That meant Raoul would eventually find out it wasn't Owen who took Margot, and he'd start to look somewhere else."

"Aurelien won't tolerate such failure," Dempsey said. "He'll get word of it soon, if he hasn't already."

"So now you see why we have to get as far away as possible," Wyatt said, finally meeting Gemma's gaze. "Whatever my father's done, I have to help him. And I want you to go with us."

"Why? So you can use me again?"

"No. Because it's dangerous for everyone now. And because…" He raised his hands. "Please, Gemma."

"You think I'd just leave my brother at a time like

this? If he knows it was werewolves who kidnapped Mal, he'll go back to—" She stopped, struggling to follow the implications of everything Wyatt had said. "I still don't understand any of this. Did Sloan know what you were doing?"

"No, unless he was keeping secrets he didn't tell anyone."

"Why would werewolves help vampires?"

"For some," Dempsey said, "it was the promise of power once Aurelien regained the throne—an alliance that would topple Sloan and set up another leader in his place. For others…" He paused, running his hand over his face. "Aurelien knew something about my past that could ruin my son's life. He would have made it known to the pack and to my…other enemies if I didn't cooperate."

"Was this secret the reason you're afraid of my brother?" She clenched her fists. "Is *that* why you want to take me with you, so he won't come after you?"

Wyatt shook his head. "You don't have to be afraid of my father," he said. "It's Ivar. Ivar's the one who blackmailed Dad. He really works for Aurelien, just as he worked for vampires in San Francisco, when—" He flushed and clamped his jaw tight.

"I let Ivar control me, then and now," Dempsey said bitterly. "He'll kill both of us if he can. All I care about now is getting my son to safety. What happens to me doesn't matter."

"Dad…" Wyatt began.

"You can do whatever you want," Gemma said. "I'm not going anywhere with you. I'm going to call my brother, and—"

Dempsey silenced her with a raised hand, his gaze suddenly sharp and alert. Wyatt sniffed the air.

"Go," Dempsey whispered. "Run back to the house and stay there."

Gemma smelled what they did: the presence of other werewolves very nearby. "Who…"

"Ivar," Wyatt said. "They've found us."

CHAPTER TWENTY-TWO

THE FEAR IN HIS WORDS was unmistakable. In spite of everything the Dempseys had done, Gemma couldn't hate Wyatt. She couldn't leave him to die.

But the smell of the intruders grew stronger, and she knew that staying with him wouldn't help. She had to find another way of fighting.

She turned and ran toward the house on feet that hardly touched the ground. The house was silent, the Spiegels still dozing in their beds. Gemma hurried to Mr. Spiegel's study, where he kept his rifles and shotguns in a long glass display case. She searched his desk and found a set of keys, one of which opened the case. She chose one of the rifles and found ammunition in a drawer.

Griffin didn't know that Starke had taught her how to handle a gun. It had been on one of her breaks from school in Switzerland, when Griffin had been establishing a new life for them in New York and she'd gone to stay with Uncle Edward in England. Edward had decided that she should know every conceivable means of defending herself, and he was an excellent shot.

But knowing how to use a rifle wasn't something Griffin would have approved of in a "proper" young lady, so they had never told him. Now she was grateful that Uncle Edward had chosen to take matters into his own hands.

She left the house at a rapid pace, slowing as she reached the woods. The voices were soft, but she heard every word.

"You were careless," someone was saying. "It wasn't difficult to follow you here."

Ivar, Gemma thought, remembering the night he'd confronted Griffin on Fifty-second Street.

"I'm surprised you don't have more important errands to carry out for your Master," Dempsey said. "We can hardly do you or him any harm now."

"But you failed him and betrayed me," Ivar said. "You let the human escape, then ran like a coward."

"I'm finished doing your dirty work, Ivar. Three murders was enough."

Ivar made a harsh noise like a strangled laugh. "It should have been five. You failed in that, too. Durant has been nothing but trouble."

"And he'd kill you and me both if he knew what we'd done."

"What *you* did, Dempsey. I was never near the house when the fire started."

"And that's the real reason you have to kill me," Dempsey said. "You gave the orders to assassinate those people to protect your secret from the San Francisco pack. You were a slave to vampires then, just as you are now. No werewolf, including Sloan, would tolerate you if they found out."

"Sloan still doesn't know, and he won't learn until it's too late." Shoes rustled among the pine needles. "I'll take the girl. Durant will suffer for his interference."

"You leave her alone," Wyatt snarled.

"You should have considered your little slut when you came here. Bruno. Teegan."

There was the sound of movement, Ivar and his two henchmen preparing for attack. Gemma walked toward the men, making no attempt to hide her footsteps.

"I thought I heard voices, Susannah," she said loudly. "Who do you think it could be?"

"I don't know, Gemma," she said, mimicking Susannah's higher pitch. "It can't be any of our neighbors. The nearest ones are two miles away, and none of them would be in our woods this early."

"Maybe we should find out who they are."

"Oh, no! Papa has caught vagrants camping here before. We should go back and tell him. He'll run them off."

Gemma turned and jogged a little way toward the house, planting her feet as heavily as she could, keeping her steps irregular to mimic the sound of two people running. Then she silently traced a wide circle back the way she'd come, working out the best path to get around Ivar.

"Move," Ivar was saying. "You'll die just as easily somewhere else."

"Guns, Ivar?" Dempsey mocked. "Are you so afraid that my son and I can defeat you and your belly scrapers?"

"A bullet's all you deserve."

Gemma stepped from behind a tree, her rifle aimed at Ivar's heart. "Are you sure you're not referring to yourself, Ivar?"

Ivar and his men spun to face her. The werewolf henchmen, Bruno and Teegan, turned back to the Dempseys almost instantly, but a moment too late; Wyatt sprang at the smaller of the men, hurling him to the ground and seizing his gun, while his father leaped aside, drawing the other man's attention.

"Move," Gemma told Ivar, "and I'll shoot you."

Ivar's mouth tightened in fury. "You don't know how to use that, little bitch."

"You want to bet on that?" She nodded toward the now weaponless Bruno. "You're the one who's outnumbered now."

"If you don't put down the rifle, Teegan will kill Dempsey."

"Why should I care? They deceived me. They're my enemies as much as you are."

Ivar laughed. "Are they? Who do you think murdered your parents?"

At first Gemma didn't understand him, and then she began to remember things Dempsey and Wyatt had said, things they had never quite explained.

Wyatt had said, *"Your brother is his enemy,"* referring to his father. And Dempsey had told Ivar, *"You gave the orders to assassinate those people to protect your secret."*

Gemma had thought he'd meant her and Griffin. But Ivar had mentioned a fire. She'd been told the story of her parents' deaths when Griffin had judged her old enough to hear it. She knew about the fire, but he'd never mentioned murder.

"You killed them," she whispered.

Ivar moved toward her, hands spread. "You're mistaken," he said in a soothing voice. "It wasn't my idea—"

"You gave the orders." Her finger twitched on the trigger. "And you," she said to Dempsey, her eyes blurring with tears, *"you* set the fire." Dempsey didn't answer, his gaze still locked on Teegan's gun. She turned on Wyatt. "You knew."

"Not until yesterday." He made a stiff, pleading gesture. "I was only a little kid when it happened. My father…he'll never forgive himself for what he did. We've never had a real home, Gemma. He's already paid—"

"I should shoot all of you," she said.

"But you aren't a murderer," Ivar said. "If you leave now, you may be left alive."

"Don't listen to him!" Wyatt cried. "He'll kill you just as he'll kill us."

Ivar ignored him. "Did you know that your brother attacked Garret Sloan and has the whole pack on his heels? How will you save *him*, Gemma?"

Gemma's grip on the rifle loosened, visions of her brother's death replacing the faces of her enemies. By the time she recovered, Ivar was halfway to her.

With sudden grim clarity she pulled the trigger.

Ivar fell. Dempsey struck at Teegan, but the gunsel's bullet took him full in the chest. Wyatt shot Teegan and then Bruno through their hearts.

Faint with shock, Gemma ran to Ivar, whose shoulder was shattered. He didn't respond to her prodding.

"Gemma!"

Holding the rifle close to her body, she joined Wyatt where he crouched beside his father. A glance was enough to tell her that Dempsey had no hope of survival.

Wyatt cradled his father in his arms, tears running down his face.

"You can heal yourself, Dad," he said. "Change. Change *now*."

But Dempsey shook his head, blood bubbling from his lips. "Won't work," he whispered. "Too weak." He lifted a hand to touch Wyatt's cheek. "I'm sorry. Sorry that you suffered…for my—"

"No." Wyatt stared wildly up at Gemma. "We have to get him somewhere where he can rest."

Dempsey looked at Gemma through eyes glazed with pain. "No right…to ask you to forgive. I'm sorry." His breath rattled. "Don't put yourself into…the enemy's hands. Stay out of Manhattan."

"But my brother—"

"Safer on his own." He rolled his head to face Wyatt again. "Find a new place. New life."

"Not without you."

Dempsey's eyes closed. A long sigh shuddered from his chest.

"Dad!"

But he was gone. Wyatt buried his face against his father's shoulder, rocking like a child. Gemma despised herself then, for she felt nothing but pity when she should have been glad that a murderer was dead.

She got up, giving the bodies a wide berth even as she realized that one was missing. Ivar was no longer there. A thick trail of blood drops led away from the crimson pool where he'd lain.

Wounded as he was, he couldn't have gone far. Allie held the rifle slack in her hands. It had been one thing to shoot Ivar in self-defense; it was quite another to hunt him down like an animal. She didn't know if she could do it.

Wyatt came to stand beside her, his voice rough with hatred. "Where is he?"

"I'm sorry," Gemma began awkwardly. "Your father—"

"You can tell your brother his enemy's dead."

Gemma met his cold gaze. "Do you think Griffin would have killed your father if he'd found him in New York?"

"Wouldn't he?"

"I don't know."

His lips thinned to a knife's edge. "You didn't kill Ivar."

"I only wanted to stop him. I thought he was unconscious."

"Unless the wound's really bad, he'll find a place to Change and force a healing."

"Then he'll get away." She kicked at the blood-stained grass under her feet. "Where will he go now?"

"He seemed to believe that he could keep Sloan's trust and continue working for Aurelien at the same time. But you and I know what a traitor he really is. He won't go back to New York."

"But I have to. If Grif's got the pack after him—"

"No. Dad said you should stay out of Manhattan, and he's right. Your brother sent you up here for a reason."

"Because he thinks I'm too weak to fight."

"His enemies could use you to get to him…Sloan, Raoul, anyone who might have it in for him because of his interference. And what about Allie? They could use you against *her,* too."

"Then I should just sit here and do nothing?"

He gazed into the woods as if he hadn't heard her. "Ivar's too much of a coward to come after us alone. He'll have to get more men, and there can't be many traitors left in the pack. He'll go to Aurelien."

"You know where Aurelien is?"

"Dad told me so I'd be sure to avoid the area if he—" Wyatt scrubbed at his face. "That's where I'll find Ivar."

"And get yourself killed?"

"My father's dead."

"So are my parents."

Wyatt was silent for several moments. "There's

another reason to follow Ivar," he said. "Maybe I'll get a chance to make up for what my father…for the mistakes I made."

"How?"

"By gathering information that can be used against Aurelien. Everything that's happened is because of him—the way Raoul's acted since he lost Margot, the attacks on De Luca's syndicate, your brother accusing the pack of kidnapping Mal. When Griffin came to get us at the vampire mansion, Raoul didn't know about Aurelien. Maybe he still doesn't. If De Luca found out, he'd want Aurelien dead. And Sloan would bring Aurelien down just because he subverted werewolves to his cause. If I get information that they can use to stop Aurelien, we could bargain with the ones who could hurt your brother and your friends."

"You don't have enough to tell them already?"

"If Sloan has started to suspect me and Dad, he won't listen to anything I have to say. And it would be suicide to approach Raoul after what happened with the letter. I need proof. Information on Aurelien's next move. An idea of how many men he has with him."

Gemma nodded. "It's a good plan," she said. "I'm coming with you."

He barked a laugh. "Do you want your brother after me, too?"

"Maybe you can still prove yourself to him. And so can I."

"What about your human friends? The shots must have woken them up."

"That's why we have to go right away."

"Won't they call Griffin?"

"They might not be able to reach him. He could be anywhere now. They'll probably think I ran away again, and it'll take them a few hours to find out I didn't go back to New York. How close is Aurelien's hideout?"

"Not far. Only a couple of hours by automobile."

"You have a car?"

"Yes. It's hidden in the woods."

Gemma bit her lip. "We have to do something with the bodies."

"And cover up this blood, or your friends will think something terrible has happened to you." His gaze drifted back to his father's still form. Gemma knew better than to speak. She helped Wyatt lift his father and carry him the quarter mile to the battered jalopy; then they returned for the other two. Wyatt used his woodsman's finely honed skills to erase all signs of the struggle.

"We moved around a lot," he explained as he took the wheel and drove out to the nearby road. "Sometimes we lived in the wilderness. I had to learn things most kids wouldn't need to. It was easier because of what we are."

Easier for a werewolf to make a home in the woods, in places no human would consider adequate shelter. Gemma had begun to see that Dempsey had, indeed, paid for his heinous crimes. He'd run away from San Francisco and never stopped running...until he'd gained and lost his second chance.

Now Wyatt was determined to atone for his father's sins. And Gemma would finally show herself worthy of her *loup-garou* blood.

ALLIE KNEW a *strigoi* was on her tail as soon as she stepped out of the taxi in front of her apartment building. Thanks to De Luca's men, she'd given the slip to the pack's agents, but the gunsels' best efforts hadn't been enough to distract an enforcer as experienced as Dorian.

He followed her into the lobby and waited while she took the elevator to the eighth floor, making no attempt to join her. That reprieve was all she needed. She went immediately to Lou's room, the pounding of her heart drowning out the tick of the clock and the clatter of her heels on the floor.

The ornate perfume vial was where Lou had always kept it, standing beside several others on her dressing table. Strange that she'd agreed to keep it here when Cato had never told her what it contained, but now Allie was grateful. Her hands weren't quite steady as she removed the stopper and lifted the bottle to her nose.

She knew at once that this was no perfume ever made. The scent was slightly bitter, and yet sweet at the same time, like blood gone rancid. She almost replaced the stopper and put the bottle back.

But the pendant still hung on its sturdy but delicate chain around her neck, reminding her that her fate was far from irrevocable.

Slowly she raised the bottle to her lips. *This is for you, Griffin. For Gemma, for Lou, for Starke. For Bruce and Nathan. For Cato and Sebastian. For everyone Raoul has destroyed or will destroy.*

The taste was as foul as the smell. Her tongue tingled as she swallowed the last drops. She set the bottle down, wiping at her lips with disgust, and waited.

Nothing happened. She felt no nausea, no dizziness, no hint of impending death. She might as well have drunk a particularly bad cup of java in some dive in the Bowery.

I hope you were right, Cato, she thought. *I hope this*

was the right bottle, or I'm giving myself up to Raoul for nothing.

She went to the kitchen, filled a glass from the tap and rinsed her mouth so that no trace of the stuff remained on her breath. Then she checked her coat pocket, feeling the slight bulk of the notes, and left the apartment.

Dorian was still waiting, his face giving nothing away. Allie smiled.

"Were you all Raoul could spare?" she asked, strolling toward him. "You must wish you were with the others, preparing to attack the usurper."

He lifted one shoulder. "It's not so terrible a trial to follow you, Miss Chase."

She clapped her hands. "A compliment! Javier wouldn't approve."

"Javier is occupied elsewhere." He started a little when she looped her arm through his. "May I ask what you're doing, Miss Chase?"

"Can't you guess?"

"It seems unwise of you to have left De Luca's hotel."

"Only if I wanted to stay hidden. But I don't, my friend." She sobered, holding his stare. "I'm going to Raoul."

Dorian's mask slipped into surprise. "Why?"

"You were there when Raoul said he'd leave my friends alone if I gave myself up. I'm going to hold him to his word."

Instead of showing satisfaction at her decision, Dorian looked grave. "Are you sure this is what you wish to do, Allegra?"

"Why, Dory, that's the first time you've ever used my first name."

He frowned. "What does Griffin Durant have to say about this?"

"He doesn't know. And I plan to keep it that way as long as possible." She tugged on his arm. "Shall we go?"

For a moment he stood unmoving, staring at nothing. He recovered before Allie could ask him what was wrong.

"Raoul will be pleased to see you," he said, "but you may suffer nevertheless."

"I think I have a proposition he won't be able to resist."

With a grunt, Dorian walked away, leading Allie toward the LaSalle parked around the corner. She stretched out in the seat beside him, concealing the nervousness that pinched her stomach and shortened her breath.

The mansion was quiet outside, but beyond the doors it was a hive of frantic activity: Raoul's enforcers gathering cases of guns and ammunition; his vassals instructing the protégés who had arrived from the nearby *strigoi* residences; strategies being discussed among Raoul's chief lieutenants. War was in the air, and Allie knew she had to work quickly.

Crispus appeared at once, his face as dour as ever. "Master Raoul is occupied," he told Allie as Dorian went to join his fellow enforcers. "You must wait."

"I think he'll want to hear what I have to say. I have a plan to get Margot away from Aurelien before this war begins."

With a grumble of disapproval, Crispus heaved himself up the stairs to consult with his Master. An enforcer returned in his place.

"You're to come with me," the young vampire said. He gestured her to precede him. She climbed to Raoul's suite on legs that no longer quivered beneath her.

Raoul didn't look up as she entered his conference room, his head bent over a large map of the state spread across a marble table. His lieutenants glanced at Allie with a certain interest, but they waited in silence until Raoul deigned to acknowledge her presence.

"So," he said at last, "you've come to your senses."

Allie took a seat in one of the comfortable armchairs scattered about the room. "I've come to take you up on your offer—I give myself to you in exchange for the permanent safety of my friends."

Raoul straightened, his eyes glittering with satisfaction. "Have you grown so weary of your dog lover?"

She shrugged. "No one tells me what to do. I'm giving myself to you of my own free will…provided you stick to your part of the bargain."

"And what if I don't want you? What if I'd rather kill you and all your pathetic sycophants?"

"You could do that, of course, except then you'd lose the chance to save Margot before you attack Aurelien and risk her life."

The room seemed to thrum with Raoul's intensity. He stalked toward Allie, his body radiating cold like an Arctic iceberg. "I suggest you speak clearly," he said, "if you want to survive the next minute."

Allie sprawled farther back in the chair. "Maybe you'd better send your men away, Raoul."

"Why?"

"Trust me."

With a scowl Raoul waved at his lieutenants. They trooped out of the room. Then he leaned over her, his hands planted on the chair's arms. "Talk."

She held his stare. "It's simple, Raoul. I know what Cato did for you. I know that Margot was your first protégée in over a decade, and that if it hadn't been for the formula, you would have been deposed as Master long since."

"You still have no proof."

"I'm not interested in exposing you, Raoul. I know you'd take revenge on everyone I care about before they brought you down. I have a better idea. You see, I'm also a product of the formula."

Raoul's expression went blank and then quickly cleared. "Cato…"

"He was like you, unable to Convert humans when he created the vaccine. He tried it first on himself, and I was the result."

Even a human would have been able to read the series of emotions that played across Raoul's face as the implications hit him one by one. Suddenly he grinned.

"You're like Margot," he said. "Your blood has the same qualities Aurelien hopes to use to duplicate the formula."

"Exactly." She sat up, forcing Raoul to give ground. "I'd be of as much value to Aurelien as Margot. I can't think of any reason why you can't propose a trade."

"You for Margot?"

"And your oath that you'll never touch my friends."

Raoul backed away, his fists clasped tightly at his back. "A very generous sacrifice," he said, "but Aurelien has no reason to give Margot up as long as he can hold her hostage against us."

"Maybe, but if that's his game, it's obviously not going to keep you from hunting him down. You value Margot, but you value your life and position more."

"I'll get her back."

"If you can find Aurelien. You know where he's been, but if he has as many spies as Elisha implied, he already knows you're coming. He won't stand around waiting for you to show up. He must have a secondary base of operations in case the first one was discovered."

"I'll find him no matter where he runs."

"And he must know that. If I were him, I'd do just about anything to buy time. He's got humans and vampires and some kind of laboratory to move all at once. I think he'd jump at the chance to take me in Margot's place, figuring you'd be distracted by her return just long enough to help him make his escape."

"Then he's a fool."

"You can also gain by this. More time for you means that your men will be better prepared for the fight."

And every minute you spend on arranging this trade will give the poison a little longer to do its work.

Raoul knotted his hands together, tendons crackling. "Even if you're correct, how do you propose I contact Aurelien?"

"Make a general announcement to everyone in the mansion that you're offering the exchange, that you swear before the entire clan to grant amnesty to anyone who's instrumental in getting Margot back to you alive. If one of Aurelien's agents is still here—and I think that's more than likely—he will know you're aware there's a traitor in your midst. The spy may decide to take the risk of carrying the message rather than waiting here for you to expose him."

"You make many assumptions, Allegra. Why should I not simply interrogate my people to find this hypothetical agent?"

"For the same reason you haven't done so already. You don't have time to question, let alone torture, every vassal, enforcer and protégé in this place. If you do, Aurelien will have even more time to prepare for your attack."

"Why should I not torture you instead?"

"Because *I* don't know where Aurelien is, and

you'll be wasting the other opportunities I'm offering." She took a deep breath. "There's only one way to ensure that it makes sense to the clan for Aurelien to give Margot up for me. Everyone knows how hard you've been pursuing me. If you make me your protégée, no one has to know about the vaccine to believe that it's pretty close to an even trade."

The huge, ornate long-case clock chimed 9:00 a.m. Raoul paced across the room, head lowered, the blue veins pulsing beneath his pale skin. "You do realize that we shall both suffer at our separation?"

"I'm prepared to deal with that if you are."

Raoul gave her a hostile look. Having lost Margot, he was surely in considerable discomfort already.

"I'll accept your proposal," he said, "*if* you agree to facilitate our attack on Aurelien once you're safely in his tender care."

"How?"

"As you've said, once I've made my announcement it's highly likely that any of Aurelien's agents who've remained in the mansion will flee to him. You'll surely meet them again in his hideout. Approach each of them and offer them this bargain: if they turn on Aurelien and help me to destroy him, I will grant them the freedom to leave New York unharmed."

"Why should they believe me?"

"You're a very clever girl, Allegra. Convince them. They must realize that I will eventually defeat Aurelien, and they will have no chance for survival then. If even one or two come over to our side, it may be enough to fatally undermine Aurelien."

Allie hid a frown, thinking that Raoul's "plan" was shaky at best. But she wasn't in a position to argue. "I'll do as you say," she said.

"Excellent." He moved toward her, his gaze locked on hers. "There is nothing more to be done but to seal our blood-bond."

The gorge rose in Allie's throat. "Not yet."

He stopped short. She fumbled for an explanation. "First make sure that you can contact Aurelien and agree to the exchange."

"If you're deceiving me…"

"I just want to make sure my sacrifice means something."

His lip curled. "Sacrifice. You won't long for your old life once you're mine."

"Maybe, but that's the deal. When you and Aurelien have struck your bargain, I'll be yours."

Raoul closed the last space between them, his eyes falling to the chain about her neck. He grabbed it before she realized his intention, pulling it out from beneath the neckline of her frock.

"Cato gave you this," he said, turning the locket over in his hand. "Sentimental to the end."

Allie held perfectly still. "He's no threat to you now."

"He never was." Raoul jerked sharply on the chain, snapping it cleanly. "You won't need this anymore." He cast it across the room, where it hit the wall and fell in a flow of silver to the carpet.

Numbness crept through Allie's body as if the poison had already begun its work. Unless she could retrieve the pendant without Raoul's knowledge, she was as good as dead.

CHAPTER TWENTY-THREE

THE FARM WAS ANCIENT, its fields overgrown with wild-flowers. Old horse-drawn plows had been abandoned among trees encroaching on the garden fence. But it was far from unoccupied. The yard and dirt road hummed with activity, trucks and other vehicles were drawn up before the faded red barn and farmhouse, and men—bare-headed humans and vampires wrapped up against the sun—loading boxes onto the trucks with an air of feverish haste.

"It's Aurelien, all right," Wyatt said, pushing Gemma lower behind a bush. "And it looks like he's heading out."

Gemma worked a kink out of her knees and stared at the open farmhouse door. "This is the middle of nowhere. Are they really afraid of being found?"

"Raoul must have learned his location. Aurelien is probably expecting an attack any minute." He glanced behind them. "He must have guards all through these woods. We're lucky they didn't see us."

Gemma didn't have to ask what would happen if Aurelien caught them. "What do we do now?"

"Wait, I guess. Then follow them and see where they end up."

So we can get that information back to Griffin, Gemma thought. "Margot must be in there," she said.

"Or waiting in one of the cars. I think they're about ready to leave."

Within ten minutes the trucks were loaded, and the last bundled figures hurried from the house.

"Margot and Aurelien," Gemma guessed. But soon the figures were lost among a crowd of others who clustered in a group and then broke apart, distributing themselves among the various automobiles. Engines rumbled to life. Three sleek black coupes set off along an overgrown track among the trees, while the trucks and another pair of automobiles started down the dirt road.

"Who do we follow?" Gemma asked.

Wyatt dug in his pocket and produced a quarter. "Heads we follow the coupes, tails the trucks." He flipped the coin deftly and slapped it on the back of his hand.

"Tails," he said. "Let's get back to the car."

GRIFFIN WOKE with a foul taste in his mouth and the feeling that he had slept far too long. He glanced at the clock, shocked to find that it was well past noon.

"Allie?"

He felt blindly across the bed. She wasn't there. He sat up, rubbing his eyes.

"Allie?"

No answer. He swung his legs over the side of the bed. Her clothes lay in a heap where she'd flung them last night. He smiled, remembering her utter lack of inhibitions and his own enjoyment of that very delightful quality.

It had been a thousand times better than he could ever have imagined. More than that. It had been heaven. Heaven he'd never believed he could find on earth.

He stretched his arms above his head, rose and

walked stiffly into the sitting room, expecting to find her sipping coffee and waiting for him to join her.

The room was empty. No coffee cup, no tray, no morning paper. His heart began to thump.

She wouldn't have gone out to feed, since she'd had her fill of him last night. There was little she could do in the hotel except sit in the lobby or visit the expensive restaurant adjoining it.

With a haste born of worry, Griffin threw on his crumpled clothing, leaving his collar, tie and hat behind, and ventured into the hall. A pair of thick-muscled hatchet men turned to face him as he closed the door.

"Mr. Durant? Can we get you anything?" one of the goliaths said.

"I'm looking for Miss Chase. Can you tell me where she is?"

The man scratched the bristles on his chin. "I believe she's with Mr. De Luca," he said.

Griffin's shoulders unlocked. "I'm sure Mr. De Luca won't mind if I join them," he said, and started toward De Luca's suite.

Goliath #1 stepped into his path. "It's a private meeting," he said.

"Oh? Then kindly inform Miss Chase that I would like to speak to her."

The other gunsel joined his partner. "Better wait in your room, Mr. Durant."

"Why?"

They began to herd him back to the door. "Boss's orders," Goliath #2 said.

Griffin held fast. "What's going on?"

"Nothing you should worry about. You—"

Without warning Griffin lunged forward, plowing between the men and sprinting for De Luca's door. Big as they were, they were no runners. He had the door open before they were halfway down the hall.

Startled faces swung toward him, and men jumped up with ready guns. De Luca was lounging in an easy chair, a drink in one hand and a cigar in the other. He waved his men down.

"So, Mr. Durant," he said. "I trust you had a pleasant sleep?"

The muscle men barged into the room, panting and red-faced. De Luca made a gesture, and they assumed positions on either side of the door, glaring at Griffin.

"Where is Allie?" Griffin demanded.

"Please sit down, Durant. You make me very tired."

"De Luca—"

Goliath #1 moved away from the wall, looking pleased at the prospect of forcing Griffin into a chair. Griffin sat.

"They told me she was with you," he said. "I don't see her."

"She was with me some time ago," De Luca said. "Do you care for a drink, or perhaps a cigar?"

"Where is she now?"

De Luca shook his head. "She knew it would come to this." He set down his glass. "Mr. Durant, Miss Chase is gone. She has devised a plan to free my daughter, and I agreed to let her try it."

"What plan?"

"She didn't go into detail, but I didn't feel it was—"

Sheer fury propelled Griffin from the chair. A trio of tommy guns brought him to a trembling halt.

"Now, now," Durant said calmly. "This was our agreement. I was to look after you, and she was to free my daughter by any means necessary."

"Where has she gone?" Griffin croaked.

"I presume to Raoul, but again, she didn't confide the details."

"Damn you!"

Huge hands closed on Griffin's shoulders and dragged him back to the chair. "You want I should clobber him, boss?" Goliath #2 said.

De Luca puffed on his cigar. "You would do well to compose yourself, Durant."

"Let me go."

"I'm afraid that would abrogate my deal with Miss Chase."

"She'll destroy herself!"

"Somehow I doubt that." De Luca tapped the cigar against a crystal ashtray. "In any case, I can't let you leave this hotel until I hear from her again. It's for your own good, Durant."

Seething with terror for Allie, Griffin forced himself to relax. As long as he fought De Luca openly, his chances of escaping the hotel were nil. "What do you expect me to do?" he asked bitterly.

"Wait. Trust Miss Chase, as I have."

Griffin swallowed a laugh. *Did you plan this all along, Allie? Was it all a trick?* He made to rise, and the muscle men moved up beside him.

"I'll return to my room, if you've no objection," he said coldly.

"By all means," De Luca said. "I suggest you rest and arm yourself with patience."

Griffin shouldered the guards out of the way and strode back to the room. He heard De Luca's men take up their posts outside his door and began to pace, trying to clear his mind.

Why, Allie? It's suicide. De Luca can't hold me. I won't stay here like a chained cur and—

Something crackled under his shoe as he passed the sofa for the twentieth time. A yellowed sheet of paper lay half under the sofa, creased as if it had been folded many times. He stooped to pick it up and spread the paper flat on the coffee table.

The writing was small and painstakingly neat. Griffin read the letter through in a minute, then read it again. The blood froze in his veins.

You see, my dear, you, too, are a product of the formulae. I had become sterile some twenty years before your rebirth, and it was upon myself that I first tested the vaccine's efficacy. My great mistake was in revealing the results to Raoul…

Griffin closed his eyes. Allie had never meant for him to find this, because she would have known that if he did…

He ran to the window overlooking the street and tore back the brocade curtains. Bright afternoon sunlight streamed into the room. There was a decorative balcony outside the window, just wide enough for a man to stand on. The next balcony was fifteen feet away. Griffin unlocked the window, stepped through and perched on the balcony rail, estimating the distance down to the street.

Too far. He would survive the fall, but his injuries might be severe enough to hamper him afterward. Quickly, he removed his coat, shoes and socks. He turned again to the next balcony, crouched and hurled himself across empty space.

He caught the railing with his fingers, swinging in empty air. Kicking up his legs, he braced his feet against the wall and looped his arms over the railing, muscles straining. He fell into the well of the balcony and lay there panting for half a minute, then rolled to his feet and repeated the process until he had crossed over four balconies.

Exhausted, he tested the window of the final suite. It was locked. Griffin removed his shirt, wrapped it around his hand and arm, and slammed his fist into the glass. It shattered, shards spraying the heavy curtains. He barely noticed that a few shards hit him, leaving his shirt spattered with blood.

An elegantly dressed woman was standing inside the room, lips parted and ready to scream. Griffin reached her in three steps and covered her mouth with his palm.

"I won't hurt you," he whispered. "Carmine De Luca's men are after me. I need your help."

She nodded, and he dropped his hand. Her eyes widened as she took in his half-dressed state. "De Luca?"

"Yes. He'll kill me if he finds me. I'll leave quietly. All I ask is that you not raise the alarm."

"But…"

"You have my gratitude." He tucked his blood-stained shirt under his arm and pressed his ear to the door. No voices, no footsteps. He opened the door cautiously, sniffed the air and looked out. De Luca's men were small, dark figures far down the dimly lit corridor. Griffin sprinted for the nearest stairwell and all but fell down the stairs. People in the lobby stared as he ran for the revolving doors.

He paused briefly on the sidewalk to pull on his shirt, not entirely sure whether he would attract more attention running down the street half-naked and bare-foot or wearing bloodstained clothing. People, particularly women, stopped to gape and titter. Griffin plunged into the afternoon crowd, his legs carrying him more swiftly than any taxi cab. A patrolman on his beat blew his whistle and pursued him for a block before he lost his wind. Knowing he could ill afford to be detained by the police, Griffin continued along back alleys until he reached Allie's building.

The elevator attendant stumbled over his greeting as he conducted Griffin to Allie's floor. The door wasn't locked. Griffin burst in and knew within seconds that Allie wasn't there. Nevertheless, he began to search for the vial of poison mentioned in Cato's letter, opening cupboards and searching drawers. An empty perfume bottle stood on Louise Moreau's dressing table. One sniff told him that it had never held perfume.

He picked up the telephone and called Ross but was compelled to leave a message. There was no time to wait. He flagged down a taxi at the curb, enduring a nervous look from the cabbie, and waved a fifty-dollar bill in the man's face. The ride was far from smooth, but the cabbie got him to Raoul's mansion in record time.

No guards stood watch at the portico, and the doors swung open at Griffin's push. The entry hall echoed with desertion. Griffin dashed up the stairs. Not a single vampire emerged to challenge him. Raoul's suite was empty, but it smelled of Allie.

Frantically Griffin circled the room, casting about for a clue as to where they had gone. Silver glittered in a corner, and he had a sudden, terrible premonition of disaster.

It was Allie's locket—the one she always wore, the one mentioned in Cato's letter. The one that made all the difference between life and death. Cato had written:

I now share with you a secret, which you may use
in extremity should Raoul threaten your freedom
and you are not able to unseat him with the evidence I have given you.

Griffin closed his fingers around the locket, remembering Cato's next words as if they had been engraved
in his mind.

I have created a toxin that is inevitably fatal to
any *strigoi* who ingests it via the blood of the one
who drinks it. You will find this poison in a vial
I have given to Louise Moreau for safekeeping,
though she does not know what it contains. I
have also hidden the antidote in the locket I asked
you to wear at all times.

Silver burned Griffin's palm as he gently undid the
latch of the locket to reveal the tiny packet within. It
had not been opened.

If you wish to kill Raoul, you need only drink the
contents of the vial and see that Raoul bites you
within twenty-four hours. Depending upon his resistance, he will be dead within a day. The toxin
will also be fatal to you unless you take the
antidote within the same twenty-four-hour period.

Griffin closed the locket again with the utmost care,
struggling to clear his mind. He knew where the vampires must have gone…after Aurelien. And Raoul
had taken Allie with him. By now he would have
claimed her in blood-bond, and they would both be
slowly dying.

Aurelien had to be somewhere within a few hours' drive of New York City. The least populated area would be to the north, but that left a vast amount of ground to cover. If Ross called up all his men, it might just be possible…

Griffin thrust the locket and chain into his pocket and hurtled down the stairs. He was almost to the door when the croak of a voice halted him in his tracks.

"Durant," the voice said. Griffin turned as a figure crawled down the stairs from the second floor, a broken stick of a man covered in open sores that exposed muscle and bone.

Struck with pity, Griffin went to the cripple's aid. The body was almost weightless in his arms, stinking of rot. He helped the vampire lean against the newel post at the bottom of the stairs.

"You came," the vampire whispered. "I called De Luca's hotel, but you weren't there."

"Who are you?"

"My name is…was…Sebastian. I worked for Klaus Aurelien, and I knew Allegra Chase."

Griffin fought his revulsion and held the man's shoulders. "What do you want, Sebastian?"

The vampire laughed, the sound ending in a racking cough. "They thought I was dead. I would have been—should have been—only Dorian—" He broke off and shook his head. "It doesn't matter. I'll be gone soon enough." He coughed again, bringing up a thin black bile. "You've come for Allie."

"Do you know where she is?"

"She's taken the blood-bond with Raoul."

"I know."

Sebastian scratched at his face, and flesh peeled

away. "They didn't think I heard, but I know. I know where they went."

"For God's sake, man, where?"

"No…God." He grabbed the front of Griffin's shirt with a last surge of strength. "Listen.…"

The directions were halting, barely audible, but they were more than adequate. They burned themselves into Griffin's mind. "Aurelien's…meeting him at the café," Sebastian said. "There's to be a trade, Allie for Margot. But Klaus can't win." He grinned with blackened teeth. "I should have known he could never win."

"Why are you helping us?"

"I…want Raoul dead. Kill him. The world will be a better—"

He doubled over, and Griffin heard the sound of bones snapping. He held Sebastian in his arms while he exhaled his last breath. When it was finished, he gently lowered Sebastian to the floor, stripped off his own shirt, and laid it over Sebastian's face and shoulders.

"Thank you, my friend. Sleep in peace."

He jumped up and ran through the door, slowing as a car pulled up at the curb.

"Griffin!" Ross called, emerging from the driver's seat. "I got your message, followed by a report of a wild man who fit your description running down East Forty-fifth Street in a bloody shirt. What the hell's going on?"

"Allie's with Raoul," Griffin said, joining Ross on the street. "Raoul's made contact with Aurelien and plans to trade her for Margot."

"Why in hell would Aurelien agree to do that?"

"It's a long story. Suffice it to say that there's something in both Margot's and Allie's blood that gives an impotent vampire the ability to create protégés."

"God." Ross passed his hand over his face. "Do you know where Allie is now?"

Griffin repeated what Sebastian had told him. "It's not only a matter of getting her away from the Masters," he said. "Allie's taken a poison that will kill both her and Raoul, and she doesn't have the antidote." He reached into his pocket. "I do, and I have less than twenty-four hours to get it to her."

Ross uttered a profanity that perfectly mirrored Griffin's own thoughts. "I'll get back to the precinct and gather all the men I can…at least the ones who know about dogs and leeches." He smiled grimly. "Are you going on ahead?"

"I have to. I'll pick up a car and a change of clothes at my office."

"What about the pack? They'll still be after you."

"I'll deal with them as I must. Will you drop me off?"

"Come on."

Ross turned on the siren, and in minutes they were at Griffin's building.

"Be careful," Ross said, leaning over the passenger seat as Griffin stepped from the car.

"I'll meet you at the café just outside town," Griffin called through the open window.

"What if they've already concluded their business?"

"I'll find Aurelien and get the information to you somehow."

Ross nodded and pulled neatly into the flow of afternoon traffic. Griffin wasted no time in getting to the garage where his Rolls-Royce stood parked and ready for his use. He was starting the engine when he saw the men reflected in the window.

He briefly considered jamming down on the accelerator, but he hesitated just a moment too long. A werewolf slipped into the seat beside him. Others surrounded the car. Cassius tapped on the window.

"Get out, Durant," he said.

Griffin opened the car door. "I have no time to argue with you now, Cassius," he said.

The werewolf laughed. "Argue? We didn't come to argue. It's over."

"Not quite." Griffin got out and forced Cassius to retreat a few reluctant steps. "I'm prepared to strike a bargain with the pack, Cassius. One I doubt even Sloan would refuse."

The light in Cassius's eyes was far from promising. "You have nothing to bargain with."

"I've never heard anyone claim that twenty million dollars was nothing."

"Are you trying to buy us off, Durant?"

"I know the pack isn't as prosperous as Sloan would like. I have the means to rectify that situation. If you'll allow me to go now, just long enough to save a friend, I'll return with you to face the pack's judgment, and I'll sign over the bulk of my fortune, as well."

Cassius was silent, his face tight with uncertainty. "You're lying."

"There is a simple way of assuring that I keep my word. You and the others can come with me."

"Where?"

"To the hiding place of the vampire who's been using werewolf renegades to further his own ambitions."

The *loups-garous* lowered their heads and rumbled. "Not good enough, Durant," Cassius said. "First you'll sign over the money—"

"If you take me now, you'll never get a red cent, no

matter what you do to me. All that money, forever out of the pack's reach."

A half-dozen expectant faces turned to Cassius. The short hairs stood up along the back of Griffin's neck.

"All right," Cassius said at last. "We'll do it your way. But if you try anything, Durant, it's over."

"Agreed." Griffin slid back into the driver's seat. "I assume you're riding with me. The others will have to follow."

Cassius barked orders to his men, four of whom scattered, while the other two got in the back of the Rolls. Immediately Griffin put them out of his mind and tore out of the garage with a squeal of tires, his heart beating out the dwindling seconds of Allie's life.

THE CAFÉ WAS TYPICAL of the roadside eateries that had sprung up along the highway during the past ten years: unpretentious, a little seedy and eager to cater to motorists on their way to and from the mountain resorts. The smell of cooking meat turned Allie's stomach as she and Raoul entered and took seats in an upholstered booth at the back of the dining room.

Aurelien hadn't yet arrived. She wondered if he would come at all. Until now, everything had gone as she'd predicted: Raoul had made his general announcement of the proposed trade with Aurelien; someone from the mansion had gotten word to the former Master; and an oblivious human messenger had returned with a proposal to meet Raoul at a small café in the tiny rural town of Shady Pines.

She'd convinced Raoul that Aurelien would make the exchange to buy time against the inevitable attack, but there was still a chance Klaus wouldn't go through with the meeting. If it weren't for Margot and the question of her safety, it almost wouldn't have mattered to her whether or not Aurelien showed up.

For Raoul was dying, even if he didn't realize it yet. His speech already had the slightest hint of a slur; an expression of bewilderment occasionally crossed his face; and his normally elegant movements had lost a little of their grace. Allie had not begun to feel the same effects, but she suspected that it was just a matter of time.

A nervous waitress sidled up to their table, avoiding Raoul's eyes. "What can I get you, miss?" she asked Allie.

"Nothing," Raoul said. "I suggest you go into the kitchen and stay there."

The girl didn't offer a single protest. She dashed behind the counter and disappeared. Raoul folded his hands on the table, his attention turned inward. Allie held her own thoughts carefully in check. The blood-bond between her and Raoul, as fresh as the bite marks on her neck, made her sensitive to his emotions, just as hers had become more obvious to him, but he was unconsciously focused on the slow changes in his body and didn't seem to notice her wary observation.

When the bell at the door jingled, he roused from his meditation and became the old Raoul once more. He stared as a man in a wide-brimmed hat and a long overcoat walked into the café, his hand gripping the arm of a thin woman who might once have been beautiful.

"Margot," Raoul whispered.

The woman looked up. Her eyes were sunken, her lips almost white. Her gaze moved past Raoul to Allie, and a trace of hope lit her weary face.

Her escort stopped, then unbuttoned the collar of his

coat and removed his hat. His hair was iron-gray, his face as proud and aquiline as the bust of an ancient Roman patriarch. Allie froze in astonishment.

"Raoul," Aurelien said in a deep, silky voice.

Raoul stood, gripping the back of his seat with one hand. "Aurelien," he said. "I didn't think you'd come."

Aurelien chuckled. "Did you really think I was afraid?"

"I could have laid a trap."

"And risk your precious protégée? That I very much doubt." Aurelien urged Margot forward, never loosening his grip on her arm. "She has been a most charming guest, but I fear she has begun to lose her usefulness."

Raoul quivered in a way Allie had never seen before, focused on Margot like a damned soul catching a glimpse of a lost paradise. "What have you done to her?"

"She's not beyond recovery, or so my scientists tell me."

Raoul surged toward Aurelien, his shoes slipping on the wooden floor. He came to an immediate halt, hands flexing. Allie felt his confusion.

Aurelien's eyes narrowed with speculation and then moved on to Allie. "You must be Miss Chase," he said with a slight bow. "How delightful to meet you."

Allie rose. "Let Margot go," she said.

"Of course." He held out his hand. "Come to me, Allegra."

With a harsh breath, Raoul barred Allie's way. "Margot first," he hissed.

"As you wish." Aurelien gave Margot a gentle push. "Go to your Master, my dear."

Margot took a hesitant step. By all the norms of *strigoi* behavior, she should have returned eagerly to her patron, not only because of what Aurelien had obviously done to her, but also to relieve the constant discomfort the blood-bond imposed on both patron and protégé when they were separated. Still, she hung back.

"Come," Raoul urged, offering his hand, "my beautiful one, my jewel."

"Allie," Margot said in a voice thin as winter sunlight.

"It's all right, Margot," Allie said. "It's all right."

There were a hundred things Margot must be longing to ask, not least among them what had become of Mal in her absence. But she pressed her bloodless lips together and moved slowly across the room. Allie went to meet her. They clasped hands, and Allie felt the fragility of Margot's bones and the sluggish pulse beneath her blue skin.

Aurelien inserted himself between them and drew Allie away, smiling gently.

"I trust you will not suffer unduly during your time with us," he said as Raoul claimed Margot and thrust her behind him. "I promise that your strength will not be wasted."

Allie said nothing. There was nothing *to* say. She was still astonished by Aurelien's resemblance to Cato…a resemblance many would have missed, as Raoul had obviously done. Cato's face had always had a certain gentleness to it, almost a meekness, that had robbed his visage of the fierce ambition that shone in Aurelien's features. If Raoul and his lieutenants had even suspected that Aurelien and Cato were related, they would never have allowed Cato to remain with the clan when Aurelien was expelled.

But Cato knew just where to find Aurelien and offer

him the formula, Allie thought. Why had he changed his mind at the last minute? "Recognized my mistake," he'd said in his letter. The notes burned in the pouch of Allie's coat pocket.

"If our business is concluded," Aurelien said, "we'll make our adieus."

Raoul turned from staring into Margot's face and glared at his rival with a hatred that made a black pit in Allie's brain. "You're free to go," he said.

Aurelien buttoned his coat and put on his hat, leading Allie toward the door. The hatred faded from Allie's mind, replaced by a dreamy sense of well-being that came very close to joy. Raoul's joy. It was as shocking as if he had declared his intention to devote the rest of his life to philanthropic works for the benefit of all mankind.

But Raoul really hadn't changed, unless the poison had altered his personality more drastically than she'd realized. He had Margot back, and for the moment that was all that mattered to him. Allie wondered if he'd prepared an ambush, and if Klaus was ready to meet the clan in an all-out fight. Raoul couldn't know the number of Aurelien's followers, but surely the clan had the advantage. Both men undoubtedly understood that the final confrontation was only days away, if not hours.

"I know where his men are," Aurelien said as if he'd heard her thoughts. "I don't think Raoul will venture his troops just yet. It's clear that he has no thought for anything save his protégée. A dangerous weakness in a Master."

"Did you expect that he would be so distracted when he got her back?" Allie asked. "Is that why you agreed to this exchange?"

"It was a factor in my decision. My agents have reported the extremity of his response to losing her. He is clearly as dependent upon her as many humans are on alcoholic beverages." He glanced keenly at Allie. "Perhaps that accounts for the fact that something is obviously wrong with him."

Allie had no time to answer, for they had reached a black coupe guarded by a pair of armed enforcers. One of the enforcers lifted his head, and Allie caught a glimpse of a face she recognized with a start: Christof, Raoul's lieutenant.

I didn't see him around after Raoul made the announcement about the trade, she thought. *He must have gone straight to Aurelien with the news. I wonder how long he's been working for the opposition?*

Her speculation was interrupted as Aurelien handed her into the backseat and took his place beside her. The enforcers climbed into the front, and the car began rolling silently along a rutted path through the woods.

The softness of the seat cushions, the sharp scent of pine, even the quality of the afternoon light, seemed incredibly vivid to Allie in spite of her growing weariness. It was a strange and cruel fact that the closer you came to death, the brighter the world became.

But she wasn't afraid. Maybe that was a side effect of the poison.

If only it had the power to make her forget that she'd never told Griffin she loved him.

CHAPTER TWENTY-FOUR

THE WRECK BLOCKED the road in a tangle of twisted metal and blown tires, one automobile overturned and the other wrapped around the trunk of a formidable tree. A motorcycle lay on its side between them, its passage marked by a ribbon of black imprinted on the pavement.

Griffin jumped out of his car, Cassius hard on his heels, and ran to the nearest victim. The first vampire lay on his back, a dagger of steel wedged upward through his jaw, his body burned almost beyond recognition by the sun. Two others sprawled in unnatural attitudes on either side of the road, necks broken. A small quantity of blood had darkened on the dry grass.

"Who are they?" Cassius asked, his nose wrinkled in disgust.

Griffin didn't recognize them. He didn't need to. It was highly unlikely that anyone could have killed these vampires except other vampires, and there were now two rival Masters fighting tooth and claw for the same territory. Either the exchange of Allie for Margot had already been completed, leaving Raoul free to attack Aurelien, or the battle had begun before the trade had taken place.

Either way, Allie remained in deadly danger.

Griffin raised his head and closed his eyes. Beneath

the stench of blood, gasoline and blistered flesh, he detected another scent, one that filled him with both hope and dread.

"A human was here," Cassius said, leaning over the motorcycle. He glanced toward the woods on the right side of the road. "He must have walked away."

Dodging the wrecked vehicles, Griffin started into the woods.

Cassius caught up. "Where do you think you're going?"

"To find the human who survived."

"What does a flatfoot have to do with saving your leech?"

Griffin paused to correct his course. "Because this particular human may be of help to me."

"You know him?"

"Yes. And he knows about us, but he's safe. You'll leave him alone, Cassius."

The other werewolf muttered something indiscernible but followed quietly as Griffin traced the scent to a stream at the edge of a meadow. Mal was lying with his arm trailing in the water, the leather of his jacket scraped raw and his trousers half torn from his body. But he was still alive.

Griffin crouched beside him. "Mal! Can you hear me?"

The brown eyes opened, focusing slowly on Griffin's face. "Grif?"

"Hold still." Griffin examined Mal's arms and legs for obvious breaks and released his breath. "Are you in pain?"

Mal grimaced and touched his bloodied forehead. "There was an accident."

"I know." Griffin helped Mal to sit, warning Cassius

with a glance to keep his distance. "Can you tell me what happened?"

Mal peered into Griffin's eyes. "What are you doing here?" He pointed his chin at Cassius. "Who's he? How did you—"

"No time for that now. You've got to tell me who was involved in the accident."

"I…I was following them when it happened."

"Who? Who were you following?"

"Raoul." He attempted a laugh. "I'd only seen him a couple of times in the paper before Margot told me what he did to her. If I'd only known…"

"Start from when you learned where Margot was from the man you questioned in the hospital."

"You know about that, huh?"

Griffin hesitated. It was on the tip of his tongue to ask Mal if he really had killed the kidnapper, but he realized he wasn't prepared to deal with the answer.

Mal gave him a curious look. "Yeah," he said. "The bastard told me where to find the farmhouse where Aurelien was keeping Margot. I got to the place just as a gray-haired man and Margot were leaving— wouldn't have known the guy from Adam if one of the other men hadn't called his name. It was pretty clear that the whole bunch of them were blowing the joint."

"They didn't see you?"

"No. I went after them, keeping my distance." He wiped at his mouth with the back of a grimy hand. "They stopped at a café in a little town off the main road and went inside. A few minutes later Aurelien came out…" He hesitated, jaw set.

"He had Allie," Griffin said, holding his voice steady.

"Yes. What the hell was she doing with *him?*"

"She gave herself to Raoul to save her friends from his threats. He offered to trade her to Aurelien for Margot."

"But why would Aurelien want Allie?"

"You'll know everything when this is over."

Mal rubbed at the torn leather of his jacket. "I had to make a choice, Grif. When Raoul walked out with Margot, I...I had to follow them. I'm sorry."

"I understand. Was Margot all right?"

"I hadn't seen her since she went to Raoul," he said. "She looked very weak, pale."

"And Allie?"

"Tired. But Raoul looked worse, almost sick. Do vampires get sick?"

Griffin glanced away, thinking of the poison that was already doing its insidious work. "Where did Raoul take Margot?"

"They headed south with three other cars. Two of the cars took sideroads, while Raoul's stayed on the highway. He'd only gone a few miles when a pair of coupes pulled onto the road in front of them. They must have been vampires, too, because they all got out and started to fight. I've never seen anything like it, Grif."

"What happened to Raoul and Margot?"

"The attackers got the upper hand and dragged them out of the car. That's when I rode in. I thought there was a chance I could get Margot away...."

"But someone stopped you."

"One of them hit me with a branch. I lost control. When I came to, Margot was gone, and Raoul was dragging himself into one of the undamaged cars."

"He escaped."

"And the other vampires took Margot."

"Aurelien," Griffin muttered. "He must always have intended to get her back after the exchange."

Mal shifted his weight, wincing as bruised muscle complained. "Is Raoul that incompetent?"

"Not usually. He should have been fully prepared for such an attack." He felt again for the pendant in his pocket. "Can you stand?"

In answer, Mal gathered his legs under him and pushed to his feet, leaning on Griffin's arm. "How do we find Aurelien now?"

"The leeches' trail is still fresh," Cassius said, earning a wary glance from Mal. "Automobiles make a stink that pollutes the air for miles. If Raoul headed south, we'll follow the car that went north. We can—" He broke off, sharply turning his head toward the east. The other six pack members stalked out of the woods, escorting a pair of familiar youngsters.

"Griffin!" Gemma cried, starting toward him. The werewolves detained her, but Cassius motioned with his hand, and they let her go, though they continued to hold Wyatt in a death grip.

"Am I glad to see you!" Gemma said, rushing into Griffin's arms. "Please don't let them hurt Wyatt!"

Griffin held her away, dismay and anger thickening his voice. "Gemma, what in God's name—"

"Don't blame Wyatt. It isn't his fault, really, it isn't."

"Wyatt Dempsey," Cassius said, baring his teeth. "The traitor's son."

Gemma whirled to face him. "*He* didn't work for any vampires. His father—"

Cassius strode to Wyatt and seized him by the throat. "Where is your father?"

"Dead," Gemma said. "And the one you really want is Ivar. He was behind the whole thing. And he…" She half turned toward Griffin. "It was Ivar who ordered what…what happened to our parents."

Shock momentarily blurred Griffin's sight. Ivar? And Dempsey was dead. The knowledge found him strangely numb.

"He'll face the judgment of the pack, just as you will, Durant," Cassius said, releasing Wyatt.

Griffin threw off his paralysis and faced his sister with icy anger. "Gemma, how did you come to be here?"

She cast another nervous glance at Cassius. "Wyatt showed up at the Spiegels'. He told me all about Aurelien and Margot. We thought we could help, so—"

"Starke never came for you?"

Her confusion was answer enough. More than likely Edward had arrived at the Spiegels' after Gemma had left. He was probably frantic with worry, but there wasn't time to take Gemma back.

"We went to the farmhouse," Wyatt said, his face pale and defiant. "The leeches were leaving, so we followed their cars to this café—"

"You must have been there at the same time I was," Mal said. "You saw Margot and Allie?"

"Yes!" Gemma said. "We tried to go after Allie, but when the cars split up, we lost her. It took us a while to pick up the trail again, and then we found the crash…" She saw the expression on Griffin's face. "I had to do it, Grif. Please try to understand."

Griffin shook his head. He had a powerful desire to turn Gemma over his knee and give her a good spanking, but it had become painfully obvious that she had a mind and will of her own that he could no longer control.

"You'll have to come with us, Gemma," he said. "It will be dangerous, but..."

"I know. I'm not afraid."

"You'd do well to be." He took a deep breath. "You are to do exactly as I say at all times. Allie's life depends on our locating Aurelien within the next few hours."

"She's really in trouble, isn't she?"

"The worst kind." He took Gemma by the arm and urged her at a half run back toward the road. Cassius and his ruffians dragged Wyatt after them.

It wasn't difficult to track the automobile that had headed north after the battle. Even when the vehicle's path veered onto a series of dirt roads that would have thrown off any human pursuit, Griffin and the others easily detected the lingering odor of gasoline and rubber. The last road, hardly more than a trail, ended in a thick stand of trees. The vampires' coupe had been pulled into the brush and covered with pine boughs.

"Three leeches went up here," Cassius called from the slope of a thickly wooded hill. Griffin and Mal followed him, leaving Wyatt, Gemma and the other *loups-garous* to wait with the cars. Griffin found no trace of Allie's scent, but it made perfect sense that Aurelien and his men would take different routes to any rendezvous in order to confound their enemies.

At the top of the hill, the screen of trees opened up to reveal a tiny valley. A lone cabin crouched by a narrow stream, shaded by beeches and sugar maples that almost obscured the building from view.

"Aurelien's backup refuge," Griffin said, praying he was right. "I don't see any guards."

"You can bet they're there, hiding all around the valley," Mal said.

"Leeches and humans," Cassius said with a curl of his lip.

"Leeches and humans with guns," Mal retorted. "There aren't enough of us to rush them."

"They'll be watching for Raoul's leeches, not *loups-garous*," Cassius said. "We may be able to distract them."

"That's all I ask," Griffin said. "Along with a pair of revolvers and some tommy guns."

"Just the two of us, then?" Mal asked with a sudden grin.

"One of us has to get through, no matter what it takes. If I fall…" Griffin glanced at Cassius, drew Mal aside and revealed the chain from his pocket. "Allie drank poison just before she went to Raoul. This locket contains the antidote. Make sure she takes it."

"You aren't dying on me, Grif. You'll give it to her yourself."

"Promise me."

"Sure. I'm a hero, remember?" He looked at Cassius. "Let's get those guns."

They raced back down the hill, Mal moving almost as silently as the werewolves. Cassius provided them with the requested weapons. Gemma's eyes widened in alarm.

"What are you doing?" she demanded.

"Going after Allie and Margot," Mal said. "This is one adventure you're staying out of."

"We can help," Wyatt said, earning a savage glance from his guards.

Griffin swallowed a harsh reply. "Gemma, do you think you could find your way back to the café?"

"I think so. Why?"

"I asked Ross to meet me there as soon as he could gather his men. He's probably there now, but he won't know where to find us."

"Wyatt and I can do it," Gemma said, eyes sparkling with excitement.

"Not the boy," Cassius said. "He stays with us."

"I won't let her go alone," Griffin said.

"You trust this mongrel with your kin?"

"As much as I trust you. I have no choice."

Cassius bristled. "*We* have no reason to help Kavanagh."

"But he can help us, and I know the elders would want to hurt Aurelien as much as they want to punish me."

With a scowl, Cassius turned to confer with his companions. "Max will accompany your sister," he said. "Rufio and Silas will stay here with Dempsey to watch the road. The rest of us will distract the leeches."

It was far from an ideal plan, but Griffin was in no position to cavil. Gemma would be in little danger while the rival vampires and their henchmen were focused on each other. And she would be safer away from the main field of battle.

"All right," Griffin said, shoving his revolver into the waistband of his trousers. He hugged Gemma hard. "You're a woman now, Gemma. Don't take foolish chances."

"I won't let you down." She darted toward Wyatt, kissing his cheek under the baleful stares of Silas and Rufio. Max fell in behind her as she ran for the car.

Griffin watched until the automobile was out of sight, then made a second check of his weapons. He and Mal climbed the hill, then started down the other side, avoiding the path of those who'd gone before. They dropped to their bellies whenever they came to breaks in the tree cover. No one challenged them. Once they passed within a few feet of a vampire who crouched on the thick branch of an oak. Only the most careful maneuvering, perfected during the War, enabled them to avoid his notice.

They reached the bottom of the hill unscathed and faced a short stretch of open meadow before the thick cluster of maples surrounding the cabin. Mal sidled closer to Griffin.

"This is it," he said. "There's not much of a chance at least one of them won't see us."

Griffin met his gaze. "If you get through—"

"I won't forget, Grif. And if you're the one who…" He clenched his hands on his gun. "Take care of Margot. Don't let her go back to those creatures."

"I won't." Griffin smiled, and Mal gave him the thumbs-up. Then they dived into the grass, throwing their hearts before them.

THE CABIN WAS DIM AND DUSTY, the windows boarded up, the furniture primitive and the facilities rustic in the extreme.

Allie walked into the main room—one of only three, from what she could observe—and took a seat on a rickety chair. Aurelien and a pair of his men followed, the guards taking up a position close to the slightly crooked door.

The heat in the room was stifling. She removed her coat and gloves, folding them carefully in her lap.

"Nice little place you've got here," she said, eyeing the walls with their festoons of cobwebs.

"It serves its purpose," Aurelien said, settling in a slightly larger chair beside the soot-filled fireplace.

"For what? Waiting around for Raoul to attack you?"

Aurelien smiled. "Are you so concerned for my well-being, Allegra?"

"Maybe I just don't want Raoul to win."

"Ah." The chair creaked as he leaned back, crossing his long legs before him. "I have wondered, since Raoul made his offer, if you willingly gave yourself to him after Cato's death."

"Did you?" She stifled a yawn behind her hand. "Why should you have been interested in me?"

"I have maintained an interest in every member of the clan since I laid my plans to return."

"I'm not… I wasn't a member of the clan."

"You were until Cato's demise, however loose your ties to it. Even had I not already begun to suspect that you were like Margot, I would have felt obligated to keep an eye on you for my brother's sake. He spoke of you so often." His dark, molten eyes fixed on hers. "I observed in the café that you'd already surmised our kinship."

Allie idly played with the hem of her coat. "So you're Cato's brother. And no one ever figured it out. Funny. Cato was there when you were Master, wasn't he?"

"Indeed. But he preferred to remain secluded in his laboratory. And since we never acknowledged any relationship other than that of vassal and liege, those who might have noticed the faint resemblance between us dismissed it as mere coincidence."

Allie wondered why Aurelien seemed so eager to confide in her, but she saw no reason to discourage him. "You implied that you felt an obligation to Cato, even though he betrayed you by serving Raoul."

"He did what was necessary to survive. For that I forgave him long ago."

"Especially since he offered you the formula."

"You are very well informed, my dear."

"Elisha spilled the beans when he came snooping around my apartment. Couldn't keep his mouth shut, in fact. Not a very reliable agent."

"He has paid the price for his incompetence." Aurelien studied his hands. "It was from him that Raoul learned of my presence in the area, was it not?"

"Raoul had already guessed something was up. He had plenty of clues, like the attacks on De Luca."

"Attacks that did succeed in distracting him," Aurelien said.

"You got quite a few humans to risk their lives for you. The men who survived the attack on De Luca killed themselves rather than risk being questioned by the cops."

Aurelien shrugged. "Who can account for the ways of humans?"

Yeah, Allie thought. *They must have been more terrified of you than of dying.*

Aurelien leaned forward. "Let us return to the formula. Whatever Elisha's many faults, he seemed certain that Cato had given you his notes for safekeeping."

"He was wrong."

"Are you quite sure, my dear? It seemed quite peculiar to me that my brother would allow himself to be killed without finding a way to deliver the information he'd promised."

Allie picked up a glove and used it as a fan. "If I had it, why wouldn't I just give it to you? I'm not exactly fond of Raoul. He pressured me into submitting to him by threatening my friends."

"Your werewolf lover?"

"You're pretty well informed."

He merely smiled. "Cato would be relieved to hear that you didn't give yourself to Raoul willingly. He was committed to preserving your freedom."

"He saved my life."

"And that is another reason why you hate Raoul, is it not? He killed my brother." He stretched. "I realize that the blood-bond encumbers you with a certain unwilling loyalty to your Master—"

"I had to obey him when he proposed this trade, but I'm not feeling any pain at our separation."

"Clearly another feature of Cato's formula. Though a dangerous one for any patron who might pursue you after Raoul's death."

"Like you, for instance?"

"Will that be necessary to obtain your cooperation?"

"You can suck me dry without my cooperation."

"I trust it won't come to such extremes. My scientists believe that they are very close to distilling the substance that will duplicate Cato's formula." His face took on an expression that was almost earnest. "What if I should suggest that you join me as my vassal?"

"Vassal, not protégée?"

"I would never wish to place such limits on your nature when your unique qualities would be of such obvious value to me."

"What unique qualities, aside from what you can get from my blood?"

"You have relationships of trust with both breeders and dogs. Such relationships are not easily acquired by those of our kind."

"So?"

"Surely a woman of your intelligence can see that Raoul must ultimately lead the clan to destruction."

"Whatever his faults, he's kept a pretty good peace with the humans and werewolves."

"But is peace with them truly desirable, Allegra? Only think—"

He broke off as someone whistled sharply from the shaded yard in front of the cabin. One of the gunsels at the door turned to Aurelien.

"They're back with the girl," he said.

"What girl?" Allie demanded, irrationally terrified that Gemma had somehow fallen into Aurelien's power.

"Come, my dear…can't you guess?"

Allie sprang up from her chair, fought off a wave of dizziness and lunged for the door. Aurelien's men fell back as she opened it, letting in a wash of dappled sunlight. Without pausing, she ran out into the yard.

A pair of enforcers were approaching with a woman enveloped in a hat, veil and ermine-trimmed coat. Allie knew who she was even before the gunsels stopped to gawk in astonishment at her own uncovered face.

"Margot!" Allie hurried to meet her and took Margot's gloved hands in her own. "What are you doing here? How—"

She lost her breath and fell to her knees. Margot tried to help her up, but one of the enforcers kept her moving, while the other pulled Allie to her feet and half carried her back to the cabin. He laid her on the mouse's nest that passed for a sofa while the world spun around her.

"She…she was standing right there, in the sun," a male voice said.

"It's killed her," another man said.

"No." Aurelien's shadow fell over her. "Her flesh should be burned and covered with open sores, yet her skin is unblemished." He touched Allie's forehead. "She is cool. Her pulse is within normal range." He laughed. "Don't you see, you fools? Sunlight can't kill her. Oh, Cato, you've given me the world!"

CHAPTER TWENTY-FIVE

ALLIE DREAMED.

She was lying naked in Griffin's arms, floating on a tide of ecstasy. She felt the strength of his body, the glory of his lovemaking, the incomparable bliss of his blood flowing through her veins.

"Never leave me," he whispered, stroking her face, her hair. "Stay with me forever."

"Forever?" She stretched, running her hands over his chest. "Even we *don't live forever, handsome."*

But he wasn't laughing. He held her gaze with those earnest gray eyes and pinned her to the bed, all wolf once more.

"Stay," he said. "If you run, I'll follow. Wherever you go, I'll be there. I'll hunt you to the ends of the earth...."

She opened her eyes as the dream left her, Griffin's words still rough and sweet in her ears. Her vision had begun to go a little dim, but enough remained that she could see Margot sitting in a chair by the sofa, her eyes filled with worry.

"Allie," Margot said. "Oh, Allie, I'm so sorry...."

Allie tried to sit up but quickly thought better of it. The room was deserted, though she thought she heard voices in another room, one of them Aurelien's.

"It's all my fault," Margot said, clasping Allie's

hand between her own. "If only I hadn't agreed to run off with Mal…if only I'd—"

"Hush." Allie turned on her side and awkwardly patted Margot's knee. "What's done is done."

"But now Aurelien has you. And he knows we can walk in sunlight." Her green eyes shimmered with unshed tears. "Aurelien told me all about Cato's vaccine and how it enabled Raoul to Convert me, but I didn't know you were like me. If only I'd been prepared…"

"Easy. Even I didn't know what I was until after you were gone." Allie made another attempt to rise and managed to prop herself up on one elbow. "What happened after I fainted? Where is Aurelien?"

"Oh, God." Margot covered her face with her hands. "He's been crowing about it ever since he realized that you weren't hurt by the sun. He made me go out, too, and when he saw…" She lowered her hands and straightened. "He knew Cato's formula would give him the power to unseat Raoul. But now he plans something much worse. He said you and I were going to be the first of a new breed. A new army of *strigoi* with the power to conquer the world."

Allie burst into laughter and winced as the sharp movements sent a spear of pain through her body. "Conquer the world?" she repeated. "Is that really what he said?"

Margot nodded. "He thinks Cato's vaccine can create hundreds more like us. Enough to compete with humans on their own ground, and to keep Converting more and more vampires without having to worry about exposure." She closed her eyes. "He talked about infiltrating human society, taking over the government and the economy… Oh, Allie, he's truly insane."

That's putting it mildly, Allie thought. "What else did he say about this new plan of his?"

"He said he'd create an army and kill any *strigoi* who objects to his scheme. Then he'd start by eliminating the werewolves and the human bosses in New York."

A chill of terrible comprehension settled in Allie's chest. She had taken poison to make sure that Raoul could never work his evil on those she loved, but she'd opened the door for something far worse.

"He asked me if I get weak the way you did when sunlight touches me," Margot continued. "I've never been any good at lying." She leaned forward anxiously. "Allie, why are you so sick? Is it the sun?"

Allie seized on Margot's question with a flare of hope. Aurelien had seen her collapse after she'd come into the cabin. He'd naturally assumed that her illness was a side effect of exposure to sunlight. When she died, Aurelien would almost certainly begin to doubt that the vaccine could create the invulnerable legion of day-walking *strigoi* he envisioned.

But even that wasn't enough. Aurelien had to be stopped. And Allie had precious little time to figure out how to do it.

"Listen to me, Margot," she said. "Somehow or other I'm going to get you out of this place." She glanced toward the adjoining room, where the voices had fallen silent. "Tell me what happened to Raoul. How were you recaptured?"

"Aurelien's men ambushed us. I think Raoul got away."

Allie felt little surprise that Aurelien had broken the agreement with Raoul. But he'd underestimated his enemy. Dying or not, Raoul wasn't going to let Margot go a second time. He wouldn't give up until he drew his last breath.

Raoul, too, might serve a useful purpose before he died.

"Why did you do it, Allie?" Margot asked. "Why did you ask for this trade?"

"It seemed like a good idea at the time." She sighed. "I would have had to give myself to Raoul sooner or later. I didn't figure that being with Aurelien would be much worse than staying with Raoul. And if there was still a chance for you and Mal…"

"Oh, Allie. How could there be?" Margot took Allie's hand again. "How is Mal? I've been afraid for him… afraid of what he'd do once he found out I really was gone."

Even Allie didn't know the answer to that question. The last she'd heard, Mal had escaped the hospital and was presumed to be on his way to Aurelien's farmhouse. "He knows that Raoul took you," she admitted.

"If only I'd had a way to explain…"

"He wouldn't have wanted you to die."

"I wish I had."

"Don't talk nonsense. You—"

She stopped as four men walked through the door from the adjoining room. Allie immediately recognized the one closest to Aurelien as Christof, Raoul's former lieutenant.

It's time to start taking a few risks, Allie, my girl. You haven't got much left to lose.

"If what Ivar says is true," Aurelien was saying, "we may expect an attack at any moment. I'll speak to the men myself." He glanced back toward the door. "The dogs have failed us. Don't allow Ivar to escape."

"Too bad Ivar didn't realize what kind of guy he was working for," Allie said.

Aurelien gave her a hard look. "I see you've recovered, Allegra. I had momentarily feared for your health."

"I'll just bet." She lifted her head, then let it fall back onto the coat bunched under her shoulders. "Margot's been telling me about your latest plans. Pretty crazy, if you ask me."

"Fortunately, I didn't ask." He looked at Christof. "You remain here with the females. I have preparations to make."

He walked out the door with his other three enforcers, leaving Christof to watch the door. Allie pushed herself into a sitting position, ignoring the nausea and dizziness that accompanied every movement.

"Christof," she said.

The lieutenant met her gaze, his expression wary. "Miss Chase."

"Why are you working for Aurelien?"

The bluntness of her question didn't seem to surprise him. "I might ask you why you gave yourself to Raoul."

"You might, but I'd like an answer to my question first."

"Raoul is a law breaker and a tyrant."

"Sure he is. But what's Aurelien? A lunatic who wants to rule the world. Or do you think he has a chance of doing what he plans?"

A silence fell between them. Christof shifted uncomfortably.

"Let me guess," Allie said. "Aurelien seemed like a perfectly reasonable alternative to Raoul until he started talking about raising an army of day walkers."

"He would give us freedom...."

"Freedom to reproduce until there's no way to hide the presence of nonhumans in the city? Freedom to murder humans and werewolves like vermin?" She shook her head. "You behaved like a man of honor when Raoul tried to take me against my will. You recognized the necessity of laws, even for our kind. Aurelien would do away with the kinds of rules that keep us safe in the human world. I don't think you really want what Aurelien wants."

Christof paced across the room and leaned against the crumbling fireplace. "Even if what you say is true," he said, "what alternative do you suggest?"

"A third choice. A Master who can find middle ground between Raoul and Aurelien. A man like you."

His head jerked up. He searched her face. "You're sincere, aren't you?"

"I can't think of a better candidate."

"Aurelien would never let me go."

"Are you his protégé?"

The insult was calculated. No lieutenant, established in rank just below that of Master, would ever consent to be a mere protégé. Christof's face darkened. "My will is intact," he said.

"Then use it. Aurelien can't succeed, and he'll destroy everything the clan has built while he's at it."

Christof turned his back, brooding. Margot gazed at Allie in surprise.

Yes, I've changed, Allie thought. *I actually care about something bigger than myself. That's why I've got to keep fighting as long as I can.*

"There's one other thing for you to consider," Allie said to Christof, throwing all caution to the winds. "Raoul is dying."

Christof started. "What?"

"He has only a few hours to live."

"You're lying."

"Why should I lie?" She held his stare. "I gave him poison just before he claimed me. You may have noticed the strange way he was acting during the trade?"

Christof sank into the nearest chair, examining her in amazement. "Yes. I still can't believe—"

"That a protégée would try to kill her patron? What was the worst that could happen to me? I'd go crazy?" She laughed. "Until I met Aurelien, I didn't think there could be anything more miserable than being Raoul's slave."

The lieutenant gave his head a quick shake. "If this is true, it means that Raoul's clan will be leaderless before morning."

"Unless you step in to fill the breach."

Christof sprang up and paced the floor from one end of the room to the other. "If Aurelien knew…"

"But he doesn't—unless you plan to tell him."

A hundred heartbeats passed in silence. At last Christof turned to face her again, his brow deeply furrowed.

"What do you want, Allegra?"

"Only three little things. You give me your gun, get Margot out of here and be ready to pick up the pieces when Raoul and Aurelien are gone."

"You plan to shoot Aurelien?"

"I'm not a bad shot. And I have a feeling he won't expect attack from my direction."

"You can't, Allie!" Margot protested. "It's too dangerous!"

"Isn't it worth the risk?" Allie took Margot's hands. "If I succeed, we'll both be free, and the world will be a much safer place for everyone."

"I won't leave you here."

"You can only get in my way."

"She's right," Christof said. "The element of surprise may be enough. Aurelien expects Raoul's attack at any moment."

"And even though Raoul is dying—even if he's figured out that something's wrong—he'll throw everything into defeating Aurelien. It's going to get ugly, either way." Allie gathered Margot in a strong hug. "You go with Christof. Find Mal and have a happy life."

"How can I do that when I know what you've sacrificed?"

"Mal will help you. He loves you, Margot." She swallowed. "There's one thing you can do for me, and you have to stay alive to do it. When…this is over, go to Griffin and tell him I loved him. I would have married him." She closed her eyes. "No. Don't tell him anything. He'll be all right. He's a survivor, too." She walked away so she wouldn't have to keep looking at Margot's ravaged face. "Christof. The gun, please."

He fingered the holster under his coat. "You can't succeed."

"I will." She leaned close to his ear. "Aurelien can't hurt me. I'm dying of the same poison that's killing Raoul." She raised her voice. "You know what you have to do."

Expressionless, Christof handed her the gun. "Miss De Luca," he said.

Margot didn't move. Christof took her in hand, easily overcoming her resistance. They vanished into the back room of the cabin. Allie counted out a minute, shoved the gun in the pocket of her coat and opened the door.

Aurelien was standing alone in a small clearing among the sugar maples, his arms outspread. "Come out, Raoul," he called. "Before all the clan, I challenge you to personal combat."

Allie crouched at the foot of the steps and listened. There was movement in the undergrowth surrounding the maple grove. No telling how many of Raoul's men were waiting there.

"Do you hear me, Raoul?" Aurelien shouted. "Or are you so afraid to reveal how unfit you are to rule? Answer my challenge, or accept that you have forfeited the right to lead!"

Bushes rustled. Raoul emerged from hiding, backed by a half-dozen enforcers. Even from a distance, Allie could see that he was trembling.

"Here I am, Klaus," he said in a hoarse voice. "I'm pleased to see that you're so eager to die."

"I'm pleased to see that you still have a few scraps of pride left after your latest defeat," Aurelien said. "Margot is mine, and she will stay mine. You have already lost, Raoul."

The next few seconds passed like images in a moving picture as Raoul charged at Aurelien, his features twisted in a way that removed all semblance of humanity. The two Masters crashed together like bulls, fingers gouging, incisors bared to slash and tear.

Allie lifted the gun. Her hand was shaking so badly that she could hardly hold the weapon straight, and her vision was darkening minute by minute. Aurelien and Raoul were a blur, a single shape constantly morphing and shifting before her eyes.

Hold still, damn it. Just give me one good shot. Just one…

Her legs seemed to belong to someone else as she

rose from her crouch. The enforcers who watched the fight stood unmoving, their gazes fixed on the combatants. Aurelien and Raoul broke apart, shirts torn and bloody slashes crisscrossing their flesh. Raoul staggered. He raised his hands as if to signal surrender. Allie strode toward Aurelien, her arm outstretched before her.

"Aurelien!"

He spun toward her, and she pulled on the trigger just as the air around her exploded with blinding light.

CHAPTER TWENTY-SIX

GRIFFIN FLUNG HIMSELF on Mal and held him down as the first of the grenades struck the ground. A dozen others followed in rapid succession, plunging to earth like a shower of meteorites.

It was the War all over again: the deafening noise, the stench of burning, the shattering flares of light that seared like acid. Griffin trembled, his vision etched with the last image he had seen.

Allie standing behind two murderous vampires. Allie with a gun in her hand.

A fresh hail of grenades fell at the edge of the clearing no more than ten yards away. Griffin raised his head, his mouth dry, his nerves screaming the same message again and again: Run. Run. *Run....*

He pressed Mal's shoulder, steadying them both. Then they rose as one and plunged forward. Nameless figures struck out at them, and they struck back, hardly knowing if they left their anonymous enemies dead or alive. It was utter chaos, just as it had been nine years ago.

"Allie!" Griffin shouted. His eyes were blinded, his throat raw, his nostrils plugged with the harsh scents of war. But then a clear space opened amid the smoke, as it sometimes did on the battlefield, and he could see clearly again.

The man who could only be Aurelien, gray haired and hawk nosed, stood at the center of the storm, bleeding from several bullet and shrapnel wounds, but standing as tall as an officer certain of victory. A dark-haired *strigoi* lay gasping at his feet: Raoul, near death from the poison that would soon claim Allie's life. Dazed enforcers gathered about them, sheep in search of a shepherd to lead them out of Hell.

Aurelien turned his head and saw Griffin. He smiled, his teeth washed in red.

"Griffin Durant, is it not?" he said, his voice strangely clear above the din. "And the troublesome breeder Malcolm Owen. You chose the wrong time to interfere." He gestured to his men. "Kill them."

The enforcers rushed at Griffin, who took the pendant from his pocket and pushed it into Mal's hand.

"Run! Get to Allie!"

Mal leaped away just as the first of the enforcers reached Griffin, who raised his gun and shot one of them point-blank, then tossed the weapon aside as the others swarmed over him.

The Hun soldiers were too numerous, overwhelming him with sheer numbers. Griffin fought like a madman, fists pummeling and feet kicking like pistons. Behind his attackers he could see the gray-haired officer, who watched safely from behind the barricade, indifferent to the ugly and meaningless deaths on both sides of the line.

Without thought, Griffin Changed, tearing his clothing from his body even as skin and muscle and bone began their transformation. He ripped into his enemies with teeth and claws, and some fell back, startled by the ferocity of the beast Griffin had become. Still, he

*was outnumbered, and the Huns beat him down again
and again.*

*His body bruised and battered, Griffin twisted fran-
tically and slipped free of those who attempted to
hold him. Suddenly another contingent of Germans
plunged into the melee, opening fire on the first group.
A grenade exploded behind them, the concussion
knocking the Huns off their feet. Griffin gasped, trying
to catch his breath. An eerie silence fell. Spirals of
smoke drifted in choking clouds, obscuring the bodies
flung like rag dolls about the clearing.*

*For a moment Griffin's vision was unobstructed.
He saw the proud Hun officer down, moving feebly, his
clothes and exposed skin blackened by the blast. The
dark-haired Jerry lay where Griffin had last seen him,
but now there was another with him: a woman, her
ministering hands moving over his body.*

Allie.

The vision of War dissolved in an instant. There
were no trenches here, no barbed wire, no doughboys
floundering across the barren fields. Only Aurelien
struggling to his feet as Allie poured a stream of dark
powder into Raoul's mouth, powder from a packet
Griffin recognized all too well.

He Changed and scrambled up, leaping over the
bullet- and shrapnel-ridden bodies. Allie looked up
as he reached her, her eyes deeply sunken, her skin
stretched taut over her fine bones. He swept her up in
his arms and continued without stopping until he'd
reached the one area of the clearing not yet on fire.

"Allie!"

She lay where he put her, breathing shallowly, as
if she'd expended her last energy giving the antidote
to Raoul.

"For God's sake," Griffin said, sick with panic. "What have you done?"

"It's my fault." Mal crawled up behind Griffin, his face a bloody mask. "I tried to give it to her. She…she fought me off. Said she had to get it to Raoul."

"Why?"

His anguished cry went unanswered. He slapped Allie across the face to rouse her, and she gasped. Aqua eyes opened.

"Griffin?"

"I'm here, beloved."

"You…shouldn't have come." Her head rolled from side to side. "I don't love you. I don't…"

Griffin lifted her against his chest and rocked her like a child. "Why? Why did you do it?"

"Aurelien had to die," she said, whispering each word as if she had gathered it from some place far beyond Griffin's reach. "I tried. I couldn't…" She gripped Griffin's arms so tightly that he could feel the pressure in his bones. "Raoul must kill him."

She was delirious, lost to sense as her final moments approached. "I don't understand," Griffin said, his voice breaking.

Allie looked into his eyes, her own suddenly clear and blazing with conviction. "Aurelien…is evil. If he wins, he rules the clan. More humans and werewolves will die." She tried to smile. "Help him. Help Raoul. The rest…doesn't matter."

In despair, Griffin turned to look behind them. The smoke was still thick, but he could make out the shapes of the two vampire Masters. Aurelien had risen to his feet, injured but ready to fight. Raoul faced him, defiant, once again at the height of his strength.

The silence was profound, broken only by the

crackling of flames from the undergrowth. Illuminated by fire, human shapes materialized from among the trees and drifted into a loose circle around the combatants.

Raoul attacked without warning. A look of astonishment crossed Aurelien's face as he met Raoul's assault.

Griffin turned back to Allie, feeling her muscles begin to slacken as she surrendered to the darkness. "Allie," he whispered. "Don't leave me."

Her head rolled against his arm. "Let me go," she said. Her fingers touched his face. "It's all right. All right."

No.

"You can't run anymore," he said. "You're going to be my wife."

Her mouth curved in a smile. "You…never give up. Still trying to seduce me with that magnificent…" Her weight settled against him. He could hardly hear her heartbeat.

"Allie. Listen to me. Almost all my life I've been fighting the same war, blaming the wolf in myself for the killer I became. But it was never the wolf." He pressed his cheek to hers. "It was hatred, Allie. Guilt. A sickness from the past I couldn't face until you walked into my life."

Her eyelids fluttered. "It's…in all of us," she whispered.

"But I let it rule me. I thought only of myself, of my own pain. I didn't think there was anything in the world stronger than hate. But there is, Allie." He rocked her gently. "There's only one battle left to fight, and we're going to win."

"You've…already won, Grif. You…" She sighed, her breath drawn out until there was nothing left.

Griffin smoothed the dark hair from her face with hands that no longer seemed a part of him. His tears mingled with the blood on his cheek and fell on her lips. She tasted the moisture, and her eyes fluttered open.

A storm of wild conjecture smothered Griffin's grief. When Allie had taken his blood that first time, after the fight in the tenement, she'd been slowly dying of blood starvation. Somehow his blood had acted as a kind of antidote, restoring her strength almost immediately.

If there was a chance, a chance in a million…

"Allie," he said, "take my blood."

The bright color of her eyes had dulled to gray. "Don't…understand."

"You don't have to. Take my blood, Allie. As much as you can hold."

He tore at the skin at the underside of his wrist and pressed the wound to Allie's lips. At first she did nothing, but then he felt the tip of her tongue stroke the wound. The anesthetic effect quickly stanched the small pain as her teeth penetrated flesh. Then the bliss came over him, easing his fear for her, bringing back memories of their last night together, the ache of joy and wonder.…

The agony of his wounds faded. He drifted in a place of inexplicable beauty for uncounted minutes, and when the dream released him, Allie was sitting beside him, her forehead resting against his.

"Allie?" He took her face between his hands, searching the new brilliance of her eyes.

She smiled. "I'm okay."

He began to shake. "You're—"

"Alive. You saved me."

"How very touching."

Griffin looked up, the rapid movement jarring him to near unconsciousness. Raoul Boucher stood over them, hale and whole, his clothing torn and bloodied but his face lit with triumph.

"Allie, my dear little traitor," Raoul said. "How very kind of you to wait for me."

Griffin made a powerful effort to rise. His weakened body betrayed him. "You're alive because of her," he rasped.

Raoul laughed. "Indeed." He gestured behind him. The vampire Griffin recognized as Raoul's lieutenant, Christof, came to join him.

"Christof," Allie said, clearly startled.

"You seem surprised," Raoul said. "Did Christof perhaps give you the impression that he was in service to Aurelien?" He chuckled. "A very clever lad, our Christof. He told me the fascinating tale of your efforts to kill me at your own expense." He tutted reprovingly. "Such a waste, my dear. We seem to be back where we started."

Allie got to her feet. "Aurelien is dead."

"Thanks to Christof. He appeared at a most opportune moment to, shall we say, assist me in putting the usurper in his place."

Allie looked beyond him to where Aurelien lay in a congealing pool of blood and then turned to stare at Christof. "Where is Margot?" she asked.

Mal shot up, ready to do something foolish. Griffin grabbed his arm.

"Christof did tell me that he helped you and Margot escape," Raoul said. "We shall find her soon enough."

Griffin struggled to rise again and fell back. "You've lost, Raoul," he said, "even if you don't know it."

"That's right," Allie said. She looked beyond Raoul's shoulder, and Griffin followed her gaze. A few straggling survivors were making their way across the corpse-littered clearing, converging on their Master like bees on their queen. "Aurelien may be out of the way, but you still have that nagging little problem of legitimacy."

Raoul stiffened. "I can still destroy your friends."

"I don't think so. You're pretty shorthanded." She raised her voice. "Maybe your friends would like to know the real reason why Aurelien was such a big threat to you. He knew that Cato made it possible for you to keep the throne even after you lost your potency, that Margot was the product of a drug, not your natural bite." She laughed. "It's all a fake, Raoul. And sooner or later the clan is going to realize it."

Raoul stepped back, his face a mask of fury. "Kill them all," he told Christof.

But the lieutenant remained where he was. The clan members drew closer, and from the looks on their faces, Griffin knew they'd heard at least part of what Allie had said.

Raoul swung about, staring. "I can defeat every one of you." He beckoned wildly. "Who will be first? You, Christof? Or you, Kyril?"

His men exchanged glances. None of them accepted the challenge.

"You see?" Raoul said, turning back to Allie. "All will be as it was. You and everyone you care about will—"

He broke off, eyes wide with astonishment as the front of his head exploded in a gush of bone, blood and brain matter. Griffin dragged Allie down and rolled on top of her. *Strigoi* screamed as their bonds to their Master were violently severed.

"What's happening?" Mal exclaimed, pressing his hands over his ears.

"Raoul is dead," Christof said, as coolly as if he were discussing the price of wheat shares on the stock market.

"Who killed him?" Allie demanded, pushing Griffin aside.

"That's what I'd like to know," Ross Kavanagh said, walking into the clearing with a half-dozen heavily armed police officers behind him. "Maybe some disgruntled vampire with an agenda of his own." He glanced from Raoul's body to Aurelien's, then eyed the distraught *strigoi* with interest. "Looks like we missed all the fun."

"Gemma?" Griffin asked, getting to his knees.

Ross offered him a hand up. "She's safe," he said. "So is the boy. They're with my men."

Thank God, Griffin thought. He looked past Ross and saw two other distinctly separate groups approaching: Carmine De Luca, with a contingent of enforcers, and Cassius, with his werewolves. Margot was leaning heavily against her father, apparently well and whole.

"Margot!" Mal cried.

"Take it easy," Allie said. "Give her a little time."

Mal subsided, straining like a greyhound on a short leash. Griffin squeezed his friend's shoulder. "How did De Luca get here?" he asked Ross.

"Seems he has connections in the department," Ross said dryly. He looked Griffin over with a critical eye and removed his trench coat. "You'd better take this. Don't want you shocking any innocent eyes."

Griffin pulled on the coat and belted it around his waist. The effort nearly sapped his strength. "Do you know who brought in the grenades?"

"Raoul, as far as we can tell. He must have been pretty desperate to risk killing his own men, as well as Aurelien's."

He might even have realized he was dying, Griffin thought.

As one, he and the others looked around the clearing. Ross's men were already beginning to make a count of the bodies and checking on the extent of the fire, which seemed not to have spread far beyond the immediate vicinity and was already burning itself out.

"Lots of vampires dead on both sides," Ross said. "There won't be much left of them come daylight." He fished a toothpick out of his coat pocket and put it in his mouth. "The survivors seem to be in a pretty bad state of confusion."

"That tends to happen when a patron dies," Allie said. "Especially by violence." She frowned. "Where's Christof?"

Raoul's former lieutenant had vanished, and Ross looked far from pleased. "We aren't letting anyone out of the area until we've got it under control," he said.

"Christof may be of some help to you there," Allie said. "He's got as good a claim on the clan as anyone." But her expression was troubled, as well it should be, considering Christof's rapid shifts of allegiance.

"Well," Ross said, "I've got a few things to take care of. You going to be all right with them?" He jerked his head toward Cassius and the *loups-garous,* who had maintained their distance.

"Yes," Griffin said. "They won't be any trouble."

"Yeah, sure. Just shout if you need a hand."

He wandered off to consult with his men. Mal stalked away in the opposite direction, leaving Allie and Griffin alone.

"Why did you do it, Allie?" Griffin asked softly.

She didn't pretend to misunderstand. "Raoul made too many threats. My life just didn't seem worth very much if something happened to you and Gemma and the others." She paused, a great weariness shadowing her eyes. "Cato left a letter telling me about a special poison he'd created just in case I ever had to get rid of Raoul. The only way I could get Raoul to fall for it was to let him have what he wanted." She hesitated. "How did you find me?"

He told her about discovering Cato's letter and about Sebastian's death.

"I'm sorry to hear that," she said. "He was a good man at heart."

Griffin swallowed, light-headed and increasingly uncertain of his footing. "Did you suggest the trade for Margot?"

"I wanted Margot free, and Raoul was less likely to realize what I'd done to him if he was busy trying to get her back. At the time I didn't realize that Aurelien would be an even worse Master than Raoul." She caught his look and gave him a wry smile. "It's a long story. I'll have to tell you about it sometime."

"There are…things I must tell you, as well." He looked past Ross to Cassius and the werewolves ranged about him. "I made a bargain with the pack, Allie. They would have kept me from coming to find you if I hadn't."

She went very still. "What sort of bargain?"

"If they allowed me the chance to help you, I would return with them to face the pack's judgment."

"That's a load of horse puckey."

"I gave my word." He clasped her shoulders. "Allie, listen to me…"

She shook him off, her beautiful eyes taking on a reddish gleam. She strode toward Cassius and came to a stop before him, hands on hips. "So you think you're taking Griffin back," she said with a smile that no one could mistake for friendliness.

Cassius glanced uneasily at his comrades. "It's our duty."

"Duty," she said with a scornful laugh. "Maybe you'd better think it over. Griffin's got a lot of friends who won't take his demise too kindly."

"No one would dare—"

"Want to make a bet on that? Everyone here has dared quite a bit lately. And Griffin has strong ties to both vampires and humans. Do you really want the other races against you?"

"We told you that Ivar is your real enemy," Gemma said, arriving with a grizzled police escort in tow. "*He's* the one who betrayed you."

"Durant attacked our leader," Cassius snapped.

"Who made Ivar his lieutenant?" Allie asked. "Who allowed traitors to stain the honor of the pack?"

"The elders gave orders to take Durant."

"And like good little dogs, you have no choice but to obey. I never knew how much werewolves are like vampires."

"You can't interfere, Allie," Griffin said quietly. "It's out of your control."

"You owe her a debt," Margot said to Cassius, coming to join them. "Aurelien planned to exterminate the pack as part of his strategy for dominance."

"And Allie made sure Raoul would win the fight, at the risk of her own life," Mal added.

Cassius's eyes looked everywhere but at Allie. "If we fail, Sloan will kill us."

"Unless Griffin kills *him*." Allie's smile widened. "What if he challenges Sloan again, for true leadership this time? Would Sloan be willing to fight him on equal terms?"

"Durant forfeited the right to a formal challenge," Cassius said.

"And that suits Sloan just fine. He's afraid of Griffin."

"It's true," one of the young men with Cassius muttered, "he's gotten weak, Cassius."

Griffin hesitated. He remembered the old battle frenzy that had claimed him tonight—the confusion, the rage, the mindless hatred. He'd been in Flanders all over again, fighting the same endless war.

Until he'd seen Allie sacrificing her one chance at life for a cause greater than herself. In that moment something had changed inside him. He was still fighting a war, but not the one that had claimed him for so many years. Now he was fighting for something far more powerful. He was fighting for love.

"Yes," he said, meeting Cassius's gaze, "I will."

Voices rose. The young *loups-garous* began to growl at each other, and soon they were arguing fiercely amongst themselves. Griffin and Allie stood side by side, not touching. Mal and Margot gazed at each other across the impossible barrier of several yards.

At last the werewolves seemed to reach an agreement.

"Very well," Cassius said. "We'll return to Manhattan ahead of you and make your offer to the elders. But if they don't agree…"

"That's a chance I'm willing to take," Griffin said. "I'll make myself available until the elders have reached a decision."

"Wyatt Dempsey must go with us."

Gemma gave a cry and rushed to stand between Cassius and Griffin. "You can't!" she protested. "Wyatt only obeyed his father until he saw what they were doing was wrong."

"What's this about Dempsey?" Ross said, flanked by two of his men.

"They want to punish him!" Gemma cried. "Just because he had the wrong father!"

Griffin took Gemma's arm, suddenly aware that he was on the verge of collapse. "No one should hate the Dempseys more than I," he said. "Conlan Dempsey helped murder my family because my parents were about to expose the pack members working for the vampire clan there. If anyone has the right to judge this boy, I do."

"And would you spare him?" Cassius demanded.

"Where is Wyatt?" Griffin asked Ross.

Ross gave a signal. Two of his officers emerged from the charred undergrowth with the boy between them.

The ghost of ancient anger passed through Griffin like the last throes of a terrible illness. The boy stared at the ground, shoulders slumped. He clearly expected no mercy. But Griffin saw no killer in Wyatt's downcast face, nor felt any lingering trace of the ruthless avenger within himself.

The War is over.

"I would do more than spare him," he said to Cassius. "I'll take personal responsibility for him. He won't cause trouble for the pack or anyone else."

"That's not good enough," Cassius said.

"Then I'll go to the elders to plead for him."

"I'm going with you," Allie said.

"And I," Gemma said.

"Count me in," Mal said.

"I'll be there," Ross added.

Wyatt raised his head. He looked like a convict just saved from the gallows by angels sent from heaven. Cassius was thoroughly disgruntled, but he knew he'd lost the battle.

"The elders will summon you," he said. "If the kid's not there…"

"He will be."

With a soft growl, Cassius and his young men retreated. Gemma ran to Wyatt, and they embraced without the slightest concern for their audience.

Allie pushed her hand through the crook of Griffin's elbow. "See?" she said. "That wasn't so hard."

Griffin covered her hand with his. "There's still no guarantee that the elders will agree to let either of us go."

"Oh, I think they will…unless they want another war."

"Why should the clan help us? They'll be in a state of chaos for weeks, if not months."

"I didn't mean the clan." Her expression made her meaning clear enough, and there was no point in arguing…at least not until his fate was decided.

He held his hand out to Gemma, who had finally let Wyatt catch his breath. She came to him with relief and joy in her eyes. "Thank you," she whispered, wrapping her arms around his waist.

Griffin couldn't bear to remind her that the danger wasn't entirely past. "You've been very foolish," he said. "And very brave."

"I wasn't brave. I was scared to death, for you and Allie and everyone. There should have been more I could do to help."

"You did quite enough, young lady." He tipped up her chin. "I underestimated you. I won't do so again."

Her eyes shone through a veil of tears. "I was stupid for a long time, Grif. I didn't understand that being an adult doesn't mean how you dress, or whether you drink and smoke."

"Some people never learn that lesson." He kissed her forehead. "We'll still have much to discuss when we get home."

"Home." She sighed and leaned her head against his shoulder. "It seems a million miles away."

So it did. And his home, not to mention his fortune, might not be his much longer, if the elders found against him.

He beckoned to Wyatt, who walked slowly toward them like a pup still expecting to be disciplined for misbehavior.

"I'm sorry," the boy said. "Sorry for what my father did to your family and Mr. Owen. I thought I could make up for it, but…" He shook his head. "Nothing I did made any difference. I couldn't even find Ivar."

"I heard Aurelien order his men to kill Ivar," Allie said. "If he's not among the dead, he must have gotten away when the bombing started."

"Cassius won't be happy if he escaped," Griffin said.

"And you?" Allie asked softly.

"The guilt is gone," he said, looking into her eyes. "So is the hatred." He summoned a smile. "Though Mal probably wouldn't have minded taking a swing at him."

"He'll get what's coming to him sooner or later," Mal said. "That kind always do."

Allie gave Griffin a wry glance, suggesting what she thought of Mal's optimism, but there was no derision in her face. "At least Raoul and Aurelien got what they deserved."

"And now you're free," Griffin said.

"Yeah. Completely free." She broke away and faced the cabin with folded arms, staring at the smoldering ruins.

Griffin swayed and caught himself, swallowing the words he would have spoken. He turned to Mal. "Margot is free, too," he said. "Don't you have a little business to attend to?"

"What bus—" Mal flushed. "I don't think De Luca wants to be disturbed."

"*You* found Margot, not him. You have a right to speak your mind."

Mal gazed soulfully at the woman standing that endless three yards away. "Maybe she doesn't feel the same anymore. Maybe—"

"Maybe she's afraid of the same thing you are," Ross said. "For God's sake, man, stand up for yourself. Go to her."

Mal went, his shoulders set as if he were about to face a platoon of German soldiers armed with mortars, all pointed at him. A brief exchange of words with his lady love resulted in a long and very passionate kiss. Mal squeezed Margot's hands, turned and marched resolutely toward Carmine De Luca.

"Romance," Ross said, wrinkling his nose. "Save me from ever falling into that trap."

You've got it all wrong, Ross, Griffin thought. *It's love that will save you.*

"What are you going to do about Mal?" Griffin asked. "He didn't kill that man in the hospital. He couldn't have."

"Fortunately, we know he didn't. We got a confession letter from Conlan Dempsey not long before we left Manhattan. Said he'd done the guy right after Mal talked to him. I think I can work it so Mal won't have to face any questioning."

"Thanks, old friend."

"It's nothing. Hey, you'd better sit down. You still look a little pale."

Griffin located a relatively clean place to sit as Ross circled the clearing, speaking to his men and jotting the occasional note with the stub of a badly chewed pencil. The surviving vampires continued to roam about in a state of dazed bewilderment, though once or twice Griffin caught sight of Christof moving among them, clearly unaffected by Raoul's death. Mal and Margot were gazing at each other with lovestruck adoration, while Gemma and Wyatt had wandered off, hand in hand.

"Cato's notes!"

Griffin started up at Allie's cry. "What about them?"

"I left them in the cabin, inside my coat!"

They both looked at what remained of the structure. There could be no doubt that anything inside it had burned beyond recognition. Griffin felt in his coat pocket and cursed.

"I had the other page," he said, "but it must have been burned up with my clothes after I Changed. I'm sorry, Allie."

"I'm not. Now there's no way that some other Master will use them to violate *strigoi* law."

Griffin followed Allie's glance to where Christof was speaking with a small group of distraught vampires. "Do you think he'll be able to pick up the pieces?" he asked.

"I don't know. I thought he might be the one to pull

it off, but even I couldn't tell which side he was working for." She gathered a handful of scorched earth and let it sift through her fingers. "Maybe when humans stop killing each other, the rest of us can learn to do the same."

Griffin took her hand. "Allie…"

She sprang to her feet. "I've got to talk to Margot before she runs off with loverboy. You just stay here and rest, okay?" She grinned, blew him a kiss and skipped away as if she'd never sampled the inside of a poison bottle.

Griffin let her go. If he survived the confrontation with the pack, there would be time. Time for Allie to decide how much she really wanted to be free.

With hope firmly lodged in an unfamiliar portion of his heart, Griffin promptly fainted.

CHAPTER TWENTY-SEVEN

GARRET SLOAN HAD RUN. That was the news Cassius brought to Oakdene when he returned from his meeting with the elders. The entire pack was in an uproar.

"He heard you were ready to fight him again," Cassius said, "and I guess he got scared. A coward, just like the leech—" he cleared his throat "—just like Miss Chase said." He straightened in the chair beside Griffin's bed. "The elders have a lot to do right now. There'll be challenges for leadership. No one has time to worry about you or the Dempsey kid. And anyway…" He grinned unexpectedly. "They all seem to think you're too much trouble, you and your vampire lady. You're bad luck for the pack."

Griffin didn't trust the young werewolf's new affability, but he'd been glad enough that the elders had sent a single messenger to convey their will. Their judgment had been far more lenient than Griffin could have hoped for.

"I assure you," he said, "I have never borne ill will toward the pack as a whole."

"If the elders thought you did, you'd be up a creek without a paddle. As it is—" Cassius shrugged "—if you pay up the way you promised when we let you go find your girlfriend, they'll consider it a done deal."

"I've already spoken to my bank. In a few days they should have a full accounting of my assets, and—"

"Oh, they don't want the whole thing." Cassius leaned back, and the chair gave an ominous creak. "I think they're afraid that too much money would ruin the pack's morals."

Griffin contained his shock. "How much?"

"Half. Though they may want to check your books to make sure you're on the level."

"That…can be arranged."

"Then the elders will be in touch." Cassius rose, almost knocking the chair to the carpet, and ambled toward the door. "You're crazy, Durant, but you survived. That's all that matters."

His footsteps padded along the hall and down the stairs. A few moments later Starke walked into the room bearing a tray of toast, eggs and juice.

"Is everything all right, Mr. Durant?"

"Quite all right, Edward. I won't even have to reduce your salary."

"That is a relief. Will you eat a little, or would you prefer to go back to sleep?"

"I'd like to dress. I've been in this bed too long."

"Twenty-four hours is hardly too long after such an ordeal. Would it not be wiser to wait?"

Griffin sat on the edge of the bed and worked the kinks out of his muscles. The faintness was gone. He'd never felt better in his life.

"This may shock you, Uncle Edward, but I'm through with wisdom." He glanced toward the window. "I've discovered that there are certain benefits to taking chances."

Starke offered his rare smile. "Very good, Griffin," he said. "Very good, indeed."

Starke selected flannel trousers and a jacket from the armoire, then produced an impeccably pressed shirt, collar and tie. Griffin accepted Starke's help with the tie, then asked to be alone. He went to the window and pushed back the drapes.

A foretaste of autumn gave a certain crispness to the early-morning air. Allie was walking along the path among the flower beds, her blue-and-green dress the one vivid spot in a garden beginning to fade with the cooler days and nights of late summer.

She'd been with him since their return to New York, fussing over him, arranging vases of flowers in his room, keeping vigil throughout the long day and night while he'd slept the sleep of the dead. She herself had recovered completely; if anything, she seemed to be stronger and more energetic than ever. It was as if some great burden had been lifted from her shoulders.

Her devoted care and attention—even the way in which she'd bullied him to stay in bed—had given him cause to hope, but he knew he didn't dare read too much into it. She had proven to be a selfless and courageous friend and companion, but she would have been just as solicitous toward anyone who'd earned her loyalty and trust. Not once had they discussed their future, or even if there was to be one.

Griffin had let the silence continue, unprepared to hear her refusal. But so much had changed; Wyatt was living with them now, given his own room far from Gemma's and firmly reminded that he had to earn his privileges. Gemma had been unusually quiet; she had made a diffident request that she be allowed to travel alone to San Francisco to visit the graves of their parents, and Griffin was still weighing the possibility.

He had given up entirely on the notion that she would

ever marry a young human of good family and excellent prospects; she'd come too far and seen too much to be content in an ordinary life, no matter how comfortable.

And Griffin had finally come to understand that his fear of the wolf within himself had been no more than the embodiment of a War he couldn't escape, memories he had been unwilling to let go—memories of his parents' deaths at the hands of his own kind, memories of the creature he had become on the battlefields of Flanders. That creature was no longer a raging force beyond his control but a part of him—thanks to Allie and the example of unshakable inner strength she had set.

As for Gemma and Wyatt, he'd insisted that they had to get to know each other properly before making a decision about whether or not they truly wanted to form the kind of lifetime partnership *loups-garous* considered the ideal. It wasn't as easy to break up that sort of arrangement as it was with human marriages.

At least some of them. Griffin never had any doubt that Mal and Margot would make a go of it, in spite of Margot's inhuman nature. Raoul's death had set her free, and she would never consent to become the protégée of another vampire. De Luca had finally granted his blessing to the couple, recognizing the futility of standing in the way of such a strong devotion.

The clan was still fragmented as Christof cemented his leadership among Raoul's former vassals and offered amnesty to Aurelien's followers. The human scientists had vanished, but since the formula had been destroyed, Christof saw no percentage in hunting them down. There was a real hope for peace…and more:

with Sloan gone, the council might be open to nego-
tiating a new and stronger truce with the clan, if only
to ensure that no *loup-garou* was suborned into serving
a vampire in the future. Everything seemed touched
with a new hope.

Only one question remained to be answered, and he
intended to get that answer before the hour was over.

He took the stairs slowly, testing his balance with
each step. His legs held up admirably, as if they understood his urgency.

Allie had paused to sit on a wrought iron bench
among the rosebushes, her gaze fixed on the late-
blooming flowers. She didn't hear Griffin approach
until he was a few feet away.

"Allie," he said, his heart beginning to pound.

"Hello, Grif." She frowned. "You shouldn't be up."

"My recovery is more likely to be impeded if I'm
confined to that room."

Allie nodded understanding and tapped the empty
spot on the bench. "You'd better sit."

"I…I prefer to stand." He glanced at the path and
then at the glossy cap of her short hair. To run his
hands through it, to touch her cheek, to kiss…

"Do you have something to tell me?" she asked, cutting short his reverie. "Any news from the elders?"

"Yes. Cassius just left—"

"And you didn't call me?" She shot to her feet and
glared at him. "You know I wanted to be there."

"It was better that I meet him alone."

She snorted. "Well? What did he say?"

He related the conversation. Allie's eyes shone with
fierce satisfaction.

"I knew it," she said. "I knew they wouldn't try to
punish you."

"There was always a chance—"

"No, there wasn't." She met his gaze. "What about the money?"

"A small price to pay for the pack's acceptance."

"So they won't be pressuring you or Gemma to join up?"

"I doubt it. As Cassius said, they have enough to deal with."

"Like the clan."

"Even Aurelien's followers must realize that they can't afford to sustain an internecine conflict for an indefinite period."

"Not in a world ruled by humans." She resumed her seat. "Aurelien really was insane."

"Hatred and prejudice know no race." He rolled a bit of gravel under his heel. "There's something I've been wanting to ask you, Allie."

She cocked her head. "This sounds serious."

"Yes."

"Well, spit it out, then."

"Yes." He swallowed. "Did you mean what you said when you…before I gave you the antidote?"

An unaccustomed blush stained her cheeks. "I don't remember."

"You said you didn't love me."

She would have risen again, but Griffin was blocking the way. She twisted her hands in her lap. "I… uh…I was a little crazy myself."

His chest tightened. "Why did you say it?"

"Because…because I… Oh, damn it!" She closed her eyes. "I had to convince you, so you wouldn't feel too bad if I died."

Griffin sank onto the bench beside her. "It was a poor attempt, Allie."

"Don't I know it. It didn't work for me, either." She opened her eyes and slowly raised her head. "I've been fighting it for about as long as we've known each other. I just didn't realize how much there was to fight against until I was about to die."

Hope was a brilliant white light flowing through Griffin's body like a taste of paradise. "Say it," he said.

She muttered something unladylike under her breath. Then… "All right. I love you. Satisfied?"

He almost laughed aloud. "Are *you?*"

She squirmed. "It shouldn't have happened. They always say vampires—"

"Can't love? Did it ever occur to you that might be a myth conjured up to keep your people from forming real attachments and caring about something other than mere survival?"

"I'm a freak in so many ways…."

He seized her hands. "You're a woman. A beautiful, courageous, vibrant woman. The rest doesn't matter."

"Oh, Grif. You're not thinking clearly."

"I'm thinking more clearly than I have in years." He leaned toward her. "I love you, Allie. Marry me."

"You never give up, do you?"

"Never."

"I can only change so much, Griffin."

"I don't want you to change."

She tried to pull away. "What would a man like you do with a wife like me?"

He held her more tightly. "I'm sure I'll find something useful, even if it doesn't meet with the complete approval of the Long Island matrons."

Her mouth curved in a wicked grin. "We could really make them sit up and take notice."

"So we could."

"I'd have to go back to Manhattan a couple of times a week to get what I need. I might attract a little too much attention here, and I can't keep using you exclusively."

"Understood."

"The clan and the pack aren't going to be happy with us."

"Since when did that ever concern you, Allegra Chase?"

She gave a great sigh, her hands beginning to tremble in his. "We can't have children, Grif."

"How do you know? How many times has a werewolf married a vampire?"

"Even if you and I were the same kind…we just don't reproduce that way."

"You're an exception to the usual run of vampires. You can walk in sunlight. You can weep. Who's to say you're not different in other ways, as well?"

"Grif…"

"I don't demand anything of you but your love."

Her eyes began to glimmer with tears. "There's still one thing you haven't considered. Maybe you never thought of it before.…"

"Tell me."

"Vampires live for hundreds of years, even thousands. Werewolves—"

"Live only a little longer than humans." He wiped a tear from her cheek with his thumb. "It's you who'd make the sacrifice, Allie. You'd have to watch me grow old while you remain young and beautiful."

"And you think that would matter?" She laughed, shedding a rain of tears. "All the things that seemed to be important to me…they don't mean anything now."

"Then we have nothing to fear." He drew her against him. "Marry me, Allie."

She pulled back and looked into his eyes. "You're sure, Grif? Absolutely sure?"

In answer, he kissed her with all the hunger and yearning he'd so thoroughly failed to deny. And Allie reminded him once again that she was every bit his equal.

IT WAS A WHITE WEDDING. All their friends were there: a rather grim Ross Kavanagh, who shook his head and mumbled about balls and chains; Mal and a well-bundled Margot, so lost in each other that they didn't notice the stares and remarks about her peculiar clothing; Louise, all smiles, with her arms filled with chrysanthemums; Bruce, Nathan, Pepper and Allie's other friends, returned from exile; Wyatt, uncomfortable in a starched collar; and Gemma, beautifully arrayed as the maid of honor.

Allie wore a daring dress with a hem cut high in front but adorned with an impressive train and a veil worthy of any society bride. Griffin showed her off before the assembled company of the social elite, most of whom were still in a mild state of shock.

"Do you see that dress?"

"Remarkable. Truly remarkable. But then again, she—"

"—really is one of us. Apparently she grew up on Long Island, but her father was a bit of a recluse. He lost the family fortune and her mother disappeared."

"Poor thing."

"She really does comport herself well, doesn't she?"

"I remember the party."

"But you shouldn't, dear. Everyone makes mistakes. I'm certain the young lady will settle down now that she knows what's expected of her."

Griffin chuckled.

Allie glanced at him, her face bright with love. "What's so funny?"

"Our guests seem convinced that you'll mend your ways now that you're a member of Long Island society."

"Oh, yeah?" She paused to smooth her stockings, showing a delightful expanse of leg. "I suppose they'll all be expecting me to give a soirée pretty soon. Or at least an afternoon tea where they can gossip their heads off."

"Undoubtedly."

"It might be kind of fun, actually."

"I'm sure you could inject an element of festivity into even the most dreary social event."

"You sure you want to let me loose?"

He turned and pulled her into his arms. "It's time for the antediluvian Old Guard to enter the twentieth century. I can't think of a better way for their lesson to begin."

"I'd say you learned *your* lesson pretty well."

"I had an excellent teacher."

She lay her cheek against his lapel. "I never thought I'd be this happy."

"Nor I." He stroked her back. "I was in a trap of my own making. You set me free."

"And I thought freedom and pleasure were the only important things in life. You taught me they aren't worth a damn without love."

He lay his finger across her lips. "Language, Mrs. Durant."

She giggled—actually giggled—and undid the

studs at the front of his collar. "Oh, that's nothing, Mr. Durant. Let's show them something that'll really knock their socks off."

Griffin lifted her in his arms and carried her into the house, leaving a trail of gasps behind them.

Dark of the Moon

by

Susan Krinard

HIS HANDS WERE stained with blood.

Dorian ran blindly through the woods, the inside of his head roaring with emptiness. Branches tore at his clothing and scraped at his skin. Bloody scratches streaked his flesh, closing before he could run another hundred paces. He felt no pain. He felt nothing except the disintegration of his mind.

Raoul was dead.

The gun had become part of Dorian's hand, metal seared into his palm like a brand.

Raoul was dead, and there was no undoing it.

He didn't know how far he traveled before he came to himself again. He stopped at the edge of a small human town, somnolent in the warm summer sun. People stared as he walked down the main street, a man bundled up in ragged clothing and mud-stained shoes. One good Samaritan, a middle-aged man with deep laugh lines around his eyes and work-roughened hands, called to Dorian as he passed by.

"Are you all right, mister?" he asked. "Need some help?"

Dorian turned to look at the human, hardly comprehending the offer. No one had ever asked such a question of him before. But when he met the man's gaze, the human flinched, backed away and quickly left Dorian to himself.

So it had always been. They were always afraid.

With that grim knowledge, Dorian's sense returned. He found a twenty-dollar bill in his wallet and walked to the town's tiny bus terminal. No one on the bus would meet his eyes. He sat quietly in his seat until the bus arrived in Manhattan. He got off and began to walk again, letting his feet carry him where they chose.

He could not go home. There was no home with Raoul dead and the clan in shambles.

How he came to the East River, he never did remember. The waterfront was raucous with human activity, heavy with the smells of oil and sweat and stagnant water. Dorian drifted alongside the river, looking down at the greasy black surface.

It was hard to kill a vampire. It was even harder for a vampire to kill himself. But Dorian had never lacked will.

He stood on the edge of the pier, the toes of his shoes hanging over the edge. One more step was all it would take.

"I wouldn't do that if I was you."

The old man came up behind Dorian, favoring a gimpy leg and squinting through a nest of wrinkles. He was lean as an old hound, dressed in a motley collection of rags.

And he wasn't afraid.

"It can't be as bad as all that," the man said, offering a smile that was missing several teeth. "Never is." He shoved his hands in his torn pockets. "Everyone's down on their luck now and then. That's why folks like us got to stick together."

Dorian stared at the man. The man stared back.

"Name's Walter. Walter Brenner." He thrust out his hand. Dorian hesitated. No human had ever done that before, either.

"I ain't got no diseases, if that's what you're scared of," Brenner said. "But I do have a little food, if you're hungry. And a place to sleep, at least for tonight. Then you can decide what's best to do. Things always look better in the morning."

Slowly Dorian took the gnarled and knotted hand. "Dorian," he said. "Dorian Black."

"Well, Dorian Black, you'd better come along with me. That's a good lad. Ol' Walter will take care of you."

Dorian went. There was nothing else to do.

He was free, but his life was over.

SUPER NOCTURNE™

Coming next month

Dark of the Moon
by Susan Krinard

Dorian once kept the warring vampire clans of 1920s
New York from one another's throats. But now, outcast
from his own kind, he haunts the back alleys of Manhattan
alone… Until the night he meets reporter Gwen, who stirs
something within him for the first time in centuries.

Gwen has stumbled headlong into a world she
doesn't understand and Dorian is determined to
keep her safe. But in order to protect her he could
be forced to do the unthinkable…

On sale 4th December 2009

millsandboon.co.uk Community

Join Us!

The Community is the perfect place to meet and chat to kindred spirits who love books and reading as much as you do, but it's also the place to:

- Get the inside scoop from authors about their latest books
- Learn how to write a romance book with advice from our editors
- Help us to continue publishing the best in women's fiction
- Share your thoughts on the books we publish
- Befriend other users

Forums: Interact with each other as well as authors, editors and a whole host of other users worldwide.

Blogs: Every registered community member has their own blog to tell the world what they're up to and what's on their mind.

Book Challenge: We're aiming to read 5,000 books and have joined forces with The Reading Agency in our inaugural Book Challenge.

Profile Page: Showcase yourself and keep a record of your recent community activity.

Social Networking: We've added buttons at the end of every post to share via digg, Facebook, Google, Yahoo, technorati and de.licio.us.

www.millsandboon.co.uk